A Tide of Treason

A. B. Daniels-Annachi

By The Same Author

RAGE: A Dark Romance Anthology

The Violents
The Myth of June
The Oath of Eve

The Plague Chronicles
Asclepius' Descent: A Short
Achilles' Heel: A Short

Non-Fiction Pen Name
Then I Was Taken by Alaina Davis

A Tide of Treason

A. B. Daniels-Annachi

First published in United States 2024

Pacific Publications

P.O. Box 1366 Corvallis, OR 97339

Edited by Lauren Donovan – The Book Foundry

ISBN 978-1-922936-84-4

For the trans boys that loved pirates *and* mermaids and wanted to be a dragon, so they could burn their own castle down.

This novel contains triggers including but not limited to:
Anxiety, Blood, Bones, Colonization, Death, Emotional/Physical/Domestic Abuse, Family Death, Genocide, Gore, Graphic Violence, Graphic Depictions of Bodily Harm, Hallucinations, Hostages, Kidnapping, Magic, Misogyny, Murder, Sex, Sexism, Sibling Death, Violence, War

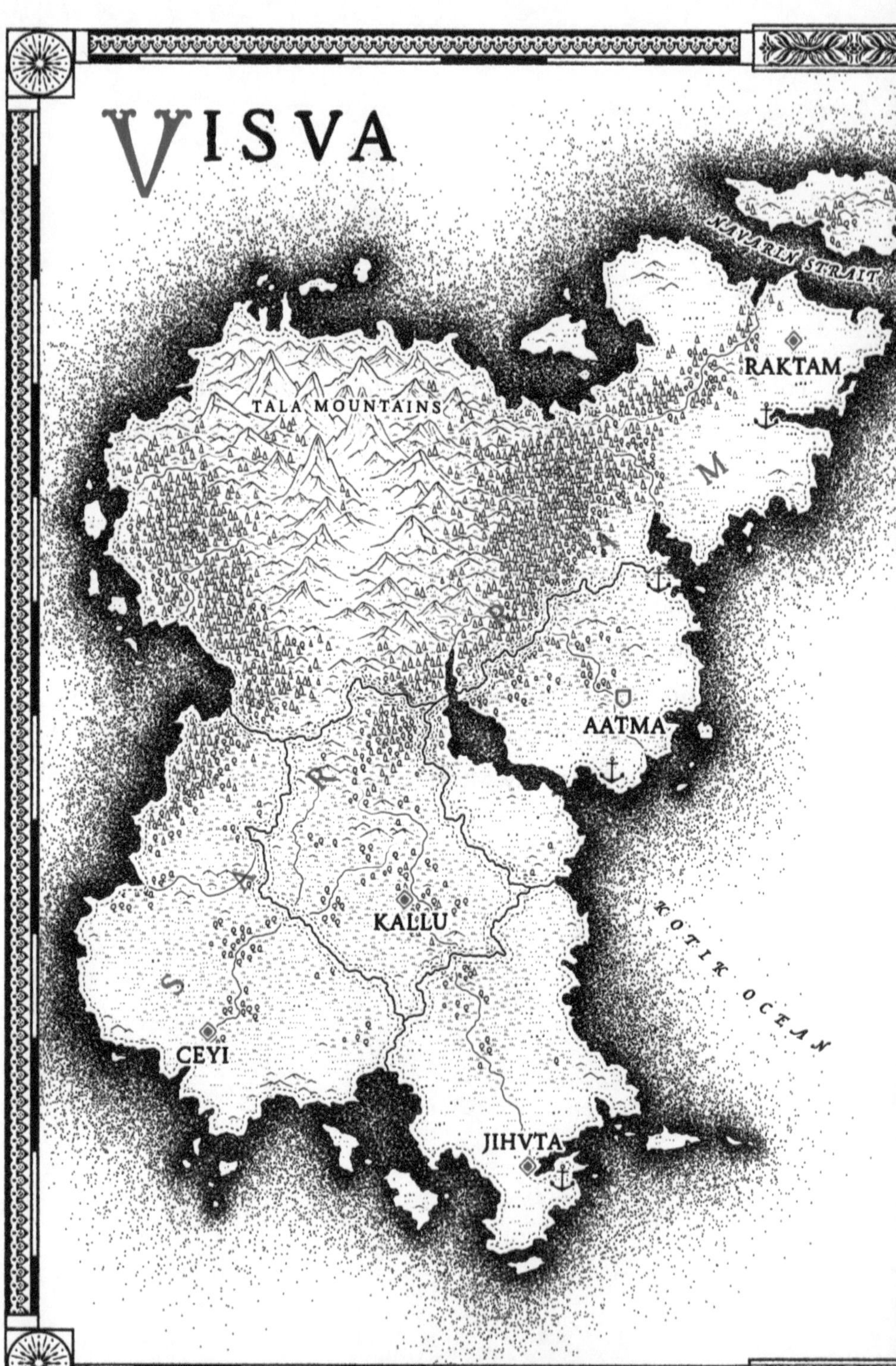
VISVA
TALA MOUNTAINS
NAVARIN STRAIT
RAKTAM
AATMA
KALLU
CEYI
JIHVTA
KOTIK OCEAN

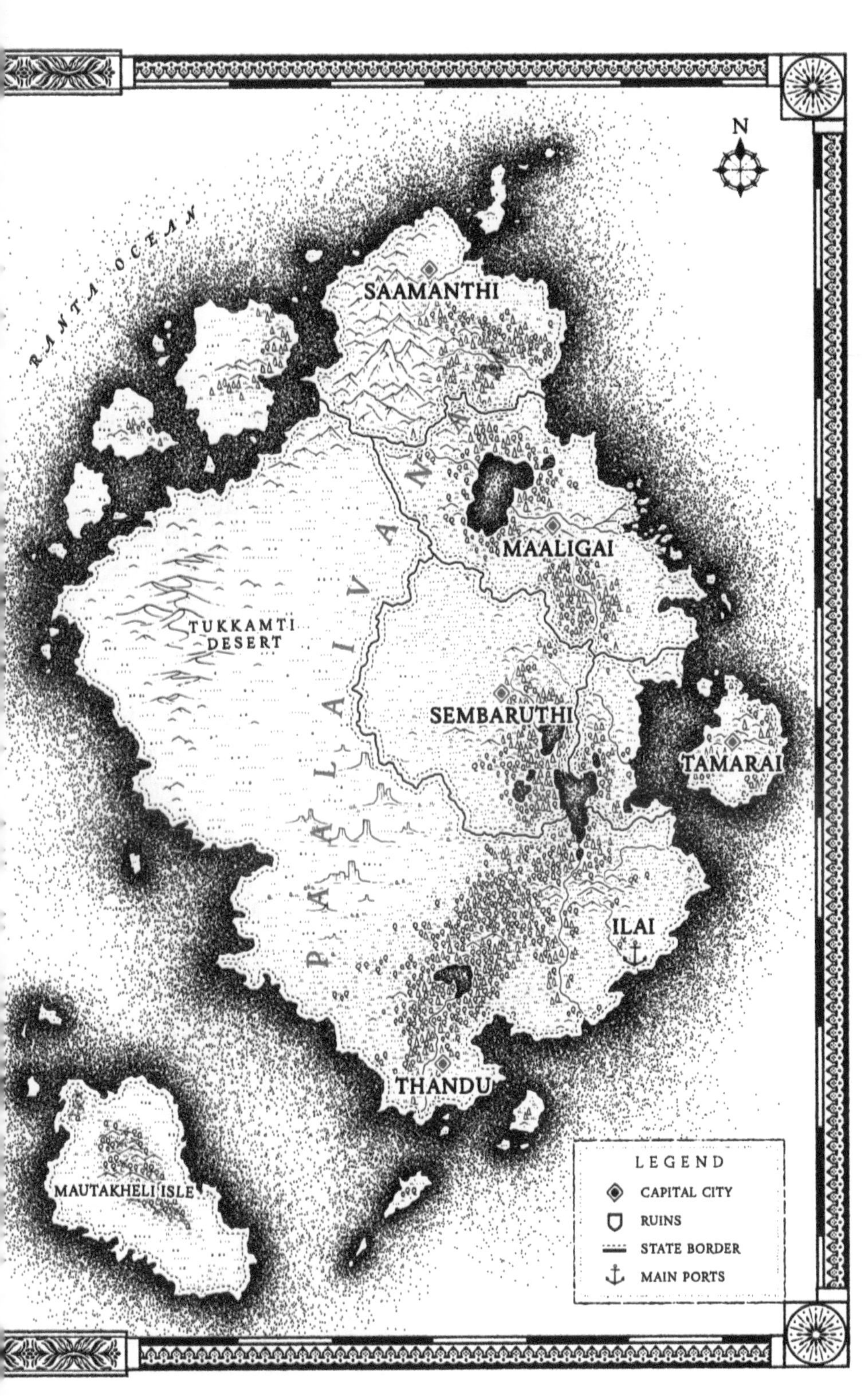
N
RANTA OCEAN
SAAMANTHI
MAALIGAI
PALAIVANAM
TUKKAMTI DESERT
SEMBARUTHI
TAMARAI
ILAI
THANDU
MAUTAKHELI ISLE
LEGEND
CAPITAL CITY
RUINS
STATE BORDER
MAIN PORTS

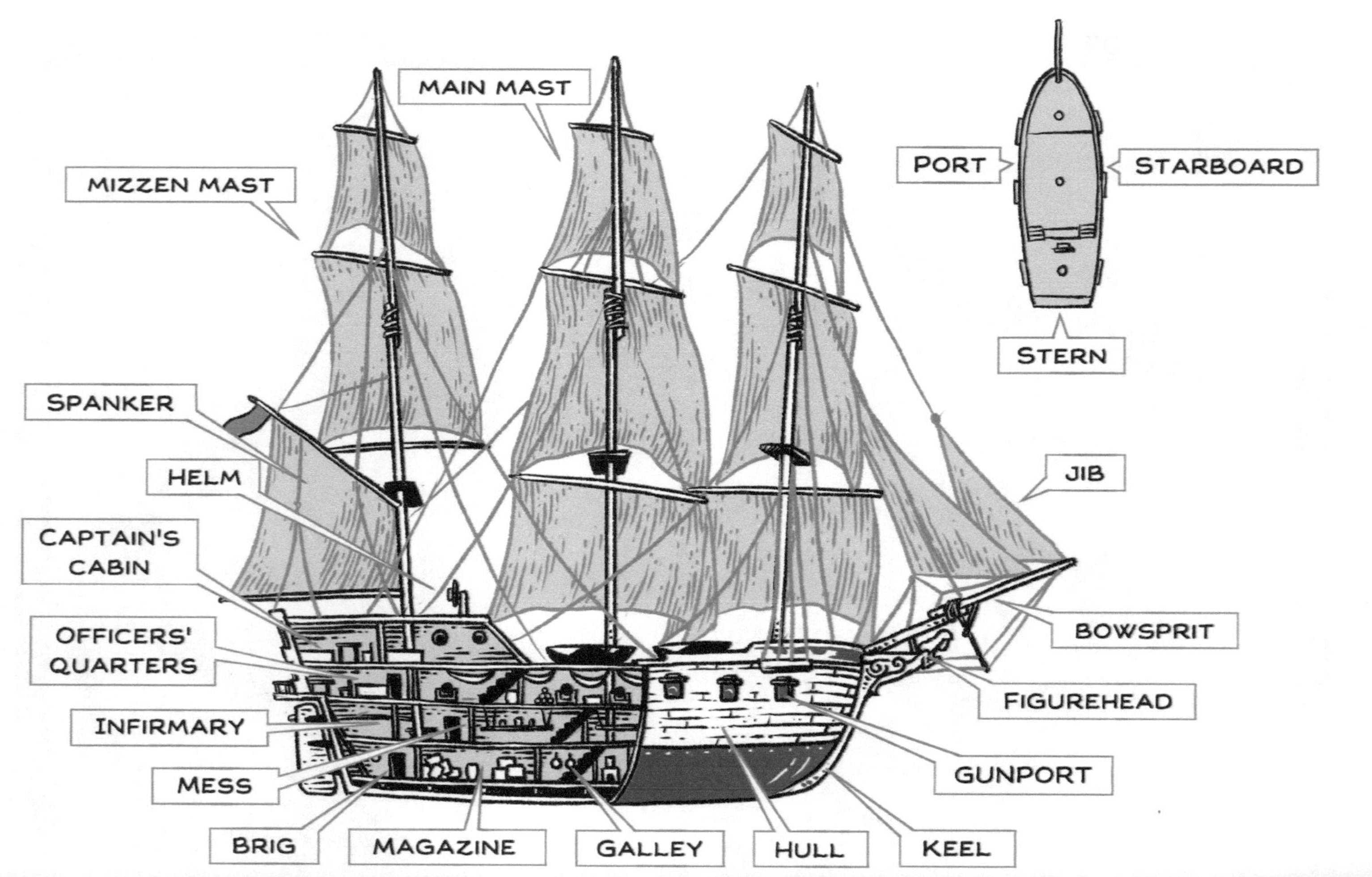
MAIN MAST
MIZZEN MAST
PORT
STARBOARD
STERN
SPANKER
HELM
JIB
CAPTAIN'S CABIN
OFFICERS' QUARTERS
BOWSPRIT
FIGUREHEAD
INFIRMARY
GUNPORT
MESS
BRIG
MAGAZINE
GALLEY
HULL
KEEL

Prologue

BURNING BLOOD RUSHED THROUGH the chamber around me. I tried desperately to cling to the walls while I was yanked forcefully through narrow veins, pushed and pulled through the dark.

My princess needs me.

Bright light flooded the room as I pooled in the palm of her hand. She pressed me into a long, thin dagger and urged me to twist around her index finger. I obeyed. Her pulse was quick, so I moved as fast as I could against her warm skin, tucking between her fingers and anticipating the threat to her safety.

"Your new husband will arrive soon, Your Highness," the maid spoke softly behind us, and Maryana turned, holding her hands out. A window opened wide in front of her, the salted breeze coasting in easily. Waves lapped at stone stairs only steps away from us, and the sun cast rainbows over the room.

Maryana's heart thumped loudly; her finger swelled with blood. The unknown of this *husband* threatened her.

She turned her palms to the sky, where a painted mural clung to the ceiling. A group of people descended from a mountain, traipsing through whorls of marigold and erecting homes on dabs of tyrian waves. The figures stopped on their trek, and magic bloomed from their fingertips, pulling trees from the mud, rain from the skies, even stitching the land together where a dark seam tore it in two. They were the first mantrik—the ministers that carried magic from the sky—that the people of Aatma descended from.

"I will not turn over Aatma to the north," she murmured, and tears fell from her cheeks to stain her palms, obscuring the bright mural.

"Of course not, ma'am," her maid returned. The younger woman stepped in close and draped a heavy brass belt around the princess's waist.

"Imogene, I fear I may be ill," Maryana cried out, and threw her hand to her chest. The tip of my blade sunk into her soft skin, and her maid gripped her arms firmly.

"You must be strong, my lady. Your people depend on you. The mantrik depend on you. We need your strength to make it through this union." Imogene's words were firm as she jerked Maryana from her panic. The princess released her grip on her own bosom and placed the hand that I was wrapped around on her maid's shoulder.

"Aatma is only a place, Maryana. But the mantrik are your people, and our magic will always be behind you. We will lift you up as you shield us from the outside."

Maryana sucked in a long breath and asked, "Do you have a scent to help the stresses of this day? Perhaps one that would also make the man amenable?"

Imogene smiled wryly and pulled a brass ball from her pocket. She focused intently on the piece of metal, working her finger around the laced edges. A moment later, flowers bloomed from inside it. "Cockscomb, for affection," she said, sprouting a burst of soft fluff like a bundle of feathers from a rooster's tail. "Marshmallow for his kindness. And a shepherd's purse, so that he falls to devotion for you."

The ball burst with tiny white flowers, and Imogene fixed it carefully to the belt at Maryana's waist before reaching up and stroking the princess's braid.

"Chamomile, to settle your nerves," she said before pulling away.

Maryana inhaled deeply, and a calm air pushed her shoulders down and relaxed the lines in her forehead.

"Thank you, my friend," Maryana whispered, reaching out to squeeze the maid's fingers.

"My power may be small, but my love for you is great." Imogene twisted the princess's floor-length braid. "If anything goes awry, I will pull new magic from the depths of my devotion to protect you."

Maryana laughed, and Imogene returned her smile. "If anyone could stretch their limits, I would believe that it could be you," she said. When she released Imogene's hand, the maid's eyes snagged against my shining surface and flashed with a knowing look.

A knock sounded on the door, a quick succession of four raps, and Imogene pulled her toward the sound. "We must be off. Your groom is near."

"Perhaps he will tumble into the sea before he can ascend the steps."

"Raktam is much colder than here, maybe he'll melt when he arrives," Imogene joked. Then her tone turned serious. "The gowns they brought are heavy and bound with laces. I believe they expect you to be ready to brave their storms."

"Too bad I didn't take after my mother. I may have been the storm instead," Maryana scoffed as the duo reached the foyer.

The door swung open wide to reveal the King and Queen of Aatma, accompanied by their board of advisors and a handful of servants.

"Maryana," the king said by way of greeting, "come, we must discuss Raktam's impending arrival."

My princess inclined her head, but I noticed her heart tick up a beat and squeezed myself tighter around her finger.

The walk to the dining room was silent. Maryana followed her father, and her mother walked beside her. The only sounds through the hall were the rustle of slippers on plush rugs and the sea slapping the shore outside the castle halls.

"Prince Eudo is to arrive any moment with his entourage," the king said, settling into his seat.

Maryana nodded, taking the seat offered to her by a servant. Her mother held her hand from the seat beside her. I curled into the princess's palm to avoid stabbing the queen.

"It is imperative that you accept his offer of marriage," he said bluntly. Maryana started, but the king raised a hand and continued. "I have not forgotten our previous discussions of choice, or your autonomy, but circumstances have changed. Word just reached our borders that if you choose to decline today, the prince intends to launch an attack."

Maryana's mouth snapped shut, and she leaned back in her chair. Her pulse was as wild as a stampede of horses under her skin, while her mother's steady tap was rhythmic atop it.

Taking a deep breath, Maryana asked, "Are you sure there is no other way? That he would invade does not make sense."

The queen frowned sympathetically, and the king nodded. "We set the board on strategizing. Aatma will suffer under Raktam's invasion. We will not fall, but we simply do not have the armies to defend ourselves. Your choice to marry is our only hope to prevent our people from suffering a great loss."

Maryana's fist closed around me, her warmth seeping into my cool surface, and she lifted her hand, pressing me against the soft flesh of her neck. "And what of my loss? What of my future?" She stood, shoving her chair back abruptly, and strode to the open window that faced the sea. "How is that a choice?"

"I would volunteer to marry in your place, Your Highness," a high voice said, and Maryana turned. She pointed her finger at a woman with long black hair and narrow eyes seated to the queen's left.

"Was this your idea? You cooked up the scheme to tax foreign merchant traders!" Maryana accused. "I would barter my left tit that you would offer me to another kingdom!"

The queen stood as well, raising a hand. "Stop! I will not sit and listen to your accusations against Navya any more. She serves our kingdom."

"She serves herself. Why can't you see that?"

"Navya is as vital to the kingdom as any courtier," the queen snapped.

"I did not arrange your marriage," Navya chimed in, "but I do not oppose it."

Maryana's chest heaved with indignation, and she faced the open air again. "No other mantrik has turned on as many as that jackal," she spat.

The king rose and shuffled around the table. "My dear, sweet Maryana. Put her from your mind now. Remember that we lean on you in this time of need. You can say no—up until the moment that the prince asks for your hand. Know this—Raktam grows stronger with each summer that passes, and they seek to erase the boundaries between each city-state, to unite our lands as one. If you insist on declining, we will stand through this attack, I know that, at least."

Maryana swallowed hard and gripped her father's hand. His skin was clammy atop hers. "Did she advise this union?"

The king hesitated before shaking his head. "She only blessed it."

"My duty is to my people," Maryana said after a beat, though she looked past the king and glared at Navya.

The queen clapped her hands together. "We will have him ushered into the throne room. You will fulfill a great destiny by saving us from invasion."

Maryana leaned into her father's embrace before they swept out, leaving her alone with her maid.

"Will you stay with me, Imogene?" Maryana asked. "I will need a friend if I am to be taken to that strange land."

The maid nodded and clasped her hand. "Of course, Your Highness."

The throne room was flooded with warm evening light when we entered it, and Maryana stroked me mindlessly. Her maid glanced nervously around the grand room, eyeing the teal-clad guard of Raktam that was stationed beneath every stone pillar.

"Your Royal Highness, I am pleased to meet you," a booming voice filled the air.

"And I, you, Prince Eudo," Maryana said curtly. "Are you enjoying our city?"

"Indeed, it is quite a stunning place. In fact, I just finished a tour of the other city-states of Sariram and found that they pale in beauty to yours. But tourism is not what brought me to Aatma, this time. I would like to say it is the heat, that I am escaping my own cold spring up north."

"Of course, it is not too far from us to you. One might be afforded travel here any time."

"Indeed," Eudo said, his voice pitching up with intrigue. "But through my travels around the continent, I heard a rumor that Aatma, while beautiful on the surface, held secrets. Secrets that I, as a future king, might want to know."

Maryana's palm slicked with sweat, and she gripped the silk of her dress. "I am unsure of what you infer, Your Highness."

"I set out to find a wife, and learn of the world, before I take the throne. I have since been told that you possess magic... That you are blessed by the gods—that all of Aatma is."

Maryana released her dress and folded her hands in front of her, allowing me a glance of Eudo. His hair was ice white, and his eyes blue as the ocean outside. "Do you seek my hand only for my power?" she asked.

"I believe that we would only benefit from uniting our states," he responded. "The south faces strife. Kallu and Jihva no longer have the resources to trade. Their armies dwindle. Residents walk the streets and beg for alms."

"And what would uniting our lands do to make life better for them?"

"I have hopes that we might join our forces, my lady, and build our resources together."

She regarded him for a moment before holding her hand out. I remained still as the heat of her magic flooded her palm. Her skin grew hot to the touch, and I began to liquefy around her finger. She pulled me back against her skin, out of my solid form.

"So it's true?" Eudo's awed voice echoed through the cool air, and he stepped closer, towering over us.

"Yes. I am mantrik." My princess's voice was calm, but her palm trembled, sloshing me to the side. "But you are mistaken, not all of Aatma was blessed to possess such power."

The man's bright eyes turned down on me, and I stretched to protect her pale skin from him. I turned toward her, noting how her soft chin was pointed up defiantly and her shoulders were squared back.

"Some families carry this gift through generations, and for some, it comes on suddenly in maturity. My mother's advisor was the butcher's child, and she presented as mantrik as a young girl, while the butcher had no magic. My maid's gift bloomed when she was an adult."

Eudo clasped her wrist, studying me. "Is all of your family gifted this way, then?"

"No. My mother is. And my mother's mother. And every woman that came before." She hesitated for a moment before pulling her hand away and willing me to spread between her fingers. "Only one man every few generations comes into a gift. And every time, it consumes him."

"My father is a docile man. I cannot imagine him with magic of any sort. I could not see magic in Raktam at all. We are an industrial state."

"Magic and technology can make progress together," Maryana offered. "And they may also destroy each other."

"My Lady Maryana, Princess of Aatma," Eudo said as he dropped to a knee. "I would be honored to have you as my wife."

Her pulse quickened, and her hand shook violently underneath me. She curtsied nearly as low as the knee he'd dropped to before responding. "Eudo Durling, it is my duty to accept your offer. Though, I have some requests if we are to marry."

A long beat passed between them, and her deep amber eyes flitted anxiously to the door before Eudo's strained voice filled the room again. "No matter, we will be a united front."

"I must request that the matriarchy of Aatma is preserved through our line. If our families join, I will not just be a consort. I will only accept the title of queen."

"Of course," Eudo said, the corner of his mouth ticking up.

"Then, I accept."

Her words were joyful, but her pulse afraid. I stretched out farther to wrap around her fingers, to protect her from this man that was scaring her so, but as I reached for the tip of one, her hand shook and turned upward, and her grip on me released.

I was dropped into a transparent vial. Eudo pinched the container in two fingers and held me up near his pointed nose, level to one giant blue eye. "I have an idea for this ability of yours, to help our people."

He opened his coat, and the world went dark around me. The heat that normally moved through me slowly leached out. I tried to scramble to the top of the bottle, to cling to the sides, but as time passed, I found myself unable to move.

When I was finally brought out from his pocket again, the light was dim. My glass prison was set down on a worn wooden table amid various machines.

I tried to look around, to see if Maryana was near, but my form had completely solidified. The glass jostled, and the stopper was removed, sending a ricochet through my form. As I was turned upside down, only a few drops of blood tipped out.

"This is astounding," Eudo muttered.

He jabbed me with the tip of a thin dagger, but couldn't pierce through. The blue eye lowered to peer at me again, and this time, shining teeth grinned to the empty room. "I hope you can serve me as I expect, Princess."

He stoppered the vial and left me on a shelf.

There was no measurement of time in the dark. I sat, rigid, in my prison until the day that Eudo finally opened the cabinet door and excited voices echoed around me. He clutched me in his sweating palm once more.

"This is it. Do you think that you could make this into a weapon?" Eudo asked, his voice shaking wildly. I was turned upright to face a balding man with a long beard. A table stretched beside him with various bowls, metal scraps, and tools. A fire roared in the corner, filling the room with heat, and a large box took up another corner.

I wasn't sure how much time had passed, hidden away in the dark of a cabinet, but Eudo had a few fine wrinkles around his mouth, and his fingers trembled with anxious energy.

The man studied him with wide eyes before looking directly at me. He took the vial and shook it, and again I didn't move—couldn't move. "Why would you want to?" he asked. "We have weapons."

"This came from the blood of a mantrik royal." Eudo's voice dropped, and he chuckled. "I couldn't pierce it—I believe it comparable to our bronze."

The bearded man sighed. "I can try."

Eudo cornered him, wrapping a fist in his black tunic and rising on his toes until their faces were nearly pressed together. "There is no 'try,' Baldric. You will tip the scales in our favor, or you will hang."

Baldric swallowed, and Eudo released him.

"You are going to help me build an empire, Baldric. You may have come from the heart of the continent, but we will turn Raktam into the new capitol of Sariram. Aatma will fall."

The bearded man was much less precious with me, and left me on a tabletop. I didn't get to look around but for a moment before something slammed down hard on top of the glass. It shattered around me, and the pressure was relieved from my sides. His grubby fingers grabbed at me, and he threw me into a metal tray before the world became very bright and very hot.

When the room dimmed and the heat began to cool, I scrambled. I didn't want to lose my ability to move before I could get to Maryana. I raced blindly toward what I believed to be an exit and found only a corner of a tray. Before I could make any escape, a spatula slammed down in front of me. It scraped down my surface, shoving me toward a mass of other metal.

Before I knew it, I was mixed with something thicker, mashed together, forced to coagulate, and we were shoved into the hot room once more.

We melted together, this other substance and me, and I became harder, denser. I was dumped into another container—this one was completely dark, and it forced me into a new shape as I cooled.

The bearded man lifted me gently from the mold and carried me in his palm from the hot room. The sun shone above, and the mist in the air clung to my sides.

"This is perfect," Eudo said.

"These scalelike pieces will be layered in armor, to replace leather and bronze. And we will find more uses," Baldric explained.

"And you are sure that no other state has this technology? You did not craft this for Aatma before coming here?"

"No, Your Majesty. You are the first."

"What did you call it?" Eudo asked, twisting me in front of his bare face.

"Iron alloy," the bearded man said. He took me from Eudo's thick fingers and held me to the light. "It is mixed with some bronze, so it's not pure. The original bottle you brought me was too volatile to use alone."

Volatile? He called me volatile.

Eudo clapped his hands. "Iron will be our savior. It will usher in a new age."

Baldric scrubbed his face and held me up between two fingers. "An age of iron? Are you sure about this, sire? I don't mean to question you, but is the queen okay with this?"

"She needn't know," said Eudo. "We've just married, and if anyone should jeopardize our new alliance..."

The thinly veiled threat was clear, and Baldric tucked me into the pocket on his chest.

When light broke around me again, the blacksmith was placing me into Maryana's palm.

She inspected me closely, and the pull of her magic called me to move.

"My queen. This is what he intends with your magic," Baldric said. "These iron rings will armor our men, but he plans to take the precious metal from you to begin with."

My queen. Her throne had grown, as had she. Her golden eyes held blue bags under them, and her chestnut hair was pinned up into an intricate pattern. Her dark skin had lightened from the lack of sun in this new land, and her hands were now frail.

"Thank you, Baldric. Your loyalty to the crown of Aatma is noted, though we are in Raktam now. I understand the transition between ruling kingdoms is difficult, but I cannot tolerate conspiracies between the king and myself."

Baldric bowed his head. "Your Majesty, I mean no disrespect. I simply want you to be aware, as he said that you were not. He brought me these drops of pure iron in a vial months ago and set me on the task of turning them into a weapon. I succeeded, but more importantly, I created a defense."

My queen regarded him before nodding. "Please, return to your station."

"What of this secret the king keeps? I fear for our homeland."

"I said enough!" Maryana snapped, and pinched me between her finger and thumb. I was offered one last look at her pallid face before she flicked me toward the blacksmith.

Baldric caught me in his fist and bowed once more before turning away from my queen. I tried to look at her again, but my solid form allowed no grace in movement. I was forced to lie flat against the man's hand as he carried me out of the castle, his racing pulse beating wildly through me.

He threw me into a dark box with no hesitation or parade.

When the lid on my cell lifted once again, the workshop had evolved. The table with the bowls where I had been melted into my new form no longer stood in the middle. Instead, roaring fires heated half the room while tables were spotted sporadically with various instruments. Shelves full of weapons and stacks of discarded iron bars filled in where one might expect chairs.

Baldric's beard was gone, leaving only a light stubble, and his hands were not as steady as before. Humming to himself, he worked quickly, but jumped any time the fire popped. He held me carefully between two small pairs of tongs, untwisting the opening at my top. As the familiar warmth of iron settled behind me, I realized that he had knitted me into another three pieces shaped like myself.

We were lifted away from the table and hung on a wall, left to watch as many people walked past. Some stopped and commented.

"Interesting design," one said.

"But how will it work?" another asked.

Baldric made a nervous *tsk* sound under his breath and pressed a finger near me. "You see, when a weapon pierces it, the chained scales will absorb some impact, or hopefully deter the weapon and cause it to ricochet away."

There were many *oohs* and *aahs*.

And then came Eudo. His eyes were still sharp and face still clean-shaven, and when he turned to Baldric, he asked, "You're sure that this will work?"

"Yes, Your Majesty."

The king reached out. The iron links below me clinked together under his touch. "It seems sturdy." He regarded Baldric coolly. "I can no longer tell if you lie to me, based on the twitch of your lip or quiver in your chin. I might recommend a trip to the groomer before we send this armor out into the field of battle."

Baldric's hand shot to his jaw, and he nodded furiously. "Right away, Your Majesty. I apologize. I was caught up here."

Eudo turned swiftly behind him, snatching an iron blade from a table, and the bustling bodies blocked my view from the blacksmith.

The first milk rays of dawn leaked in through the front door around a parade of men, and they lined up around the room.

"This one is mine, then?" a blond-haired boy with a full face of freckles asked, stopping in front of me.

"That's it. Suit up, we march to Aatma at daybreak," an older voice bellowed behind him.

The boy's freckled fingers were gentle as he lifted the chains I was secured to. We moved like a piece of cloth, sifting through his touch, and he wrapped us around his body. He found a helmet of iron and shoulder pads before someone shoved a sword into his hand.

When he moved, we moved with him, contouring to his chest and breathing his ragged breaths.

The morning was grim. Sunrise smeared red as blood on the horizon and the ground was dimmed by the shadows of heavy swords raised high in the air. The din of men's cries echoed as figures covered in iron marched around me. I could not see behind or next to me, but the knit scales ahead told me enough.

I rode through a field coated in mud, affixed to my soldier's chest, and the army around me halted many times before the yells finally matched the clanging of metal.

Brown brass glinted off the blue reflection of iron around us, stabbing for the armies' belts, swinging for their shining helmets, and spearing their chests coated in protective scales.

Sunlight flashed over a tarnished weapon as it aimed for me, but it clinked off, and the sword of the man I was attached to swung wide around before burying his blade into the leather chest of his enemy. I could only watch as he impaled body after body. I couldn't be sure how battle worked, but it was clear that I had been taken from my queen and should no longer protect her, but was meant to protect this sword-slashing demon in her name. How he was able to lay down tens of enemies in a row was a miraculous feat.

I rustled against the scales behind me, this way and that, as the man wove through the crowd, and when the sun reached its apex, I expected to soften, but realized I still couldn't move. The brass that Baldric had mixed me with held steadfast. I would perform my duty, whether I wished to or not.

The man whom I protected slashed through another enemy, and his body vibrated with a yell of triumph. As he turned, his pride was cut short. I could not gather exactly what happened—one moment, his arm was stretched out in front of him, and his scream filled the air. The next, he spun, and I was shoved away from his chest as something sharp mangled the clasp that kept me attached to the other scales around his heart.

Had I been the first created as well as the first discarded? I had to wonder at my fate as I flew through the air. The battle raged underneath me, and I was offered the view of shining iron clashing with polished bronze and torn leather.

There was a clear overwhelm as the bronze began to retreat, but I saw no more as I fell into the mud, and my world was dimmed once again.

I was lost to light and sound until a wave of heavy water finally washed over me. Sea-foam cleansed the grit from my surface, and the pressure of the wash tore me from where I had been buried in the sand. The current tossed me gently about. It took a long time to sink to the bottom, and many fish kicked me up when I neared the sand anyway.

I passed coral reefs, where I might have settled, but I found myself a slave to the ocean's way and the form that Baldric had forced me into, spinning this way and that.

The darkness of night in the ocean was incomparable, broken only by the bioluminescence of deep-sea fungi and loose, glowing algae. Shafts of daylight filtered between waves like stars burning out, highlighting the sparkle of sand and creatures that would never be seen by man.

A snail with a thousand tongues and a volcano on its back spewed steam at me, spinning me into higher currents, where one of six fins of a strange, blue being slapped me toward an island. Deep, swinging voices carried through the foam, and I tossed about the waves on the tails of people of the sea, then was scooped into the bill of a screeching gull.

By the time I found land again, the sun burned hotter than before.

"Careful with that rigging! Fall my mast and I'll drop you like an anchor!" a voice yelled from nearby.

"Load those barrels quick! The Maharajah arrives at dusk!"

Boots shuffled around and over me, and I was kicked into a pile of rocks. The sky stretched vast and blue above, without a cloud to darken it, and the air was humid. Though my world was bright once more, and full of colorful sails, I remained unnoticed as rust overtook me.

Forty-Nine

Years Later

1

Dorian

A BLADE SWISHED PAST my ear, narrowly missing my neck and sending a shiver down my spine. Hari recovered his arc, turning the sword back and aiming it for my shoulder. I dodged the blow and flicked the ground beneath our feet with the tip of my own blade, showering him with pebbles and sand.

He shouted in surprise and shielded his eyes, allowing me a moment to regain my footing after his last onslaught. I backed up until my feet were near the ring of charcoal rocks. "That was a cheap trick," he accused, shaking the sand from his crop of blond hair.

I grinned and motioned for him to continue, and he rushed me, sword raised. He jabbed it forward, but I was ready. I turned and lifted my longsword, knocking the flat side of it against the hilt of Hari's and sending his weapon clattering to the ground and him sprawling outside the sparring boundary.

"I'm sure I've bested you thrice now," I said with a grin, reaching out a hand.

He gripped my arm from where he lay on the ground, rising and sheathing his sword before clapping a hand on my back. "You cheated, and I've gone easy on you. I'll truly let you have it tomorrow," Hari replied.

My chest warmed at the thought of spending more time with him, and I threw my arm around his broad shoulders. "I look forward to it. I missed you while you were away."

"Shall we make a run for the Cloak and Dagger? You yanked me into training so quickly that I didn't get a chance to eat this morning."

I glanced at the guards stationed around us. Their iron helmets glinted in the midmorning sun, and their teal capes barely rustled in the breeze. Not one of them gave a hint that they overheard our conversation, but I dropped my voice anyway.

"I could go for an ale while you tell me of your time away," I mused, and Hari slapped my back before gripping my neck and steering me away from the sparring ring with a laugh.

A clear path circled the castle grounds to the front gardens, passing a maze that would direct any unfamiliar guest back into the rows, but we wove through the hedge like thieves in the night, ducking between blackthorn bushes as a few promenading couples wandered past.

"I didn't mean to interrupt your march home, but three months felt like three years when I saw you."

Hari had joined the royal guard on a training mission for the summer, and it was the first time we'd been separated since we were in leading strings. Now his presence was intoxicating, and as I covered his body with mine in a narrow crevice between the hedges, hiding us from sight, I couldn't help but take a deep breath in, committing the smell of his after-training musk to memory.

I studied his face for as long as I could. The deep amber of his eyes, the few freckles across the curved bridge of his nose. The voices behind us faded, and Hari looked up at me before pointing down the path. I grinned and stepped away. "Right, we should go."

"Not that I don't enjoy you pinning me into confined spaces, Your Highness," he joked with a lopsided grin.

"How indecent of you!" I returned, chuckling as we emerged onto the main road.

Thick slabs of stone beckoned us to the center of town, angled away from the looming shadow of Castle Durling. Hari looped his arm through mine, and I fell into an easy run beside him.

Brick buildings nearly stacked on top of each other rose up on either side of us, filled in with iron bars for support. Rusting signs croaked outside of businesses, swinging in the salty breeze, and restaurant owners placed seats and rolled tables in the streets outside their doors.

We turned down one of the many side streets of central Raktam, ignoring the lush homes at the end of the lane, and ducked under the sign depicting a dagger stabbing through a piece of cloth.

The room inside was dark and nearly empty of patrons. Tables were still stacked with chairs, the lanterns low on whale fat, and the Cloak's owner scrubbed the bar fruitlessly.

"Good day!" I called out as Hari fixed the door shut.

Bromios looked up and glared as we took seats at an open table.

"For a man who chose to brew beer, you would think he would be happier to have customers," I murmured under my breath.

The older man slammed two jugs of liquid down in front of us a moment later. "Perhaps I would be happier if my patrons paid their tabs and did not whisper my name," he spat, and stormed back behind the bar, leaving me stunned.

Hari chuckled, and I turned, sputtering. "Have I not paid for all my drinks?"

My friend shrugged. "We may have stumbled out too drunk once or twice."

"Sky's above," I swore, and shook my head. I lifted my glass to Hari, ignoring the daggers of Bromios's glare at my back. "We must toast to your return! It is not every day that my gentleman-in-waiting returns from military training."

Hari tapped the edge of his glass to mine and offered me a grim smile before knocking back his drink. I took a swig myself and closed my eyes against the heady burn of alcohol on my tongue, swallowing the bubbles and setting my mug down before Hari cleared his throat.

"I'm just glad I didn't come back as an official guard," he said.

I chuckled, shaking my head. "I always wondered what happened at camp. The men leave like pups chasing a bone. I worried you'd have your balls clamped in a vice or something," I nudged his hand.

He shook his head. "By the sky, something strange was out there. Not just at camp, but beyond the walls. From the moment we left, I felt unease. The duke took us out to the base of Tala, and just the weather of the mountains was enough to drive a man mad. Snowdrifts fell over our camp, broken only by floods from the river Tapti. The exercises he put us through with the higher officers were something else, too. Men fell to each other's blade. Others were lost to the forest. Then they stopped talking a few days before we returned."

My mouth went dry at his description of his time away. "I thought that the training of the guard was meant to be a ritual experience. Not break their spirits."

Hari shrugged and drained the last of his beer. "Perhaps it is only since Hastings took over. I don't remember the guard so stoic when we were young, either. I can't remember the last time I heard one of the men at the king's side speak."

I pushed my drink toward him and nodded in agreement, looking through the window beside us. The film of grime nearly obscured my view, but it was still clear that the street outside was almost empty. I glanced around the pub, realizing that we were still the only patrons. "I wonder where everyone is..." I mused.

Loud bells chimed in the distance, and Hari shot up out of his seat.

I swore loudly as he turned and bounded toward the door. "Is Girish's wedding today?" I called after him. I nearly tripped over my chair as I moved to follow, but then remembered our tab and fished a few coins from my pocket. They fell to the table with a clatter, and I dashed out of the tavern.

Hari was already on the main road when I caught up to him, his cheeks tinged pink. "I was supposed to march with the procession!" he exclaimed.

"Fuck the guard! I can't miss my uncle's wedding!" I yelled.

He ignored me and kept running, darting up the stone steps of the castle. He disappeared down one of the many hallways of the foyer.

My breath came ragged by the time I reached my room, and I had to pause outside the door, pressing my palms to my chest and leaning over to breathe deeply.

When I swung the door open, the room was empty. I sighed in relief, having expected my stewardess or groomer to be present, and strode to the bed. Someone had laid out clothing for me, and I stripped out of my sweat-soaked blouse quickly, tossing it onto the leather chaise at my side. Dirt crumbled from the heels of my boots into the carpet, and I threw my breeches atop them.

I looked down at my short underwear. They really weren't suitable to wear under the woven trousers that had been put out for my evening dress, but...

The castle bells rang in succession, chiming a song that warned the wedding would start soon, and I yanked my pants from the bed and struggled with the legs. The brocade heels I stumbled into could only be my father's idea, and I swore as I shrugged on my shirt and tore out into the hallway.

The brass button of my vest snagged, and I twisted it as far as I could as I reached the courtyard. I slowed as my stewardess came into view in front of the doorway, forcing myself to take a deep breath. Her lips pinched together as she advanced on me.

"Where have you been?" she demanded. "The ceremony's beginning, and your father was seated nearly twenty minutes ago!"

I mumbled an excuse while trying to button the vest again, and she huffed and shoved my fingers out of the way. "Honestly, I can't help you if you won't help yourself." Her voice was sharp, but when her gaze fixed on me, I found only kind golden eyes. The color of honey and set with deep wrinkles like waves on the ocean. I smiled warmly at her and dipped my head.

"Thank you, Imogene."

She brushed a sandy curl from my face before stepping back so I could walk through the door. "Cut your hair," she said by way of goodbye, and I gave her hand a squeeze before hurrying down the steps of the garden.

The scent of rosemary filled the air from the bushes lining the path, followed by guava and hibiscus. I rounded the low wall of the garden and snagged one of the pink flowers, tucking it into my pocket in hopes it would help my presentation.

I was relieved to find that she had exaggerated slightly, as the music that drifted through the courtyard was not a wedding march and the bride was nowhere to be seen. I lifted a hand in greeting to the groom, who rubbed his hands together anxiously, and hurried down the aisle to the second row. An empty seat sat open next to Hari.

"You okay?" he asked, placing a hand on my knee.

I calmed at his touch, not realizing how fast my heart had been racing until I had a chance to catch my breath.

"Imogene," I laughed, "chastised me as if I were still her ward. Honestly!"

He shook his head. "Why you chose her as your stewardess and not someone new, I'll never understand."

I shrugged. "She's tough, but I trust her. Who else to advise me but the woman who raised me?" Then, shaking free of Hari's grasp, I rose to meet the groom with an outstretched hand. "Uncle Girish! Happy wedding day."

The older man's smile stretched the wrinkles in his cheeks, and his brown eyes shone in the bright sun. "Thank you, m'boy. I am a happy man indeed."

"Have you planned the honeymoon?"

"Oh yes, my future missus lined it all up. We set sail immediately for an extended tour of the ports of Sariram."

A sour bite of jealousy stung my tongue at that. "How nice that you have such an opportunity to leave Raktam," I said. I cleared my throat and tried to smother the spite in my tone. "I wish you calm seas during your travels, Uncle."

He gripped my arm in a tight embrace and looked deep into my eyes. "I am only sorry that your mother cannot be here to celebrate this day."

A knot in my stomach twisted as he slid the dagger so eloquently between my ribs.

"Of course," I choked out.

Girish hurried away as the city bells began to chime again, this time in three loud gongs, followed by the normal chimes that marked noon. I turned to my right as my father approached. His demeanor was abrasive, his dress uniform extruding an air of warning. I nodded an acknowledgment and nearly stood and bowed, but decided against it at the last second as he took his seat. He cleared his throat and straightened the iron buckle on his jacket, leaning over the arm of his chair toward me.

"Where were you?" he asked.

I swallowed hard and found myself lost for words. I glanced up at my father and immediately regretted meeting his hard, gray gaze. As if on cue, Hari's hand found mine, and the calloused pads of his fingers kneaded into my palms, pushing that familiar feeling of calm through me. I took a deep breath and leaned toward my father.

"I had to catch up on sparring. I was out of practice," I whispered. It was a half-truth. I hadn't sparred since Hari left.

He sat back and grunted as the music began. Violins sung from behind us, and brass notes echoed through the trees. The back of a red gown shimmered as the bride walked toward the arch of vines, and the couple faced each other as our royal priest began to speak.

"We are here today to join the hands of Councilor of Raktam, Duke Girish Aatma with Viscountess Sabine Rothnam. Should anyone object to this marriage, speak now," he said, his voice high and clear above the chattering of birds.

My father leaned in close again and spoke under his breath. "You'll be up there next, eh?"

I nodded, but stars danced into vision at his suggestion. I did not want to marry; I had no desire to stand up under that archway and exchange meaningless vows.

My uncle and the viscountess suddenly separated from my reality and sprouted strings from their arms and legs. They were thrown about like puppets as the sky flooded with darkness above them.

A figure with arms covered in jewelry and his hair tied in a knot atop his head rose up and lifted their braces.

"Do you agree to be played like a marionette?" he asked as my uncle's jaw moved in a nonsensical fashion.

"I do," the viscountess returned.

Girish raised his arms and shimmied oddly, almost as if he were excited, while the god behind them pulled their strings this way and that. The viscountess turned to face me.

"And do you agree to be played like a marionette, my lord?" she asked.

I jerked back, gaping at her. Her jaw opened and closed, and it felt as if I were being mocked.

"Well? My lord?" she asked again, and I blinked, moving in my seat. The stars spun above us, and I blinked rapidly, finally realizing I was still sitting at the ceremony. The viscountess was, in fact, addressing me. Her red ball gown was bunched in one hand as she squeezed between rows of chairs, and she clasped her other hand at her breast, covering the open spot of her corset as she leaned down to speak. I blinked again and shot upright, aware that my mind had left this place for a moment.

Hari and my father had walked away, and the ceremony had wrapped up. Most guests were mingling.

"I asked what you thought of the wedding, my lord," the viscountess said, her cheeks turning a shade of pink similar to her lips.

I nodded. "Of course, my apologies. I got caught up in the emotions of it all. It was beautiful, congratulations on your nuptials," I offered, then rushed out, "and your new title."

She inclined her head. "Of course. Taking on the role of Duchess will come with its own responsibilities atop the rest of it," she said with a smile.

Our conversation lulled, and I realized that I wasn't sure what to say. Should I offer congratulations again, or ask if she wanted this marriage? What was appropriate when she was a member of my court?

Lady Rothnam cleared her throat and saved me from thinking of it. "I see my mother. Please excuse me, Your Highness."

"Of course," I said, moving out of the way and releasing a heavy breath as she swayed down the aisle toward an aged woman.

My eyes skated over the rest of the crowd milling about and landed on my father a few meters away. His gray military coat shone silver in the sun, and the teal sash that covered one of his shoulders had been thrown back and pinned with a purple broach, denoting his rank. I moved to step toward him, thinking of some conversation I might make, but a page ran past me.

"Your Majesty!" the boy exclaimed.

My father turned, the crown on his head glinting as he did so, and the guest he spoke to ducked away.

"News! An urgent notice from the commander," the page said, gasping for air.

Father snatched the letter from him and mumbled as I approached.

"—sighting of katalval. Sky's above," he swore. He looked at the boy, then around the courtyard. "Gather the naval officers and the council. We'll have a meeting tonight."

The page nodded, dashing away before he could be asked anything again.

The alarm in my father's eyes was enough to raise the hair on my neck as he fixed his intense gaze on me. "You'll be there as well. Straight from dinner, and bring Hari. You'll need him."

I bowed my head. "Yes, Father."

2

VESHAK

SALTED WIND WHIPPED MY hair back and stung my eyes as I looked out over the darkened sea. The round of my spyglass framed a narrow passage to the northwest: the Navarin Strait. Bordered by callous rocks and treacherous cliffs on either side. It was danger enough to attempt sailing through without the hordes of hungry seabirds it was named after nesting in its high cliffs. Crashing waves in the distance warned of rough travel if we continued en route, but our next payday was currently sailing directly toward it.

I dropped from my perch on the rail and faced my first mate, Cayde, and my crewmen. Silence stretched on as the two navigators examined maps stretched out across a few crates and the astronomer lifted his astrolabe to the sky, turning its dial to line up the horizon.

I met Cayde's gaze as the silence stretched on, and he shrugged. After a long minute, I finally dropped my spyglass down onto the crate, causing them to jump.

"Can we cross the strait or not?" I asked.

I cleared my throat, dropping my voice as low as I could when I saw the look on the men's faces. It was my job to keep them calm, and a crack in my voice would only make them worry. But I was starting to panic—we served the emperor of Paalaivanam, and had not taken a prize back to our sponsor in six months. Worse than not returning home, my men had received no pay in half as long.

Ehann lowered his brass dial from the sky and turned his gaze on me. The way the stars reflected off his nearly black eyes as he spoke was unsettling. “No, if we continue, we'll be dashed on the rocks, as that merchant will be.”

A groan escaped my lips, and I shoved away from the crate, pacing a few steps before turning on my lead navigator. “We're overdue for pay and a report back to the courts. What if we venture west?”

He cleared his throat and pointed to the map, which depicted the divide between the oceans. We were currently on the northernmost border of the Ranta Ocean, and if we moved any farther south or west, we'd cross into Kotik waters. “We can risk it. There's a trade route along here,” he said, tracing a line from Taimur Bay to a coastal town south of Aatma's ruins. “But if we get caught by a royal ship, they won't recognize our marque of the Maharajah. We'll be branded pirates.”

I scratched my chin, and Cayde peered over my shoulder. “It's been a long time since we last graced Kotik,” he murmured.

“Aye,” I agreed. “And it was bloody before.”

I glanced over at our second ship, a smaller, faster vessel. “Last time we only had the sloop,” I said, motioning to the two-mast ship. “I reckon with a galleon underfoot, we'll be easier respected.”

“As pirates or as privateers?” Cayde asked.

I looked at the map again, at the mark that the navigator had made for the western trade route, and grimaced. “Does it matter?”

“Captain?” the younger navigator asked. “What happened?”

I blinked at him, then quickly remembered we'd only taken him on at port last year. Cayde and Ehann exchanged a glance, and I sighed, sitting heavily on one of the crates. Noise picked up from the lower deck. A barrel of wine had been cracked open, and tins of drink were circulating.

"You don't need to worry about it. Go, join the party."

He hesitated, dropping his freckled hands to his sides. "I mean no disrespect, Cap. But if I'm to face pirate waters and come out ahead, I think I should know the stakes," the boy said.

Cayde lifted a brow at me, and I scrubbed my eyes. The music picked up from across the ship, and a stomping dance began. I sighed heavily, recalling our battle from years before.

"Nearly a decade ago, when I was just shy of twenty, I gathered one hundred men to sail," I said.

"And a few women," Ehann interrupted. I shot him a dirty look, and his mouth snapped shut.

"We boarded the sloop at Thanam with a list of orders from the Maharajah—my father. We only carried supplies for two months, and a satchel of hope. The sea was fair to begin with, and my crew was rosy-cheeked and merry. We even employed a couple of musikers at the Port of Ilai to keep spirits up. But when we hit the open ocean, our mission took a turn that we could have never expected."

The memory rolled out in front of me as I spoke, replaying as if it were happening right then.

The open ocean was vast and blue, with stiff sea-foam peaks hugging the sloop's belly and fish flanking us as we left the safety of land. I turned from the bow and faced the crew, scanning the deserts of Paalaivanam before I turned my full attention to the crew that I was expected to captain. The chill of the sea had already set into my bones, and I rubbed my hands to warm them.

"We have orders to capture a vessel heading south," I declared, my voice barely loud enough to command a rava bird, let alone the mismatched looking men and women before me.

My appointed right hand straightened next to me and leaned in. "Perhaps we should tell them why, Your Highness?"

I spun on him, eyes wide before grimacing. "Of course." Of course he would know how to address me, though I climbed aboard this ship to escape the rigidity of titles and court.

I yanked a slip of papyrus from the pocket of my coat and lifted it high in the air. "A merchant has been reported circling the Mautakheli Isle. Our Maharajah advises that they carry beer and lard from the Sariram state of Raktam. They took a long route through our waters, likely to divert attention from the wealth on board."

My voice wavered as I spoke, but none of the crew looked away nor challenged me. As I finished my speech, a few clapped their hands to their chests, others saluted with two fingers to their brows before dispersing about the deck of the sloop.

Three men were left standing in front of me, including my right hand. I hesitated before raising a brow at Cayde. He motioned to the shorter of the two at his right; with long black curls and big eyes the color of the sea, he looked at home on board.

"This is your bos'n, Captain. Any orders for the crew can go direct to him, or to me, and I'll pass them on."

The man inclined his head, and as his tight ringlets flopped forward, a tattoo of a compass was revealed on the back of his neck. He held a hand out, and I saw lines like the route of a map traced down his forearm, and around his hand. "Orion, Cap. Pleased to be here," he said.

I shook his hand, aware of how strong his grip was. "Do you have navigational experience?" I asked, nodding to the tattoos.

"Aye, I was raised as an apprentice cartographer, under my father. I served on board the *Royal Naga* last."

"Wow, I'm sure my father was pleased with your service to bring you here," I returned.

He gave me a tight-lipped smile and released my hand, allowing me to turn to the last man, who Cayde introduced as Felix. He was tall and lean, towering over me by at least eighteen inches, with cords of muscle wrapping up his arms. His cut-off linen pants revealed similar strength in his legs.

"Our physician, whom we're very lucky to have," Cayde said warmly.

"What doctor needs all that muscle?" I joked, and Felix's face went grim. Wrinkles formed around his dark-brown eyes, and his gray beard trembled as he spoke.

"When you're knocked out by a kraken, do you want him or me draggin' you out an' carryin' you a'shore?" he asked.

"Understood," I said. My gaze lingered on his honey-toned eyes. "Are you from Aatma?" I asked.

He nodded sharply. "My family moved to Paalaivanam before the war. We were sorry to hear of the state falling."

"It was a travesty, but we're lucky to be sheltered from Sariram's politics," I agreed.

Felix and Orion regarded me before disappearing among the crew, leaving me to watch the land fade into the distance. I had to wonder what I signed up for. The Maharajah had agreed to let me sail, but only after much arguing. Now I wondered if perhaps I would have been better off in the Mahal, safely tucked inside the vast corridors and gardens of my home, awaiting a marriage that would benefit our empire.

I pondered the thought, imagining my brother on the throne of Thandu while I joined another state, and watched the sun set.

Though I was meant to be in charge of the ship, it felt as though it ran itself; any time I spent on deck was time that I was in the way.

I attempted to watch the sea from the stern, and the musikers played in short bursts, stopping to ask if they were too loud, too quiet, or if I had requests.

"Please, pretend as though I am not here," I begged.

"Of course, Captain," the violinist responded.

The drum player banged out a beat, and the trumpet blew a few shrill notes before I felt all their eyes on me again. I cut a path back down the steps quickly, making way for an open spot on the deck, and leaned over the rail. Peace only lasted for a few moments, as water was tossed over my boots. I leaped back, and a young boy apologized profusely.

"I'm sorry, Cap! T'was an accident. I gotta swab here s'all!" He dropped to his knees and scrubbed the stone in his hand around near my boots, trying to slosh the water in a different direction, but I walked away. The bow was the same, as I found a few men staring at maps and inspecting the sky, supervised by Orion.

As I gave up on finding peace on the ship, Cayde rounded on me, throwing an arm around my shoulder. His small oval spectacles slid down his pointed nose, and his golden eyes seemed to capture and hold the sun in them.

"We're due to come up on the merchant vessel soon. What's your call?"

I blanched at him and shrank back under his arm. "What do you mean?" I asked.

He dropped away from me, leaning on the side of the ship and crossing his arms. "Do you wish us to slow our speed, rest, and make way when dawn breaks? Or should we raise the sails and race the sun to ambush them at dusk? If we hit eleven knots, we might just make it."

My brow furrowed, and I nodded along to his suggestions. It made sense to me to let the crew rest, to hold our energy, in case we had a big fight ahead of us, but I hesitated and met his gaze.

"What would you do?" I asked.

"Chase it," he said confidently.

I held reservations when Cayde volunteered to join this crew, as he was my older brother's friend, and I trusted nothing about Aagneya, but Cayde also sailed in my father's navy. He wouldn't do anything that would harm us.

"We should do that, then," I said.

As he moved to turn around, I thought of Aagneya once more, and reached out to touch his arm. "Why?"

He shrugged. "It's our first mission. The men are hungry for adventure, they are not yet battle-worn, and the ship has not had the chance to take on any wear. We are in the best shape we ever will be."

I grinned. "Good, then this will be easy."

"Stow your cargo, release the sails, brace for speed!" Cayde screamed above the whipping wind.

As soon as the words left his lips, the sloop jerked under my boots, and I threw my hands out to grip the railing in front of me. The air was filled with the sound of tearing cloth and vicious waves slapping against the belly of our ship. I knew that a sloop of war was fast, but I didn't realize how fast.

We gained speed quickly, and Orion darted past me to a gate that I hadn't noticed before. I leaned over the rail and sucked in a sharp breath as I watched one of the deckhands climb down a rope to hang over the hungrily stirring sea. Mist sprayed him, and sea-foam curled like fingers, tearing at his clothes as he perched precariously on a single plank attached to our starboard side.

"Count!" Orion yelled down.

Orion flipped an hourglass, and the boy lifted a reel with knotted rope. He threw the chunk of wood attached to the end, and it flew out behind the ship. The boy's bare toes gripped the wood beneath his feet, and he held his position fast, with fingers wrapped around the line as it slipped into the water below.

"Speed!" Orion screamed over the sound of the sails ripping through the wind.

The boy stopped the reel, releasing the knot in his hand and winding it with the crank. "Nine!" he called up.

Orion swore and turned away, while a few other crew members tossed a ladder over the side. "We need to lighten the load if we're going to make eleven and dusk," Orion declared.

He and Cayde looked at me, and I stuttered out, "Toss the biscuits?" They'd be the first to go bad and could hold a bit of weight.

Cayde shook his head a fraction of an inch. "The wine will be heavier, and we're chasing a beer merchant."

I nodded quickly. "Toss the wine."

"Dump the wine!" Cayde yelled, and a collective groan went up before the crew scrambled to the hold below. A working line was formed in a matter of minutes, and buckets of wine were passed from hand to hand to be poured overboard.

The next speed check took us to eleven knots, and our race against the sun began. I expected the ship to fall still at night. Instead, nearly half the crew stirred about the deck, lugging cannonballs and sharpening swords, or stowing ropes and stitching sails.

I wandered past my cabin, unable to force myself to go in. I should rest, but something about the brass plaque above the door, with CAPTAIN hammered into it in crooked letters made me uneasy. I paced instead, until I found Cayde watching the ocean from the quarterdeck, behind the wheel.

"I worry I won't know the right call," I said, addressing Cayde's back. He looked over his shoulder and smiled. "Perhaps you'd make a better captain," I finished.

"My last captain had been at sea for over twenty years before I joined his crew. The one before that was forty-eight. It's your first voyage." He released the wheel and motioned for me to take it. I grabbed one of the handles and was nearly bowled over before I straightened.

Cayde jerked his chin toward it. "Your place is steering this, commanding the crew. If I wanted to be in charge, I could have taken a ship years ago, but I am here to serve the crown, as my father did, as his did before him."

I laughed at that. "I bet my father never thought his son would ask for a ship instead of a plot of land and one of the cities."

Cayde raised a brow and eyed me up and down before lowering his voice. "I don't mean to speak out of place, Your Highness, but I only knew of His Majesty having one son and one daughter. I thought Yuvaraja Aagneya had already started training to join the court this year."

My face burned hot as my stomach, and I looked at my feet. "He has two sons now. I'd prefer if the crew only knew such as well."

Cayde clasped his hands behind his back and inclined his head. "Of course. As I said, I am here to serve the throne."

"Ship ho'!" someone called from the crow's nest, and we both looked up. Just off the bow was the obvious bright spot of white on the dark sea that indicated a ship. We were gaining on her, fast.

We did not beat the sun, but it was to our advantage. Wind whipped around our ship, offering us more speed than we could have hoped as the night wore on, and my crew wound themselves tightly in anticipation. The sails were raised when the enemy ship came into view, and only our dark flag flew above us, so if they saw us, they should know that while they sailed in Paalaivanam waters, the black ship of Thandu was near.

When the moon reached its peak, we coasted up to the ship's portside. She was named HM *Lunae* and flew the flag of Raktam. I snorted, looking up. What a disgrace to Prajapati. Clearly it was a ship that came from the west that had long since forgotten the gods and only praised the God of Night, of Death, and of Destruction: Rudra.

The crew gathered behind me and waited. I raised a fist, to hold their position. We slowed as silently as possible, passing planks from hand over hand and lowering them to the other ship's rail. Finally, I flattened my arm and allowed the crew to climb aboard the *Lunae*.

We did not make haste, hesitant to wake the other crew, but more scared to rock their ship more than the sea, lest we set off any hidden traps. Cayde stuck to my shadow, and we crept along like mice in the dark.

The watchmen on the ship raised no alarm, and as the minutes ticked by and I began to wonder why, I tripped over my answer—one of their men had been left with a severed neck. Bile rose in my throat, and Cayde caught me by the back of my shirt.

"A fall will wake them," he said, pointing to our feet. I looked down to where my foot balanced on the hilt of his sword and nodded, then scanned the deck, where our crew was working to silence more watchmen.

Panic began to flutter in my stomach, and I spun on Cayde. "I can't do this," I said, in a loud whisper.

His eyes widened, and he shook his head. "It's too late." He jerked a thumb over his shoulder at the now empty deck. "We have half our crew on this ship, we're in this with them."

I swallowed thickly and moved to step around him, but a rush of boots on wood pulled both of our attention.

"Captain!" voices whispered in unison. "They're hauling weapons!"

"There are no supplies!"

The crew stampeded toward the planks. An uproar began below my feet, and I stumbled back. Cayde caught my arm and dragged me toward our ship. Time moved so fast that I barely caught a glance of a crew clad in teal pouring over the steps before a rope was shoved into my fist and I was flung over the side of the ship. Instinct kicked in as I fell, and I twisted myself around, swinging over the sloop and rolling, trying to save myself any broken bones.

The crew was wild around me, dropping sails and throwing swords. The deep vibrato of cannon wheels rumbled through the wood at my knees, and I scrambled up, grabbing the arm of a man nearby. "What's going on?" I asked.

His mouth moved, but his words were barely audible over the raucous that played around us. "Battle!" I caught. My heart raced, and I released him. This was it, it was my time to be a captain. It had come quicker than I thought.

The HM *Lunae* was in the midst of waking—her crew was working to drop sails and lift their anchor. I made eye contact with one of their crew members as they attempted to release the planks we had thrown between our ships. Most of my crew worked to prepare our ship for offense. I ran for the bow, yelling as I moved.

"Man the cannons, burn the powder!" I stopped behind the wheel, where my extra weapons had been stored, and began to strap throwing blades to my thighs, sliding extras into my boots, and stuffing cannon powder satchels into my pockets.

"What are you on about?" Cayde roared, stomping up the deck.

"If they mean for battle, then we'll sink them!" I threw back, rushing for the mid-mast, where I worked to release the sails. Some of the boys ran to help me, and we began to turnabout slowly, facing our cannons at the ship's stern.

Cayde grimaced, hesitating as if he meant to protest, then echoed my cries to the crew. They leaped into action, piling cannonballs into empty crates, preparing kegs of powder. The King of Raktam's ship fled as we took aim. Booms rang through the air, deafening the shouts of both of our crews, but ours landed true in their hull.

Cries rang from their deck, and their longboats were flung into the waves. My heart lodged into my throat while their men scrambled to escape. They didn't try to fight back, and no one made it off the ship before another round of fire echoed. Thunder cracked followed by splintering wood as one of our cannons broke through their magazine, and explosions erupted throughout the hull in a whoosh of flame.

The ship fractured like porcelain dropped on stone and became engulfed in flame far quicker than should have been possible.

Their men screamed but fell into the wreckage, unable to board the lifeboats that floated away aimlessly. The ship crumbled and broke apart, sinking fast, and soon enough, night swallowed the *Lunae* and her crew whole.

"No survivors?" a voice asked from my elbow.

I glanced back to find my ship's writer waiting with a logbook open in one hand and a quill in the other, ready to write. I looked back to the sea, where only a mast broke the waves, and nodded. "I think it's safe to say there were none."

We watched in silence, Orion and Cayde arriving after a moment. The pieces of wood and stray canvas floating toward us left an uneasy feeling in my gut, and I finally worked up the courage to ask what bothered me.

"I've never sunk a ship before, but I feel a ton of beer shouldn't flame as it did. One of the crew said battle. He wasn't talking about battle with us, was he?" I looked to Cayde, whose gaze was fixed on the sea.

Orion spoke instead, leaning against the rail. "We only saw a hold full of weapons. Enough to flatten a city."

The writer continued, "Their captain's log marked a route to Thandu. I believe they intended to attack on behalf of their crown."

I whistled low and considered the orders we had sailed on. "Raktam is aiming to conquer more than just Aatma."

Cayde clapped my back. "The Maharajah must have suspected."

I cleared my throat and straightened from the barrel I sat on, pulling myself from the memory, and looked at the group in front of me. "So, there you have it."

The younger navigator raised a brow. "I thought you said it was bloody."

Cayde chuckled. "You're not good at inference, are you? We had to chase down the ships heading for our home. We intercepted a handful, killed everyone on board. We never did get the beer the Maharajah promised, but we gained new crew, earned the galleon, and weapons enough to equip a man-o'-war."

The boy's jaw dropped. "That's why you have your reputation as a pirate? You stopped the Iron King from an invasion?"

I nodded. I had left out the part of my story where I asked Cayde not to reveal the truth of my identity, and he was faithful from then on, so my reputation went deeper, but I did not need this young man to know that.

“I’d do it again. If Eudo were to set into the sea himself, I would have his head,” I said, grim. “If I had the armies he did, I would march around the world just to see him sent beyond the veil for what he did to Aatma, and to our Maharani, my mother.”

3

Zara

Warm currents wrapped around my fingers while my gaze fixed intently on the world beyond the filmy foam. Fluffy white clouds swirled through the powder blue sky, seeming to stretch on forever. I reached a hand up, fingertips breaking the calm surface, and the contrast of the hot air outside the cool water sent a shiver through my body. The bubbles that escaped my lips scrambled up to pop into the other world—the human world.

Which reminded me that my lungs had been protesting for nearly twenty minutes. It was time to stop lounging and refill my air supply.

I smoothed the fine hairs on my face down before tipping my curved nose up first, letting the rest of me follow with the push of the current. I had made the mistake of going up the wrong way a few times when I was young, and tried hard to avoid it now. Having your fur pushed sideways or backward by a stray wave was a less-than-comfortable experience.

Water sloughed off my head, and I gasped, my lungs burning at the intake. My lashes fluttered of their own accord, beating salty droplets from my eyes, and I shook my head to adjust to the dry world quickly. My vision was blurry at first, but by the time I had my fill of hungry breaths and my lungs were aching from being too full, I could see clearly.

The Kotik Ocean stretched out as far as I could see in front of me, midday sun spraying droplets of gold over its surface. I flicked my tail to hold steady as the sharp cries of navarin birds pierced through the sky as they flew east, but their wings flapped too fast to catch more than a blur of red. I froze as they descended in the distance—I swore I could see the glint of shining iron in the direction they flew, but I shook my head at my own anxiety. There was no way that I could see any part of Sariram from here.

I made a rude gesture in the continent's general direction anyway and turned my face to the sky. The sun's rays warmed my cheeks and relaxed my shoulders. Although I hated the dry world for the humans that it held, the heat outside offered a nice respite from my sister's company.

The tufts of hair on the back of my neck spiked when a splash of water crept near my scalp, interrupting my singular moment of peace. I snorted out a droplet of water and looked around, nearly expecting Juhi to shove me under the surface.

The sun had inched across the sky—I had stayed out longer than I expected—but I was still alone.

"Goodbye, Prajapati," I called to the god in the sky. He did not respond, of course. He never did. A small part of me wondered if he was truly up there, if he truly was the god that became the sun, as my mother had told me, or if the sun had simply always existed. But I did not dare question his position out loud while swimming in the oceans he had created.

I took one last breath of the fresh air, knowing that I wouldn't get to break the surface again until nightfall, and ducked back underwater.

The sudden cold on my scalp set every hair on my body up straight while I was blinded by fine bubbles flooding out of my fur. I patted myself down with my eyes closed, smoothing over the insulating layer of fur from my stomach, down my rear, over my tail joint, and flicked my fin up to press the clumps between my flippers flat. The bubbles in my eyes finally cleared so that I could see through the waters around me. Not a fish was in sight, all likely tucked in their homes, since the sun was going to start dropping soon. Teal ocean stretched far in every direction, including down, where I was sure that much larger creatures lurked, if I really felt like seeking company.

I pulled at the frayed cloth strip that hung from my shoulder to my hip and wrapped it over my head. Bunching my coarse hair into two clumps, I carefully wove it with the black cloth. A small smile ticked the corner of my mouth up as I tied the end off.

The open sea was ominously quiet as I swam toward home. Completely unbroken no matter what direction I looked. After a few minutes, I spied a reef covered in anemones and urchins and shot over dunes of sand and patches of rocks, spinning occasionally to break up the monotonous swim.

Something about my journey toward the island today felt different. I slowed as I reached the edge of the reef. Coral jutted out from the sandy cliff, dropping off into an abyss below me. I peered over the ledge of the trench into darkness that sent a shudder down my spine.

It was an unsettling dark that seemed to reach over the edge of the reef, stretching out to snatch anything that it might be able to drag into its never-ending depth. No one had ever been to the bottom of the trench, and it stretched endlessly to either continent.

The likelihood of falling in was slim. But there was always a chance. In those depths was the unknown. It could be residence to a kraken that feasted on katalval bones, or some witch that had transformed herself into a monster to seek revenge on the creatures of the sea.

I swallowed hard, swimming up and preparing to cross. My heart clenched at the width from reef to reef. It was simply unlike swimming over open ocean.

As I flicked my tail, something wrapped around my arm, and I released a scream. All of the air in my lungs burbled up from my throat. I lashed my tail out, and more restraints wrapped around my wrists, and seawater stung my nose. I gasped and flailed, darting toward the surface. Visions of drowning swept through my mind, and I was blinded by a flood of bubbles before the hair on my face stung at the root.

"Zara! Calm down!" Sai's voice broke around me as I choked on air, and her sharp nails dug into the muscles on my shoulders. I blinked the salt from my eyes, and the grip of her tail on mine loosened.

"What were you thinking?" I demanded, my vision clearing. My youngest sister's face came into focus, and I bit the inside of my cheek, fighting the urge to chastise her.

Her lower lip stuck out, and her long hair was wild from where I had gripped her to fight back.

"I meant to surprise you, not terrify you," Sai said, her voice barely more than a whisper.

I stifled another cough with a heavy sigh and reached out to tuck the hair back from her face. "I'm sorry," I said, smoothing the rough sand in my own voice.

Sai pressed the back of my hand against her cheek and smiled softly. "I forgive you. But you must hurry."

She ducked under my arm and dove beneath the surface before I could ask any questions. I had only a moment to decide whether or not to follow. Her shadow crossed the trench, and I took a deep breath before closing my eyes and diving toward her.

We tumbled toward the reef together, my stomach clenching as my tail fin grazed the rocky edge of the trench. I exhaled a stream of bubbles, and Sai gripped my back.

"You made it over," she said, her voice quivering as much as my body.

I choked out a laugh and pulled back to look at her. "Cheeky Chinna," I goaded, calling up her childhood nickname. Sai grinned and floated above me, holding out a hand, and we swam together toward home.

"You were late, so I thought the trench might be stopping you again," Sai said.

I shot her a sidelong look and swallowed hard. That deep hole in the ocean should not bother me as much as it did. There were far scarier things than the dark. And clearly my fear was affecting my family, if my young sister felt the need to come after me.

I finally shook my head, realizing that I had been quiet for a while, and motioned to the surface. "I was enjoying my time scouting, and had quite a bit of time in the sun. The navarin were flying north."

Sai smiled and nudged my arm. "That's good, I'm sure the sun will help your mood."

"I do not know what you speak of," I replied curtly.

I watched her shoulder lift from the corner of my eye before dropping, and I fixed my gaze ahead, hoping that she would not press the topic. It should not be any of her concern if I had a poor mood most days, if I struggled to smile or find joy in the things that I used to.

Once, happiness ruled my days. I swam freely, without purpose. But now... the responsibility of our people dying weighed too heavily on my shoulders to allow space for anything else.

A bright canvas of colors bloomed in the distance, and the tails of other katalval darted this way and that through our underwater home. The reef rose in different levels, arcing and spiraling around itself like a hundred conchs stacked together.

Domes made of rock were buried under layers of coral and anemones, housing different fish or brown-skinned katalval. We swam through an arch cut between two massive boulders, and the sea around us stilled. I kept my eyes peeled for any signs of the rot—tiny flecks of red-coated shards of iron that floated around, too easy to miss, through open water—but I knew our home below the island was safe.

The innermost part of the reef was vast and open, and hundreds of our people used it as a thoroughfare, swimming this way and that to reach their respective destinations.

An elder darted around me with a knitted seaweed bag full of debris tucked under her arm. A young boy stumbled past, his fins struggling to keep him afloat under the weight of a bundle of palm leaf.

My gaze drifted up, to the shadows, and I met my father's eyes.

He leaned against the kelp-covered opening to a council room, a frown affixed to his face.

"I should have told you before we made it here," Sai murmured under her breath, "a council meeting was called, and your presence was requested."

I quirked a brow at her. "What about Juhi? If you and I must be there, surely she should be as well," I said, referring to our other sister.

Sai shook her head. "She is still at Cankili. It is not a family meeting, it is for council and ruler."

I stopped swimming and gripped Sai's arms. "Take the throne," I said, sharply.

"You must stop that jest." Sai brushed me off and darted toward the meeting room, leaving me alone in the middle of the hall, jostled about by fast-moving katalval.

I threw my head back in frustration and followed her in.

"It is not a jest, and you know that," I snapped at my sister, settling onto a large rock beside her. Our father towered over us on my right, and the democratic council circled the rest of the room, leaving only one empty seat at the head of the assembly.

"I am lucky to have my advisory seat," Sai whispered. "Don't push my luck. *Please.*"

"What can anyone do? I am the heir, I am your sister!" I insisted.

Our father cleared his throat beside us, and a hush fell around the room.

"Let us begin." A woman named Navya rose, her braids floating behind her and large black eyes landing on each of us in turn. "Today is the second anniversary of Raanee's death, may she rest with Matsya in the waves."

Murmurs honoring the god that made up our seas echoed around the room, and I whispered mine in turn, "Om namo Matsya."

"We must thank Barun for serving as our leader for the last two years, through mourning his wife, and learning how to counsel our people."

A modest murmur of agreement circled the room, and Navya waited. She had gained her seat as the second of the council by possessing a power that no other katalval could imagine—she could change the form of herself and others, and therefore, she was our most respected elder. Behind the head of the council.

Navya resumed her seat, allowing our father to rise and clear his throat.

"Thank you, Navya. And thank you, all, for your advice over the years and assistance in guiding our people. Though it has been difficult, it is an honor to fill my wife's fins, until the day that my daughter is ready, which I am sure is quite soon."

He fixed his gaze on me, and the depth of his stare sunk into my stomach like iron sinking between the waves. I said nothing, and averted my eyes. Barun nodded briefly and clasped his hands.

"That is not the true reason we are here today, anyway. There has also been a sighting of ships, just north—"

A series of gasps cut Barun off, and he cleared his throat, waiting for the council to regain their composure.

"North of the island. Until now, the reefs have protected us, and I do not suspect that we face any attack by the humans aboard, but I am asking for volunteers to scout the ships and report back. The katalval that warned us advised the travel of two ships heading west by southwest, and we must ensure that our deterrents are lain on the other side of the trench."

Urchin pins pricked along my skin, and I jolted from my seat. "I will go!" I exclaimed. "I volunteer, I mean, to scout the ships and learn their motivations."

Barun's jaw snapped shut, and red tinged his cheeks. Applause broke out around the room, accompanied by cheers from the council.

"Our brave leader-to-be!"

"The heir apparent would volunteer!"

Barun's eyes hardened, and he jerked a thumb to the kelp curtain, flitting out behind it. I pushed my way through the throng of advisors, patting the back of wrinkled hands and returning the kisses the aunties pecked onto my cheek.

A hand gripped my wrist before I could leave the room, and I looked up into a pointed face. Navya held me in place.

"Do not let your father get to you," she said.

"Of course, Auntie," I responded. What else was there to say?

My father looked far smaller than he should, leaning against the wall in an empty room. The tide was out, leaving the water only waist-high, and his skin was damp with nerves and pallid in the moonlight.

He slumped over further as I treaded the low water and stopped in front of him.

"Father, I—"

"Why?" he asked in a low voice.

"Pardon?"

He pinched the bridge of his wide nose between his middle finger and thumb and turned his face to the sky. "Why do you insist on putting yourself in danger? Do you think that I don't hear about how you stray from our island? The liberties you take in crossing the trench or traveling past the southern border? Is it not enough that you have been allowed more time in mourning than anyone else? Can't you find happiness in the simple role that you have been given by your mother?"

I swallowed hard and twisted my fingers in front of me. "I wish to help our people, and I can't do that here. Sitting in a coral bed all day does nothing for them when I could be out there, finding a way to save them from the same fate as Mother."

"Juhi took up her place as a guard years before your mother passed. Sai has taken up station on the council. You are the only one who has not taken your position." Barun turned his watery gaze on me. "Please, daughter, tell me why you cannot find peace in filling your role. Must you subject me to losing my wife and also fearing for the future of my daughter?"

My stomach dropped, but I backed away and shook my head. I had carried the guilt of letting him fill my position for so long. It would not end now. "As long as our people die from the rot of those... those humans," I sputtered, "I shall know no peace."

Sai was waiting in the reef when I tore past, and I almost didn't see her through the tears in my eyes.

"What are you doing?" I asked, as she darted to catch up with me.

"I'm coming with, obviously." Sai reached out and handed me a bundle of banana leaf, and I slowed to an easier glide. "We'll stop for Juhi, too."

My fingers shook as I unwrapped the leaf and revealed pieces of sakka fruit. I thanked Sai and lifted a chunk, touching my palm to my forehead and offering the meal to the gods.

"Annam Prajapati, rasah Matsya, bhoktodevo Rudra."

"Annam rasah bhokta," Sai echoed my sentiments quickly, and pressed the piece of fruit to her tongue.

I chewed the sakka slowly, savoring the sweetness of the fruit's flesh, careful to tuck the seed from its pit into my cheek. The sinewy ribbons of its mild meat shredded easily between my teeth, and I swallowed my first piece, then a second, and a third, before I pressed the seeds back into the leaf and looked at Sai.

"Why did you stop saying the names of the gods when praying over your meals?"

We swam in silence for a long while, and I wondered if she had missed my question. The sun began to fade overhead, and Sai dropped the seeds from her fruit along our path, letting them sink below us.

She finally spoke when we reached the trench, and I hesitated before following her over.

"You live in fear of darkness every day. I knew your fear from the first moments I could dream, myself. I remember you scrambling in your sleep and nearly slipping beneath the water as you reached for light that did not exist."

Sai dropped a seed, and I watched it sink into the pit beneath us. I swallowed thickly.

"I have watched you struggle to cross a trench that no one should truly worry about, simply because it is dark."

I opened my mouth to protest. It was not so simple, there was more to fear, but she quieted me with a sideways glance.

"Do you ever wonder, if the gods truly existed, why would they strike such a fear into you? That you might struggle to travel to and from home without a companion. That you might nearly drown yourself every night, unless someone nearby grasps your hand and holds you throughout the worst of your night terrors?"

I slowed my swimming as my heart thudded hard and fast inside my chest.

"You hold my hand in the night?" I asked.

"Juhi and I both have. Before us, there was Mother," Sai said.

Something hot and achy bloomed in my lower stomach. Revulsion against my own needs, shame for my younger sisters seeing such vulnerability, and fear for what was to come from Sai's mouth next. I stopped moving and reached out for her.

She gripped my fingers, and a wry smile ticked her mouth up.

"Don't you think, if the gods were real, that they could craft us into exactly who we wanted to be? That I would not have been born in the wrong body? That you would not suffer from debilitating fears? That Mother would have fought off the rot and lived?"

The blood in my veins turned cold.

"Why should I make offerings to the gods, then, when they made me suffer a childhood measuring myself against sisters that had an unfair advantage?"

"I'm sorry, Sai. I never knew you felt that way." I stumbled over my words, and she released me, pulling her braid around and tugging on the end of it.

"And what of Navya?" I asked. "She helped transform your body into what you needed, yes? What if Matsya brought her to us for that reason?"

Sai scoffed before beginning to swim. "The gods are imperfect, and so long as they fail us, I will fail them."

"Wait," I said, "what do you mean by that?"

Her eyes were so dark when they turned on me that my stomach clenched into a knot. "Until you know the pain of Navya's ability, you will never understand. That Prajapati, Matsya, even Rudra, has forsaken us."

I let my youngest sister swim ahead then. I watched the weight of her burden bow her back in, her words stung my ears, and for the first time since our mother's death, I finally realized how old four and twenty looked on her.

Grief for her lodged in my throat, and I was quiet as I followed her.

The water became more murky the closer we got to Cankili. Sharp rocks and ledges jutted out from around it menacingly. The surface was devoid of any plant or marine life, which was ominous in its own right. Sai slowed her pace to a wobbly drift, and I kept my eyes peeled for any creatures that might have wandered this way.

It was rare for any katalval to travel this far north, but Juhi had an important role.

When she was only ten years old, she had begun to train with spears and knives—reclaimed from the sea floor—under the guide of our oldest warriors. She excelled with the blade, and with Mother's blessing, she joined our guard as the youngest and strongest.

The guard did not take an offensive role against the humans, ever. They existed only to protect the sea creatures that could not protect themselves. And our primary predator was no predator at all.

Once, all the waters of the Ranta Ocean had been clear. Before I had been allowed to swim alone, my father told me stories of his childhood. While he accompanied me around our island, the bay, or near reef cliffs, he spoke of when he was young. The sands had been free of debris and soft and clean enough to nap on. Wildlife roamed freely. There wasn't a place in the ocean that was unsafe for our people. All were protected and welcome.

I looked down at the seafloor as I remembered his words, and my stomach turned. Now pieces of metal winked from the ground. Half buried in the sand were forgotten knives, barrel belts, and other various broken and sharp things. And rings. The sun caught them from high above and made them sparkle like fish scales; from far away, that was what they looked like. But close up, they had an opening in them like a hook that could slice into flesh far easier than any blade or claw.

I grimaced and ignored the pull to swim down to the shine, instead yanking the makeshift filter from my neck up to cover my mouth and nose. It was courtesy of more human throwaways. The strips on either side tied behind my head, securing it so no floating pieces of ring rust could get into my airway. It was just too bad there was nothing I could use to cover my eyes with.

I swam up to Sai to ensure that her own filter was pulled tightly over her mouth and nose. She nodded to me and pointed ahead.

The wall loomed in front of us, and it was hard not to shiver in its shadow. Rainbows danced across its surface as we swam past, reflected from the metal waste below, and all the dancing lights were difficult to resist. But we were strong.

I forced myself to flit through the gulf entry, and it was like swimming straight through a curtain of sand. The water there was so thick with pollution that I could only see clearly about ten feet in front of me. I glanced down at the floor of the gulf and shuddered.

Where there should have been coral reefs housing schools of fish, and octopodes blending in with anemones, and blue bottle jellyfish, I couldn't see a speck of sand. The entirety of Cankili was buried in tiny looped pieces of metal, nearly closed into a full circle. Tens of thousands of the rings lay in piles, sprouting rust that filled the water around me. It mixed with the other waste collecting in the stagnant pool and turned the lower half of the gulf to toxic sludge.

So many rings. Tiny little things. Yet they caused so much damage. They produced slivers of rusted iron at an incredibly rapid rate, which filled our water. The polluted water was then breathed in by the creatures that lived here, making them sick. Or they would accidentally swallow a ring, and its sharp edge would slice through their intestines in a matter of minutes, and they would die of internal bleeding before anyone realized what had happened.

Or, like within the confines of the gulf, the rings began to pile up, slowly suffocating the sea beds until life simply couldn't exist anymore.

Thirty years ago, the gulf had been safe. There had been little rubbish from the humans there, just like everywhere else in the oceans from Ranta to Kotik to the South Seas. But the gulf had been a hub of activity for all marine life. Since the beaches were deserted, katalval could lounge there with sea stars, or potentially spot a jagarving—the great winged beings of Paalaivanam—since they loved the desert heat. I didn't remember the times myself, as I was very young, but my father told me stories. That was before the waste from the human wars began to suffocate us.

"Zara!" Sai exclaimed, grabbing my arm.

I looked up from the seafloor to where Sai pointed, and saw a tailed silhouette in the distance, and smiled.

The clear outline of Juhi's thick, muscled tail was perched against the wall in the distance.

"I think she hid from us," I said, voice muffled through the cloth of my filter.

Sai chuckled and nodded before slapping her fin through a current and taking off. I raced after her, cutting the waves expertly with my lashes pressed together, filtering the sand and allowing only a sliver of light in.

I reached Juhi first and tumbled over her. Sai collided with me, and we fell through the waves in a tangle of limbs and fins.

"What in the seas is wrong with you two?" Juhi asked, squirming out from between us with a chuckle. She lifted the filter that was fitted to her face, revealing a wide mouth and two sets of razor-sharp teeth under a pointed nose.

I looked between my sisters and heaved a sigh. "It has been a long day."

"I haven't seen you in two days," Juhi said, raising a brow, shoving Sai back before grabbing her into a proper hug that made our younger sister's eyes bulge.

"Right, of course," Sai agreed. "And I know it's been so long since you've been home—"

"But I am swimming to the north, where Ranta and Kotik meet. Barun said there was a sighting there," I finished.

Juhi gasped. "Why would he send you? Why not one of the guards? Like me?"

I lifted a shoulder, and Sai nudged me. "You had to be there, Juhi! Father said he wanted volunteers, and Zara just took the role like no one else was in the room."

Juhi's face drained of color, and she gripped my arms. "Is he angry?"

"I'm fine, but he's not happy."

"Since we're heading north, it made sense to gather you," Sai finished.

Juhi lifted a satchel from her hip and held it out. "Can you go find a place for these shells? I collected them yesterday from the debris and think they'll make good homes for the hermit crabs."

Sai snatched the bag and grumbled as she swam away, out of earshot.

Juhi pressed her hand to her chest, gripping the shell that hung on a necklace and twisting it. I tried not to smile at her familiar sign of nerves. "Do you have a death wish?"

I snorted. "I wouldn't wear a mask into the gulf if I did, would I?"

Her gaze darkened, and she leaned in. "Why would you leave the island, then? You know how dangerous it is out here."

I felt sheepish under my younger sister's glare. Why did I volunteer? Now that Sai and I had spent half the day swimming, and night was beginning to fall, the rush of doing something new was fading.

But as I studied Juhi's scarred hands that gripped my own, and looked at the hard sinew of her tail, I thought of how fiercely she protected our people, and how terribly I wanted to do the same.

"I can't continue treading the shallows, waiting for the tide to reach me."

Juhi slapped me on the back and grinned. "Well, it's about time you showed up." Then she laughed and yanked a spear from the holster on her back. "At least Barun can't say you're not fulfilling your destiny, or whatever he says anymore."

I smiled weakly and agreed, taking the spear that she shoved into my arms.

"And what of Sai? Why is she here?" she asked.

I hesitated before shrugging. "She needs to be included." The moment we had shared felt too private to let Juhi into. While Sai was sensitive and empathetic, Juhi was strong-willed and often abrasive.

"Alright, then... To the north," Juhi said.

To the north, indeed.

4

Dorian

Fragments of light shone on the walls and ceiling, reflected from the bejeweled costumes of the contortionist trio moving about on the council table. They wore white as pure as the snow atop the Tala Mountains—a stark contrast to the rich tapestries that decorated the room around us.

I leaned back in my seat, gripping the carved sides with tight fingers as the advisory board shuffled in, and forced my eyes from our entertainers. Father took the head of the table. Other members passed me by, nodding or throwing murmured acknowledgments my way as they found a seat. When the last chair scraped into position, a violin was stroked behind me, and soft music filled the air, just under the hum of conversation.

"We must read the agenda, and take names," Duke Hastings said, prodding the arm of Father's gentleman-in-waiting, Lewis.

Lewis's nose wrinkled in return, and he pulled his scroll away, turning to face the middle of the table and clearing his throat.

The woman on the table moved, twisting her arms above her head and fanning her hands out like wings. She lifted a leg, furthering her parallel to a bird, and winked at me.

"We have a few items to attend to. Of utmost importance, marked by the king—"

"Long may he reign," the duke interrupted.

"Aubrey," the king warned. Duke Hastings's already translucent face paled, and I stifled a chuckle.

The board shuffled at the interruption, and I straightened. "Really, Hastings. Can't we have one meeting where you know your place?" I folded my hands and met his gaze, which he narrowed.

He opened his mouth, as if to snap back at me, but Lewis unrolled the scroll and began to speak again. "In the matter of the king's concern, a hybrid was spotted off the coast of Paalaivanam by our Captain and Commander of Ships, Trevor Nottley."

Heads turned to the weathered sailor, whose windburned cheeks turned up with his grin and chest puffed out with pride.

The door opened behind me, breaking the chords from our small band, and I felt a clap on my shoulder before Hari took the seat beside me, the dissonance from scraping his chair causing an itch in my ear.

I fixed my palm to my chair, fighting against the urge to reach out to touch him, and looked at the large painting of the sea behind the naval commander. My eyes traced the peaks and dips of the waves, and a deep longing filled my chest. I sighed and turned back to the table. There was nowhere to look in this room that didn't cause some sort of discomfort.

"Sir Trevor Nottley reported back immediately of the sighting, and a decision must now be made of how to proceed." Lewis looked around the table, catching my eye, the captain's, my father's, and avoiding the duke.

Hastings cleared his throat, and Lewis ignored him, continuing.

"His Majesty the King would like to open the floor to suggestions, beginning with that of sending our navy out to hunt the hybrid."

Hastings cleared his throat again, and Lewis dropped his scroll, releasing an exasperated sigh. "Sky's above, my lord, what is so crucial that you must interrupt my every sentence? Does a fire burn under your chair?"

The rest of the table laughed as Hastings shifted in his seat, and his jaw twitched before he spoke. "What of the rest of the council, Majesty? Should we not wait?" He spoke only to the king, and I rolled my eyes, looking back to the entertainers atop our table.

The first woman lay flat out, allowing the second to bend backward above her, with hands wrapped around her own ankles. Her white-painted lashes fluttered at me, and I inclined my head to her, turning to look back to the pair of advisors now in dispute.

But my gaze lingered on the man contorting himself behind the women. His skin was pale as a scallop, and eyes a piercing yellow. I found my stomach twisting in a copy of his arm behind his neck, unable to look away. Hunger burned in my belly for his crooked smile. He turned his face slightly, allowing me to drink in the way his nose curved up and lips pouted. His golden hair caught the light, and he planted his silk-clad toes against the mahogany table, lifting en pointe and snaking his hands from his head to behind his knees.

As the cello was stroked, the man spread his legs and dropped his head, pushing his feet behind his neck. His breeches shifted open at the thighs, and the longing in my gut suddenly eased. I looked away as a sour taste filled my mouth.

Duke Hastings was staring at me. I blinked, realizing his thin mouth was moving.

"What?" I asked.

He sighed heavily. "We were discussing the implication of sending a fleet to find this hybrid, Highness." Though he addressed me as a prince, his voice held distaste, and I raised a brow.

I turned to the rest of the council. Seven others sat around the table, which was headed by King Durling. "And what if we don't?"

I thought hard, trying to remember where it was spotted, but could conjure nothing but golden eyes from memory.

My father leaned forward. "We can send a ship to the Isle and see if we spot one there."

I nodded. "That sounds like it would save resources, no?"

Lewis answered. "We have been doing as such for years, every other moon, on the king's command. This is the first time a sighting has occurred near Paalaivanam, Highness. There is also the matter of farming, from inland."

"Which is what we have been discussing," Trevor added.

I clasped my hands and nodded. "That sounds like quite the situation."

My father turned toward me. "So, what would you have done?"

Hastings's head swung between us quickly as I sat back, glancing again to the contorted man. His body twisted, arms bent, and hips open, like an invitation.

I forced myself to return to my father as my mind raced. I should have been paying attention. A wrinkle formed between his brows, below the jewel of his crown.

I just didn't care. I didn't want to deal with the farming, whatever the issue may be, or the hybrid. He had been chasing them my entire life and talked of sightings at least once a year. I was tired of it all.

"I'm not sure how I'm to answer, or even why my answer matters," I finally said.

My father regarded me coolly, leaning against the arm of his high-backed chair. "How can we allow you to take the throne if you can't make a tactical decision?"

I shrugged, moving to stand. "Send the fleet, it's not like it affects my position in this castle."

He rose in tandem and slapped his hands on the table. "Sit down." He motioned around the room. "This room is filled with only excellence, and I will not have my only heir detracting from the greatness I have built. You must contribute!"

I obeyed but splayed my fingers on the wooden top. "Might I go with the fleet? Will their travel allow me out on the open sea?" I asked, glancing around the room.

Lewis cleared his throat, ignoring my request, and said, "We might propose a reward to the city-states. Troops, money, and a visit from His Majesty the King—"

The duke raised his hand to his chest, mouth opening to speak, and my father reached over his chair, slapping him loud enough that the crack cut off Lewis's words.

The duke gasped loudly at the impact, throwing his own hand to cover his cheek.

I stifled a laugh, and Lewis continued. "It might help aid our searches. Free labor for the conquest of capturing one of the monsters."

Eudo pursed his lips, pressing his fingertips to them. The bejeweled man on the table bent backward, and his tongue glided across his bottom lip. The women at his sides stroked his spread calves before pressing their own chests against either side of his head. His eyes burned a hole into my clothing, and heat crept up my neck.

"We will reconvene on the matter," Eudo said with a sigh.

Lewis lifted his scroll. "His Highness must still observe the potentials for the queen, at His Majesty's request."

My eyes widened a fraction as I tore my gaze from the show. "You jest," I demanded of my father, whose mouth flattened in response. When did we get to this topic?

"Quiet, boy. My daughter is among these fine ladies of Raktam," Hastings snapped.

The king slammed a hand on the table, turning on the duke. "You will not forget your place, Aubrey."

Hastings lowered his head, mumbling an apology, as the guards at the door moved.

"First to appear shall be the daughter of the duke, Miss Bernadette Hastings."

I rolled my eyes, glancing at Hari, who frowned and shrugged. My father's jaw was set as he stared at the door opening across the room, and I lifted my gaze back to the center of the table, staring into the contortionist's golden eyes intently. I would not entertain the idea of marrying the duke's daughter just to ascend. The man in white stretched his arms out on the table; keeping his legs behind his head, he folded himself in half. More of his skin was revealed along his calves and forearms as he bent further, and my heart rate picked up.

Why did I have to marry to take the throne? What an archaic rule it was to take a wife. Why not a husband, or no one at all?

5

VESHAK

FLAMES DANCED AROUND MY vision while a deep buzz filled my ears, and a steady thudding beat drilled pain into the base of my skull. I couldn't tell if it was from yesterday's hangover or today's drink, but as I tipped my head back and looked at the stars, and belched, heat climbed my throat, and I thought that it must be both. I swallowed back the flames that threatened to pour from my mouth and looked around at my crew. Some danced, some stood around by the cannons, and the rest sat around the fire that burned in the middle of the deck.

Whoever engineered the basin that held the fire had a death wish for all of us, or they forgot how flammable the ship was. I grinned to myself at that thought, tempted to sit directly in the tub of flames and warm my constantly damp skin.

I shook my head and kicked my feet off the wheel, sweeping my hat from my knee and standing with a groan. The crew needed me to be responsible. I plopped it back on my head, but a hiccup escaped me and knocked it askew as I stumbled down the steps. As soon as my feet hit the main deck, the crew's voices fell to a murmur. It only irked me a little. I was planning to turn in to my cabin immediately, but sucked a breath in through my teeth and rolled my neck before taking a lap around. The click of my boots on the planks with the wild music, loud laughter—noticeably behind me—created the worst kind of orchestra. The pain in my head traveled behind my eyes as I turned at the stern. A group of sailors jostled about the cannons, clearly drunk on our dwindling supply of wine. Sky's above, I hoped they weren't intending to shoot those off. We were aching for ammo as it was.

The creak of my door pierced deep into my brain, and I winced as I tried to latch it quietly. The crew swung back into their full, loud spirits once the door was shut, and it did not go unnoticed by me, no matter how unsteady my steps might have been.

I needed to lay off the drink. But months at sea without a break in luck really brought morale down. I could feel it affecting the crew, which is why I couldn't blame them for their cold shoulders. We were all hurting for a good payday. There'd been nary another ship out worth capturing, no raids to be had. I had half a mind to just raze the beaches of Raktam down and steal from the Iron King himself. But my ship was better than that. I was better than that. I had to be.

A voice outside jerked my head up, and I realized I hadn't moved from holding the door closed. I froze in place as it became clearer.

"He's gone off the plank. It's been two months since last pay. We have to do something." I recognized the voice of my watch lead, Ward, and I held my breath, pressing my ear to the door to listen. Blood rushed through my ears, and I mentally cursed the seas for the bad inclinations that dulled my senses.

"What can we do?" someone else asked.

"We could protest. There's a way. We could take the ship. Some of the..." His voice fell away with the sound of receding boots. I could only assume that they'd moved past my cabin.

I gripped my head and turned from the door, swearing. Of course they were mad. Furious, more like. They had a right to be. When I was given the ship, I swore that the crew would never go without. I had to earn my place as their captain, and here I was... failing.

Shit, how naive had I been to make that stupid vow? I hadn't realized just how bad it could get at sea. Even working for the royal house, we could suffer.

I moved to the cot roughly, nearly stumbling over the corner of my desk. A ledger fell to the ground while I tried to unravel the mental threads of how to avoid a mutiny. I fell on my back on the window cushion, studying the knotted wood ceiling through blurred vision. A sigh escaped me, and I kicked a foot up on the wall. I needed to take better care of my crew. They needed assurances.

Darkness crept into my vision as I considered what to do next. The ship rocked. My head pounded. The drums faded to a dull thud.

Thump.

Thump.

Thump.

"Veshak!"

The pounding was back in my head, tenfold worse than before sleep took me.

The same lulling sway of the sea that put me to sleep sloshed the contents of my stomach, and as I rolled to the side, bile rose in my throat. A groan slipped through my lips as the pounding got louder.

"Veshak!"

I realized it wasn't just my head then. Someone was banging on the door. And I had made the disastrous mistake of latching it... which meant I had to get out of my cot.

I rolled from the cushions and dropped on all fours, belching as I moved.

As I crawled to the door, cracking my sleep-coated eyes, he yelled again. "Rajakumara, get your gods damned rear up!"

An involuntary hiss escaped my lips as I bolted upright and lurched for the handle, jerking it open and grabbing a fistful of Cayde's shirt.

"Don't call me that." The words cut through gritted teeth, and it took me a moment to realize he was laughing.

"Don't act like royalty, then. Come, there's news. We need you topside."

He pried my fingers loose from his blouse and danced back a step before I was able to swipe out a fist. As he jogged away, I doubled over, retching.

I did not expect the night before to do such a number on me, and my head was as murky as the waters around Cankili. I tried hard to keep up with the crew when it came to their nightly habits, but I was just not built the same.

A bead of sweat rolled down my spine, urging me to move, so I ducked back into the room and snatched up a canteen, guzzling like a man stranded before moving for the upper deck. As I cleared the landing, the first thing to strike me was how silent the ship was. My eyes adjusted to the sun, and I quickly realized that no one was at their station. Instead, forty-odd backs faced me, leaning over the starboard rails.

"What in the— AYE!" My voice snapped out over the crowd, and nearly every spine straightened. "Get back to work!" I scanned the group for Cayde as they began to disperse among low grumbles. He was crouched next to Orion, hugging the rail as if he might climb right over it, while Orion's eye was firmly attached to a spyglass. Neither of them moved.

I swore under my breath and hobbled toward them, arm wound tight over my stomach.

"What do you want?" My question was gruffer than I intended, and Cayde raised a brow at me, while Orion jumped to attention.

"There's a ship on the horizon, Captain," he said, voice shaking.

"No bloody way. Let me see that." I reached for the glass, and he fumbled it into my hand. Cayde pointed southwest.

"If we shift sails, we can probably catch them. Looks like a square-rigger from inland. If they're coming up the south side of Aatma, they're definitely not a Raktam vessel, which means they likely haven't been discharged yet. Could have valuables. Or at least food."

In the distance was a long ship with three tall masts. Their multitude of wide sails would make them slow, and their plain belly showed a lack of status. They seemed to be on a path perpendicular to us, and with the size of them, they would have the space to carry half a year's worth of meat. They had to be a trader.

"Or nothing at all. They could be a pickup vessel." I finished for him, snapping the spyglass closed. They were certainly not a Raktam ship, lacking the typical iron decorum that the ruddy kingdom prided itself on sullying everything with, including small merchants. But why they would be coming up from the south confused me. The closest place on that side of the Kotik was Kallu. And the city was located so far inland that traveling by sea made no sense.

"You don't think they might be braving the ruins, do you?" Cayde piped up, interrupting my thoughts. My brow furrowed, and I shook my head.

"I don't see why anyone would. There's no reason to." I looked up again, studying the speck on the horizon. It looked tiny without the magnifier.

The thought of anyone sailing around to scavenge in the ruins of the old Aatma Kingdom was asinine. For one, the place had been destroyed an entire generation before, when my mother was my age.

For two, a shipyard lay between the open ocean and any docking point. Navigating it was asking for certain death.

I nodded firmly. "Alright. Call it. Turn the rudder, hoist the sails. We're after a merchant and a payday." Orion straightened again. "We'll need to board the sloop. The galleon doesn't have the speed, and she needs a clean," I said. "Plot the course for interception just after Aatma and west of the Isle. Don't let them get any closer to Raktam." I said with finality.

They both saluted and ran to alert the crew, leaving me to look out over the sea for another moment. Ships moving from the south just didn't make sense. But we could block them off quickly. I'd get an answer from their captain, and gather pay for my men.

Cayde started yelling then, and a flurry of movement kicked up behind me. I pressed my fingers to my tender skull to stifle the pain there, but a grin forced its way over my face at the sudden spike of energy. Feet pounded across the deck, and the rip of canvas unfurling from nearby forced my heart into my throat. The trumpeter threw a wild tune into the air as he sprinted across the ship, and I heard the fiddle join him from below. I couldn't help but think that everyone would be in good spirits that night, if we could just get a score.

I strode across the deck to our portside. Yanking a rope from the mid-mast, I secured a knot in it and tossed it over the sloop's foreyard before swinging over the gap between the boats.

A heavy drumbeat, accompanied by the vibration of a trumpet, traveled through the fibers of the deck and reverberated through my chest once I landed. Cayde was already at the wheel, preparing our course. Ward rushed past, his muscled form nearly knocking me aside, with a group of cannon hands behind him.

We could sail the sloop with a skeleton crew of sixteen, but a full deck greeted me when I took my place beside Cayde: eighty sets of eyes staring. Orion saluted from the galleon before pulling the boarding planks back and motioning for the sails to drop. They would stay where we left them until we returned.

"You have served as ideal privateers under the Maharajah, taking only what I've commanded, returning information to the Royal Mahal, and arresting enemies of his crown. Today, we sail back into enemy waters, where we would be branded as pirates." My voice carried evenly over the ship, and crew from the galleon even stopped to listen from the rails above. "We will not be caught!" I yelled.

My men cheered back.

"We take to survive. We do not start wars with no cause. And we do not trade in people! We may be bloodthirsty pirates to them, but so long as our flag carries the marque of Paalaivanam, we sail with honor!"

Our ship cut through the sea hungry as a shark chasing a trail of blood. The sails choked on the air that filled them, nearly tearing at the seams, and great swaths of foam chafed the keel beneath us.

We came upon the ship much sooner than we expected, south of where we left our galleon.

The cacophony my men returned howled through my ears and strummed my nerves, tuning my pulse to the musikers metronome. The trumpets played violently below the spanker brace, building to a crescendo meant to terrify the ship we were approaching, and my own body reacted accordingly. A quick glance through my spyglass showed a flagless three-masted barque with a copper plate wrapped around her. It was definitely a merchant. But why they were out this far at sea made no sense. If they were traveling from Jihva, a large city on the southern coast, they should have stayed closer to the continent. Instead... they were nearly within a stone's throw of Mautakheli Isle.

Cayde let out a hum next to me, drawing my attention from the trader. He motioned at the waves peeling away below us.

"It's been a long time since our rig moved like this."

I nodded and slapped the rail, wincing at the pain still shooting down the side of my skull.

"A long time since you came on the little one, anyway," he continued.

"Indeed."

I sighed and turned to the rest of the boat, taking in the crew manning their stations: yanking ropes, stuffing cannons, running supplies, and sharpening hand weapons. We were minutes from pulling alongside the other vessel, and it was nearly time to board. The single-level deck settled something on my heart. This boat was great for running attacks. But that was all.

"Ready the plank!" I bellowed, descending toward the bow. Orion had stayed on the galleon but sent us with one of his cox'ns, who I think was named Lance. "Keep her steady up their port."

"Aye," Lance said, releasing the wheel and letting it turn with the wind. I slapped him on the shoulder as a gunner approached.

"Are we not giving a chance of surrender?" he asked. His eyes were wide, and I glanced at his smooth skin, flush from the wind at our stern.

I cleared my throat and spoke loud enough that anyone near us would hear me. "This crew needs some action, it's been long enough. Today is raid first, questions later!"

A cheer raised from the cannon group nearby, and a grin crept up my face. The broad side of the merchant ship rose up next to us. An officer of the opposing ship hung off a rope ladder slung on the center mast, arm waving wildly. He yelled something indiscernible over the music and gestured up. I followed his gaze to our black flag with a padma maut surrounded by swirling designs, the torn edges flapping freely in the breeze, and winked at him. They had still not raised any colors.

"Take what you will!" I shouted, and the band behind me ferociously picked up their tune. My crew let out a collective bellow; a few stray, high screams sounded; and feet stomped. I raised the sword in my hand and looked across the plank that had been slapped down to watch the recognition register in the other crew's faces as they realized what was happening.

We had done this many times before. They thought we were another cruiser approaching to talk trade routes. We boarded with blades burning and pipes screaming. Then the inferior crew fell in minutes.

I was rooted to the deck, watching my people crawl up the plank, some ignoring it altogether and jumping from the side of our boat to sink daggers into the broad side of our enemy, bleeding her of salty water she had taken on and using their blades as picks to crawl up and over the rail. Their roars intertwined with the sound of the waves crashing up between our ships, and our trumpeter and drummer's tunes thrummed through the air. As the cannons swiveled into place, ready to sink the other if they overwhelmed us, I finally moved and dashed up the bridge. I leaped off their railing and crashed down in front of a man in an open shirt.

The sharp edge of my blade lodged into his gut easily. It pulled his lower intestine out upon exit and turned the cream of his linen clothes a deep maroon color. His full lips were still open around yellowed teeth in shock when he dropped to his knees. I spun to meet another enemy before he stopped breathing, yanking a dagger from my boot and throwing it into a spin to lodge into someone's bright-blue eye before decapitating a woman that tried to sweep a thin sword at my shins. Clearly these people were not prepared. They were attacking haphazardly instead of in union. Jihva should be better versed in what to expect on the open ocean.

A bellow to my left drew my attention, and another member of the linen-clad crew charged me with a short sword raised in front of his face, looking down the blade like it was an arrow strung on a bow. As if running with a pommel at his eye socket could achieve anything but self-harm.

I stepped aside as he stumbled past, jammed my elbow into the middle of his back, and kicked out to trip him. When he fell to the deck, I yanked out another dagger from my belt and slid it in the base of his neck before he had a chance to move. I almost felt bad for the ship's crew. They were slow and unorganized.

Cayde whistled and pointed up to a beefy man with a large belly standing atop the foreyard. He was just finishing a spirited yell. He banged on his chest once. I squinted. He twisted a rope around his fist, and before I could hazard a guess at what would come next, he launched himself from the nest.

"What in the depths?" I muttered.

He swung, sliding down the rope, arcing too wide. He scrambled at the last second, and his torso met the deck's railing with a sickening crunch. He fell back in a heap, groaning.

I met Cayde's gaze, and it hit me then. Only one ship could sail so inexperienced.

"Kallu!" I yelled.

My entire crew stiffened, and I was able to easily pick them out of my peripherals, spotted around the deck. Sky's above, what would we do? We had a reputation, but Kallu would have no idea. It was no wonder they were so brazenly attacking us and had no clue how to manage a fight. They were a smaller city-state—really a town—set so far inland on Sariram that they only ventured to sea once a decade, if that. It was no wonder that they were in an unmarked ship. They likely only had the one, and it would have been set aside for use by their only royal.

Shit, what a disaster! Attacking them was unethical slaughter. But we had a job to do as well. I had men to feed and pay.

"Rudra's balls," I cursed under my breath, stowing my sword. Two months without a job, and this is what I was faced with.

I grimaced and let out a shrill whistle, mimicking Cayde's signal that our entire crew used to get each other's attention. Mine was higher pitched than the other and drew all eyes.

I had only a moment to make a decision. They needed the pay, we needed goods, but we could not continue fighting men that could not fight back. My head spun and heart thudded hard in my chest.

I finally raised my hand in the air and closed my fist, motioning back to the ship, indicating that we should ease our attack.

A few of the crew nodded, and I checked the confused looks before lifting my hat at the others. Finally, recognition registered across every face I could see, and we moved back into the fray as a unit, less furious than before. The whole interaction took only a moment, and my heart thundered in my ears the entire time. I had to be grateful they understood me without words.

I was rushed immediately upon turning away from the stern. I didn't aim for a kill like before, instead yanking a rope from my waist. I threw an open hand up at the man's throat and stopped him in his tracks as he gasped for air at the sudden impact, and I had ample time to run around and bind his hands, bringing him to his knees and securing his wrists to his ankles.

"We may be vicious, but we are not monsters," I told the man as I finished tying the knots. He ignored me, but I nodded to myself. This was the right choice.

Their entire ship's contents were still ours for the taking... But I wasn't heartless. They'd be left alive with rations to return to where they came from. First, we'd capture the crew, then I was going to question their captain.

6

Zara

My fingers twitched around the spear that Juhi forced me to carry. The spear itself was rough in my hand. It was a weapon of the time before iron, with a heavy wooden handle and sharp steel point, recycled from an old harpoon. Something about its weight felt threatening, as if it would turn on me as I swam.

"I don't know about this," Sai said, holding her weapon away from her body. "I still don't know how to use it." The curved dagger in her palm was small and less of a threat than a defense.

Juhi rolled her eyes. "Every woman should! Just holster it, you may need the protection."

Sai grimaced and tucked it into the leather strap at her waist, and Juhi lifted the satchel she carried, carefully pulling out a solid ball of dead coral. Steel rods from the refuse of weapons before the iron war had been jammed into it, and it resembled a hand-sized urchin now.

"I brought some sea spikes too," she said with a grin.

"Where did you get those?" Sai blanched.

"I stow them in the gulf," Juhi said with a shrug.

I shook my head. "You're diabolical, for no good reason."

Sai touched my elbow, pointing to the surface above us. The sun was beginning to dip low. I nodded and led the way to the open ocean.

The water dropped in temperature as we swam, forcing the hair on my tail to puff up to further protect me. As the sun dripped his last light into the sea, the edge of the reef rose up in front of us. Juhi flashed an impish grin at me before flicking her flipper and shooting past me in a burst of speed. A flurry of bubbles assaulted my face, and I smiled through closed teeth before racing to catch up to her. Sai yelled something behind me, but I kept swimming. The water was the clearest I had seen all day. The reef grew around us, and fish peeked out of their homes as we raced by, but no matter how hard I pushed myself, I couldn't catch up with her. I knew she would tease me later for being slow—I blamed her head start.

We shot over the edge of the reef, and Sai gained on my tail. I saw her braid in my peripheral for a second before I kicked hard and passed her by again. I reached out, nearly touching Juhi before she made a hairpin turn, heading for the surface. My heart skipped a beat, and I spun in her wake, using the momentum to follow. I managed to break into the balmy air moments after her. With my heart racing, my lungs screamed for air from the exertion of the swim, and I gasped, floundering above the surface for a moment. I blinked fast to adjust my vision at the same moment her flipper crashed into mine, and I was thrown back. Salt water rained around us. A laugh burbled from my lips, and I grabbed her wrists and spun us until I was above her. I still couldn't see, but I could feel a fine coating of bubbles on my face from the flailing, and her tail joint dug into my stomach.

Cold air broke the tension around my face, and I gasped, throwing myself away from her. Juhi moved to tackle me again, but I raised my hands.

"Zara!" Juhi yelled from where she held me.

"I concede!" I cried. Juhi grinned wide and shoved me one last time.

“Imagine trying to fight a warrior,” she scoffed.

I rolled my eyes and raised my palms to flatten the hair on my face, turning to find Sai and make sure she hadn’t been lost.

I stuttered to a stop. In the distance, sails loomed on the surface of the water, fabric flicking in the wind.

“By Matsya, I didn’t believe it...” I said.

Juhi twisted the shell that rested between her breasts.

“Fuck, we’re going to die,” Sai said.

“No, we are not,” I snapped. “Let’s go.”

Foam streams jetted behind me for the second time, though now I wasn’t racing for fun, but for the good of my people. The implication of humans so close to our home was unimaginable.

An uncomfortable urgency settled around us the moment we saw the ship. I felt the change in the sea. There was no physical marker to move through, nor magic; it was a sense that we were leaving safety and storming toward the gallows ahead.

We swam through the dark, open ocean for twenty minutes with silence stretching between us. The water did us no favor of retaining sunlight, so we had to rely on our eyes to invert the dark shadows of night—when they presented themselves.

I kept my gaze ahead for most of the swim.

The curved underside of a boat emerged, and I pursed my lips with disapproval, pushing ahead of my sisters to put a layer of protection between them and the danger. The spear in my palm grew heavier. I knew the chances of an encounter were low, but after four years without seeing a human, or other beings with legs, I couldn’t help but heed the sea snails wriggling around my gut. Then I noticed there was a strange shadow under the ship. I squinted.

I stuttered to a stop as I realized there were two of the long beams sticking into our ocean.

Two ships.

Two batches of unwelcome humans.

I braced myself and surfaced. Juhi broke next to me a moment later, immediately followed by Sai. We were directly next to the smaller boat, at its flat back. Thank the gods it was dark enough that no human would be able to see us with their notably terrible vision.

As soon as the barrier of water fell from my ears, I slapped my hands against them at the raucousness that assaulted us. The air was filled with an earsplitting combination of terrified screams and unfamiliar commands being thrown about, barely overshadowed by grunts and bellowed orders. The noise was further layered with the sound of tearing and rippling cloth. The voices were all fighting to avoid drowning under some unnaturally brassy tones, scratching and screeching trills, and some wheezing lung that was about to give out. The loudest of it came from above where we surfaced.

I looked to my sisters desperately, but their faces were pulled in the same pained way mine was. The fine hairs on their cheeks stood straight up, their brows raised and their mouths dropped open. Juhi's hands were clasped to the sides of her head, sharp nails digging into the wet hair that was plastered to her temples. Sai's eyes bore into mine, begging for reprieve from the chaos. I finally gritted my jaw and dropped my hands. The onslaught was painful and kicked up an ache at the base of my skull that I'd never experienced before.

How these humans existed, I'd never understand. All I wanted to do was dive back under the water where it was quiet and safe. But instead I pulled out my spear and gripped it tightly, nodded to my sisters, and swept around the side of the massive container. The insane caterwaul continued as we swam, and we paused under one of the weapons that jutted out from the ship's side.

A scream rang out from above, followed by a clear yell of, "Man overboard!"

A body flew above us. My back seized, and I threw my arm out to hold my sisters and I up against the wood grain as the human arced over the water. We watched with dropped jaws as his limp form was swallowed by hungry waves. A second later, Juhi shoved me out of the way and dove toward him.

The seconds ticked by. My heart raced, and Sai twisted her fingers into mine.

If I followed her, it could jeopardize her safety. A minute passed, then two. As I raised my tail to shoot under the water, she surfaced. Holding the man's severed head.

"We couldn't risk him swimming and carrying tales to the surface," she whispered once she was near.

I nodded, and she dropped the grotesque thing. It sank quickly, and Sai covered her mouth in horror.

"Fiercest warrior," I reminded her, and myself. The title assigned by the last ruler, our mother, when Juhi became old enough to fight, had regularly slipped my mind. She'd been our fastest and strongest for a long time, but as the oldest sister, I wanted to protect her.

With the memory, I glanced at Sai. My stomach twisted at the fear in her eyes, the way she chewed on her lower lip. Her curls fell flat around her face, and I lifted one, twisting it. "You shouldn't be here," I said, as quietly as the roar above us would allow.

The color drained from her face, and Juhi placed a hand on her shoulder.

"I want to help," Sai retorted, fighting against Juhi's might.

"You are counsel to Barun," Juhi said. "If something happens to us, you'll be needed at home."

I nodded. "Plus, you'll be needed to lead our people."

Her eyes widened as she searched my face. "But..." Her protest died on her tongue, and I made a *tsk* sound.

I gripped her hand tightly. "You must stop fighting it. I have tried to pass the role to you so many times. I will never be able to lead our people, and now, more than ever, proves that we need you in Mother's seat."

Tears swam in her eyes, and she nodded firmly. "I shall inform the council what's happened."

Juhi moved away. "Swim with care, sister."

I nodded my agreement before giving her a squeeze and releasing her.

"Be safe," Sai said, then dove back beneath the surface.

I took a steadying breath before turning to Juhi.

"Ready?" she asked. The corner of her mouth quirked up, and she led me farther down the side of the boat. The noise quieted suddenly, and we stilled under yet another weapon. Some humans spoke low in the distance, but the sharp screeching tones were no longer around to dampen them. Then two voices were carried over the edge to us.

"Why would you be so close to the Isle?" They spoke low, soft, and dangerous. This one was definitely in charge.

"I-I heard of a hybrid." This voice was scared but gruff.

My body stiffened. That's what they called us. Hybrids. It sounded like a dirty word from their mouths, as if we were mixed with something unknown or unliked. We weren't anything hybrid. We were proud katalval. Not that the Sarians understood that.

"A hybrid?" Soft asked.

Gruff whimpered.

"Why did you seek them?" Soft pressed.

"Raktam promised coin. Enough to retire on. A proclamation was sent all across Sariram. We've never even been on the sea. Do you know how landlocked we are in Kallu? But we fell destitute after the war from Raktam, just like everyone else, and our lord would do anything to dig us out of poverty." The pleading in Gruff's voice was sickening, and Soft grunted in response. Why humans held power over one another was a mystery to me. There was a beat of silence before I heard something heavy thunk across the wood.

"The promise of coin is a joke. Leave this ridiculous quest and return home. Those people are not to be hunted," Soft growled. My pulse thudded. A human that wouldn't hunt us? They had to be lying. They were going to turn around and take the quest for themself.

Soft's voice rang out loud and clear then. "We leave this ship here and sail north."

A chorus of groans rose from elsewhere on the ship, and I finally released my breath. I turned wide eyes on Juhi, and she nodded. They would both be leaving, which meant good news for us and our people. We could take that back to Barun and no one would have to worry.

We shoved away from the side of the boat as another voice breezed over the wet slap of the waves. "Hey, where is Lance?"

Footsteps rushed across the wood, and Juhi and I swam in a frenzy. I shoved her in front of me, forcing her head under the water, and her tail quickly followed, splashing furiously as she swam hard. I turned in time to see eyes peek over the rail.

The face contorted. Ruddy cheeks swelled and temples strained. "Hybrid!" they yelled. I submerged myself and chased my sister. There was a flash of light reflected in the wave peaks, then a dull thud sent a shiver down my spine. Juhi turned as if she was going to ask what happened, but we didn't get to speak before a heavy ball the size of my head broke Kotik's surface in front of her.

We stopped as it plunged hard and fast. If we hadn't slowed, it could have crushed her. The flash and muffled boom sounded again, and I reached out to grab her, looking around frantically. The next ball sank into the sea to our left. What were these things? I shot out and pressed my palm to it, letting it drag me down. Its surface was cool to the touch, likely only from how cold the water was, as it was emitting heat from its core. It seemed to be one solid piece of the same iron the rings were made from. Which meant it would soon start growing rot.

I released it and watched it sink. The flash happened again, this time immediately followed by two more. I hissed from an unexpected sharp pain and looked down to see an arrow poking out of my fin before meeting Juhi's eyes. It was made entirely of the shining silver, except for the very back two inches, which was the same wood of the ship and flocked with bloodred feathers from a navarin, the sea bird that flies at sunrise. Stupid, stupid humans.

Juhi wove over, dropping below my tail with a disapproving look, and examined it as more arrows began to rain down around us. She touched the seam between the wood and that foreign cause of rot, clearly finding some notch to pull at, as a moment later she had the feathered side free.

"Hold still." Her voice was rough.

I clenched my jaw as she pushed the stick farther through the sensitive skin of my flipper. Without the protruding feathers, it burned, but fell through easily. She gave it one hard yank, and with a pool of blood, it fell off, sinking like the balls.

"Thanks," I panted. She pointed east and jetted off. I didn't hesitate before following, racing close enough that I could reach out and touch her tail.

Weaving through the open ocean was scarier than if we could hide near the bay. There was no reef to shield us. Not a single boulder to dive behind, nor other sea life to help us fight off the enemy we couldn't see. We couldn't risk going deeper, lest one of the heavy things catch us and drag us down. It might hurt us, and if not, could trap us with how fast they sank. We would drown being stuck in the deep, if the high pressure didn't kill us first. And we had no way to know where they were raining from. My mother's voice crept into the back of my mind then. "Fear the land for the monsters he molds." She had warned me since I could swim alone.

The flashes eased after a few minutes of swimming, and when I glanced back, I could no longer see either ship that was sending the projectiles our way. I flicked my tail. It was sore, but manageable. We were going to be just fine.

As I turned back, my body crumpled hard. I let out an exclamation, taking on water through my nose. I blinked hard and snorted out to keep the burning salt from my lungs. Water flurried in my eyes, and it took a moment to realize that Juhi was frozen in front of me and I'd crashed into her. I circled around to find her fingers wrapped in an iron grip around her throat.

"Juhi? What's wrong?"

She gasped and scratched at the skin on her neck, and her face turned a few shades lighter.

"Juhi?" Panic gripped me. I looked to the sky, grabbed her waist, and tore us both toward the surface. She must've mismanaged her last breath; she was just running out of air. I would get her to fresh air and she'd be able to breathe and she'd be fine.

We broke into the night, and my own breath caught in my throat as I waited for her inhale.

But she continued to claw at her throat, drawing small drops of blood from fine cuts, strangled sounds escaping her in bursts.

Juhi's name left my lips in a scream that should have woken Matsya from the foam and then chilled her bones.

"Please, Juhi, breathe!" I begged of her.

I pulled her hands from her throat to get a better look at it, but she only tore them away from me and continued to rip them down her neck. I tried to blink back my tears and crane my neck to look into her mouth, to see if she was choking on something, but all was clear.

There was nothing I could do but hold my sister, beg her to breathe, and pray for her. I kept my arms braced, ready to catch her should she start sinking. A shiver racked her every few moments, and I wasn't sure if it was that or the wheezing that made my heart pound in my chest.

I didn't know if minutes had passed, or hours. I only knew that tear tracks dried on my face in the cool air. I realized that I couldn't cry anymore at about the same time my throat went raw from screaming. At the same time her hands slowed their clawing at her own throat.

My body trembled as I forced myself to look down at her. But I had to see. She was my little sister, and I had to look at her.

Her normally brown skin had gone pallid, the fine hairs on her body limp. Her eyes were barely cracked open and glassy. Head tilted back, resting on my shoulder, as she faced the skies.

She gasped again, her body seized, and I scrambled to wrap my arms tight around her. Brushing her hair from her face. Blood began to trickle from the corner of her mouth, and she searched around frantically.

"Juhi! Jah. Look, I'm right here, sweet. I'm sorry. I'm so sorry." Tears scalded my cheeks again, burning their way through my fur and filling the chapped cracks of my lips as I watched Juhi cough up more blood and try to squirm and roll away from me. I dug my fingers into her arms to keep her as long as possible, begging her to somehow recover from this unseen demon that had taken her. If she'd stayed home, she'd be safe. Or maybe if I'd been leading. What force could have infected her so badly?

It hit me then, and I loosened my grip enough that she turned and began spewing something up. The smell of metal filled the air, and she continued coughing and shivering.

She had swallowed a stray ring.

We had discarded our masks outside of Cankili. In the dark, there was no way she would have seen it, and they constantly got into fish's airways, causing internal bleeding in a matter of minutes. I raised my shaking fingers in front of my face, and a strangled sound left me at the coating of blood on my skin. I looked down to see it was spreading around us, turning the water black.

A sob shook me then. If I could have just gotten her to the doctor, they may have been able to help her. But she couldn't hold her breath in this state. If this had happened closer to the Isle, we would have been okay. I would have blocked her nose and carried her through the sea myself. But we were still an hour's swim away from home. I wrapped myself around her tightly, crying as her shaking began to subside.

"Juhi, I'm so sorry," I mumbled into her hair, peppering her cheeks and nose with kisses until the warmth seeped out of her skin. I pressed the curve of my nose against the flat of hers and let my tears soak the fine hairs on her face. I stroked her forehead roughly and whispered reminders of our family that waited at home, the promise she made that she would protect our people. No matter how much I begged, she wouldn't speak to me.

Her chest stuttered and fell. The seconds ticked by while I waited for her lungs to expand again. The air around us grew colder. Her body grew heavy, and I had to curl my tail up to prevent her from sinking.

I held her until my tears stopped flowing and the sky turned a dusty blue color, the first rays of the morning sun peeking over the horizon and kissing the moon's glow.

I pleaded with all the gods. Matsya to restore her health, Rudra to seal the veil so that she couldn't leave me, Prajapati to create a new world to escape to if it meant she had more time. They stayed quiet, leaving me to mourn alone.

A shiver cracked my spine as I leaned over Juhi's cold form. I held her limp hand and tried to ask once more. "Please." The sores in my throat from screaming barely let a whisper scrape past.

The sun began to warm my back, and I sucked in a shaky breath and straightened, looking over Juhi. There was no light behind her eyes anymore, and she hadn't breathed for hours. Blood was dried on her chin, and I carefully licked my thumb and rubbed it away before gathering her in my arms.

"Rudra guide her." I prayed to our god of death and kissed her forehead.

My mind was a whirlpool as I swam slowly. I couldn't help but look down at her blank stare every few minutes. How could we have ended up here?

My heart fractured over and over again for the future that now lay dead in my arms, and by the time I reached the reef that sheltered the Isle, I was barely treading water. A crowd of somber faces waited at the edge of the bay. I looked around slowly and found the hooded eyes of Barun. A sob broke from my lips as he rushed toward me, and he gathered Juhi in his hands the same moment I fell to the sand below.

"We thought you'd been lost," he said gruffly.

I began to choke on salt, and two women grabbed me and yanked me up to fresh air. I sobbed harder as I recognized Sai's gentle grip, and Navya. They held me between them, clapping my back to force me to breathe while one of the doctors spoke to Barun. I couldn't gather my wits to try and remember his name, and his words hammered my ears between my gasps.

"Zara, it's extremely important. Cetea Juhi has no external wounds. Can you tell me what might be wrong?" His words were gentle, and I knew he spoke her full name in respect, but they sliced into me like a knife.

I looked past his shoulder. His black curls were floating in the way, but I could see Juhi had been laid across a rock. The corded shell on her neck floated a couple inches above her chest. The gift I'd given her on her last birthday. Her bosom and stomach had begun to sink in, and her skin looked sickly yellow under the water. She had lost so much blood.

"Zara?"

I glanced at him and tried to focus, but my intestines hurt. A large, warm hand came to rest on my shoulder. I looked up to see Father floating next to me, back straight, a pillar of strength. He held me up as my spine began to bow.

"Um, we were swimming home as fast as possible, and I turned to look back, and then collided with her." My throat was raw as I spoke. "She was tearing at her neck, and when I took her above, she was struggling to breathe. I think it was a ring."

He nodded empathetically, and Barun squeezed my arm. "Was she showing any signs of the rot before?" the doctor asked.

I thought back to the last time she was home. She'd been acting normal and had followed all protocols leading up to today to stay safe. Even further back, all three of us had gone on a great long swim to the islands north of Paalaivanam two weeks before, and it was full of long chats and laughs. She'd shown no signs of exhaustion or less lung capacity. No decreased appetite or bad vision.

I looked to Sai.

"I also visited with her just last week. She was her normal, strong self. Full of light. Nothing was wrong." Sai spoke clearly, and I reached out and took her hand, giving it a squeeze. Tears swam in her eyes, and I scrubbed my face and looked around.

The doctor cleared his throat and pursed his lips, scanning my face. "And are you okay? Physically?"

My flipper flicked of its own accord, sending a zip of pain up my tail, and I remembered the hole then. "I was struck. I forgot." I curled my fin up to show him, and he motioned over another physician. "Rayan can help patch you up. Rest, while we examine your sister and prepare to lay her with the passed."

I nodded numbly, and Sai tugged my arm. I turned to catch a last glimpse of Juhi being held up by three council members as they whispered prayers to Matsya. Tears pricked the backs of my eyes, the grief sitting heavy in my gut beginning to twist up into a sharp point. I tried to swim to her, but Barun's grip tightened.

"Let them do their job. It's easier to grieve later." His voice was strained, and I wondered if losing my mother helped him handle the loss of his daughter a bit more calmly. I clenched my fists in response.

We would still have Juhi if it weren't for the rings.

7

Dorian

Biting wind whipped my curls around, throwing a chestnut lock across my face and blocking my view for a moment. I brushed the hair from my lashes, devouring every detail like a starved man. I refused to miss a moment.

The barnacles peeking up from the lap of the Taimur Bay's surface. The splintered and worn grains of wood stretching out across her thick belly. The slats of the rail acting as a protective arm wrapped around the deck. The ship was regal in only the way that a ship could be.

My lungs began to scream, and I released my breath through tight lips. I was so caught up in admiring her that I forgot my most basic functions.

Her...

I didn't even know the ship's name. I glanced at the stern and took a step in that direction. I felt as if I were moving through sand, but I needed to know what she was called, to lock in the reality of this dream. More than I had ever needed anything.

A billowing sound filled the air, followed by a snap. I stopped in my tracks to watch the mainsail get yanked into position. The air around me stilled, pregnant with anticipation. The ship, whatever her name, was about to set off on a grand adventure. And I'd be boarding her. A grin crept across my face.

A flash of movement near the mast caught my eye. Someone on the deck approached the rail, waving. He pulled the tall hat from his head, revealing a tight topknot of hair, while the thick scarf around his neck obscured his face.

I whipped my satchel tight over my shoulder and ran for the gangway at the windbeaten side of the ship. It wobbled under my feet at my first step, and my stomach quivered with it. It was unbelievable that after all this time, I was finally getting to leave Raktam. I had my chance to sail, to live on the wide ocean, if only for a time. I wouldn't have to be Prince Dorian Durling, heir to the throne, waiting to ascend and start draining myself for the good of the people in my father's stead.

I'd only be Dorian, a sailor-in-training.

Sweat slicked my palms as I walked farther up the plank, reaching the first ridge. It creaked, and a voice like my father's called out.

"Dorian."

I stepped, my movements becoming sluggish, and the Eudo-reminiscent voice creaked again. "Dorian!"

I whipped my head around, salt stinging my eyes, and the ship wavered in front of me, beginning to sink down into a void of stars. The sky darkened, and I blinked away the wisps of night from my vision, groaning as I realized I had drifted into a daydream.

Hardened gray eyes surrounded by fine wrinkles and liver spots replaced the sails. I jerked back.

The world around me shifted. The brisk wind died down, replaced by the heavy smell of old texts. The strap of my travel bag fell through my fingers, and the dock became a settee under my feet. I wobbled and braced myself, my hands digging into its coarse embroidered covering. The fog around the docks lifted completely and left me in the library with my father, and when I turned back to look at the ship, it had squeezed itself into a glass bottle, tucked between two travelogues. It was only a small thing, eye level, just out of reach on a wooden bookshelf. There were no waves lapping its side. No captain hailing me to come sail. And there was no adventure waiting for me beyond the horizon.

"Are you paying attention, boy?" The king's gruff voice forced my jaw to clench.

I released my grip on the back of the chair and lowered myself into a stiff sitting position, my limbs still trembling and mind disoriented.

I cleared my throat. "Yes, Father. I apologize."

His mouth flattened into a line, forcing more wrinkles into his sagging cheeks. "Your mind is always flying away. Sometimes I wonder if your body will follow. That behavior will have to stop, come your birthday."

I dipped my head, trying not to let the frustration show on my face. "Yes, of course."

He fixed me with a wary eye before clearing his throat and tapping his temple. "I was saying that we need to plan the coronation."

I nodded, uninterested in whatever he meant to happen. We still had months.

"I married your mother a week before my own." Another rasp came from his throat, and his fingers twitched on the arm of the chair. "We should not break the tradition. It was one of her few requests when I asked for her hand."

A throbbing started at the front of my skull as I realized where this conversation was going. I fought to keep my eyes in focus, staring at the gaudy, gilded crown on his head, with the single gemstone hanging down to his widow's peak.

His jowls shook as he chewed his lip and rolled his shoulders back before speaking. It seemed like very out of place behavior for the king. "You said nothing of the women we presented yesterday. I wonder if you've noticed any of the eligible bachelorettes that we have hosted over the summer?" he pressed. "Many have now become betrothed. Did any from the meeting catch your eye?"

I shook my head on instinct before I could think of the question. We had, in fact, hosted many balls over the last few months. All of which I had attended in physical presence, with my gentleman-in-waiting. Now that I thought of it, I didn't remember a single face. I'm sure I danced with someone. Maybe many someones. The fact was that my mind had been elsewhere completely.

He began to speak of Duke Hasting's daughter, and of a widowed viscountess. "Dorian." Eudo's voice startled me, and I met his disapproving gaze.

I dipped my head and apologized once again. I'd been fighting hard to stay in the room but had faded away at first chance.

"Do you, perhaps, prefer Hari?" he asked anxiously. "I'm sure it can be arranged..."

That must be why he was so nervous. If I said yes, he'd have to turn to a cousin to continue our line.

I shook my head harshly and pulled my ankle to my knee, releasing a breath. "Sky's above, Father. No. I simply don't care one way or another which woman you choose to warm my bed for the rest of my miserable life."

The shock on his face likely mirrored my own, as I couldn't remember a time I'd spoken so brazenly, but I forged on.

"I know what you'll say about my own misery and company, but that's all I foresee. How should I consider a marriage when I can't even feign excitement about the turn of my decade, or bringing Raktam under new rule?"

He leaned back and rubbed the dimple in his chin with his thumb, a deep crease forming between his brows as he nodded. "I see. But you understand that it is your mother's declaration that you should marry before you take the throne?"

"Yes."

He raised a brow. "And you'd prefer that I choose your bride?"

By Rudra's balls, Eudo, what don't you understand?

"Yes." I kept my tone even, fighting to stay in the room.

A long beat of silence passed between us before he spoke again.

"I wish you cared more about the inner workings of the kingdom. This is your future, and your heir's future, you know."

The corner of my mouth twitched down, and I shook my head slowly. "Father, I speak openly in hopes you might understand me better tomorrow than yesterday, as the king to be, over the son you raised. I know that you take great pride in ruling. But you should know that all I wish is to leave. I want to be on the sea." I motioned up at the ship in the bottle and held my breath, waiting for backlash. "I don't particularly care who I'm forced to fuck an heir into."

I almost expected him to slap me, but the look he gave me was appraising. "Your mother did not speak of ruling with such vitriol, but I believe she held some of your feelings in marriage."

"Why would she ask that I wed before ascending to the throne, then?" I asked.

"Matriarchy was of utmost importance in her family. The crown did not follow the man of the house, but the woman."

"It makes sense that you would fail as a king the moment she left," I muttered.

He stood with a grunt, taking a moment to adjust the iron buckles on his stomach, and to pull his coattails behind him, before pacing toward the door. "Come, walk with me."

I hesitated for a moment and glanced through the large window on the far wall. It afforded me a fleeting glimpse of the dark sea, beyond the castle gardens and city walls and windswept beach. My chest twinged. And I followed my father away from freedom, into the depths of the winding hallways of our home.

I kept pace with him as we walked, but his slow movement started a tick in my jaw. The man appeared twenty years older than he was. He reminded me of a tree that had been weathered by the elements, with a curved trunk for a spine and drooping limbs. His head had been bald for years as well, and I could only imagine how sparse his beard might be, if he were to skip a week's shave.

It had to be the damned ruling. Running a kingdom killed him inside, but he wouldn't ever admit it. And I was expected to willingly walk into the same fate.

He finally spoke, slowing even more, as if the effort of holding conversation and walking at the same time was too much. "I know you have worked hard to fulfill your duties and prepare for the end of summer. I hope you know how sorry I am that you were never afforded the luxury of leaving the kingdom for pleasure's sake."

He turned the corner to the eastern wing.

"I am meant to get out in the lower city sometime this week, to see the people. But I've been tired, and now must hold council about this katalval situation, so I think you should go."

I ground to a halt and blinked at him. The sudden change shocked me. I could swear he was beginning to lose pieces of his mind, and it took a moment for me to catch up.

"You want me to go... to the beaches? Are you not worried that I may make a mistake?" It wasn't the freedom that I craved, but it was something. To leave the inner ring of the kingdom was more than I expected.

He chuckled and reached for the handle of his door. "You're more than capable of kissing a few babies and keeping your tongue in check. Just don't start daydreaming."

I inclined my head, trying to keep my heart from leaping. "Of course. I'll go tomorrow." The last time I had been allowed near the beach was nearly five years before. When I was caught by the guards swimming, and had been banned. My heart had ached since. I would have killed a man to place my bare feet in the sand, to touch the freezing cold seawater. And Eudo was sending me there freely.

The bolt of Eudo's lock slid heavily into place, and I spun toward the opposite wing. I had to prepare to face the people.

I unbuttoned my sleeves at the wrist and swept toward my suite, heels muffled by plush purple rugs. The paintings of the hallways were a blur as I strode past, the colored tapestries barely noticeable as I turned the corners. My door swung open easily, and I froze, my cravat still in hand.

Everything was as I had left it, all wrought iron furniture perfectly in place, teal and purple pillows and plush quilts scattered about, with silver fabrics draped from the chandelier to the outer walls and slung up over rods by the vast windows. Sconces threw shadows across the dark velvet. The color was the only touch of decor I had input on, and it could help me imagine I was underwater late at night when the fire had gone out. In the middle of the afternoon it felt a bit silly and old age.

What wasn't as I had left it was my barber and my groomer standing at attention behind my vanity chair.

My mouth flattened into a line, and I unbuttoned my vest, throwing the heavy piece of wool onto the bed as I walked to the chair.

"I take it you two already knew what was happening?" I glanced at the groomer but addressed the barber, who was new to his station.

The barber inclined his head before stepping up behind me. He paled when our eyes met in the mirror, and looked down, quickly taking up thick handfuls of my hair. A long pause passed between us, and I cleared my throat. It must have occurred to him that I wanted an answer, and he finally swallowed and spoke.

"Yes, Your Highness. His Majesty summoned us just after you left for your morning walk in the gardens."

My jaw ticked of its own accord again as he picked up a scalloped comb and began to twist my hair this way and that, trying to straighten the coils, no doubt. The walk had been before breakfast. Hours before my meeting with *His Majesty* in the study. Eudo wasn't easing my concerns about marriage or attempting to comfort me over my dead mother—he was plotting, always one step ahead, per usual.

The minutes ticked by painfully as the barber pulled my hair and air hissed between my teeth. I watched him intently in the mirror, noting every time his thin fingers snagged a curl and my scalp pricked with pain. He never met my gaze. I didn't even know his name, but it wouldn't matter. Yet another one incapable of dealing with my hair. He'd be out of the castle before nightfall.

He finally finished, bowing his head, before he stepped back and scurried from the room. I reached up and touched my tender head before examining the threads stretching from my crown to meet a single twist that sat between my shoulder blades.

"It's not a bad job, really," I muttered. It was too bad that he couldn't be gentler.

The groomer chuckled and set a basket on the table next to me, and I turned to flash a look of disdain at him as he laid out an assortment of razors, bowls with water and foam, brushes, and towels.

"Play nice and he might practice enough to know how to touch you." He touched his index finger to the side of his jaw, tracing the chiseled muscle in his chin. I returned the gesture with a chuckle, and he winked.

I settled back in the chair, and he planted a firm finger in the soft spot under my chin, turning it to the ceiling sharply.

"You know, Simon, I favor the way you skip formalities over the stiffness of the other staff," I said. His finger on my throat strained my voice.

"Yes, sir. I am well aware," he drawled, leaning down to look at me from the side. "It was you who complained of formalities when your first whiskers needed trimming."

I looked over, and my eyes skated down his perfect jaw, with the tiny patch of red under his lower lip.

"Tell me, Simon, has there ever been a bearded king?"

One of his brows lifted, and he poked his finger into my cheek, forcing me to look back up at the ceiling before he stood. I caught a glimpse of his bemused expression before he wrapped a steaming towel around my face. The warmth seeped into my skin and forced my shoulders to relax as his footsteps receded. "No. You would be the first to consider it. Eudo believes that rulers owe honesty to the people, and vice versa. If you cover part of the face, you might be hiding something. Just—"

"Like the generations before, yeah." My voice sounded muffled under the cloth, and I waved my hand at the notion. "Facial hair should not correlate to honesty. What if I simply prefer the look? I enjoy things differently, that's all."

The sound of metal clicking answered me, and a porcelain tapping sound began a few feet away. Simon was foaming the soap.

"Well, Dorian, that would be—"

I didn't get to hear what it would be, as he was cut off by the bedroom door slamming against the wall. In a flurry, I threw the towel from my face, blinking its fog from my vision.

I was roaring before I could even see who had entered. "Who dare comes una—" I stopped with a leg swung over the chair and the towel clutched in my fist as my gaze landed on Hari.

His thick arms folded across a broad chest, and he kicked one riding boot in front of the other before leaning against the frame. "Good afternoon, *Your Highness.*"

I rolled my eyes and shuffled back to my seat, shooting Simon an apologetic look as I tried to fold the towel neatly. "Why, by the seas, are you barging into my room?"

I could hear him moving behind me, and a telltale creak sounded. My wicker chair groaned for help, and I turned, ready to snap at him for sitting on the dainty thing—it was the only piece of nonmetal furniture in my room—only to see that he had tracked mud across my rug as well. I let out a long-suffering sigh and leaned my head back instead, moving to let Simon resume his shaving preparations. Moments like this were the only thing I didn't miss when Hari was gone.

"Have you heard the news?" I could hear the smile in his voice.

"So help me, if you are about to tell me about going down to the beaches, I will gut you like the cod you act."

Simon brushed soap along my jawline. He lifted the towel, and I watched his brows furrow in concentration as he worked, a crease forming over his slightly crooked nose. The cool foam tickled my chin.

"So, what are we to do about this? If the hybrid is important enough that the king cancels his normal duties—"

"He canceled his duties last time there was a sighting too," I reminded him. A fist clenched around my heart as I remembered the wild look in my father's eye when news of my mother's death had been brought back from the docks.

I had only been three when she left for a month-long voyage, and a week after my fourth birthday, she was reported lost at sea. Eudo blamed the hybrids. Everyone else, logically, blamed the storms she had been charted to sail through.

"He's canceled being a father every time there has been a sighting," I murmured into the towel.

The cold touch of Simon's blade brought me back from the memories of my father locking himself in his office, and I felt Hari's hand on my shoulder.

"Times are changing," he said. "Perhaps we set off on an adventure to chase the tail?"

His voice pierced through my skull, immediately swirling ideas from the depths of my mind. An adventure to chase it? To set sail, absolutely. And to capture a hybrid would be to capture my father's attention.

An adventure...

I jumped from my chair, sending foam flying, and turned. Simon froze to my left, a straight blade in his hand. I shook my head at him and advanced, a finger pointed at Hari. "You daft genius. That may just be the way."

His eyes flicked around the room wildly.

I rolled my own eyes at his lack of imagination. He'd just connected all the dots to my freedom and he didn't even realize it.

"What has the king sought for the last twenty-six years with more ferocity than a pirate seeking treasure?" A grin crept across my face while I waited for him to answer, but he was silent.

I glanced back at Simon, who had retired the razor and taken up residence in my vanity chair. The poor man was massaging his temples until I spoke to him. "Not a word of this. You're in cahoots now."

He had the good grace to bow his head and salute in acknowledgment, though he shot a dry look to the skies. I knew I could trust Simon.

I jumped onto the bed, miming as if I were perched on a deck rail. "Imagine, Ri! Out on the open sea for a month, maybe two. The cool wind whipping through our hair and the waves rocking our ship wildly, swirling the ale in our bellies as intensely as in our barrels. Swinging from ropes and chanting shanties." I swung around a bedpost and winked at him. "Docking a bed or two 'a port as well."

I could see it as the room around me shifted and I faced the open sea that was stretching out over my bedroom floor, my rug turning to the sand that would lead us to freedom. "Here and there we'll drop a net, and maybe we'll swing by the old dead island from fishermen's tales. In the name of King Eudo." I could see the Isle's silhouette in the distance, but Hari exclaimed, interrupting my vision.

"We'll have a grand hunting adventure!" He jumped and jerked me by the arm. I turned from the sleek gray flipper splitting the water's surface and gave him a lopsided salute.

"Aye."

His face split into that grin again, and his eyes flicked to Simon before he nodded. "He's wanted to find them nearly as long as your mum's been missing. It'd be amazing for you to get a bit of that freedom you've been craving. I know you've been going mad being cooped up here."

I dropped down from the mattress heavily, nearly pressing my nose right up to his and forcing him to step back. "Mad is an excessive term, especially from you, dear friend." My voice was low, and a growl built in the back of my throat. I swallowed it down and straightened my shirt. "I must see a bit of the world before I kick the bucket, yeah? I think the kingdom can afford me the same freedoms of the people. And if I fulfill the king's quest..." I stepped back with a shrug, and an indiscernible look flickered through Hari's eyes.

He touched my shoulder, gently this time. "Of course. I understand. Worry about your shave and the people today. Leave the king and word of travel to me."

I gripped Hari's arms, staring deep into his amber eyes, before pulling him into an embrace. "Thank you."

He scrubbed the flush from his face and left the room in a hurry.

"Why don't you take his hand?" Simon asked as I settled back into the chair.

Warmth rose into my own cheeks, and I lifted a shoulder. "It isn't like that," I said.

Simon pursed his lips and said nothing as he hid the redness of my cheeks beneath another towel.

Morning over Raktam dawned as bleak as any other, with mist rolling in from the sea and the dull cries of sea birds filling the air. I took my breakfast in my room, then dressed in silence, staring out over the gray-washed buildings.

I could only wonder if the rest of our state was as depressing as our city. Did the village that farmed our corn struggle to rise, as I did? Did the town my uncle presided over despise their leader, too?

I did not want to find out.

The castle was quiet as I wound my way to the stable door. Imogene waited just outside, looking as impatient as she always did.

"I chose the guard you are to travel with," she said, pulling at the tassels on my cloak. "There are five that are not to leave your side. Under any circumstance. Do you understand?" Her golden gaze bore into me, and I swallowed hard, unsure why she was so insistent. I nodded.

"Good. Hari will accompany you to the lower kingdom. Keep your sword clear, but do not panic by any unexpected challenges that might arise."

"What do you mean?" I asked, and she raised a hand.

Garden soil stained her fingertips, and a bundle of flowers poked out of her apron.

"I want you to set off quickly and quietly before anyone interferes."

I nodded, and Imogene patted my cheek before retreating down the garden path. I thought I heard the tapping of a cane, some scuffle, but it faded, and I turned down the opposite path to the stables.

As she had warned, five teal-clad guards waited outside of a royal carriage, accompanied by two footmen and Hari.

I was shut inside the cart, alone, and I swallowed hard as the great wheels began to roll and rumble beneath me.

The iron work around the carriage squeezed the walls tight. It was curved in an arch at every corner, worked into every crevice, meeting in a swirl at the center of the ceiling and encircling a piece of glass to let in light. The seats across from me were covered in a soft woven cloth, and small adornments of the Raktam crest dotted every few inches, reminding me that so long as I rode in this cart, I would be cradled by the guard and carried wherever the king willed.

I brushed my thumb over the arm rest and immediately snatched my hand away. Even the rounded ends were studded with metal. A long-suffering sigh escaped me, and I glared at the little iron shield above the opposite bench. It was engraved with a horse and held a chain hanging from each point. The crests were made to look like brocade, but just like so many other things in the kingdom after we'd won the war against Aatma and Father had been dubbed "the Iron King," the stupid things had been made from real iron. As soon as I took the throne, I'd change the symbol and have every crest smelted and tossed in the harbor. It was just another reminder of our bloody history.

If it hadn't been for the iron we manufactured, we wouldn't have earned the upper hand against our old ruler and overthrown them, wouldn't have had the protections we did. At the end of it all, my mother wouldn't have felt that we needed to make connections with the other continents, and she wouldn't have left.

Her face tried to float to the surface of my mind. Dark curls, like mine. A soft nose and dimpled chin. Eyes like the sun. I didn't have my own memory of her, only what the paintings in the castle held.

My lip curled of its own accord, and I slapped my hand to the carriage door. I couldn't stay in here any longer, drowning in the smell of metal with only hand-sized glass to stare through. The wheels ground to a halt, and the horses snorted in indignation as the driver yelled for the procession to slow. Hari popped his head through the hatch and raised a brow, but I shoved past, stomping onto the stone road before he could ask what was wrong.

We'd traveled far enough away from the castle that my father wouldn't have a chance of seeing me, and we were steep enough down the hill that I could justify wanting an easy walk, if a guard asked.

I cracked my neck and looked around. We were stopped at the inner kingdom, where most residents were patrons of the Durlings' or held titles themselves. The most important lords and ladies of Raktam lived just a block or two from where I stood. I scoffed. Barons and marchionesses, plus the widowed viscountess that Eudo refused to stop asking me about, among others. I thought her name might be Mildred or something of the like. I cleared my throat and began walking down the road. The divide from the inner kingdom to the Mid was only a ten-minute walk away.

The sky was dull, seeming like it might drizzle at any moment, and the gray rock of the city's roads were slick with a fine mist floating in from the Taimur Bay that caused a thin slip of mud and rubble to grind under my boots.

Hari looped his arm through mine and cleared his throat. "Bit much in the cart, huh?"

I shot him a sidelong glance before rolling my eyes. He lacked tact when prying into my mind. He might be a large brute, but he sure was emotional. In any case, my mind had wandered so far since I left the carriage that the reason I climbed out had escaped me.

"You could say that," I said in a low voice.

"What's wrong?" he pressed.

I was suddenly aware of the way his fingers massaged the muscle of my shoulder, and a sense of ease warmed my chest as he pressed his other palm against my forearm.

I sighed loudly and glanced at the guards flanking us. They were sitting atop large shires with studded saddles and leads, artfully ignoring our conversation. I didn't actually know how likely it was that they would report back to the king, or, gods forbid, the duke, but I hated to risk it. While I could see the other members of the court selling our secrets for a loaf of bread, though that could be more of a reflection of myself than the people, I trusted Hari implicitly.

I finally spoke. "I feel so suffocated here."

He stayed silent as we walked, and I looked around at the homes we passed. In the Mid they were tall, narrow, but wealthy by much of the kingdom's standards. The middle kingdom, or Mid as most everyone called it, was the largest part of Raktam, aside from the farmlands located well outside of the walls. It was where the business districts lay, most trading residents, and where anyone that could afford to do business with other cities or even the castle itself lived. Politicians, sailors, taverners, historians—nearly anyone that could—lived in the Mid. If you left it, not by choice, anyway, there likely was no coming back.

The buildings on either side of the road still held history from the war, as each one was armored with protective beams made of iron outside their corners, and the roofs were made of corrugated sheets of the stuff. Some people who'd opened businesses on the lower levels of their buildings had taken to mounting iron sconces or engraved signs that creaked in the light breeze, and the eerie sound made me wince. I noted that some of the hinges had started rusting, and wondered if there was a supplier of grease to take care of that. Rust could spread quickly and become a nuisance, and the business owners would have to pay to replace their signs before the paint wore down.

We passed a bakery with tables spilling out onto the path, packed between street lamps. The customers seemed unbothered by the damp air. Men looked dapper in dark wool suits with silver accents, and I noticed a few of them had interesting-looking hats and wore a new style of buckles and chains on their boots. The ladies had leather harnesses with iron clips and external braces over their gowns.

"Has there been some change in fashion I missed?" I nudged Hari and nodded to a trio. "I don't remember ever seeing tall hats and hanging chains, and women in metal like this. They could strap daggers into those holsters."

Hari chuckled. "It seems to be a fairly new trend. I quite like it. I'm considering some boots for myself."

I looked at his loafers and pursed my lips. The dress reminded me of pirates, in an odd way. I couldn't say if I liked it or not. I felt out of place in my own sky-blue breeches and puffed sleeves.

We continued down the main road, and I peeked through the side streets that led to more shops. We passed a blacksmith, tailor, and chemist. I could smell a strong ale and roast from one alley, and my stomach grumbled as a lively airy tune reached my ears. If given the chance, I'd stop at that pub in a heartbeat. The royal guards' stiff spines told me they were not as keen as I.

The music followed us around and down a bend toward the thick outer wall that protected the bulk of the kingdom, and just as the sky dimmed to dusk, we reached the spiked gate.

In times of war, before my memory started, the top of the wall was armed with catapults that shot greased balls of fire into the fields beyond. They were said to fly fast and true and take out eighths of an army at a time, and the troops that they didn't lay flat were beheaded at the gate and stuck upon the spears as a warning to the next wave that might approach.

"Raise the gate!" a keeper yelled, and I shuddered. Eudo was rumored to have been a vicious commander.

The chains creaked as they rose above us. I was momentarily struck with the vision of walking through the opening and being skewered. Hari was looking at me curiously, a crease above his wide nose, and I shook my head at him. I clenched my fists and fought to resist the urge to run through the arch, lest the vision come true, and counted my breaths instead.

Four exhales later and the smell of the beaches hit me. The keepers immediately lowered the gate, and my stomach knotted. The last time I was out, I had caused a riot with insensitive remarks about the section being poor. They did not like my defense that I didn't know they were not as well off as the inner rank. Which must be why Father had mentioned biting my tongue.

I had made a stupid mistake in thinking that Eudo took care of the kingdom in equal parts back then. When I was banned from swimming at the beach that was just outside the gates, Eudo decided I should do more work for the kingdom. So he sent me to the outer ring. I had no idea of the level of poverty the people were in there. There was no peerage. There were no lords or ladies listening to the people's complaints, there were no merchants selling quality cloth, no blacksmiths with good steel. The homes were small and in ruin, without available carpenters and materials to repair them. Fresh, good food was nonexistent.

There was food, but it was nothing like what we had in the castle or even right inside the walls.

I tried to make suggestions, to better the conditions, which were not taken well. Then I tried to give them gold. I think that they thought I mocked them. I was lost for words that day. Eudo would have had my head if I weren't his son. I didn't know what else to do. I was yanked away by the guards while the people threw everything they could and burned the carriage left behind.

Eudo should have prepared me.

I looked at the sea in front of me and breathed deeply. Back then, the beaches in front of the kingdom were in a decent state, just smelling of sea. Now the desperate stench of death from the north edge of the kingdom had reached even these lower sands.

The farther we moved from the wall of the city, the more the guards around me tensed. Even the air around me tightened and became thick with hot manufacturing pollution, and Hari's grip on my arm reflected that. I finally pried his fingers from my bicep and shook him off, and he grimaced at me with an apology in his warm eyes.

My group circled around the east wall of the kingdom, trekking as the sun dipped to kiss the horizon. Night would fall soon.

"Why did Eudo want to come out here?" I broke the silence to ask.

Hari looked startled by the question, and I followed his gaze to the officer closest to us. He stiffened atop his horse, and I prodded my friend's chest. "What? What's going on?"

"Eudo just wanted you to visit." He spoke slowly.

I raised a brow and tried to meet the guard's gaze, but he looked away. "Really?" I asked Hari. "That sounds like a lie for a perfectly reasonable question."

He shrugged and fell silent. I stared at him for another minute, waiting for some sign that he was lying, or for him to continue, but it was clear that I would get no more conversation out of him.

I shook my head and fixed my gaze on the ocean, enjoying the splash of salty spray that reached our high path and licked my calves. Everyone with me was gracious enough not to say anything when I got distracted and slowed down to watch a whale breach, and again when a particularly strong gust of wind shoved me into the seagrass off the gravel cliffside.

Hari finally cleared his throat and took my arm again on the third distraction, pointing at the docks that were creeping nearer as we reached the proper outer city, hiding in the shadow of the high northern wall of Raktam.

"I promise if you keep walking, the end of our journey will be far more fulfilling than these little moments," he said.

I cocked my head, confused. "We're just going to greet residents, how could they possibly beat sea life that I haven't seen in years?"

He grinned and motioned to the docks again. "You'll see in about two minutes."

I shook my head as a large ship came into view. Three tall masts with heavy sails saluted me, an army of cannons stood at attention on her berth, and a crew of at least two hundred clad in the Royal Navy's teal-and-gray uniform stood at attention on the deck.

Hari led me to stop in front of a ramp that was leaning against the main deck. I stared at the wood panels in front of me, frozen in place. I was speechless. It was so similar to my daydreams, but it felt so real.

"Ri, tell me this isn't a dream."

"It's not, Dori." He cupped my elbow and pressed his chin into my shoulder.

I nodded. Of course, that's what someone in a dream would say. I licked my lips and raised my hand to brush a curl from my face.

"Eudo agreed. What better person to bring in the kill than the crown prince?"

My fingers shook. Hari squeezed my arm.

"Rudra's balls, this better be fucking real." The words left my mouth in a whisper, and a few chuckles sounded around me. I took in the ship, then the memories of my dreams slammed into my mind, and I looked up at her head. The name *Clover* was plastered there, and

I breathed a sigh of relief as reality crashed around me. I was finally going to board a ship.

I looked at Hari and grinned, and he motioned to the ramp. "We have everything ready. Let's go."

The slab of wood wobbled slightly under my feet, just as I had imagined, and I couldn't keep a skin-splitting grin from my face as I climbed it quickly. The crew on the deck didn't move as I passed through the rail and greeted Trevor Nottley, our Captain and Commander of Ships, who had been ordered by the king to keep me safe on this journey.

The next hour of disembarking speeches and instructions passed in a blur, and I only came to with the snap and billow of sails.

I scrambled to grab Hari's hand as the docks of lower Raktam shrank into the distance and we sailed away from everything I'd ever known.

8

VESHAK

I CROUCHED ON THE bowsprit of the galleon, my fingers digging into the salt-weathered pine, and the heel of my boots notched tightly to keep me from falling into the waves below. My coat flapped in the wind, and a steady spray kept my face drenched. Even so, my eyes were wide open, scanning the water for any sign of the katalval we'd seen the night before.

A plan had begun to brew as soon as we reached our galleon.

My mother had once ruled over Raktam, alongside their bloodthirsty King Eudo. She told my brother and I tales of his hunger for war when we were children, and our father, the Maharajah, brought home reports of Eudo's devastation to further validate her stories. She said that Eudo invaded Aatma for the mantrik; Father told us that the final generation of Aatma children had been given jobs in royal households. Mother said Eudo planned to unite all of Sariram; Father reported that the borders between their states had fallen. Mother said he would hunt her for her mantrik, if he knew that she lived. So Father kept her safe in the Mahal.

I believed that ship captain and his news that Kallu was poor and desperate for a reward from Eudo. Why a katalval, I had no idea, but there was no doubt that any Sarian would skin the katalval alive and sell their bones if it meant some shred of equity from the king.

Clearly, I had to catch the katalval before that could happen.

"Aye! Veshak!" Orion called from behind me, and I turned on my narrow perch to see him wildly waving a piece of linen above his head.

I sighed and stood just enough to move my knees comfortably, to pace carefully back toward him. My leap over the deck rail made him flinch back, sending his crown of black ringlets flailing.

"Sorry. I didn't mean to scare you." I rubbed the back of my neck and lifted a shoulder apologetically.

He shook his head and laid the cloth out on a nearby barrel. "You didn't, you just reek of fish guts more than normal."

I snapped my mouth shut and put a foot of distance between us, craning my neck at where he was pointing. He was a short man, the same height as I, but he seemed to forget I had trouble looking over his arm as he shielded part of the drawing.

The square he had been shaking about was a map, marked in rich black ink taken from the trading town of Ilai and waxed to protect from sea spray. He'd used a pin to mark our position.

He traced a wide path at the center point between two continents. "I've plotted our path to the next interception, if you wish to stay at sea. But we can't put off the clean any longer, before another long haul. If we avoid docking, we must careen."

"South of Raktam?" I asked, with a sigh. I worried about trying to pull our ships inland on the east of the continent. Too many ships, and sailors went missing there.

"Got it. I'll trust you to get word to Ward on the sloop. Let me know if you need anything." I said.

He nodded, and I clapped him on the back, turning for my cabin. I didn't make it far before spotting a part of the crew gathered on the main deck. The smell of fried dough filled my nose, and roasting spices sizzled through the air. A few handfuls of my men sat shoulder to shoulder, too quiet, and I changed course, my stomach rumbling loud enough to hear over the ocean.

Flames licked the belly of the bronze bowl, and my chest warmed in response. An extra clay pot had been fitted into a shelf below the fire, where I saw chapati bubbling and crisping. The smells of chili, onion, and ghee overtook me. Cook whistled at me and motioned at the big pot next to the fire.

"Pull up a seat, Cap. You need to eat like everyone else."

I did not need to be told twice. Someone shoved a stool under me before my ass could hit the deck, and I grinned and took the bowl handed over, helping myself to a ladle full of masala that made my mouth water before it even touched my tongue. Sky's above, I was grateful for Cook.

"Taking advantage of the calm seas?" I asked.

He winked and scooped some chicken out for another of the crew.

Not only were spiced foods better tasting than naval slop, but the chili helped keep everyone illness-free, and kept our rations preserved for a few mealtimes without spoiling.

I tore off a piece of chapati and used it to scoop some masala, and the bite exploded with flavor in my mouth. I let out a groan of appreciation, and Clarence grinned at me, raising his own flatbread.

"Good, innit? Kallu had ginger root."

I nodded enthusiastically. "Good call, taking their chickens. It could have been another month before we docked."

He flicked his twin braids to his back and puffed out his chest.

I dug in and ate like a man stranded in the desert until the navigator-in-training spoke up.

"So, Captain?"

I turned to look at him. He had the telltale blue eyes of East Sariram, like Clarence, with mousey waves tied back in a knot at the nape of his neck.

"You have pretty strict opinions on these sea things?" The way he ended sentences in a question made my brain itch. I nodded.

"Why?"

I swallowed my last bite of onion and dusted flour from the chapati off my hands, reaching for a jug of ale.

"You came from Sariram, right?" I asked.

He nodded. "My family is from the east, a little village near Ceyi."

"Your education lacked in childhood. Sariram filters out the most important part of history," I said. I swallowed a bite of chili that seared my throat.

The boy leaned forward, watching me expectantly.

I finally set my chapati down. "At the creation of our world, there was Prajapati, who made all. Matsya came and breathed life into us, and Rudra destroyed and carried the dead beyond the veil. All were vital to the workings of our world."

"They created us, yes," he said, interrupting.

I raised a finger. "All of Sariram knows they created the humans. They are not told the rest. They do not know that jagarving fly free in the deserts of Paalaivanam, or that katalval swim through our seas. They are unaware that mantrik poured from the void that Rudra tore with his scythe and built their home in Aatma.

"The same mantrik that are aboard our ships, like our good doctor, or Willy-Will," I said, nodding to our oldest crew member. The furrows around his eyes creased, and he raised a wrinkled hand in greeting. "You might not know that Willy-Will could tear this ship apart with a storm, if he wanted to."

A look of apprehension and mixed anxiety rippled over the boy's face before I cleared my throat and continued.

"Our Maharani is mantrik as well. And she tells the story like this—Eudo came to learn of the magic that was scattered around Sariram. Such power was rooted in the rich streets of Aatma, traveling the trade routes between the other city-states, and he was jealous of the capitol that had been built there. Raktam was beginning to grow poor, as the city-state was too far north on the continent from the main routes of travel. Bad weather locked them into place and stunted their farming ability. They possessed no magic to help their own lands, and no partnerships to increase trade. But they had people, and people made armies.

"He spent years building up an army that would threaten the rest of the continent, then knocked at Aatma's door with a plan. If they refused partnership, he would attack. But they accepted, and offered their princess in marriage. Many of her close advisors moved to Raktam with them, and he gained the greatest alliance he would ever have.

"A few years later, he equipped his military with new weapons and stormed Aatma anyway, razing the city. The last people standing were employed in Raktam, given jobs that would suit their magic, and Aatma was wiped from their maps."

"How could he overwhelm Aatma if they had alliances with everyone else?" the boy asked.

"He used their greatest weapon against them—the princess," I said. "No one in Raktam, Aatma, or all of Sariram knew that he married her for the magic that turned the tide in his favor: iron. She came from a royal mantrik family, and her ability reflected that. He stole the magic straight from her blood and turned it into the weapons and armor that equipped his armies. She nearly died before his war on Sariram was over.

"Once the kingdom grew and riches flowed, their now queen was growing sicker by the day. She begged Eudo to stop taking the iron from her veins, but he needed it to run his country. So she appealed to his power hungry side. 'Let me make contact with the other continent,' she begged him.

"After a time, he relented, on the condition that she would return in a month. She was to sail under the guise of exploring Paalaivanam, to search for people there and offer an olive branch. But a storm swept her ship off course and nearly killed her and her crew at sea."

"It was the katalval that saved her," I said.

"They carried her to Mautakheli Isle, along with the few survivors of the shipwreck. They fed and cared for her. One full year she spent, stranded on the Isle with only the company of the people sent with her by the Iron King, and those that lived in the sea. Until our Maharajah set sail for Aatma.

"He did not know of the war, of the capitol falling, or of the hostile takeover of the Sarian states, and planned to make contact as well as establish trade. But he sailed close enough to see smoke from what was meant to be a desolate island and sent a boat out to rescue them.

"Our Maharajah married Raktam's former queen within the month, crowning our Maharani and introducing the first mantrik to Paalaivanam. He called back all attempts to create peace with Sariram and has hidden my mother ever since."

He was silent for a moment before clearing his throat. "What exactly do you mean by magic?" he asked. "I have never seen it on this ship."

"I mean exactly what you think," I said.

"It is a metaphor? You can't mean real magic. People don't fly, or live in the ocean."

"Of course they do!" I argued. Flames roiled in my belly. I wasn't a liar, and I would not have him make a fool of me in front of everyone here. I leaned back, looking to the sky, and a heat rose into my throat. It was always there, simmering low in my belly. I just had to let it loose.

My jaw popped as a belch of flame crackled from my mouth and into the air above me. Fire climbed to the sky, reaching for the clouds above, only to be extinguished a moment later.

Gasps rippled through the crew. Clearly some of these men had not been around the last time I released my flame, and I licked my lips, grinning at the boy.

"Did that look like a metaphor?"

One of the crew from Paalaivanam nudged him. "You need to go into the city when we dock at Thandu next, jagarving fly all over."

I strode away and left him sitting with his jaw agape.

Cayde looked unhappy when I found him leaning next to a cannon.

"Didn't you enjoy my show?" I asked, clapping his shoulder.

"You're a fool," he snapped. "Have you forgotten that you could send us all up in flames? You must keep that contained, especially when the deck was just rubbed down."

I felt my face sour, but I knew he was right. I didn't use my magic because this ship was as flammable as paper, but I wouldn't have the men make a fool of me, either.

"I have a plan I wish to discuss," I said, changing the subject.

His eyes widened, and he straightened. "No. Absolutely not."

"You haven't heard my idea!" I said, following him as he moved toward the helm.

"I know you too well, Veshak. It is something that will get us all killed. You have that look in your eye." Cayde dashed up the steps and lifted himself onto a barrel beside Orion, who shot a glance between us and rolled his eyes.

"What if it is a plan that will bring us riches enough to retire?" I pressed.

Cayde pinched the bridge of his nose under his glasses and looked to the sky. "You wish to be rid of me? So I must find another captain?"

Orion dropped the charcoal in his hand and crossed his arms. "Cayde could buy his own ship?"

"Exactly. A fleet of them, truly," I said.

"I don't want my own ship," Cayde said.

Orion cocked his head, and the corner of his mouth ticked down. "You deserve your own ship. You have sailed more years than any other. It is a disgrace that you were the Maharajah's first mate and now you serve his son, too."

"Shut it! I'll listen if you both stop pestering me," Cayde finally said, exasperated.

Orion nodded to me, and I pulled the map over that he had been marking. "The Kallu captain got me thinking about this prize from Raktam. My poor mother has been terrified to sail since she fled from Eudo's grasp, and I certainly can't waltz through his halls and do anything about it in our current state."

"Oh no," Cayde groaned, and I smacked his shoulder.

"Listen! I want to capture that katalval that we saw, and take them to Raktam. I will use them as a ploy to draw Eudo out, and then kill him! We can collect our own prize from their coffers, return the katalval to sea, and head back to Thandu."

"Do you not see how flawed your plan is?" Cayde asked.

"It took ten years of sailing to spot one yesterday. How do you intend to *capture* them?" Orion asked.

"We'll figure it out," I said, grinning.

"What about trading them for a prize? Don't you think Eudo would have protection in place to avoid such treason within his own walls?"

"We will find a way." I waved off his concern. "We will find another ship to take along the way, perhaps another from Kallu. Since all of Sariram has been informed of this prize, I'm sure there are more ships than ever out. Perhaps we will overtake a Jihvan ship and sail under their flag."

"Why kill a king we have never seen?" Cayde grumbled.

I slammed my palms down on the barrel and looked into his brown eyes. The wrinkles around them were freckled from years in the sun, and his frown deepened. "If I had the opportunity to kill him ten years ago, I would have. This is the first, and possibly only, chance I will ever have to free my mother from her past. Our Maharani deserves to travel freely and without fear. She spent years trapped under Eudo's thumb, and now is trapped in a different place, for the same reason."

I choked on the sentence that would have come next. *I was nearly resigned to a life just like her, locked up in that Mahal.* Somebody had to do something about Eudo's hold over others.

"Okay," Cayde said, reaching out to squeeze my shoulder. "Then, we kill the Iron King and bring your family peace. And we hope that our crew is ready, too."

"I'll plot the courses for hunting, but we must clean the ship first," Orion warned.

Tears pricked the back of my eyes as I gathered both of my friends into my arms and squeezed them tight.

"Alright, alright," Orion groaned, and I backed away with a chuckle.

"You must feel how much I love you," I said with a wink. I tipped my hat and turned to the wheel. "Plot the course, and prepare the men."

They both saluted, and Cayde took off across the deck, leaving me with a warmth in my chest as the sun set over calm seas.

I kept our course heading west on mild winds throughout dusk. When the stars began popping into existence above us, Ward made his way toward me. His thick mustache obscured his mouth, so I could not see his lips when he spoke. And shadows pulled over his eyes in the dark.

"I've come to relieve you," he said.

"What of Orion?" I returned. The standard shift change called for a navigator at night.

Ward shrugged, letting his shoulder drop quickly. "I dunno, I was asked to fill in by Felix."

"Keep the bow west. Do not change course, we have a course set."

He hesitated before taking the wheel. "What is the prize?"

I frowned and looked out over the ship, remembering Ward's whispers outside my cabin. "Right now, we chase a low tide," I said, turning away.

I heard him scoff as I took the steps to my cabin below, but I did my best to ignore the unsettled feeling I had. I had always been a fair captain, I thought, and this was the first time in my decade at sea that someone had threatened a mutiny.

I released a deep breath in the solitude of my room. My journal was undisturbed atop my desk, next to a pile of silk, books, and trinkets taken from the Kallu ship that I had yet to sort through.

I yanked a silver chain from around my neck, pulled the key hanging off it from beneath my vest, and unlocked the bottom drawer of the desk. I shrugged off my heavy coat and discarded it onto the chair, along with my hat. The three buttons of my wool vest twisted open easily, joining the already large pile of wool. I trailed my fingers along the checked silk sash around my waist, the smooth cloth gliding against my calloused pads sending a shiver down my spine, before finally untying the knot and letting the piece of fabric flutter to the floor.

A mirror hung on the wall opposite me, and I glared into it. My first night undressing in the cabin, I tried to wrench it from the wall, to no avail. Nothing would stay hung over the top to cover it, either. So, I turned away as I untied the lace of my linen shirt and threw it to the floor. I was left standing in only my breeches and binding wrap, neither of which I enjoyed taking off at the end of the day, but both of which I had to shed or I risked immense pain in the morning.

I took a deep breath and fumbled for the edge of the cloth, tucked under my arm. I had to pry at its frayed edge with my nails, and it stung to unwrap myself. Freeing the cloth from where it pressed into the fragile skin of my chest felt both damning and like breathing for the first time.

As I unwrapped myself, I remembered telling my mother how I felt about my body. Memories of wrapping a piece of linen so tight around myself that I cried from the pain flashed through my mind. Cayde presenting the women that had joined our crew and learned my secret, before he threw them overboard. Building the crew that respected me as the man I was.

I took a shuddering breath as I tucked the wrap into the drawer and secured the lock, placing the key back around my neck.

I would not allow Ward to take what I had worked so hard for.

Cayde stood at the helm of the galleon, arm outstretched toward an inlet north of Aatma's ruins.

"That'll be the place. It gives us visibility of the northern seas, but allows the sloop to protect our back."

I scrubbed my palms together, considering. The small beach would be a fine place to careen our galleon, but I couldn't settle the anxiety that pooled in my gut. We normally aimed further south. Something about being so close to Raktam didn't sit right with me.

"Aye," I said. Turning to the crew that awaited instruction, I checked the sword in my scabbard out of habit and cleared my throat. "Orion has been alerted to protect our back at the grave." I motioned to the cliffs off our portside, where the ruins that claimed so many ships lay. There was a spot just large enough to hide the sloop. "We'll station a boat at the reef for watch, anchor to the pines, and the rest of you will scrub like your life depends on it."

A round of shouts went up, and the crew broke. Moments later, our great ship began to turn into the bay, barely protected by a dead reef and lowering tide.

The crew rode in to the beach on longboats, ferrying supplies back and forth. Tents were pitched under the rising sun, and the tide pulled away from the belly of the galleon slowly. She was finally free of the sea by midday, and we set to clean.

Cries and grunts of effort echoed across the beach as the men pulled ropes from over the galleon's rails. I stood meters away with a canvas crumpled in my arms and watched the trees they attempted to anchor to.

"Alright, Cap?" a voice behind me asked.

I startled, turning to see our oldest member. His skin was like leather, worn by his years at sea, and wrinkled further as he chewed on a betel leaf. He raised a hand to shield his eyes, and I pulled the hat from my head and held it out to him.

He shook his head, but I insisted. "I need the sun, anyway. I've been at sea too long."

I motioned to the largest tree that Ward was walking toward. He hoisted a rope and pulley up, which was attached to the main mast.

Willy-Will observed for a moment. "You think they're going about it wrong?"

I looked back to the beach. A line of hefty pine trees stood guard at the edge of the sand on the other side of the beach. Their needles pointed to the sky, and stocky trunks meant they had been there hundreds of years, while the palm trunks were narrow enough to wrap my arms around.

I nodded. "The palms are too low on the coast line. They were only planted by the tides in the last few years."

The old man's eyes fixed intently on mine, and he reached a hand out for the cloth, which I released. "Let me fix your tent, Cap."

I opened my mouth, but my words were snatched away as shouts sounded from the other side of the beach.

The ship had been tilted, tied to the palms that grew from the sand. As I turned, the rope that held the main mast began to fray. Ward's hand on the pulley released, and the tension loosened. The mizzenmast rope snapped, releasing with a crack and whipping through the air. Sharp cries and screams rose from my crew, and I broke into a run toward them.

Willy-Will yelled from behind me, but I ignored him. The sand shifted unevenly beneath my boots, and wind blew through my shirt, pushing me sideways off the beach.

"Who's under?" I yelled.

No one responded, too busy snatching tools up or grappling for the ropes that remained. The wet wood of the galleon began to creak from the pressure of being held by so few ropes, and I fought against the dry sand to run faster.

I made eye contact with Cayde and threw my fist in the air in an arc. He turned up the beach screaming, "Go! Run! A ship's not worth your life!"

I made it to the rudder as the groaning of the aged wood bending on itself filled the air, and looked down the length of the ship. I saw nobody, and a heavy breath left my lips, but as I turned away, a voice cried out.

"Help! Ward!"

The memory flooded me of listening at my door a week before, hearing that voice plot mutiny with my watch lead, and I hesitated for a fraction of a second. It was so familiar, but without a face, I couldn't place it. The ship groaned above me, and a rope snapped again, and I leaped into action, running far out toward the coastline, looking for who the voice came from.

Screams flooded my ears, and my heart raced, blood burning as I ran as fast as I could. My heels dug hard into the sand, but it gave way too much.

"I'm coming!" I yelled.

The ship creaked in response, and the keel began to fall toward the shoreline. I heard the last rope snap, and the voice cried out again, and I saw him.

The navigator's apprentice was half buried, trapped under the ship's stores. His legs had been crushed by the ship first, and the sand stained red. Tears flooded his face, snot flowed freely, and I stuttered to a stop as he reached his arm out.

"Veshak!" he begged.

"I'm here!" I called, leaping forward.

As I moved, the ship released one last shudder, and fell to the ground with a thud. The boy's final scream was barely audible over the crash.

Sand plumed in the air, flying into my face, and I cried out in protest, throwing my hands to shield my eyes. Blood pooled under the ship, painting the sand and flowing into the water around my knees. I choked back bile that rose in my throat and fell to the ground, pressing my palms down. The sand was cool and gritty between my fingers, and I scooped a handful up, rising slowly.

Chaos broke from the crew as soon as I rounded the ship and proved my survival, and they ran to gather around me.

"Stupid bastard," Cayde chastised.

"Who was it?" a cannon boy asked.

Ward stood with his arms crossed in front of a small group, including Ehann and Clarence. I ignored the questions and approached him, lifting my chin to gaze into his eyes. I raised the handful of the boy's blood. I didn't even know his name.

"I made a vow to you when you boarded, do you remember? I will always chase a payday for you, I will always direct you for safety, and I will never sacrifice myself for you. No life on this ship is greater than another."

Ward swallowed and nodded, casting his eyes down. "Yes, Captain."

"Anchor to the pines. Next time you disregard me, it might be you under the keel."

I strode away from the silent group, toward a fully constructed tent.

"Thanks, Willy-Will, but I think I'll be heading for the sloop," I said.

The old man nodded. "There's a longboat down the beach."

"I want you to accompany me. Cayde too. Fetch the hands not needed here." I lifted my hat and swiped the sweat from my brow as he walked away, turning to watch the waves as they lowered into the bay.

We left quickly, and the steady lapping of the sea against our boat covered the creak of the galleon being pulled on her side once again.

I took a deep breath, enjoying the mist from the bay on my face and the silence of our small group. Until one of the cannon boys opened his mouth.

"Do you think that was on purpose?" he asked.

I exhaled loudly and spun to look at him. His face was sweat-soaked, as was the neck of his blouse, but he didn't stop rowing.

"I don't think we need to speculate," I said, scrubbing my eyes.

Cayde flashed me a look, eyes wide and mouth flat, before gazing out over the ocean.

"I just think it's odd—"

"I think it's odd that we can't row in peace," I interrupted, looking pointedly at the reef we approached.

His mouth snapped shut, and Willy-Will chuckled.

The water was clear beneath us, and I hung my head over the side. Colorful fish passed us by, and our boat nearly grazed the coral of the reef that shielded the bay as we passed into the ocean.

9

Zara

FOAM KISSED THE SEAM around the widest part of my waist, where the fur thickened to cover my tail, and I trailed my fingers through the dense green bubbles. The patch around me was littered with pieces of dried palm leaf and broken shells. The sun was dipping low in the sky, ready to close my full first day without Juhi. I shivered as Prajapati took the warmth with him toward the horizon while pulling bumps across my flesh. I had to fight against the urge to crush the small white flower in my hand.

Sai reached out and wrapped her fingers in mine on the right, while Barun gripped my left arm. The council waded at our back, each with their own white flowers, and I knew more people supported us behind them, but I could not bring myself to turn and face the crowd.

As the sun touched the sea, Barun released me and turned to put his back at Paalaivanam. Sai shivered, and I pulled her in closer. The council swam ahead, Juhi held aloft by binds of seaweed between them. They released her body in front of Barun, where she floated on a bed of foam, and I choked back a sob.

Barun looked to the sun. My heart thudded. Sai squeezed my hand.

He opened his mouth to begin the prayer to Prajapati, and I sucked in a breath. He gave thanks to the god of creation for the world that we lived in, for it afforded space for Juhi's existence. The bumps on my arms tingled. The wind blew.

The sea churned around us as Barun addressed Matsya, giving thanks for the life that she had given Juhi and releasing her essence back to the god of preservation. He began to move away, preparing to release Juhi to the waves. The sun slipped lower as he beckoned Sai forward. No words were spoken as she placed the flower in our sister's hair. She returned with tears in her eyes.

Barun cleared his throat, and I realized that it was my turn. "Please, place your padma," he whispered with a cracking voice.

Swimming toward Juhi felt as if it took hours. I was moving through thick sand, and I nearly dropped my flower multiple times. I couldn't look up at her, so I focused on the curled petals in my palm. Juhi had said once that they were her favorite flower, and she just wished they weren't also a symbol of death, as she'd like to wear one every day. I wish I never had to know what they looked like against her dark ringlets.

I finally reached the top of her head. Her curls were fanned out like an anemone's arms, with an empty spot at her crown. Her skin had lost its normally warm undertone and was now a sickly yellow color.

It struck me as I nestled the token into Juhi's hair that this was the second death in our family that my father had performed the rites for. I studied the tearstained tracks on Barun's cheeks as I waded close. His shoulders suddenly looked much more hunched than before.

I threw my arms around him, stopping his prayer, and the sob that racked his frame shook my own body as he returned my embrace. Pain twisted through my chest, pouring acidic tears from my eyes. I wanted to beg his forgiveness for causing Juhi's death, I wanted to apologize for the fact he had led two funerals in as many years, I wanted to clean the whole ocean of the rot that had taken our family from us.

I said nothing and let go instead, and returned to my sister, pulling her in close.

Barun swallowed hard, lifting his own padma from the water and moving toward Juhi. I stiffened when his hand touched Juhi's hair as he placed the flower. Touching a deceased body after the rites were performed was forbidden, and everyone knew so, as it could interfere with Rudra collecting their essence.

"Om namo Rudra," Barun began to speak the final prayer, and I stifled a gasp as my gaze flicked back to where his arms were hidden in her hair.

A moment later, he turned, and the shell that Juhi wore on a cord was clasped in his hand. Barun finished the prayer, and murmurs of "Om shanti om" rippled through the crowd. His hands were clasped in front of him under the water, then folded over one another in the next moment. The theft happened so fast that I could have imagined it. Except when I squinted at Juhi's light-bathed body, I could see the absence of the shell.

My heart thudded and palms slicked with sweat. If anyone else did that, they would be banished. But he was my father, and our leader. Would Juhi have given the necklace to him?

Her chest was bare as it had always been, but her breasts looked naked for the first time in four years. Her missing shell was too obvious. I fought against the urge to clench my fists and looked back at Barun. There was a smudge of orange standing out against the slate of his fur. The mini twist of the conch curled against his chest like a finger, and my heart thumped with nervous anger and guilt.

Barun nodded once, backing away from where he was blocking the current. The council released their own flowers, and a mound of padma rode the current around Juhi, scattering like a protective barrier. I touched my fingers to my lips and let my tears fall as my young sister's body turned, surrounded by shades of the sunset and glowing in early evening light.

The sun dropped over the horizon, where she became a speck. The ocean went silent and stilled completely for a moment as the top of the orb was enveloped. The crowd froze. I swallowed my tears, holding fast. A green light flashed from where the sun had been and chased itself away.

"Barun!"

I spun with my father and Sai and sucked in a sharp breath.

Navya swam away from the rest of the council, who bobbed hesitantly in place.

"It seems her essence was accepted by Rudra," she said. Her face was pinched, as if she had hoped for something different.

"Thank the gods, yes," Barun said.

"Though you interfered with her rites," Navya said.

Sai gasped beside me, and my stomach dropped. Barun moved in front of us, his arm lifting protectively.

"I do not know what you speak of, Navya. But I do believe that the council has a meeting tonight."

"You stole from Juhi's corpse, and I'll not stand for it. You must release the necklace," Navya pressed, advancing on our father.

Barun's face was still, and Sai swam in between them, holding her hands up. "What's going on? Father?" She looked up, eyes brimming with concern.

"He took the shell from Juhi's not-yet-cold form," Navya declared, "and our laws state that anyone touching a body after the rites must be banished." She pointed at the cord tied around Barun's neck and moved on him. I ducked around and grabbed her arm to hold her in place.

"This is a serious accusation, what you imply is treason," Sai said, looking around helplessly.

Navya turned on me, baring her teeth. "Do not flounder by, you are meant to be our leader. You must have seen him."

I hesitated, looking into the depths of Sai's eyes, and jerked my chin down a fraction of an inch. Shadows pulled over her gaze, and she backed away from our father. I released Navya as the council approached.

I sunk my teeth into my lip to keep quiet, tasting sour blood on my tongue. He was grieving; he didn't deserve banishment. Did he?

Navya's voice lifted. "Cetea Barun has committed a crime against the gods." Cold pricked my skin, and the other katalval were deathly still. "It is divine law to let the dead rest. To take from their body is evil. Barun chose to desecrate our most beloved deceased, by stealing a gift from Juhi."

A hushed gasp rippled around our people, and I lifted my gaze. The pain in my father's eyes was unbearable, and I understood why he did it.

"It was a lapse in judgment, Navya. He deserves mercy," I interrupted.

She turned appraising eyes on me but continued to speak over me.

"For violating our most ancient rules, from the ruling of the council, Barun will be banished."

Shame heated my neck, and the crowd began to stir. Sai lifted a hand to silence the disagreements. "Until such a time that the laws are changed, we have no way to argue this ruling. Barun will be banished—immediately and alone."

Barun's gaze sunk into the sea, and his shoulders sagged. Sai approached me and took my hand, and I realized that my fists were still clenched. I unfurled my fingers and looked at the marks my nails had made in my palms.

"Are you okay?" I asked her, voice low and shaky.

The crowd began to converge at the same moment, spinning in close to Barun, all wanting a piece of him, to grab him and yank him below the depths where he would be shoved across the trench.

I turned from the sight of our father being dragged away and shielded Sai's view, pulling her into a hug. "I am so sorry."

She pressed her forehead against mine and touched my chin. "He knew better."

"But does he deserve to leave?"

She did not answer as the crowd moved away. My mind spun, and I reached up and gripped Sai's arms, searching her eyes. "I never thought this would happen. I could have never guessed our father would do such a thing."

She shook her head and gripped my hands. "I hope you'd do the same at my rites."

Tears stung my eyes, and I laughed. "I love you too much to let anyone interfere." I wiped a stray tear from my cheek and swallowed. "Sai, I have to leave."

Her large eyes grew wider, and her frown exaggerated the dimple in her chin. "You can't be serious."

"If our father was not in mourning, he would never break a rule. He's not the first we have banished for similar causes, and we shouldn't have to worry about such things, because our people should not be dying!"

"What would you do?" Sai asked. "It is a sickness that plagues our seas, rot in our water that kills them."

"I will stop it," I declared. "I'll go to Sariram and stop their dumping of iron."

She suddenly slapped my hands away. "You are stupid!" Her scream was more shocking than her slap, and my jaw dropped. "You cannot change the state of the entire ocean by will. You're just looking for a reason to leave as you do every single day. Why can't you just be happy and make your life here like everybody else?"

Guilt simmered in my stomach as tears streamed down her face, and I chewed on my lip. "I should have been banished too," I said.

"What do you mean?"

I raised a hand to the strip of cloth in my hair. "I took this from Mother's waist when she died."

Sai's mouth snapped shut, and she backed away.

"She never should have died. Neither should have Juhi. Things here must change, and we are the only ones who can make it happen."

"You can't be serious," she cried.

I gripped the cloth in my fist and looked deep into my little sister's brown eyes. "I should have been banished. I'll end this rot as my penance instead."

She began to protest, but I continued. "You must take the seat at head of the council." Before Sai could say anything else, I darted forward and wrapped my arms around her, tears stinging my eyes. "I love you so much, Chinna. Please, live well. I will try to return."

She stiffened in my grasp, and I released her, taking in one last look of her soft features before swimming away. Pain dug into my chest like one of Juhi's spears, but I did my best to ignore it.

The sea felt thick against my fur, and salty tears poured freely from my eyes as I swam. Night encroached on the waves too quickly, making my heart pound. I didn't know where I should go, and I had not taken time to prepare supplies. I didn't know where the iron came from, or why it came to our seas. Sai had a point, but I could not go back and admit that to her.

I pulled to a stop in front of the trench, squinting over its dark depths.

Someone swam toward me in the distance, and panic gripped me. They were coming at me fast, barreling through the water, and I nearly turned and swam away, but then I saw long black hair and the glint of a spear, and released a breath.

Navya slowed in front of me, tucking her weapon away.

"Where are you going?" she asked at the same moment I asked, "Where have you been?"

I shrugged, and she looked around. "The crowd dispersed quickly," she murmured.

A sneer tugged the corner of my lip. "No thanks to you."

Navya sighed heavily and reached out, but I ducked away from her touch. "I hold no ill feeling toward your father, and I'm sorry for how that turned out. But I could not play favorites and ignore what he did."

"It was a lapse of judgment in a moment of grief," I pressed.

"I wish I had said nothing," Navya said.

I grimaced, and she stiffened. "You aren't chasing after him, are you?" she asked.

I jerked my head to the side.

"Where are you going?" Her voice sounded panicked, and I raised a brow.

"To stop the rot from the humans." A swell of pride filled me as I said it, but my chest deflated at the laugh Navya released.

"You can't do that!" she exclaimed.

"Why not? They're killing us. Someone must end it," I retorted.

"You certainly can't do anything like that"—she motioned up and down my body—"The iron began flooding these oceans years before you were born by men that marched throughout the west continent. You can barely pull yourself ashore without a struggle."

My tail flicked beneath me of its own accord, and heat rose in my cheeks. I knew she was right, and I should have considered it, but I was far from caring at this point.

She suddenly swam close, circling me, and I turned with her. Her gaze trailed up and down my body, lingering on my tail. "You'll need help, if you have any hope of traversing their world."

"What do you mean?" I asked.

"The surface, of course," she said with a smirk. She gripped my shoulders and shook me gently. "I used to change people all the time, I can do it for you too."

I swallowed hard at the thought of losing my tail. I knew about her helping Sai, changing her body to how she saw fit, but to change to a whole different being?

"That's not possible," I choked out.

"Of course it is," she whispered. "How do you think I live here?"

My mouth went dry, and I struggled for words. She had been lying about being katalval? But of course she had... how else would she have magic. Did anyone else know? I had to warn them. She held a council seat.

"It's been a long time since I've used magic to transform a body instead of contort it," Navya stated bluntly. I blanched at her, finally closing my mouth.

"Excuse me?" I stuttered.

"I will give you legs, if that is what you wish. You can go and try to change whatever it is you want."

My pulse quickened, and my head spun. This was it. This was how I would fix things. No more of our people would die. But what of this impostor living among us, who had just chased my father away?

"I need you to do something for me," she said.

"What?"

"Don't come back," she said, narrowing her eyes at me.

"Why wouldn't I? I have a sister to return to!"

"You must trust me, if you wish to go. Magic has a price. What is given cannot be undone. If you come back here, I will have no way to return you to your old form."

I released a breath as visions of a possible future ran through my mind. I could die up there and never see Sai again. Our people would not know that Navya was not katalval.

But if I succeeded, she would never have to perform at another funeral.

"Okay," I whispered.

Her hand suddenly wrapped around my wrist. "Hold still, look into my eyes," she warned, "and remember our deal."

The water began churning around my tail, bubbling, and my skin prickled, then began to glow.

Then the pain started. Hot and searing, my bones screamed and I screamed in turn, face turned to the sky; it was unlike anything I had ever experienced. As if someone was breaking every piece of my tail over and over and yanking the muscles into a new place.

The follicles my fur grew from felt as if they were twisting, and the spot where my waist ended and my tail began itched furiously. The fine dusting of hair on my stomach bristled, and my ribcage compressed. I couldn't breathe, I doubled over, my screams turned silent, and I begged for her to stop. The light around me became blinding, and the salt from my tears burned my face. A great tear shredded its way through the middle of my tail, and Navya dug her nails harder into my skin while her words drilled into my skull. She was saying something about death. If she died. But it didn't matter, because *I* was *dying*.

My arms prickled, my stomach twisted, my ribs cracked. Then suddenly all the pain stopped as quickly as it started. I took in a gasping breath, a dull ache replacing the sharp cracks that had been filling me, and as I straightened, I sank.

The sea swallowed me, the water was thick, and it filled my nose and mouth without mercy. I sank hard and fast, and suddenly I crumpled against the pebbled sand at the edge of the trench. Two foreign-feeling joints folded beneath me, banging into sharp rocks, sending shooting pain up my body. My arms flew above my head. I flailed, trying desperately to flap my tail, but I couldn't feel it anymore. The last thing I saw before darkness enveloped me was Navya swimming overhead.

10

Dorian

THE CREW WAS LOUD, the boat tossed me about like a sack of flour, and the salty air had begun to suck the liquid from my skin.

I felt alive in a way I had never known was possible.

I was stuck to the back rail, slung up over the side with my face to the sea when Hari found me for the fifth time in half as many days.

"That bad, Your Highness?" he asked, with a slap on my back.

The movement shoved my gut into the hard wood of the rail, and I groaned in pain, turning bleary eyes on him. I didn't understand how he could be so... upright. I said as much in fewer words.

He laughed and crossed his arms. "I guess I'm more excited about this than you. Or maybe I'm tougher."

I belched and shoved myself farther over the rail. I didn't have the energy to challenge him. He sighed loudly and leaned down, nudging my shoulder. "I'm worried, Dorian. I've never seen you ill. Have you had any visions?"

I shook my head, another wave of nausea hitting with the movement. "Not since boarding."

"Perhaps you should have some ale. It might be good for you."

I hadn't considered that. I nodded, and inhaled through my mouth, trying to ignore the mix of smells from around me. It was an assault, with fish from the sea, sweat from the men, wet metal and mildew—I assumed from the joints and build of the boat itself.

"If this continues, we can turn back." His voice was low. I glared at him from the corner of my eye, scared to move. My nostrils flared in indignation, and my neck heated. He pursed his lips.

"Got it. I'll find some drink."

He wandered off and left me to wallow alone. I watched the foam churn from under the ship, turning outward before mixing into great ribbons of bubbles, which made me feel sick all over again.

I clenched my eyes shut and wondered where I could have gone wrong with my expectations. How could I have climbed on this ship and ended up so unbalanced? I had always loved the sea. Spending time swimming calmed my nerves. Or on the balcony offset my room, looking over the ocean in the distance at the end of the day when everyone had retired. I even enjoyed the silent carriage rides at dawn when I could watch the pink painted sky through the window above and that ride swayed me to and fro.

A twinge of pain in my lower back reminded me that I had been leaning for an hour, and I straightened, my eyes still closed. The movement was significantly less sickening when I couldn't see. I think it was the fact that no matter what direction I looked in, I was surrounded by blue. Up, down, east and west on the horizon. There was nothing to break it up. No solid foundation to fixate on.

I thought again through everything I loved as I popped my hip. I'd spent a lot of time dreaming of this. Even the daydream just a few days earlier, on the ship in the library, on waves in my sleep. When I thought back, though... it was silent. In fact, every memory that was happy, the only consistency was that my father wasn't there. And the really good ones were quiet.

"Here." Something hard nudged my hand, and I opened my fingers to grasp the smooth wood of a carved mug.

I cracked my eyes open in time to watch Hari lift his own and throw it back.

"Thanks." My throat was raw when I spoke, and I took a careful sip. The drink was sour and dark, slightly warm, but bubbly. I realized why he suggested it then.

"On the bright side, you have stubble."

I snorted into my cup. Bright side, indeed. I'd wanted to grow a beard for nearly fifteen years. "I guess missing a few mandatory shaves will do that."

He chuckled. "I wonder if Simon thinks of you."

I swirled my drink and watched it. That was another thing that had made me unhappy. Not Simon, but being forced to stay clean-shaven.

I lowered myself to the deck and sat cross-legged, leaning my head against the damp wall and taking a deep breath. "Ri, when are you most happy?" I asked, squinting up at him.

He lifted a brow and sat with me. He scratched his head and took another swig before rocking back and resting his forearms on his knees. "That's a tough one. Do you want the honest answer or the royal answer?"

I froze, confused. What on earth could he mean by that? What could possibly be the difference?

He must have noticed, as he quickly shook his head. "Never mind. I'll say training. Spending time with you. That's what comes to mind first."

"Really?"

He gave me a tight-lipped smile and nodded. "I adore you, Dorian." His hand fell to my thigh. "Though, I would enjoy our time together more if you would allow us to relax and explore more together."

"Hm." I pondered for a moment, sipping and letting the bubbles settle my stomach. As the sickness faded slowly, the world came into sharper focus, the sounds of the crew floated into my consciousness, and I realized how ridiculous I must look. It wasn't just me and Hari here. There were some two hundred others running around the massive wooden beast, making it work, and I'd tuned them out for well over twenty-four hours.

I swallowed hard and leaned over to peek down the steps. Teal uniforms were walking all over the main deck, and the one steel gray coat of the captain was turned away from me just in front of one of the masts.

I looked back at Hari and grimaced. "I've been a terrible sailing guest, haven't I?"

He laughed loudly and shook his head. "It's probably for the best, they're a very organized lot. One misstep and Nottley would have your head."

I leaned back again and watched the sky for a moment, thinking about life. I wondered what it would have been like had I not been born into the royal family. Would I still have craved escape so hard that I attached myself to the idea of a ship like this and then regretted it? Might I have had a father that I loved? Perhaps a mother that didn't go missing.

Hari kicked my foot, and I frowned at him. "What?"

"Where'd you go?"

"Not into a dream, if that's what you're worried about."

He shook his head. "No, I mean emotionally. You looked to be in pain."

"Oh. I just... I wonder about life. If I could have been something else. If I should have been someone else." I chewed my cheek and looked down at my hands.

"How do you mean?"

I sighed and shrugged. "Maybe if I weren't a prince, if I'd been a commoner, or even born inland. Maybe I'd be happier."

"Maybe you'd be married with three kids screaming at your feet." He grinned, and I kicked his foot back.

"Yeah, right. I'm already supposed to do that, and I am sure that Eudo will have it all arranged for me by the time we return."

His laugh faded, and we both turned to watch the sea. I was grateful he'd found a solution for my stomach. And talked to me. It was nice to exist outside of the castle, without prying ears. I glanced past him to see that there really wasn't anyone around. Since we had left the royal guard at port, with Hari assuring them he could keep me safe on his own, it was truly just him and me among strangers.

I stretched my legs out and yawned, rolling my shoulders back. Leaning forward, I tapped his knee. His blue eyes widened.

"Hey. Thank you for this. I felt so confined even in conversation before."

He sniffed and shuffled before lifting a shoulder. "It's nothing. Only my duty as your man-in-waiting," he said, his tone joking.

I nodded firmly and reached above my head to grab the railing, hoisting myself up. We both knew it was more than that. I felt significantly better than before. Though, as soon as I was standing, a milder version of the nausea returned. Hari must have noticed, as he snatched up my mug and lifted it.

"Your face is pale. I'll be back."

I nodded and watched as the crew continued to mill about. Some tying ropes, some moving barrels and boxes, some chatting or motioning about. My eyes roamed about the large ship and landed on the captain at the other end. I could barely make him out, but could see two others flanking him. He seemed stiff, and I looked past him to the blue horizon he seemed fixated on. I squinted. It wasn't unbroken anymore.

I walked across the back deck to get a better view. I swore I could see a black dot in the distance. Could we be coming up on land? Perhaps the island of rumored hybrids? But I would have imagined it to be a few more days of travel still. I kept squinting, but it didn't move. I looked back at the captain, who was standing as still as a statue.

Hari walked up the steps directly in front of me and followed my gaze before raising a brow and asking what I was doing.

"I think there's land in the distance, and first I wondered if I was seeing something, but look at Nottley."

Hari turned shoulder to shoulder with me and grunted. "Huh, you're right. That's odd. He seemed very relaxed earlier."

"You don't think it's a concern, right?" I asked. I was sure if it was, we would be warned. Plus, what dangers could lie out here?

Hari nodded and handed me my ale. "Of course not. If you're worried, we can go and ask. Otherwise, there is food in the galley."

I dropped my gaze from the captain and grinned, tapping my cup to my friend's before taking a deep draw. The ale coated my stomach like silk, and it momentarily numbed the sharpness of my worries.

"I might be up for a bit of grub. I wonder if there is space to spar."

He opened his mouth but was interrupted by a shout across the ship. A yell was returned from a crew member closer to me, and suddenly an uproar began. Hari wrapped a veined hand around my arm, pulling me to the back corner, while one of the uniforms ran up. He looked frantic, with bloodshot eyes, and his hat knocked askew.

"Highness, we need to prepare. You'll have to go below deck!" He gestured wildly behind him, and I glanced up to see sails dropping, ropes being pulled, cannonballs being carried this way and that.

"Why?" Hari stepped in front of me, and the man cringed back.

"There's an unmarked ship to the south."

My heart stuttered and the world went dim as I looked out over the ocean. I grasped at Hari's arm, and his fingers tangled desperately in mine.

"I see it now," Hari muttered.

The world began to haze through stars in my vision, and I clutched Hari's arm, trying to stay grounded.

The sound of drums took over the beat in my chest, and a hot pipe whistled loudly. "It can't be pirates, right?"

I couldn't hear Hari's response as I grew dizzy. A great black flag rose up in front of me, gripped in the giant hand of Rudra. His knotted black hair bobbed atop his head, and his pointed grin pulled into a sneer.

"Your destiny awaits," he taunted.

I swallowed hard as the sea rose around him, churning violently. The stars flooded the sky, flashing into great balls of flame that burned too bright to be real. Suddenly the flag in his hand wrapped around him, searing into his back and flapping like wings. The skin pulled back from his mouth, and his chin elongated into the maw of a beast. I tried to scream but was frozen in place, my pulse keeping beat with that terrifying music. His maw unhinged, and flame erupted from his throat and washed around me.

11

Veshak

Ward grimaced at the cloth cross between our feet. Colored pieces of wood sat in different blocks of the quilted pattern. The navigator assisted him, while Felix sat on my team. I was in the lead, with all four either home or in the belly of my arm of the cross. Felix had returned two of his to home and was five points from returning another. Ward's team had barely moved throughout our game. He would need forty points to capture one of Felix's pawns and move closer to his own belly. He lifted his fist and looked to the sky. "Let's go, Prajapati, grant me this boon."

He scrubbed his palms together and released the seven shells. The cowries fell, clinking against each other, their curled backs taunting us all as they bounced and spun around, until they finally fell into the cloth with a gentle thud.

Seven blank sides faced up, and I released a belly laugh as Ward punched the air. "Twenty-five, and another turn!" he cried, while the rest of us shook our heads.

"I suspect a cheat, or Prajapati must really hold you in his favor," I joked.

He tapped his wooden piece across the board by twenty-five spaces, grinning as he moved, and picked up the cowrie shells again.

"I will best you at Pachisi once this year," Ward taunted, glee sparking in his eye.

I grinned and leaned in, digging through my pockets. "Let's make this interesting, then," I said, producing a gold anklet set with precious gems and dangling it out. "If you win, this is yours."

He set his jaw, and I grinned as he shook the die once more.

"Captain!" Cayde yelled. I stood before the brass hit the deck and turned to see Cayde motioning wildly from the bow.

"Shit," I muttered in the same moment that Ward swore and announced, "Only three."

I pocketed the chain once more, and Ward stood. "Hey, our wager!"

I waved him off and dashed toward Cayde, snatching his spyglass once I got to his side.

"It's a royal ship," he murmured.

The great royal flag of Raktam, adorned with a gray crest on teal cloth, snapped at me in the distance. They sailed straight south, turned only a few degrees away from us.

Ten years at sea, and for the first time in under a week I had seen both katalval and a royal ship from Raktam, and had been threatened with mutiny. "By the sea's, someone has angered the gods," I said, lowering the spyglass.

"Or they are very pleased," Cayde offered.

I chewed on my lip and sat back on a barrel. "That is a man-o'-war. They'll have more than a hundred guns aboard."

"We can hide, with the galleon still beached, our sloop doesn't stand a chance."

"The king must be on that ship," I mused. "Why else would they sail a warship under their royal flag?"

Cayde's brow furrowed, and he placed a hand on my shoulder. "They could have more firepower than we expect, and take up a strong defense. We'll face a wall of cannons," he said.

I nodded grimly, looking out over the sea. My heart ached. This could be the missing piece of my plan. Instead of invading Raktam, their king had come to us.

We were faced with two potential routes in order to confront him, and we had mere hours to execute either plan. On one hand, we could go on the offense and take chase with both of our ships. The tide would go in soon, and the galleon could sail again, and from our current position, we were only able to see that Raktam had one vessel out.

As with our strategy of hiding the sloop, there was the possibility that they were pulling a smaller boat behind them, and we'd end up overpowered in surprise.

On the other hand, we could board under the flag of pirates.

"I think there is something to be said for drawing them in," I said. "We lower our flag, play at a ship in need, and attack under a white flag."

Orion approached and looked between us, eyes narrowing as he realized what we were discussing.

Cayde hummed and scratched his beard, which had grown scruff since our last docking. "I feel our chances at success are slim. The king is not known for his mercy, at sea or otherwise. What if he ignores us and passes by?" he asked.

With the galleon still careened, we could wave white, beg for assistance, then ambush them from the beach.

I motioned to a barrel on deck and pulled a few coins from my pocket. Setting the trinkets up in a makeshift model, I placed the smallest to the left of the barrel, and the two larger at the top and bottom, to indicate. "Since they're heading south." I drew a line with my finger toward the coin near the bottom of the barrel. I moved the larger coin closer to the small one and pulled the anklet out as well, using the chain to form a barrier around part of the larger coin. "We'll be vulnerable, so we have to time it perfectly. This will be a two-pronged attack. Our beached crew is going to shoot from the bay, while we attack from the deck. Then, after they've been overtaken, we can regroup."

I glanced at Cayde as he opened his mouth to protest again, and raised a finger.

"Having the galleon exposed is the advantage. If the royals *do* take the bait, the worst risk is the loss of our smaller vessel, and if they don't, and pass us by, we are ready to take chase with the galleon."

Cayde brushed a hand through his red hair, pushing it away from his forehead, while Orion crossed his arms.

"You know I'll follow you to the gallows, Captain," Cayde declared, straightening.

Orion scratched the back of his neck before nodding once. "How do you want to split the crew?"

The air compressed from my lungs hard, and I leaned an elbow over the barrel. "That's a harder discussion. We're going to lose good men today, no matter how we strategize."

Orion checked the sword at his side and motioned behind his shoulder. "I'll rally the crew and send a boat to warn Ward and the galleon. They'll need to be filled in."

I reached out to shake his hand, gripping his forearm before waving him off and leaning over the rail of the deck. Cayde's presence bore over my shoulder, and my shoulders sagged with the weight of his gaze before I finally glanced back at him.

"What is it?" I asked.

He hesitated before joining me. Shifting uncomfortably, he looked out over the sea, then at me, and gripped the salt-worn rail tightly. "Are you ready for this?"

A scoff escaped my lips before I could stop it, and I covered the reaction with a cough. "Why wouldn't I be?"

He raised a brow and shook his head. I straightened and pressed two fingers into his shoulder. "Do you think I cannot handle it?" I pressed.

Cayde looked to his hands, rubbing his fingertips into his palm, where he'd likely lifted moisture from the wood, before he met my gaze. "I just wonder if you've considered what we are about to undertake. We will face Eudo on that ship. You proposed the plan, but to talk about it is different than to act."

I swallowed hard before I nodded.

"I know," I said, "but I must kill Eudo, for my mother's sake. As long as he lives, I cannot rest."

He turned away to prepare, and I caressed the pommel of my sword and looked at the ship from Raktam. We would meet them before dusk. The tide would stay out until the moon rose, leaving the galleon beached and the navigator that had sacrificed himself stuck with the ship. I hoped we did not have too many others to bury at sea.

I heaved a sigh before turning from the rail and whistling shrilly.

One hundred and twenty pairs of eyes turned on me, and I spread my arms wide. "Today we chase the greatest prize of your careers!" A round of cheers went up from the crowd, and I clapped my hands together. "Royals from Raktam approach."

A hush fell over the crew and murmurs broke out as I spoke. "By dusk tonight we will board their ship, infiltrate their navy, and kill their king! Show them no mercy!"

Earsplitting cheers and applause erupted from the deck, and I dropped down from the bow, moving about the crew to distribute individual orders. I needed my men excited and on alert as we prepared. And I made sure to clasp hands with each one, as it might be the last time I saw them.

As the sun set, our black flag from Paalaivanam was lowered. Our sails were hoisted at half-mast, and we moved out meter by meter into the path of the Royal Navy.

The king's ship slowed as they approached, and I barely breathed. The sun began to set, and we turned in tandem, pulling our starboard sides together.

Hundreds of men in iron breastplates and teal jackets stood at attention across the thin strip of sea that separated us. My heart thudded wildly in my ear. Moments ticked by, and then the unfurling of cloth filled the air, followed by the screams of my men, gasps of the royals, and thuds of planks and ropes being thrown across.

I watched with a clenched jaw as my crew threw themselves to the deck of the man-o'-war in some manner: swinging on ropes, running across slabs of wood—some just leaped with their weapons haphazardly tucked into various belts.

They had taken me seriously when I said to have no mercy. The teal-clad military began to fall before they could react and pull out a defense. Heads were freed from spines and rolled across the deck while the officers registered that this wasn't a normal invasion. Intestines were spilled from torsos, like souls torn through Rudra's veil, while the Raktam Navy threw warnings among their own crew. Blood began to flood their freshly oiled deck, offering it a darker stain.

I launched myself from the rail I stood on, yanking a rope from nearby and twisting around a mast. My wrist wrapped once in the thick hemp, and my legs swung out from under my body, pointed over the deck. I released the rope and flew in a high arc over the space between our ships, spinning in midair.

The landing was hard, sending tremors from the balls of my feet up to my jaw, but well worth the shock on the naval officer's face when he spun away from my ship to find me behind him, a dagger already drawn from my calf and poised at the soft spot where his rib cage joined together.

"Tell me who's aboard your ship." I leaned in and demanded, raising my face so we were almost nose to nose.

"Just the navy. F-from Raktam," he stuttered. I glanced at his hand, seeing his fingers were trembling against the hilt of his sword. He hadn't even cleared the handle of it.

"Liar," I spat. "You couldn't be louder about where you're from and prouder to hold passengers from Castle Durling." I motioned to the flag that bore the royal crest above us and slapped his hand away from his belt, where he'd tried to draw his sword.

Backing up a step, I drew his sword in one smooth movement and raised my dagger to the bulge at his throat while pointing his own weapon at the one in his pants. "Tell me who you house aboard or choose to lose your manhood."

I needed him to say the name. To confirm that it was Eudo.

He stumbled, but the rail behind him caught his back. His lips were pursed tightly, and though his body shook, he said nothing.

"Hold your tongue and it will be your life," I growled.

His throat bobbed. "The Crown Prince Dorian," he breathed. Had I not been watching his lips, I would have missed it.

I faltered, disappointment clouding my judgment for a moment as the corner of my mouth ticked down. I nodded, lowering the sword. Then I watched him exhale before jamming the knife deep into his neck.

"No mercy," I said dryly as he choked.

My plan would continue to be forced to change. The king was not aboard, but his son was... But what good would it do me to kill him? I frowned and shook my head, anger flooding my body. The king was a coward, or too lazy to sail himself.

I turned away before the man's body hit the deck and let the roar of enclosed battle flood into my ears. I sliced and stabbed my way through the crowd, spinning off the backs of my own men. Their intensity was palpable as they fought; they needed this bloodshed just as much as I did.

Cries rang out from all sides followed by squelching and thuds, and a flash of metal passed my peripherals. I tried to duck, but a hot spray slapped across my face. I grimaced and turned to see Willy-Will raise his rapier sheepishly. "Sorry, Cap. Tried to stop it." A body lay crumpled at his feet, a deep wound at the neck.

I nodded his way and kept moving, slicking the blood from my face and swallowing hard. I ducked under the arm of a boy, slicing at his thighs with my dagger. One of my sailors-in-training yelled a "Thank you" at my back, and then I heard the telltale thud. My crew was doing well—my family was doing well.

One more weave between teal coats and I found myself at the back of a squat man with a purple naval cap on. His hairline was trimmed under it, and the hand hanging at his side held thick fingers and a single silver signet ring on his pinky. I wasted no time in hooking my sword upward, to sheathe my blade in his ribs.

A flash of metal swung through the air from my left, knocking my sword to the side. I staggered back with a gasp and spun.

A mountain of a man stood over me, his crop of blond hair flecked with blood. Muscles rippled under his brown skin as he shoved my blade down to the deck.

"I'll thank you not to murder my captain," he said, drawing back his sword. "Call your men off."

I turned to face him fully, and his eyes widened a fraction before he straightened and readied his stance.

"I'll thank you not to give me orders," I retorted, swinging my sword.

He lifted his own and blocked me easily, but opened his right side to attack. I swung and slashed, pushing him back a step. His long legs and high hips had him moving like a tiger, and the corner of my mouth ticked down.

Our swords locked in the air at the steps to the helm, and he leaned in, forcing me to brace myself. I grinned, playing off as if I was exerting no effort to hold him off.

"I should know the name of the man I am fighting," I said, digging my heels into the deck.

"Hari Freemantle," he said, grinding his sword off mine and slashing it down toward me. I was forced back a step until I recovered my block. "And who am I about to slay?"

I gritted my teeth and backed up. "Captain Veshak Annitiki, Privateer."

He jerked his chin down and pulled back, allowing me the opening I needed to dive forward. Before I could sink my blade into his side, Hari spun away, and pain erupted from the middle of my spine. I gasped for air as stars swam in my vision, and I fell to my knees.

The chaos of fighting around me dimmed to a buzz, and shouting above became clear. I felt blindly nearby, trying to grasp for the handle of my sword, but a boot crunched down on my fingers, and I cried out in agony as my knuckles popped.

I looked up through my blurred vision at Hari, the grim expression on his face, and tried to make out the words coming from between his lips. His babble fell to the ground between us, and he stepped back, relieving his weight from my hand.

I gasped as the sounds of battle suddenly flooded into my ears again, and I grabbed for my sword, scrambling upward. It swung uselessly beside me for a moment until I shook the feeling back into my arm. My spine still hurt, but not like I had been stabbed. He had just hit me.

He was still speaking. "—while he's down," he said, motioning around. "You should retreat now."

I blinked at him, trying to make sense of his words. "What did you say?"

"You should retreat while you have the chance. I won't kill a man while he's down, but I can't speak for the rest of this crew."

I gritted my teeth and inhaled sharply, pulling my sword up and swinging it in a low arc. It dinged off the flat of his, allowing me to gather air and pull down hard and fast. He let out a cry as I grazed his arm. He staggered back, lifting his sword and looking down.

"Captain!" Willy-Will's voice pierced through the air, and I turned to see him on his knees. Blood poured from the side of his head, turning his black skin ruby.

I searched desperately for someone to save him, panic rising in my throat. For the men still engaged in combat, just as many lay on the deck, equally roped in the clothes of my crew as clad in teal. They lay with their eyes open and void of essence, limbs detached or mouth agape and leaking blood.

The gray-coated men of the Royal Navy moved as one, swinging and slashing their blades violently. I watched another handful of my men fall and felt their pain as my own, twisting in my chest like a dagger.

I choked back a plea for help, staggering against my sword as it dug between planks at my feet. The sickening sound of bone crunching behind me filled my ears, and I tensed, preparing to fall. Someone must have hit me. Hari had just struck a killing blow.

Moments passed like sand through an hourglass, but I felt no pain, no warmth of blood on my neck, so I spun around slowly.

Orion stood over Hari with a beam clutched in his hands. His face burned red with anger, and he threw the chunk of wood down, producing a rope from his belt after.

"The men need you!" he called over the din of battle. I stood, shell-shocked, as Orion tied the man's hands together, then rolled him on his stomach and secured his wrists to his ankles.

I shook myself from my daze and dashed for Willy-Will.

The man above him lifted an axe into the air, ready to swing it for the older man's head, and I slid to my knees behind him and reached past my mate. My blade glided easily through his stomach, stretching up, lodging through his intestines. He choked out a rasped sound before blood trickled from between his lips, pouring over Willy-Will's head, and he fell sideways.

I let my sword fall with him, grasping my friend and lowering him down in my arms. "Are you okay?" I nearly screamed the words, and he shook, nodding.

"Let me rest, please." His fingers trembled on my arm, his mouth quivered, and he curled into himself between the boots of one man and the legs of another.

A shiver ran through me as I tried to stand again; tears pricked the back of my eyes, and my fingers shook around the hilt of my sword as I freed it from the soldier's gut.

Blood squelched under my boots, and everywhere I looked, I saw the death-stricken faces of my crew.

Rage filled me. Anger heated my core, and my shiver quickened to a feral growl in my chest. We could not—would not—lose anymore. My men's sacrifice would not go to waste.

I raised my blade above my head and let the flames in my stomach free. Fire climbed my throat and erupted into the sky, licking the edge of my blade and turning it red. The sail above set aflame, and the men around me began to break apart from each other.

I ran into the fray, slashing my sword through the backs of gray coats, opening fatal wounds or blinding men with the heat from its broadside.

"Retreat!" I screamed.

I did not stay to see what happened, turning instead for the helm. A door sat behind the wheel, and I had not yet seen the prince aboard the ship. He had to be hiding, nay, cowering in that cabin.

I bolted toward the door and found Orion engaged with the captain that I had been stopped from killing. I took a deep breath, ignoring the screaming protest of my muscles, and raised my sword.

It speared through the back of his ribcage. His breath caught, and he turned his face, allowing me a glimpse of a single, wide, ice-blue eye surrounded by windburned skin. Chapped lips with untrimmed red stubble dropped in shock.

"Nottley!" A deep voice bellowed from behind me.

The captain slumped back over my blade.

I twisted my sword before dislodging it and yelled over my shoulder. "Cayde!"

A beat passed before he appeared at my side.

"Aye."

"The prince is in there," I said, motioning to the door.

"Not the king?" he asked.

"Not the king," I confirmed. "We take the prince and retreat."

"Aye," Cayde said.

He lifted a leg and kicked at the door. He grappled loudly with the prince for a moment before throwing one hard punch to his face.

The man sprawled out on the floor, his royal clothes bloodied, and his eye quickly swelling.

"Rudra's balls, why's he look like you?" Cayde said in the same moment I murmured, "Fuck..."

12

Dorian

STARS SWAM IN MY vision as I sat up, pain ricocheting around my skull. I tried to lift my hand to press my palm over my eye, but found it bound to my side. I wriggled and quickly realized that my whole body was secured in hemp. I could not move from where I had been propped upright on a bench.

"Hari?" I croaked.

It all came back to me very suddenly then. The screams of the men, the clash of swords, the door blowing in off its hinges, and the man that threw his fist into my face.

The room around me was dark and dank. A puddle pooled at my feet, and salt crusted on the walls. There was no natural light—no windows—but a shaft of light from a sputtering lantern shone over a bucket in the corner.

I shuddered as my eyes fixed on the bars in front of me. I'd been locked in the brig. Worse, I had been tied up and had no way to move.

A door creaked at the end of the hall, and I tried to stand but fell back to my seat hard.

"He must be awake now," a low voice said.

Someone grunted an agreement, and I ground my teeth, fighting against my bonds.

"Let me out of here! You have committed treason! You will face the gallows for your crime!"

"You may wish to withhold your judgment," a man said, stepping into the wane light.

I sucked in a sharp breath as I fell back against the wall.

He had dark amber curls to his shoulders, with a deep peak on his forehead to rival my own. His curved nose with a bump on the bridge froze me in place. I lifted my fists wrapped in rope in an attempt to touch the bump on my own freckled nose, noting that he even had a single freckle larger than the rest on his right nostril. A dimpled chin fell below plump lips with a pronounced bow, and I pressed my trembling lips together.

The world spun around me.

"Who are you?" I asked.

"Your brother," he said, raising a brow, a grin tugging at his mouth.

Heat crept up my neck as anger and confusion swirled inside me. "Impossible!"

"Not at all. *You* are Prince Dorian Durling of Raktam," he said, pointing at me and then himself. "I am Rajakumara Veshak Annitiki of Thandu, the equivalent of a prince. How are princes born?" Veshak asked, arrogance tainting his voice.

My mind raced faster than my pulse, and sweat beaded on my brow. "It's not possible, my father has no other children..."

Veshak's brow wrinkled in confusion. "Did Eudo send you to sea for being simple?"

"Do not speak of my father!" I yelled, lunging toward him. I momentarily forgot my position—my arms stuck to my sides, legs bound with thorough knots from my knees to ankles—and my face hit the ground hard, leaving me writhing in pain.

"Sky's above, man, get a hold of yourself!" Veshak exclaimed, sliding the lock open and stumbling in to lift me up. He shoved me back onto the bench and leaned me against the wall, bending in to search my eyes.

I saw the differences between us then. He had a softer face than me, his lips were more plump, and one eye was different—ghastly, almost, with a sweeping scar that had caused it to lose its brown color and turn a pale shade of gold.

His palms pressed hard into my collarbones, holding me back against the wooden bench. A shadow fell over the doorway, and the man who had knocked me unconscious filled the space. I swallowed hard.

"Do you understand that we share a mother?" Veshak asked, drawing my attention back to him.

My eyes widened, and my heart stuttered. No. That wasn't possible. I could have no siblings, because that would mean that Eudo had lied to me. Or that Mother had.

"No," I whispered, looking deep into his mismatched eyes. "I have no brother."

"Our mother told me stories of you when I was young. But she also told me stories of Eudo, and his atrocities."

"N-no," I stuttered. "You're wrong! My mother would have come home!" I strained against the ropes, fighting to get free, fighting to hurt him. How could this stranger take me from my ship and make up such egregious lies?

I leaned forward, and pain erupted on the side of my face as he slapped me.

"Calm down!" he yelled.

"What do you want from me?" I cried out, whimpering as I tasted blood in my mouth. I wriggled forward again and felt more hands grasping at me.

"To kill your father."

Stars clouded my vision as I fell to the ground and pain exploded through my head. Darkness flooded the sky around me, and the creaking floorboards gave way to sand and rock.

"No," I groaned, lifting my suddenly unbound hand to rub my temple. I was drifting into more visions when I needed to stay put. "Please, no!"

A model of the Tala Mountains wavered in the distance, the peaks and valleys of Sariram stretching out around them. As I stood, water rushed to flood the land around me, rising to my knees, and I groaned. Matsya rose from the waves, standing on a great black tail, a trident clutched in her hands.

Rudra moved through the continents, stomping around and creating sinkholes, squashing people, and knocking down trees while Prajapati moved around him, attempting to slow his rampage.

As I watched the scene unfold in front of me, watched the gods fight over our world, I could still hear murmurs from my cell. The vague pressure of Veshak's fingers pressed into my arms was a strange sensation as I took a step toward the battle that currently raged over Sariram.

"Leave my creation be!" Prajapati boomed.

"Get help!" Veshak called from far away.

I shook his quiet voice from my ears and let myself fully absorb what played out in front of me.

Matsya began to weep, and tailed beings emerged from where her tears mixed with the sea-foam. They looked exactly like her, with black skin and long hair, naked except for a coating of fur, but they all had a set of sharp teeth and daggerlike nails.

I swallowed hard as one swam past me. But they paid me no mind.

Rudra swung his fist to the ground at the same moment that Prajapati dove in front of him. The brothers collided and fell into combat, with Prajapati defending himself and the people running about his feet and Rudra throwing wild blows.

Matsya continued to weep beside me, and I cast her a sidelong glance. I wanted to ask why she did not intervene, but instead I held my tongue and watched the brothers battle.

Rudra raised his arm, and the limb stretched to the sky, elongating into a flat blade which he slashed down toward his brother. I stifled my gasp as he cleaved Prajapati in two, lifting the god's head and turning to throw it across the world. It landed with a thud on the continent of Paalaivanam. Rudra picked up the rest of his brother's body and swung it wide, throwing it with a sickened smirk into the sky.

Bright light suddenly flared above us as Prajapati burned, and I blinked back tears in my eyes as I stared directly into the sun.

Rudra let out a cackle, moving to flatten a forest, and Matsya let out a bloodcurdling scream. A shudder ran down my spine as she raised herself from the sea and opened her mouth wide. From the depths of her throat, another god appeared far more terrifying than even Rudra.

"Makali, protect them," Matsya begged before falling into the sea. Her hair spread around her body, her arms circled the tailed beings she had birthed from her tears, and her skin fell to pieces of sand.

Makali rose up in front of Rudra, towering over him like a mother standing over her son, with ten arms and skin black as night. Unlike a mother, she had weapons clasped in every hand but two. He didn't stand a chance against her discipline. He had done something terrible and would answer for his crimes, for the gods didn't have parents to help them, so Matsya had created her own.

Rudra cowered back, and the colorful ornament atop his head bobbed and swayed as he dodged between her blades. His small stature seemed to aid him in weaving around Makali's many limbs, and he leaped nimbly atop a hill to avoid a low swipe from a cleaver. The hill exploded into a rain of rock around them, sending boulders tumbling, and tiny people ran and screamed at their feet.

I fixed my gaze on where Rudra's toes barely touched the lush fields. Every spot sunk into a valley, rooted with a dark sickness of some sort. Bogs formed at his heels when he allowed them to fall, but anywhere Makali covered his steps, forests sprouted. She let a scream of frustration loose, and the sun, newly embedded into the sky, burned brighter for her.

As Rudra jumped from the hill, Makali lashed out and sunk a tapered sword into his eye. He fell to the ground, thrashing and screaming, as she stood over him. The blood that fell from Rudra's face soaked the earth, and a moment later, a deep river formed. Makali fell next to him and lapped at the drops, staunching the flow of the river to the sea, but quickly fell back, hissing loudly as her tongue began to dissolve in the middle.

"Quick, someone come!" Veshak was yelling again. I could tell it was him, but the tone was that of a fly buzzing.

"I'm fine." I wasn't sure if I said it out loud or not.

Rudra staggered up, and as his fist formed, a rod grew from his fingers, elongating into a scythe. He grinned and advanced on Makali, swinging his blade while cackling as she still crouched with her tongue clenched in her fist. He swung it high over his head, snagging it on a piece of sky. The sun flared, and when he tore his blade down, a sliver of black night shone through a crack behind the path of his swing. A void of stars sunk into the ground, opening into a rift that stretched from the northernmost point of Sariram where a town was already forming.

I watched the gods continue to struggle for a moment before I stood. I realized I'd been sitting in the middle of the ocean, and the ass of my breeches were properly soaked. Tiny people scrambled at my feet as I walked inland, just as they'd run from the gods. My steps were careful around them. I treaded past the jagged hill and waded through the forest. Makali had Rudra pressed down on a knee, his scythe cocked horizontally, barely keeping her dual blades from sinking into his shoulders.

"Leave me alone!" A high voice called from elsewhere, and I swung around to meet it.

No one was behind me. The battle between the gods continued. People ran around in the soil. I turned back to look at the sea I had been sitting in, but I could no longer see the bench I had occupied, and Veshak was nowhere to be found.

I heard the voice again; it sounded both far and near, large and small. I couldn't place it.

Rudra bolted past me, arms raised and bloodied at the elbow. His wrists joined above his head, and his skin stitched together to form his blade. He swung it wide around him, ignoring my presence completely, bellowing at the incarnation from his sister.

Makali dodged the fatal swing, and it tore into the ground instead.

A scream rang out, and I stumbled back before spinning.

The scythe had shredded through the earth, widening the tear, and the scream was coming from that place beyond.

I bounded across the fields, over a last sunken valley and around the god's wild stabs, and skidded to a halt in front of the rift between the mountains. I blinked. The stars beyond swirled and danced, tiny points of glowing hot white light in a mass of purple space. I caressed the edge of the torn ground, and my fingers hummed with energy. Something about it was calling me.

I reached out to touch a spot of light, letting it spark up my arm, and the black space formed a tendril, wrapping around my wrist.

And I was sucked forward and down into the earth.

Darkness swirled around me as I was pulled hard in every direction. The tendrils of ink held me and continued to push me along. I tried to scream, and my mouth flooded with starlight, tasting of smoked flesh and burning metal. I spun through the portal, for what could have been an eternity, with my eyes clenched shut until I landed hard on the balls of my feet. I dug my heels into a plush rug and wheeled around to see a wooden door with iron inlays.

"Where am I?"

The midnight coils released me, and I shook the last spots of starlight from my vision. I wriggled my toes against red fibers and glanced up at the arched ceiling, carved and painted, the corners laid with ornate emblems of silver tones.

The door in front of me held a handle in the same color as the rest of the metal streaked through the hall, and a single teal-colored panel sat in the center.

It hit me then—I was looking at Eudo's bedroom door.

Before I could formulate a proper thought, I heard the woman's hushed cry inside the room again, and I reached for the handle.

"You have to stop this, Eudo. I'm being drained."

The door swung open on silent hinges. My mother held her hands toward my father, the backs facing him, and my jaw dropped.

He was much younger, perhaps only thirty-five, with a straight spine and head full of thick hair. He held a bucket in his hand and dropped it at my mother's feet.

My mother, the queen... She was beautiful and soft, and yet... she looked frail. No painting nor faded memory depicted her so sickly. Her cheeks were sunken, and her hands were bruised with protruding veins.

"You'll be fine. The kingdom needs iron. It is your duty to provide it," Eudo snapped, and pulled her toward the bucket, reaching for a knife at his belt.

"Please. I can't keep doing this. Think of Dorian. He needs his mother."

Eudo swung around and slapped her then, and I gasped before starting forward.

"He needs no such thing. He would do just fine without you," Eudo said. I froze. "He has a nursemaid, tutor, and a strong father." Eudo advanced on Maryana, pressing her back into the post of the bed, grabbing her jaw and turning her face up to meet his gaze. "You would do well to remember who saved you from joining the rubble of Aatma. You have purpose here. There, you'd join the worms."

"Leave her be!" I yelled.

Eudo's head snapped around, and his sneer fell.

"What are you doing here?" His voice shook.

"Let go of her!" I yelled.

My brow furrowed as he stepped back, but instead of running to me as I expected, Mother began to fade. Her body grew frail so quickly, and blood coated her arms while iron rivulets cut through her skin. A halo shimmered around her as I stumbled forward. I reached out an arm, trying to grasp her fingers as she fell backward, but she disappeared before her body hit the floor.

I turned on Eudo, and my face heated. The colors leached from the room, and his body sagged.

"What was that? Where did she go?" I demanded.

"She wasn't here, boy," he said. He leaned slowly and fell back on the edge of the bed. Wrinkles stretched themselves across his face, and a light stubble sprouted under his chin. His jowls wobbled as he looked up. "She was a shadow. Nothing more than a memory."

"No. No, I saw her, right there. You hit her."

He shook his head. "You saw a wisp of what I remember her looking like. The rest..." He trailed off.

My heart sank. "Tell me that wasn't a memory. Tell me you're a righteous king." I leveled my father with a hard stare and realized his eyes had brimmed with tears.

"I am a just king, but a flawed man." His face was still. "She is mantrik anyway."

"What does that matter?" My stomach sunk as I asked the question. Of course she was; how else would she have an ability to produce iron?

Eudo fixed me with a flat look. "Have you learned nothing?"

I flexed my fingers and took a step toward him. I knew it in my gut. I did not want to believe it. He had to be lying, but if Veshak was truly my brother, then Eudo must have hidden other things from me, too.

"Tell me. Why hurt her? Why hurt us?"

"Aatma was filled with the mantrik. All of them wildly manipulating energy with no constraint, and they ruled that way since the beginning of time."

A shiver ran down my spine as the extent of his confession began to sink in. "You killed all of those innocent people because they possessed abilities that you didn't?"

Eudo scoffed. "Innocent? They started the war."

"How?" I pressed. How could he justify slaughtering tens of thousands and earning the name 'Iron King'?

"They refused to step down." His voice was devoid of emotion, and my own stomach hurt at how nonchalantly he spoke.

I looked around again, spinning as the corners of the room filled with shadows. He leaned on the bed post and nudged a log toward the fireplace that was already brimming with kindling.

"And you married Mother despite her power?"

"I married her *for* her power. She had utility. They all needed direction. Look at Hari."

I clenched my fists at my side. "No, you're lying," I argued, but he raised the poker, and I saw the truth in his eyes. Hari had been recovered from Aatma—more than likely torn from his family—he must have been kept alive for a reason.

"Why are you telling me this now? You've had thirty years."

"I am dreaming anyway." Eudo stated bluntly. His shaking fingers wrapped around the brace on the bed frame. "You've left for sea."

I released the hold my nails had on my palms and nodded. Perhaps this was a dream. Who was to say. Every time I folded into my own mind, I saw something new, such as the gods fighting or my family turned to puppets. This was the first time I had spoken to anyone this way, so perhaps this Eudo was only a reflection of my own mind, of what I wanted to hear.

I looked back at him. He gripped his knees, and I could see through his pants that they had grown more brittle. He sucked in a shaky breath and began to wheeze. He covered his mouth while he coughed. The spots on his hands had grown to cover more of his pale skin, and his protruding veins rolled when his fingers shook.

My mind would never conjure such a weak version of my father, no matter how much I disliked him.

Cold dread curled a finger into my stomach as the image of Mother's hand flashed in my mind, drained of life like a corpse, like him. "You did not answer me about Mother. Was that truly a memory?"

Eudo recovered himself and held my gaze for a moment, and I searched for some sign of his thoughts. His gray eyes were devoid of empathy, still as hard as the day I set sail. But he looked another ten years older.

"No," he stated. His arm dropped from his face, and a nerve between his left nostril and top lip twitched. I nearly missed the movement cloaked by the fine stubble covering the lower half of his face.

"No? You mean to say it was a farce? Not true?" I pressed, stepping forward. Pricks of anger crept up my back, needling my scalp. Did he just lie? Was that a memory? Was Veshak the one I should trust instead?

"It was false." Eudo's head dropped, and the spot above his lip twitched again.

I closed my eyes for a moment, blinking back tears. He was lying to me. I understood then, the need for a clean face. The beard taking root nearly hid his reaction to the dishonesty falling from his own lips. He had harmed my mother. He had torn down her home in injustice. He had chased her away. He had groomed me to keep me docile and turned me in on myself.

My mind would never conjure a father that lied.

The starlight I had fallen into seeped through the floorboards, and hot rage filled me. I roared and lunged at him, wrapping my fingers tight around his throat.

13

VESHAK

FLAMES BURNED ON THE surface of the sea, lighting up the horizon as ash rained over the wreckage of the prince's ship.

I'd kidnapped my brother.

I took a hard, shaky breath and hung my head as I thought of how my mother spoke of Dorian. How she reminisced on her short time in his life, how she desperately wished to save him from Eudo. How she thought we would become close if we met.

She said that we looked nearly identical.

My mother's oldest son, whom she had not seen since before I was born, whom she wished to return to one day, did not know me and hallucinated from the stress of learning the truth. My brother who I had kidnapped and silenced by force slept in my brig. And I'd set fire to his ship.

I scrubbed my face in frustration. Why did this have to get so complicated?

Boot heels clicked on the deck behind me, and I swung around before I could be asked for anything.

"By Rudra's balls, if you have a request, shove it up your own ass," I demanded.

Orion froze and threw his hands up. "Not at all, but I will pass that along," he said with a chuckle before his face fell. "It is time to bury our dead."

I nodded and followed him.

The crew gathered on the deck below the helm, allowing myself, Cayde, Orion, and Ward to ascend to the quarter deck at the rear of the ship. Cayde produced a sheet of papyrus with names scrawled over it, and a line formed from where the recovered bodies from the royal ship lay, awaiting their last rites.

"Phillip Thatch, navigator-in-training, buried on the coast of Aatma," he called out, and the crew went silent, bowing their heads for a long moment. "Renaud Pavani, cannon hand."

The men shuffled about and worked to pass up the slight body of a boy. I remembered shaking his hand, and I touched his shoulder before Ward let him slide over the end of the ship and Cayde called for another moment of silence.

Twenty-eight names were called, while only seven bodies were buried in the sea.

I stood and looked out over the railing as the crew dispersed behind me, guilt roiling in my gut. Orion hovered nearby, wringing his hands together.

"What has you twisted in knots, Cap?"

I just wanted to kill Eudo to let my mother free, and now somehow I had no katalval to infiltrate the kingdom with, a quarter of my sloop crew gone, and no king to kill.

"The plan has gone to shit," I said.

Orion regarded me for a moment before producing a flask from his pocket. He uncapped it, took a swig, and passed it to me. I lifted the bottle in thanks before taking a drink. Bitterness spread on my tongue before dripping warmth down my throat, and I breathed a puff of hot air back out through my nose.

He chuckled at the smoke that I half hiccuped over a moment later, and I passed his flask back.

"You have yourself a look-alike."

I shook my head, struggling to meet his eyes. "A whole lot of good that will do me."

"You have never been a man to give up, let alone feel discouraged by a change of plans," he said. He gestured around. "We have new hands from their ship, whether willing or not. So what if the king was a prince? You can find leverage in that."

I snorted and surveyed the crew working, the gray coats scrubbing the deck, and then my eyes narrowed on Hari, milling around the foremast. His vest looked out of place among my crew, but he towered over many of them, and his eyes fixed on Orion.

"You have yourself a shadow," I said with a nod in the man's direction.

Orion swung around and shook his head. "That one seems to be lost without the prince. He is his personal hand. Said they have never been separated or something."

Hari leaned against a railing and watched Orion, his shoulders bowed in like a lost child, and I was suddenly struck with an idea.

"We took their flag, correct? Before the ship went down?"

Orion nodded, then hesitated. "I believe so. I will have to check the logs."

"You do that. Check for uniforms as well. I've just been struck with an idea."

"Sky's above, Cayde is right—you and your ideas are terrifying."

I reached out and gripped his shoulders, a grin spreading across my face. "I can take the prince's place! If we plan appropriately."

Orion groaned and turned. "I'm going to fetch Cayde, he is better suited to listen to your nonsense."

There would be some issues with taking his place; there were still clear differences between us. His skin was the color of a canvas sail before it was bleached by the sun, so many shades lighter than mine. And we only had one eye of the same color.

I also lacked knowledge about Raktam and would have to learn how the kingdom operated, quickly.

Looking at Dorian Durling was like looking into a warped mirror. I would have to polish the reflection perfectly to fool the kingdom, let alone Eudo.

I did not wait for Cayde, racing toward the steps behind the helm and descending into the dark.

Sparse lantern light flickered through the jail in the belly of the galleon. I crept past empty cells as quietly as possible, but could not silence the click of my boots against damp floorboards.

"Who's there?" Dorian called out.

I released a heavy breath and stepped into the light in front of his cell.

"Hello, brother," I murmured.

He was exactly where I had left him—laid out over the bench, hands bound but legs freed. When he had his fit and fell to the ground with blackened eyes, I was unsure what to do for him but to let him rest. Hari said that he did not possess any magic, but his eyes said otherwise, and I could not trust him to be completely free inside the cell.

"No," Dorian snapped, staggering upward. "Why do you keep saying that?"

I looked around and found a spare bucket, which I turned upside down and sat on to face him.

"Because it is the truth. We share a mother, but that is not why I am here. I need your help," I said, leaning in and placing my hands on my knees. I tried to make myself as calm as possible, as receptive as possible.

Dorian's body trembled with clear anger. "My mother died at sea. Killed by hybrids."

My brows shot up at that, and I shook my head. "No, I don't know how Eudo would have that information, but it is incorrect. The katalval are primarily peaceful, and they are the reason Mother survived before my father rescued her."

Dorian said nothing, but I noticed a nerve in his jaw twitch.

"You know about the origins of the katalval? So you must know that they were created from love."

"You could have just asked me to kneel," he said. "Why would you lock your brother behind bars if you truly believe that is what I am to you?'

"Where's the fun in that?" I said with a smile. "As I understand, you only kneel to King Eudo, whom I believed to be on board your ship. I did not intend to capture you."

He stood and took a step forward, and I forced myself to stay put, to allow him to close the distance between us.

"Why do you want to kill my father?" Though the question could have been a threat, he asked it with great curiosity.

I took a deep breath and stood as well. "Your father is the only reason that our mother has never left Thandu."

He began to shake his head, mumbling to himself as he moved back toward the bench, and I continued.

"You must know it to be true—our mother is mantrik, and iron runs in her veins. I inherited a great power from her as well, and flame pours from my mouth on a whim. Her iron is what gave Raktam the upper hand when Eudo started the war against Aatma." I pulled the key to the cell from my pocket and twisted the lock open. Dorian sat as I opened the door and stepped inside.

"I do not want to hurt you," I said. "Mother misses you dearly. But she cannot leave home until Eudo is dead."

His shoulders slumped, and he leaned against the wall.

"Is Eudo still alive?" I asked.

His face went somber, and he nodded.

"And why were you sailing?" I asked.

"An escape, before I take the throne."

I breathed in, trying to think about how to approach this.

"She spoke of you, but never left. She mostly spoke of her fear of Eudo. I only boarded your ship today to kill Eudo myself."

"You will fail," he murmured. "He cannot be killed, and you will be caught as an intruder."

My brows knit together, but I ignored that. "That is where you come in. I need your help."

Dorian's head snapped up, and I froze where I stood. "What do you mean?"

"It seems that although our mother couldn't give us a childhood together"—I gestured to him and then myself—"she gave us both her very distinct Aatman look."

We really were the spitting image of each other, aside from the couple of details that could be altered or explained away. If he were to remain locked on the ship, I could return to Raktam and execute the one person I held resentment toward: the man who had hurt my mother.

"I don't know you, and I do not wish to. I have dealt enough with my other troublesome brother. But unfortunately Castle Durling sent the wrong royal, and the idea has struck me that perhaps Mother did me a massive favor, having you by Eudo. I need you to tell me about Raktam, all that you can, so that I can take your place there."

Dorian's head swung around, and he spat in my face.

"What the fuck!" I jumped back. "Were you raised in a stable?" I hissed, wiping thick mucus from my face.

"A castle. The one you'll be jailed in for raiding my ship." He wriggled in his binds, and I turned away. The cell door shut heavily behind me.

I glanced back at Dorian and frowned. "I'll be going to Raktam with or without your help, but the sooner you answer my questions, the sooner you might be free."

"You can't take my place!" Dorian spat behind me. "I have a wife waiting, the law demands a marriage!"

The deck was silent as I emerged into the bright afternoon, and I felt a hundred sets of eyes on me as I tracked Cayde through the crowd. Men stood stiffly against the rails, eyes downcast, as though they had each been dealt a blow.

"What is going on?" I asked between ragged breaths.

He grimaced and grabbed my arm, hauling me to my cabin. The crew parted easily, clearing the path with murmured condolences. The door slammed loudly behind us, and I gasped.

Hari sat back in my chair while Orion mopped blood from his brow with a damp cloth, and Felix stood behind him with a needle and thread pulled between his fingers. A musiker sat across the room, hands tied and a bloodied fiddle in his lap.

"There was an altercation—" Felix said, and I rounded on the musiker.

"Did you attack this man?" I demanded.

The fiddle player hesitated before nodding. "He don't belong here, Cap."

"Hari surrendered," Orion quipped.

Hot rage filled my gut, and I grabbed the musiker by the back of his shirt, dragging him out of the cabin and in front of the helm so that everyone on deck might see.

"You lot better listen now and hear me clearly! Unprovoked attacks will not stand in my fleet!" I roared, and heat poured from my mouth. "Everyone on this crew is here by my choice, and if you have a problem with a mate, you bring it to me or you're welcome to fucking leave!" I pointed over the side of the ship before shoving the musiker away.

"Tie him to the foremast tonight. I don't want to see his face," I spat before returning to the cabin.

Cayde's eyes snapped up when I opened the door, and alarm was evident in his features.

"What?" I asked, moving to look at the damage that had been done.

"What did you do with him?"

"Nothing, just strapped to the mast for a night," I murmured, studying the gash on the man's head.

"Veshak... you must follow through. They will sense weakness if you do not throw him over. Dunk him, or maroon him. There are already talks of mutiny," Cayde pleaded, and unease filled the air around us.

I waved him off. "We have already lost too many men. Let them rest. If it happens again, I will tie the ropes to their necks myself," I said, finally meeting his gaze. He pursed his lips and nodded, but his eyes betrayed his concern.

14

ZARA

WATER TICKLED MY FINGERS first, then I felt the burn of the sun. I rolled my eyes in their lids and stretched out—pain shot up through my bones in a wave of stinging needle points akin to the shock from a jellyfish. I cracked my eyelids open, gasping at how dry and grainy they felt, and ran my tongue over painfully chapped lips. The sun was beating down on me relentlessly, and I felt as if I'd dried up from the inside out.

I raised a hand to my nose, grimacing at the lack of moisture on my skin, how different it felt to normal. Small pieces of salt came away from the crevices of my face, having settled while I slept. I touched the crown of my head, my jaw dropping at how thick and coarse my hair was. It had never fully dried before, as I'd always been at least somewhat submerged in water. Is this how the humans felt all the time? I stretched my cheeks and rubbed my temples. Surely there must be a way to not feel so... *dry*.

The land beneath me shuddered, then shook side to side, and I sat bolt upright, pushing the hair from my face. My fingers sunk into slick blue flesh, and I sucked in a breath—the great body of a blue dragon stretched out around me.

Navya had spoken of them before, how she rode on their backs to travel faster than swimming. I had never seen one, but he was unmistakable, with three sets of wings stretched out on either side of his body, thin spiny fingers, a whiplike tail, a body in shades of blue that blended with the surface of the ocean, and tiny pins that crackled with electricity protruding from his back.

A shiver ran down my spine. He made me think of a jagarving, if they had never learned to shift to human forms.

I shoved to my knees, wincing at the electric feeling still tingling through my body. I almost wondered if he had shocked me in my sleep.

The dragon skated the surface of the ocean but did not move slowly. The current coursed over his back, nearly ripping me from his spine many times over. I fought against the pull with my new appendages, using the strange joints to grip his small back ridge until they ached. I practiced flexing my muscles as we moved and watched the cold air lift bumps along the new skin on my body, raising the hair on my stomach and arms from the chill in a different way than I was used to.

Sitting on my tail joint, with my legs arched in front of me, hands planted on either side, and my feet gripping the small fin, I flexed my new toes. Everything felt so strange. The way my body moved, the trade of my fur for fine hair, the difference of the fat in my stomach and rear. I felt foreign in my bones.

He finally hit a calm stride, and I took a deep breath, trying to slow my racing heart as he settled between low waves.

"Am I going to regret this?" I whispered. I wondered what Juhi would say to my leaving the Isle to pursue the humans. I knew though, she'd be excited for adventure.

The dragon didn't respond.

"Am I going to die, facing them?" I smoothed down his barbs, and a low grumble vibrated through him. I wasn't sure if that was a yes or a no or a warning to stop touching him.

I sighed again and looked out over the horizon. We would near Raktam soon, and I wasn't sure what would occur once we were there. I had no idea how to fit in among the humans. Sky's above, I didn't even know how to move like one.

I glanced at his flat back, and the thought occurred to me that he was as good as a moving island. I could very well practice walking before I ever hit the continent. I hooked my legs under myself, cringing at how the hairs turned backward. It felt as uncomfortable as when I broke the sea's surface the wrong way. I stood on my knees first, wobbling, and ducked up and down a few times. The movement made my muscles burn in different ways than swimming did.

When I placed a foot under my new body, a rumble traveled through my legs, and I sent a silent prayer to Matsya to soothe the being so he wouldn't electrocute me, or worse, toss me into the sea to drown.

I practiced on my legs for hours, falling over repeatedly and sending pain shooting up through my body. The dragon grumbled disapprovingly each time my elbow dug into his flesh, and I apologized profusely.

As the sun peaked overhead, a familiar sound thrummed through the air, and the buzz of electricity bristled under my palms.

I turned fully around, and a loud gasp left my lips as I realized why the dragon jolted—rising in our path was a massive ship flying a black flag with torn edges.

"We have to go another way. They'll kill me!" I could not get near that boat of humans. Gods knew who would be aboard, but I'd have no escape.

He continued speeding along, and another anxious sound rippled through him. I looked around frantically, as if something nearby would give me an escape. Only water greeted us on all sides.

"We have to go the long way around. Humans are hunting kataval!"

He huffed, sending foam shooting out from under his head.

"Please, go around," I urged, pressing my fingers into his back. His barbs raised, and I yanked my hands away in pain.

I didn't know exactly what he understood, if Navya had set him on a certain route, if he was capable of changing course, but he seemed to gain speed, heading toward the ship, and my stomach dropped.

"Please..." I whispered. He didn't respond. I leaned down near his head and pleaded.

The ship's noise reached us clearly a moment later, and I gasped as he began dropping under the surface. "No! I can't swim like this!" I scrambled for a hold on his smooth back, but as my fingers wrapped around his small fin, he vibrated with another groan and put on a burst of speed.

Water flooded my nose and mouth, filling my airway and snatching my breath. Salt stung my cracked eyes, and suddenly everything that had been so dry was very wet. I clung to the fingerbreadths of fin I could grasp as my legs flung helplessly behind me, the current tearing at every inch of my bare skin. I bobbed up and down like a mollusk picked up in a fast current. My hair wrapped around my throat, and the only sound around me was the roar of rushing water.

And as my fingers began to slip, and black edged my vision, we stopped. I gasped, taking on more sea into my lungs, and sputtered into a flurry of bubbles. The world was empty as I tried desperately to breathe and searched with blind hands for something to hold again. I rasped out a plea and found nothing in the void around me while I kicked furiously to stay above the surface.

As my muscles screamed and I began to fall back into the water, I felt something smooth just under my toes. I spread my foot out and realized he was underneath me. Floating still, silently, in case I sunk. As I searched with my other foot, my arms pinwheeling wildly, a shout rang out somewhere near me.

"Man overboard! Grab the ropes!" a deep voice yelled, and a flurry of movement began above.

I continued coughing and fisted my eyes to clear my vision.

As the broad side of the ship came into focus, speckled with sea weeds and barnacles, a thick heavy rope hit the water next to me. I peered up and saw a group of faces looking over the rail.

"Are you okay?" one asked.

"Come on!" another called.

I opened my mouth to say something but another fit of coughs overtook me, and I raised my weak arms instead, grasping the rope. I wound it around my fists, and as soon as my weight was displaced slightly, I felt the dragon drop out from under me.

Two pairs of arms hoisted me over the rail as a third threw a sheet around my body. I looked around and realized every human was clothed, while I still only had my wrap tied from shoulder to hip.

"Bloody hell, you're a woman," someone near me breathed.

"What's a woman doing out here?"

"Is there a shipwreck nearby?"

"Is there anyone else?"

The chorus of voices was overwhelming, and my head spun. My throat burned from taking in so much of the salt water. A rumble of laughter wove through the growing crowd, and I felt my face begin to burn as the men squeezed in tighter. My back was to the wooden rail, and I looked down at my bare legs and feet. I didn't know how to escape danger on these things, didn't know if they would support me.

"Alright, let's give the sea-woman some room to breathe. Cap won't be happy if we rescue someone just to kill her a minute later."

My head snapped up to meet the rich blue gaze of a man the same height as me. Shaggy black hair fell into his eyes, and he puffed out his chest as he nudged through the men. "Or send her jumping back overboard."

"C'mon, Orion, we haven't had a woman forever," an older one said. He licked his lips and shoved back thinning hair.

A round of cheers went up near him, and the one he had called Orion shouldered his way through the crowd.

My mind raced. I didn't know how I would get off the ship. When I said I needed to get to the humans, this was not what I meant! I tried to speak again, but my vocal cords grated together.

The blue-eyed man marched toward me, and I pressed back against the rail as he looped his arm around my shoulders. "C'mon, then, let's get you dry and warm."

I felt the color drain from my face at the prospect of feeling so dried out again, but couldn't force words up to protest. He dragged me through the people, many of which towered over me, and across the hard floor of the boat. The pads of my feet ached as we walked. Every step sent a pain up my legs into the low of my back, and I stumbled to keep his pace as he kept his grip on my upper body.

"So where did you come from?" His voice was quiet, and I flinched back at his proximity to my face. A long moment of silence passed before he said, "We'll need answers. Our captain won't hesitate to kill an uncooperative intruder." He narrowed his eyes at me, and my mind raced. Someone had mentioned a shipwreck.

"I—" My voice rasped as I tried to form my mouth around the words, but I shook my head, touching my throat. It still burned.

He nodded and pursed his lips. "Bit shy, are we? I haven't even introduced myself." He held out a hand. "I'm Orion, ship navigator. What's your name?"

I shook my head again, baring my neck to him. I motioned at it as he swung a door open.

"What's wrong with you? Jackal took your tongue?"

I wrinkled my nose at his words. Nothing had taken my tongue; I'd simply swallowed enough water to drown a navarin and was paying the price.

He shook his head, muttering under his breath, "Bad luck," as he shoved me into a small room, motioning around to some soft-looking spots. "Take a seat. The captain will come in soon." He snapped the door shut again, leaving me alone with the sound of water slapping wood and my own roaring thoughts.

15

VESHAK

I LOOKED AT THE shirt in my hands and then up at Cayde with a raised brow.

"You can't be serious." I pinched the hideous vest between my forefinger and thumb and snorted.

"If you don't want to wear it, then don't," Cayde snapped. "You're the one who is set on storming the castle and becoming king. At least you'll look the part."

"Covered in fancy brocade," the writer quipped.

Cayde smirked and threw the crumpled trousers at me, which I caught before they smacked me in the face. They had the same woven pattern down the side that the vest did, and the mild scent of oak clung to the thick wool.

"You'll look the part on the throne," Cayde remarked.

I chuckled and rolled the clothes into a bundle, throwing them onto his desk before nodding at the logbook. "What else did we get?"

The writer dragged his finger down the page. "The flag was put in the navigation room, along with a chest of recovered biscuits. There wasn't much else that was taken, save for a few weapons, which were sent to the berth."

I leaned back against the desk and pressed my fingertips together. "How many uniforms are there?"

"At least twenty. They'll need to be repaired, they were taken from the men that climbed aboard our ship."

I nodded and looked at Cayde. "I want you to prepare a small crew and Orion to go ashore with me. You stay on the ship and manage the rest of the lot. Ward can head the sloop, but keep an eye on him."

Cayde saluted with two fingers, and I stood. "I don't expect this to be flawless," I said. "I need information about Raktam from Dorian before we go, and the men need time to sew their uniforms. We must think of a good excuse for the loss of the royal ship as well."

The door was thrown open suddenly, and all three of our heads swiveled to see Orion with a pale face.

The writer dipped his head and left, but Cayde hesitated.

"You look as if you've seen a ghost," I said.

Orion shook his head and shut the door quietly behind him. "Veshak," he murmured, and I straightened. He rarely addressed me by name. "There is a woman on board."

Panic struck me, and I glanced at Cayde. The last time a woman had been in our crew, she nearly outed me to the rest of the men. How had one slipped past?

"Impossible," Cayde scoffed.

"She came up from the sea. A shipwreck or something," Orion explained. I felt the fist around my heart ease and moved to leave.

"Hey, Veshak?" he asked.

"Speak freely." I turned to give him my full attention.

His shoulders seemed to relax at that, and he cleared his throat.

"I left her in your cabin. But you should know that there was no debris around."

I nodded slowly, and he wrung his hands. "We shouldn't have encountered anyone near here. There's no way she came from the naval wreck and then made it this far east again."

"I'll get an answer." I clapped his back and smiled before leaving.

I nodded to Ward, who stood behind the helm, then rapped on my cabin door.

"Coming in!" I called.

Frozen by the desk stood the woman from the sea. The deep black pools of her eyes widened as I met her gaze. I looked over her awkward pose: the way her hand was fixed on her hip and her body was half bent over. A thick curtain of tight waves hung around her shoulders to her knees, and I frowned as she shifted her weight and grunted.

"Are you okay?"

She straightened but didn't say anything, and I swallowed at her lack of clothing. The sheet wrapped around her at least seemed warm. I closed the door behind me and took a step deeper into the room.

"I'm Veshak," I offered. "I am the captain of this ship."

She shifted her weight again and still did not say a word. Was she mute, or deaf? Perhaps I needed to find someone on the ship that could translate another language.

"Are you hungry?" I asked.

Her stomach growled loudly, and I smiled at the confirmation as she wrapped her arms around her midriff. I stuck my head into the hall and called to a navigator, who whistled for someone else. It took only a minute for Cook's assistant to come running with an armful of copper bowls.

The woman lifted her fingers to her lips and further widened her eyes while the food was laid out on the desk. I pulled the extra chair from the corner of the room and set it in front of the table for her, waiting. Finally, she dropped her arm and sat.

"Grab some clothing and blankets as well," I commanded as the boy scurried away.

Silence stretched between us as she looked at the bowls of rice and sambar, her hands folded in her lap. I picked up my own bowl and poured the vegetable stew over rice, taking a bite before asking, "Are you going to eat?"

Her eyes flicked all over the table, and I realized how much she reminded me of the tropical rava birds I had grown up seeing. They were beautiful, tall and rare creatures. They sang all night, a low tune full of melancholy. But as soon as they were caught, they fell silent. It was rare that anyone tried to cage them, because the city sounded far sadder when it was quiet at night than filled with the mourning song.

"You're free to eat or not," I said as gently as I could. "This is my cabin, you're a guest here. Safe, and welcome to stay."

She blinked at me and sat back.

"What do you mean?" she asked. Her voice was raspy, as if she'd only drunk sea water for weeks.

I smiled at the sound. "We wouldn't rescue you from the sea if we meant to throw you in the brig. You must be starving, gods know how long you were out there." I motioned at the food that she still hadn't touched. "Please, make yourself at home."

She dipped her head and picked up her bowl, only pausing for a moment before taking a bite. She chewed slowly and looked out the window. I watched her for any signs of dislike, but she looked content.

"What is this?" she asked.

"Sambar. It is an old recipe from my home."

She copied what I had done, pouring the stew over her rice and eating with her hand. I briefly wondered at the possibility that she came from some part of Paalaivanam as she finished her meal. She certainly had the look: the cool-toned dark skin, large deep-set eyes, and long features.

I watched her fluid movements for a minute more before clearing my throat. "So, where did you come from?" I asked.

She coughed. I balked, and when she started choking, I leaped from my seat and slapped her back. She waved her hands wildly, and her breath hitched as she leaned over the table to recover herself.

"I'm sorry! I didn't mean to catch you off guard," I said.

She waved her hand as she caught her breath. I handed her a glass of water and pulled her chair out, waiting before I spoke again.

"What ship did you come from? You couldn't float up from the middle of the ocean," I asked anxiously as she sat.

She angled her leg out and inhaled hard, and I looked down as she winced. In the middle of her foot was a wound the size of my pinky: red, angry, and swollen.

"You're injured?" I asked, then pursed my lips after. Why did I ask such a stupid question? Of course she was injured.

She looked down and then shrugged. "I suppose so."

My mouth gaped for a minute as I tried to think of what to do. How was she so calm about it? "Haven't you had trouble walking?"

My gaze roamed over her, this woman that barely spoke, and I tried to grapple for some explanation as to how she could have survived in this state.

Before she had a chance to answer, footsteps began banging on the deck above, and shouts sounded from outside. The door swung open, and I turned to Cayde stooped in the door, water dripping from his head.

"Veshak, we have a leak," he said, strained.

I jumped from my seat again, wrapping my fingers behind my neck and letting out an exasperated sigh. "How many catastrophes can occur in one day?" I cried out before shaking my head and sitting again. "Handle it," I said.

Cayde looked from me to the woman before pursing his lips and ducking out of the room once again.

"What does that mean?" she asked.

"Somewhere in the bottom of our ship, likely the cargo hold, there is a puncture hole that needs to be patched. There are plenty of capable men who can oversee the repair," I explained. I leaned forward and pushed a bowl of jackfruit toward her, and her eyes widened.

"Is that something you enjoy?" I asked, and she nodded before taking a bite. Tears swam in her eyes as she chewed, and we were silent for a long while.

"My name is Zara," she finally said.

I inclined my head and smiled. "It's nice to meet you, Zara. Can I wrap your foot up with a bandage?"

Zara nodded, and I rose from the table. I moved slowly, pulling the key from underneath my shirt, and felt her gaze tracking my movements. When I ducked behind the desk to unlock my drawer, I heard her chair scrape, but she settled back when I stood again with a linen wrap in my hand.

"I'll compress this around your foot and ankle," I said as I knelt in front of her. She said nothing, but I felt the muscles in her body tense as I touched her heel. I tucked the cloth around her foot similarly to how I wrapped my chest, then braced the joint before padding the wound with an extra wrap. "How is that?" I asked.

She stretched and nodded once. "Better, thank you."

I smiled up at her before resuming my seat. Something about Zara made me think that she might run at any moment and I must move carefully.

"You're safe here, on this ship," I said.

She chewed slowly, her dark eyes fixed on me, and I swallowed hard.

"I must go to Raktam," she said, finally, setting her bowl down.

The knot in my stomach eased, and I wiped the sweat from my palms onto my trousers. "You are welcome to stay with us, we will sail that way in just a few days' time."

Zara was quiet until she finished eating, and I felt the opportunity for conversation slip away. I rose once the bowls were empty and moved toward the door. "Please, rest." I nodded to the bed. "We can converse in the morning."

16

Zara

I TOSSED AROUND ON the cot in the captain's cabin, turning to look through the window on my right. The moon seemed to taunt me from the horizon, and I pressed my hand to the glass. The captain said I was safe.

Taking in the stale cabin air, I finally rose. The wood under my feet was nearly as cool as the night air, and a shiver trembled through me. Normally the air felt so warm, but without the sea to compare to, I felt as if I might freeze, and I wrapped the sheet tighter around myself.

The door opened easily, only releasing one long squeak, and I slipped into brisk night air. I breathed easier outside. I might not be a prisoner, but I was surrounded by sea on all sides that I was unable to traverse alone.

Even my internal direction was gone. I could not tell which way was north and which direction each continent was in.

The ship was far stranger than I could have ever imagined. Everywhere I looked, I recognized some debris from the seafloor. The same nets that suffocated reefs were tied to a mast, leading to a seat in the air. The same spears we trained with hung from racks or piled in barrels. The wood I walked on was smooth and damp with grease, so different from the splintered remains of ships I'd seen sunken in the sea.

I found myself at a railing, looking out over the dark ocean. A few men milled about the deck, but I ignored their leering gazes and listened to the sea lapping the side of the ship. I stretched a hand over the side of the boat, but the surface of the Kotik was still so far out of reach that only a few droplets of spray landed on my fingertips when foam splashed into the air. A sigh escaped my lips as I rubbed the saltwater into my cheek.

"Can't sleep?" a voice asked, and I jumped back. My heart skipped a beat, and I swung around to meet Veshak's mismatched eyes.

His gaze was intense, one brown eye and one golden looking straight into my essence, and I swallowed hard, shaking my head. "No," I said. "It's the sea."

He looked out into the dark, nodding. "It unsettles me, too, sometimes. It's alive, and I fear the nights she's angry."

The corner of my mouth lifted. His eyes snapped back to me, and a shiver racked my spine again, causing his gaze to wander over my body. "Did no one fetch you clothing? You must be freezing." He did not wait for a response, turning to a nearby boy that leaned down on his hands and knees. "Go and find our guest something appropriate to wear."

The boy jumped up, dropping the stone from his hand with a thud, and ran away. Raj shook his head, lifted his hat, and wiped his forehead. "I truly apologize. I left Cayde in charge of your care, but there was that emergency below decks, and then night fell."

I nodded, assuming that Cayde was the surly man who had burst into the cabin. Veshak leaned on the railing and looked back out, gaze wandering to the stars. I tightened my grip on the cloth around my body, moving to secure it at my waist and free my hands.

"I worried that you wouldn't tell me your name, before," he said, breaking the silence around us. "I thought 'even the stars are all named, yet you've come to us without one.'" He looked at me, bemused. "I had considered that I may have to name you. I think that 'treasure' would suit, as you came from the sea."

I laughed, and it sounded strange so far above the water. "Just Zara is fine." As the words left my mouth as easily as my laugh, the smile fell from my face. I tried to search in my mind for the anger I felt at Juhi's death; I should not feel so relaxed around this strange human. I had to keep my guard up.

"Okay, Zara. When you're ready, I'd still like to know where you come from as well—why you're going to Raktam," he said. His gaze lingered on mine a moment longer, and he motioned to the horizon before reaching a hand out to the approaching boy. "The morning mist will be rolling in soon, you'll want to bundle up if you continue standing out here."

He handed a package of cloth to me, and I thanked him. I let the sheet drop from my body, and a furious blush rushed up Veshak's neck. He stooped down and picked up the sheet, holding it in front of me as I wriggled into the clothing.

"Normally we get dressed behind closed doors," he murmured, his face turned away.

The human clothes were strange, made of much lighter fabric than that which was tied around my shoulder. The trousers allowed a breeze to pass through but insulated my legs similarly to my fur. It was not nearly as constricting as I expected, and as I ran my fingers over the flowing shirt—which fell to my knees and was split at the hip—I realized that was likely due to the fact these garments were dry.

There was a pair of shoes in the bundle as well, with hard soles and tall sides, but I disregarded them, unsure of how I would walk.

"Is your body a secret?" I asked, lifting a coat to examine the fine stitching at its seams.

He said nothing, and I finished dressing. Once I was done, I held the black strip of fabric in my fist and turned to look at the ocean once more.

"I am done," I told him, settling the cloth over my head and preparing to braid its ends into my hair.

He shuffled next to me and threw the blanket over his shoulder, watching my fingers work. His brow furrowed when I pulled a string loose from the frayed end, and he snagged it from where I set it on the railing. The thick thread hung on his fingertip, and he peered at it curiously before watching me tie a knot into the end of my hair.

"This piece you use looks like our sails," he remarked.

I shrugged and tossed my braid behind me, where it fell with a *thump* against my knees.

"My mother found it tangled in a bed of coral when I was young."

He reached out and asked, "May I?" When I nodded, he pinched the knot of fabric between his fingers, and I froze.

Veshak's gaze wandered up, and he let out a low chuckle, pointing to the sky. "Look at our flag."

I did as he commanded and watched for a moment as the black cloth billowed against the pitch black of the night. It was mesmerizing, until he motioned to the edges of the flag, which were jagged and torn. "This flag has flown on this ship since it was set to sail. I wonder if your hair tie came from it."

I swallowed and looked back at him, unsure of what to say.

"Perhaps it is destiny that you found us," he offered.

"Perhaps," I agreed, but my stomach dropped. Surely the gods would not be so cruel as to take my mother and sister just to put me in the path of humans. A strip of cloth could not be confirmation of their intentions, could it?

He smiled again and shrugged. "Or perhaps the gods are fickle beings and we all live by free will."

I returned his smile at that and dipped my head. I would not voice my concern out loud as brazenly as he, but I released a breath of relief that I did not have to lie.

"Come, I will give you a tour of the ship, since we are both awake."

I followed him, careful to stay a step behind. "Behind the helm is my cabin, of course," he said, pointing past a large wooden wheel to the wall I had exited from. We had to climb to reach it, and we passed the descending steps hidden there, stepping up onto another shorter set. "This is called the poop deck. You'll often see Orion up here with other navigators, and myself. This is the highest deck of the ship."

The rest of the ship stretched on from where we stood, so far that I could barely see the front.

He pointed to the column in the middle of the ship. "The crow's nest is up there—we have someone on watch at the top of that mast, so you needn't worry if you're out and about. You'll be safe." He paused and glanced around, and I noticed a few men on deck look away from us, and Veshak's voice dropped. "You are more than welcome to traverse the ship as you please, though I think you may be safest in the cabin. These men have not seen a woman in a very long while. And if I am honest, there has been unrest brewing for some time."

"What sort of unrest?" I asked, my interest piqued. Perhaps there was something that I could use here.

He shook his head. "Nothing to worry about, I won't let it amount to anything."

My shoulders slumped, and he led me down the steps again. He stomped on the ground in front of the helm and pointed back. "Below us are Orion's and Cayde's quarters, should you need anything. Even lower is the infirmary, then the brig, and mess. The mess is where we eat. But again, I want you to feel comfortable, so I can have your meals brought up."

I bristled at that. "That sounds like what you would do for a prisoner," I noted.

He shook his head. "You are not a prisoner. If you wish to dine belowdecks, by all means." His cheek tugged up a lopsided grin. "Be prepared for rowdy men, if that's the case."

Heat burned up my neck, and I crossed my arms. "I can fight." As I said the words, I noted the ache in my hips and shoulders that I had never felt before, and I winced.

Veshak watched me for a moment longer before leading me across the deck.

A handful of men lowered their heads as we passed, pausing their work, and I wondered at their behavior. "Do they always quiet when you walk through?" I asked.

He nodded, glancing around before slowing. "It is disconcerting, but it does not stop. I believe that they hate me."

I observed the way a few of the men threw glances at me before looking at Veshak and then back down at what they were doing. "Perhaps it is respect?" I offered. "Perhaps if you were not walking here with me, they would not work."

His grin faded, and he turned back to the tour. "To either side are longboats. We use them to ferry to and from shore, and in case of emergency."

"Like the leak?" I asked.

"Like if the leak was too big to patch," he said.

A man knelt over one of the boats, his hands smoothing over the wood of its rail. He mumbled to himself as light emitted from his palms.

"You have mantrik on board?" I asked.

"Of course," Veshak said. "That is our carpenter. He works with plants, but that also lends him the ability to warp the wood he works with easily. We have mantrik who manipulate weather and communicate with animals. Felix, the doctor, can heal physical injuries. Cook, or Clarence, is adept at leaching poisons from food. Many mantrik fled for the sea when Eudo tore down Aatma. So many people had to find new homes in order to escape his tyranny..."

"That is awful," I whispered, watching the man's hands work. Wood rose and knit together under his fingertips, snapping as it tightened.

"Yes, it is. But at the same time, my mother fled as well. My family came to be because she joined the diaspora. She may have been displaced against her will at first, but then she left a second time for her betterment."

I nodded, and he tapped the rail to our left, changing the subject. "You'll find weapons clipped underneath these, also for emergencies."

We reached a large hole in the center of the deck, covered with a block of crossed bars. "That is how we access the cargo hold. I don't imagine you'll need to go down there—it takes a couple of men to move that grate."

I said nothing, but swallowed hard as I imagined being stuck down in the dark, only able to reach a hand up through the bars.

"And, finally, we have the bow," Veshak said while motioning to the narrow deck in front of us. He climbed a few steps and pointed out over the edge. "On this side is the anchor, and that side the head, for when you need to go. There's a lantern here," he lifted a sputtering light from beside the rail, and I blanched.

"Sorry, what do you mean? What is the head?"

He frowned and pointed over the edge of the rail, and I followed his finger to find a small perch, with a handle attached to the side of the ship. "Y'know, for when one needs to use the facilities?" he asked. "But we don't have one on board, so all the men go here."

My stomach churned as understanding dawned on me. In the ocean, our waste was buried in sand.

"You mean that you just let it fall wherever it may?"

"Yes..." he said, then hastily continued. "You're staying in my quarters, where I have a private head that you may use. We empty it once it is full."

I felt as if I might faint at that. How much more disgusting could these human bodies get?

As I had the thought, my stomach growled, and we both looked down at it.

"Come, let's get you some food," Veshak said before leading the way to the set of steps at the back of the ship.

I was unsure of how late it was, but as we descended into the belly of the ship, I expected silence. Instead, a wild raucous shook the ground we walked on. I had to fight the urge to grasp Veshak's hand to steady myself, as my knees nearly gave out.

He led me down a dark hallway, lit only by barely flickering lanterns on the wall, and fear trembled through my bones. I clenched my fist, expecting sharp nails to dig into my palm, but only flat, useless fingers pinched the soft skin of my new hands.

"Where are you taking me?" I asked, forcing a bravery into my voice that I did not feel.

Veshak glanced back with a furrowed brow before stepping aside to reveal a hall full of tables. "To the mess," he said.

A spread of tables with benches on either side stretched out, split by a narrow walkway. Men crowded around each bench, laughing and chatting, throwing food or papers or trinkets at one another. Platters of meats and fruits and foods I did not recognize decorated the tabletops, and Veshak approached the nearest open seat, motioning for me to join him.

Silence fell over the table, and the rest of the room followed suit in quieting to a low murmur in a few moments.

I felt foolish as the captain began to pile food on top of a clean plate for me, and embarrassment tainted my tongue when he paused with a knife in his hand. "I did not ask before, do you eat meat?"

I shook my head. "No. Vegetables only," then, "Excuse me. I must go."

Veshak raised a brow, then his eyes widened. "Oh, of course."

I stepped away from the crowded room and wandered down the narrow hallway. I passed a dark room full of hot pans where a fire burned. I could not find the steps to go back up to my cabin, but another set led down farther, so I descended quietly.

Sparse lantern light cast flickering shadows on the walls around me, and I was reminded of the great trench. I swallowed hard, fighting the urge to run. My bare foot landed in a puddle, and I froze as someone called out, "Hari?"

A narrow walkway split walls of open bars, and I crept toward the sound of breathing.

Each set of bars held an empty room, a bench, and a bucket. I shivered, wondering if this is where prisoners truly stayed.

The last lantern shone directly into one of the rooms, and I stepped in front of the door, sucking in a sharp breath. A man sat inside, his arms wrapped around his legs, his long curls thrown back to reveal a face like the captain's.

"Veshak?" I asked, confused.

Nervous energy pricked my skin, and I stepped away as he murmured, "No."

It wasn't possible, of course. I had left Veshak only moments before.

The man looked me up and down, and I suddenly felt very uncomfortable under his scrutiny.

"Sorry, you look so much like him. Who are you?" I asked.

He was silent, observing, and did not answer as he unfurled his limbs and leaned back on the bench. I turned to walk away, nearly stumbling over my own feet.

"Wait!" the man called out. "Do you have a key?"

I paused and shook my head. "No, I am just wandering. I have nothing with me."

He slumped back on the bench and nodded. "Very well."

I cocked my head, looking over him once again, then up at the bars that stretched from floor to ceiling. "Why are you in there?"

"Why don't you ask Veshak?" he sneered, turning to pull his legs up on the bench.

I startled at his sudden change in demeanor and backed away, stumbling toward the steps at the end of the hall. Why would Veshak have someone in a cage? And someone that looked so much like him? Would he put me in there if he knew I was not human...

17

Dorian

HARI SAT ACROSS FROM the door of my cell with his arms crossed while I paced, my teeth grinding.

"He's lying."

"So what if he is?" Hari asked in a whisper.

My mind tossed as hard as the waves against the ship's side. There was simply no way that Eudo was the man Veshak said he was. He was firm, but he had to be to rule. He was also fragile. This captain would say anything to get into my head.

"We don't look that much alike."

"There's no way to know without Queen Maryana's confirmation," Hari returned.

"Eudo would have committed crimes then, things that we hang citizens for with less proof. And Mother would never have left me voluntarily." My words were barely above a breath.

"And she loved you more than life itself," Hari confirmed.

"A king must sit above abusing his wife."

Hari nodded when I glanced at him, then nudged the tray that he had set inside my cell. "Please eat, Dorian. I barely snuck down here."

I ignored him and continued pacing. "Mother wouldn't be alive out there, right? Waiting to be rescued? Or hiding from me?" I asked. I hoped my voice sounded confident.

I spun at one end and turned, beginning my round again, and he threw his hands up.

"For the love of the gods, would you sit down? You won't get out faster by walking a hole in the floor."

"Better I dig a hole with my heels. I don't see a key in your hand," I snapped back.

I flopped onto the bench and glared at him. He leaned back against the wall while I picked at the leg of some loose linen pants that had replaced my rich wool ones. They pooled around my ankles uncomfortably and made me want to yank the threads on their seams to pull them apart.

A huff left me.

The people would know that Veshak wasn't me—even if he slit Eudo's throat from behind and paraded around in my clothing.

"I'm worried," Hari said.

I lifted a brow at him. "About what?"

He motioned to the locked door, and I snorted. "At least you are on the other side. Why do you get to roam free, anyway?"

Hari lifted a shoulder. "They give all prisoners of battle the choice to join or die. I opted for the former."

Anger brewed in my gut, and then my familiar nerves kicked in. "Have you heard anything about why I am being kept here?"

He shook his head, and I let out a shuddering laugh. "He intends to masquerade as me and kill Father."

Hari's face drained of color, and he heaved himself off the ground. Standing, he towered over me, and I stood to try and meet his eyes. I found my hand stretching out of its own accord, reaching to touch him. I hungered for some sort of contact, but he turned away before I could graze the back of his arm, and I let mine fall through the bars.

He turned back with a serious expression, pressing his fingers to his chin. "Perhaps he will let you go once he is done?"

I scoffed. "Why would he do that? He benefits the most from taking my throne, doesn't he?" I laughed, but it faded quickly.

If he took the throne, I would not have to.

Hari said as much a moment later, and I pressed my face against the damp wood of the cell door, relishing the lack of iron around me.

"There's nothing waiting for us at home, anyway," I said.

Something unfamiliar flickered across Hari's face, but he nodded his agreement.

"I was supposed to protect you. Eudo only allowed us to leave on my word that you would be safe." His tone was hesitant. "I think he might have me hanged if he learns what happened."

I reached out and tried to touch him again, but he was still too far. "Ri... You could have never anticipated that pirates would overtake us." My lip curled up involuntarily. "Let alone my 'long-lost brother.'"

Stomping feet echoed through the wood above us, and we stood at the same time. "I will find a way to get you out," he breathed.

I gripped the bars of my cage and peered at him. "Wait..."

He stopped and reached out to wrap one of his large hands around one of mine.

"Just keep coming to see me," I pleaded. "And be careful."

"I will, I promise."

I squeezed myself against the door and watched as long as I could as he walked down the corridor. His footsteps were loud on the steps at the end of the hallway, and I slumped back against the wall. The lingering smell from Hari filled my nostrils, and I pressed the back of my hand to my lips, savoring the small contact he had given me.

I craved more, but I would settle, for now. There was nothing either of us could do to break me out; I had to believe that. The boat rocked below me, and I knew that trying to escape in the middle of the ocean would be a death wish. At least one of us was free.

My stomach growled, interrupting my thoughts, and I glanced up at the tray he had brought me.

A flatbread lay atop a pile of rice, with a bowl of some sort of golden soup, and I frowned. It was nothing like what I would eat at home, but as the gnawing hunger set into my gut, I pulled the silver tray closer and picked up the bread. It had begun to stale in the dank air of my cell, so I dipped it into my glass of water to soften it up, chewing it as quickly as I could.

When I took a sip of the soup, I nearly choked—fire erupted on my tongue, and tears sprung into my eyes. I dropped the tin over my rice in shock and swore, scrambling to clean the mess up and separate the food.

The rice soaked up the soup too quickly, and the tears that stung my eyes began to fall, not from spice, but from hopelessness. I gave up from separating the spoiled grains and began to lick the rice from the plate, slurping the soup up between my sobs.

"Rudra," I called out, throwing away the dirtied tray, "why have you abandoned me?"

I noticed that the soup did not burn when mixed with the rice, but I didn't care enough to finish eating. I had no water left, no bread left, and my stomach still ached.

Footsteps echoed down the hallway, and I scrambled upward, wrapping my fingers through the bars of my cage.

"Hari?" I called, desperation tainting my voice. "Have you returned?"

Veshak stepped into the light and tapped his hand on the lock, clinking a ring on his finger loudly against it. "Hari, huh?" He looked over my cell and clicked his tongue. "I was unaware that he had been put on meal duty."

I swallowed hard as I realized my mistake. "No, it was a slip of the tongue." I backed away, and Veshak pressed his face into the bars, staring at me with his mismatched eyes. He held a dagger in his hand, but he turned the blade away as he watched me.

"You care for Hari?" he mused.

I shook my head.

"I don't care, it does nothing for me, so long as you tell me about Raktam."

I swallowed hard and lowered myself to the bench, sitting on my hands. Nerves and fury mixed in my stomach, and I had to fight to stay present. Hari's safety counted on it. "What do you want? Why?"

Veshak knelt to eye level and frowned. "I don't want to hurt you. Please understand that my goal to free our mother is sincere. I would like to release you."

I motioned to the door, and he shook his head.

"*After* I kill your father."

"He is well protected by a fleet of guards."

"That's a start," Veshak said. "And what of this marriage that you mentioned?"

I hesitated. I didn't want the throne, why did it matter if he married the wife that Eudo lined up for me?

But Hari...

"You must swear that Hari will face no harm."

"I will ensure his safety as much as any crew member, so long as you help me," Veshak promised, sheathing his blade.

I took a deep breath before crawling toward him and kneeling before my brother.

"I am meant to take the throne at the end of the summer, but my wedding will occur a week before. I told Eudo to find me a wife, because I do not care for sex."

"Tell me about the kingdom, the guards. Anyone important to you."

I shook as I shared everything about my life. I told him about Imogene, my stewardess. How Simon had been my groomer since I first grew a beard, how meals worked and who my family was.

He listened intently, asking a few questions. When I had told him all I could think of, he rose and turned away. I launched myself toward the bars, fear flooding my body and electrifying my skin.

"And Hari?" I cried out.

Veshak looked back and nodded. "You have my word. One of the crew."

He disappeared, leaving me in the dark, and I finally released the tears that pricked at my eyes. I was so scared, so terrified that I would never see Hari again, that it was some sick joke just to further Veshak's quest.

I knelt, ready to pray to the gods, to beg for help, when I heard a thump against the wall. More banging began above me, and I crouched on my hands and knees, the hair on my arms standing on end.

I looked around, but I had nowhere to run, and I was tossed to the side.

A tremor shook the ship, the room tilted around me, and I was thrown up and into the air. I sucked in a sharp breath before I was thrown down. Hard.

Stars encroached on my vision, and I scrambled toward the bench. I tried to tuck myself underneath it, to find shelter as my head spun, but we rolled on the tide once more, and my head smacked hard into the thick slab of wood.

Water flooded my nose, and my world went dark.

I've died, I thought as I floated through and between blackened waves. There could be no other explanation for the sudden disappearance of my jail, for the way I could breathe the sea around me, for the ease with which my body moved on the current.

Light flashed beyond the peaks of foam above me, and a distant thump followed, but I closed my eyes and ignored whatever chaos tried to pull me away from my death. I let my shoulders relax for the first time in weeks and sank deeper into the ocean.

The depths were calming, silent. I wondered, briefly, if this was how the hybrids felt when they swam.

"Yes, it is an enjoyable existence," someone said.

My eyes flew open, and I scrambled upright, finding myself staring into the large, red eyes of a god. The ornament on his head bobbed in the sea, and I kicked away from him.

I sucked in a breath and coughed, expecting to choke. But still, my body was suspended. He moved to swim past me, and the stars faded from my view, leaving only deep waters around us.

"This is a vision," I realized out loud.

I turned, terrified, but a hybrid floated where the god had been. Her wild hair drifted freely around her, and she bared her fangs at me.

"I do not know what vision you speak of, I am in the midst of directing a shipwreck," she said. "Go die quietly."

I stuttered and blinked, trying to find an answer for what was happening. As she swam, her thick, furred tail slapped me away. I paddled my arms and watched as she wove her fingers through the water, pointing at Veshak's ship. A mass of tentacles in the distance rose and moved in response, swimming toward the boat.

"Is this why I was knocked into the stars?" I mumbled to no one in particular. "Where did I go?"

The hybrid whipped around, dropping her hands and releasing the tentacles.

"What do you mean? Speak plainly!" Her voice was shrill through the waves, and I slapped my hands over my ears.

"I mean that your beast there knocked the ship this way and that, and I fell through the stars again."

She descended on me, grabbing the collar of my shirt. "You are on that ship? Right now? Who are you?"

"I-I think so," I stuttered and nodded furiously, suddenly scared. Her sharp nails pricked the thin skin on my neck, and her large eyes bore into me. "I am the Prince of Raktam... Dorian."

She looked me up and down, then touched my face and peered deep into my eyes. "Yes, I see it now. You are also mantrik."

"No—"

Your power comes from the void, from Rudra himself. You must have a very powerful family."

"You're wrong!"

"I have a task for you, Prince of Raktam." She cut me off and released me, and reached up to smooth my shirt, sending a shiver through my body.

"I am stuck in the brig. There is not much I can do," I said, fighting the tremor in my voice. It was all too much. The fight, Veshak, Hari. I could not handle anything more.

She cocked her head. "Why would they jail their prince?" then, "Never mind. There is a woman on board. Kill her."

I blanched. "I am jailed. Stuck behind bars. I am incapable of killing anyone. I am not quite sure how I ended up here."

"Are you daft? You used magic. Clearly it is a defense of some sort for you. You are mantrik, just like me."

I pulled away, looking past her, to the ship that was tilted nearly into the sky, and the pieces all fell together.

When I felt threatened by Eudo, I fell through the void. When I craved escape.

When I feared for my life.

It couldn't be true, but when I looked back into her wide black eyes, terror filled me.

"If you can escape the jail when you feel a threat, you can do it at other times, too," she said, coming closer. I backed away, suddenly aware of my body still lying on the hard floor on the ship and the fact that she had access to my mind.

"Who are you?"

"That does not matter."

She stroked my arm and twisted her long fingers in my tunic. "I need the katalval on board to die," she spat. "There is too high of a chance that she may return to the sea, though we have a deal that she won't. And if she does, my plan will fail."

I tried to pull my arm free, but her grip was strong. I felt for my body, stretching my mind out, and it became easier to feel, but her grasp on me was too solid to return.

"I cannot escape," I insisted.

"I cannot kill her myself. Magic has a price, and mine will be paid if I spill her blood. But you have no such tie." Her nails dug into my skin, and she wrapped her tail around my legs. Pain erupted through my body, and I cried out as the bones in my feet began to splinter.

"Please," I begged.

She did not relent, squeezing harder until tears streamed down my face. "You will find Zara and ensure she does not return to the water. Kill her, or I will kill you and take your kingdom for myself."

18

Veshak

I DID NOT KNOW beauty until I first laid eyes on Zara.

I gripped the wheel tightly and studied her. She stood only a few steps away, still on the quarter deck, but far enough that I could stare openly and not be caught.

The breeze tossed stray hairs around her neck, curling around her ears and braid. Sunlight cast golden rays on her skin, and she rubbed her fingers together before turning to face me.

"What are you looking at?" she asked.

I shrugged and nodded toward the bow, where Hari and Orion plotted our course together. "I wonder how the new recruits are handling the change of command."

The corner of her mouth lifted, and she moved to sit on a crate next to me. "I believe the change to be well. I heard them laughing together yesterday."

"And how are you?" I asked, looking into her dark eyes.

She was so quiet when we first found her, aside from the questions that only told me she did not come from a ship.

"The last few days have been better than the first," Zara said. "But I do wonder when we might reach Raktam."

I swallowed hard, but tried not to let my smile falter. I was not ready for us to part ways just yet.

"Orion is plotting the course as we speak. I hoped that you and I might discuss our goals, once we dock. I have a plan for myself, of course. Sariram is not so kind to women who travel alone, and if I know what you need, I may be able to assist you."

Her spine straightened, but she nodded once before turning and striding down the steps.

"Zara!" I called after her. She ignored me and continued walking across the deck.

"Sky's above," I muttered, searching for the wheel lock. When I finally found it tucked between the crates, a shuffle came from near the main mast.

"Stop!" Zara cried out.

I was running before I could make out the scene in front of me.

A handful of men gathered around Zara, jeering and hollering at her.

"I've got a bed for you," one of the soldiers taunted.

"I saved your sheet," another cooed.

Zara pressed her back into the mast, and I watched her fingers twitch toward an oar.

I shoved between her and the men, spinning to face them and drawing my sword.

"Leave her alone!" I swung my blade in an arc, nearly grazing the tips of their noses. "Zara is a guest on this ship and will be treated with respect."

Ward dropped down from a rope nearby and yanked a whip from his belt, and I jerked my chin at him. "Give 'em a lashing," I seethed before throwing an arm around Zara and guiding her away.

"I could have handled myself," she grumbled.

"There were five of them and one of you," I said, glancing at her. I wanted to laugh, but a shiver ran up my spine. What would have happened if I hadn't stepped in?

"Thank you," she mumbled.

I did not respond, touching her shoulder gently instead and opening the door to the cabin.

I stopped in the entryway as she stepped inside, and she paused, looking at me. "Are you coming in?"

"This is your cabin now," I said with a shake of my head.

"Right..." She chewed her lip for a moment and reached out. Her thumb grazed my cheekbone, and I braced myself against the doorframe, scared to move. Her touch was as light as a feather and sent a shiver down my spine.

"Have you slept? Where did you move your bed to?" she asked. "The skin around your eyes is black."

I smiled and pulled away from her, ignoring her question. "You're more than welcome to roam the ship, but you may be safest here."

"Have you been sleeping in the jail?" she asked, and I felt as if she'd slapped me.

"What do you mean?"

"I mistook someone for you, it was so dark."

I shook my head quickly. "I forgot that you might go down there." I turned to ensure no one was listening before stepping into the cabin and latching the door behind us.

We were so close—her chest pressed into mine, her face turned up so her lips were near my chin. Finally, she stepped aside, and I released a breath and strode to my bed. The soft cushion sank beneath my weight, and a groan escaped my lips. My bones craved the rest, but I couldn't let myself sleep.

Zara settled into the chair across from me, and I spread my hands over my lap.

"I have a plan for Raktam, and I hope that you do not dive off the ship with a scream upon your lips when I share it."

She waited patiently as every fiber of my being ached for me to reach out and touch her, but I took a steadying breath instead.

"That man was taken from a royal ship. We will return him to Raktam."

I explained everything. I told her how we had invaded Dorian's ship and kidnapped him, and my new plan to take his place and slay his father. She remained composed as I spoke, not betraying a single emotion. I hesitated as I reached the end of my plan. Her face was so open, so curious, and I couldn't do it. I could not betray her trust or turn her away from me.

So I withheld her role in my plan.

Zara pressed her fingertips to her mouth and nodded. "I cannot imagine living a life at sea such as yours. The trials you must face, the decisions you must make..."

Her voice was barely a whisper, and guilt twisted in my gut.

"I must kill Eudo. Once he is gone, my mother will be free, and I can return to my life."

She took a step back and nodded again, slowly. "I need to go to Raktam, but I am unsure where my journey will take me once I am there."

I stifled the urge to reach out, instead saying, "Let me help you. When we dock, I will go wherever you need."

Zara did not answer, but I left her on that vow, letting the door snap gently. I heard the latch click into place before I faced Ward at the wheel. Heat coiled in my belly, rising up my neck in shame, and he glanced back at me.

"Trouble in paradise?" he asked.

I scoffed and swallowed, moving to take the wheel, but he did not budge.

"You abandoned your post," Ward said.

My brow furrowed, and I looked up at him. "I had to help her. The men attacked."

He lifted a shoulder. "She was fine, they did not lay a hand on her."

I reached for the wheel again, and he moved to block my way. "We have rules, Veshak."

The fire in my gut rose at his lack of respect, but I hesitated. He was right. Should I not hold myself to the same standard as the crew? But as I observed him, the puff in his chest, I couldn't help the nagging in my mind, his voice outside my cabin.

"Where do you stand on my captaincy?" I asked.

Ward's hand slipped on the wheel, and he glanced at me. He opened his mouth to speak, but that was all I needed to know.

I turned to walk away, and my legs were swept out from under me. A yell of surprise caught in my throat, my fingers already on the handle of my sword. But it was not the blow from Ward as I expected.

The ship trembled below us, and I scrambled upward.

"What in the seas?" I bellowed, and Ward yanked the wheel to the side, fighting an invisible current to keep us upright.

"We've hit something!"

I hesitated for a moment, torn between running back to Zara and ensuring her safety, and leaping into the fray of my men who were preparing for the unknown on deck. I felt Ward's eyes on me, and I shook myself out of the spell, dashing down the steps to the main deck.

"Report!" I yelled up at the crow's nest.

"Nothing, Cap!"

"Bloody lies it's nothing! Look again!" I screamed, turning to the crew nearby. "Batten the hatches!"

I loosed a dagger from my belt and ran toward the bow. My heart stuttered as a roar from beneath shook the ship. A great tentacle snaked up over the starboard side, reaching high into the air, and I loosed a warning yell as it snatched one of the cannon boys.

The boy flailed in the air, tied up tightly in coils of orange and red flesh. A suction cup fixed to his face, he kicked his legs wildly, and I cocked my arm back and threw my knife as hard as I could at the beast.

The blade sunk deep into its arm, but the monster did not react. It pulled the boy over the rail and into the sea.

"Kraken!" I cried, and my scream was echoed by the men around me as they drew their weapons.

A mass of four tentacles shot up through the waves and latched on to the bow of the deck, pulling us toward the sea and wriggling for every body it could reach. Men were flung into the ocean, while others rushed the kraken with weapons drawn. Arrows flew freely, and the cannons were loaded.

Ward yanked on the wheel and screamed at me to go.

I ran hard and fast across the ship, drawing my sword as I moved. Cayde emerged from the cargo hold as I reached the main deck.

"What in the skies is going on?" he bellowed.

I dashed past him and launched myself onto the bow, slashing at another tentacle that was beginning to snake up from the surface. My blade severed the tip off, and the beast screamed from the depths—a high, bloodcurdling sound—before the tentacle whipped back and slapped the belly of the galleon.

I was knocked backward, staggering to stay upright. Cayde roared behind me, and a dagger whizzed past my ear a moment later. Hari bolted past me, sword drawn and slashing at the next rising tentacle, with Orion at his back.

A volley of arrows followed them both, and the stomps of my men signaled that they were ready for battle.

19

ZARA

THE SHIP GROANED UNDERNEATH me, and I was thrown, my new body unable to keep up with the rumble that shook the floor as we shifted. The room tilted, and I rolled to the side, crawling toward the door while waves crashed against the window. Men threw commands on the other side of the wall, and metal scraped wood. I hesitated before throwing the door open.

The iron tang of blood and salt filled my nose before I understood what I was seeing. A massacre was strewn over the deck of the ship. Waves tumbled over the hull, and crew members were struggling to run against the uphill turn of the deck. A thick tentacle curled over the railing to my right, and I sucked in a sharp breath. A man with two long braids down his back yanked a sword from his belt and swung it in a high arc before slashing it down into the soft red skin of the beast. The tentacle barely moved as the blade pierced layers of skin and muscle. He slid it back out and lifted it high, and my heart raced as I watched him prepare to stab it back down. Before metal met flesh, the tentacle swung and knocked him to the side.

I scanned the rest of the ship. Some men were gathering at the cannons, others stood behind the rail with bows and throwing daggers drawn, while other tentacles inched and pulled themselves over the side of the ship.

"What are you doing?" Veshak yelled.

My head snapped up, and I found him hanging from a net in front of a mast, muscled hand wrapped in the hemp.

"I want to help!" I called back.

His motioned to the chaos with his blade. The thumping of the drums and screams of the men forced my heart to beat wildly in my chest, and I could barely hear him.

"Can you wield a sword?"

I shook my head. "A spear."

His brow furrowed, and he slid down the rope, landing directly in front of me. I nearly stumbled back, but his hand flattened against my hip, holding me in place.

"A spear will do you no good here," he said, fixing his mismatched eyes on me. His breath tickled my nose, and I pursed my lips. "Plus, your foot is injured."

I shrugged. "I can walk on it."

We stared at each other for a moment, and my racing pulse at his touch almost drowned out the war cries from around the deck.

"My people are fighters. My sister was our best warrior," I murmured.

His jaw ticked before he backed away and yanked a sheath from his right hip. He thrust the hilt of a sword at me and grunted, "Don't die" before turning back to the fight.

I looked down at the weapon in my hand and slid it from its cover. It was light, the handle curving around my hand protectively, and the blade was thin and tapered to a point. Not a spear, but long like one, with a deadly sharp edge down its length.

Another tentacle slapped against the hull of the ship, sending tremors through my legs. I eyed the largest arm, reaching for the main mast.

A group of three ran past, swords raised and voices bellowing. I brandished my new weapon in front of my shoulder and followed them.

The great beast raised an arm from the depths and reached over the side of the ship again, feeling along the railing. A suction cup the size of a palm frond sucked down onto the deck before more of the tentacle arced up into the sky. It felt its way through the trio as they took turns stabbing their weapons into it. A pang struck through my chest as I watched the tallest slide a short sword through a suction cup, and the creature twisted around. Muscle curled out from the wound, and a cheer went up.

I hesitated before following them to jab my own weapon toward our attacker. I did not want to hurt another being of Matsya. But if it took down the ship that I was standing on, I would die.

I skirted the men as well as I could, dragging my blade over the squirming arm that swung wildly at us. As we slashed at it together, the tentacle flew backward, retreating into the sea once more. I turned in excitement, expecting the men I had worked with to have grins plastered on their faces, but two had already run off. The sun glinted off their swords as they ran across the deck toward another attacking tentacle.

Before I could move to join the closest fight, something like thunder cracked a moment before groaning filled the air. The ship began to teeter under my feet, and I flung my arms out on either side of my body to keep my balance. The cries from battle shifted to yells to take cover, and the crew sheathed their weapons to run up the deck. I looked around frantically as the ship began to slope further, and from the portside, where the first tentacle I saw had been, a bulbous head rose from the ocean.

Water cascaded over the loose skin, and the sun glinted off the reflective surface of a massive eye as it dragged itself over the edge of the ship. A yell reverberated through the air as a body swung by on a rope, and I nearly dropped my sword.

The kraken let out its own bellow, tentacles flailing wildly, thrashing about and reaching for the mast and belly of the ship. Veshak scrambled away, but one tentacle flung out and wrapped around his body.

My heart dropped into my stomach as the captain who just saved me was yanked close to the kraken's body.

The rest of the crew turned and climbed up the deck, which still careened downward, as the beast's body weighed it down. No one made a move for Veshak, and I looked to the sea, sending a silent prayer to Matsya, before digging my heels into the slick wood and releasing my hold. I lifted the blade above the kraken with both hands, pointed toward its eye, and released it.

My sword struck true, and its scream of pain shook the ship in its hold. Its tentacle jerked just enough that Veshak could shove his way out. He grabbed for the rope that he'd swung in on and twisted it around his arm before sprinting to the far end of the deck.

The tentacles fell away, and the kraken's screams cracked through the air. Pain shot up my leg as I scrambled for a grip on the rail. A great wave splashed over me, washing away debris, and yells from the crew filled the air, mingling with my own. Veshak collapsed beside me, throwing his arms out on either side of his body, but his eyes rolled into the back of his head, and his knees buckled underneath him.

I gasped loudly as he fell and tried to catch him before his head hit the deck. The large black-skinned man who had helped pull me from the ocean ran over as the deck finally settled, and he lifted Veshak's shoulders.

"What's wrong with him?" I asked.

"I dunno. We'll figure it out," he said, shooting me a strained look. He hoisted Veshak into his arms and jogged to the cabin where I was meant to be sleeping.

"I'm Felix," the man said, and I opened the door for him.

"Zara."

He laid Veshak out on the bed, and I twisted my fingers together. The ship still rocked unsteadily beneath us, and I jumped when the door opened again.

Cayde burst into the room, eyes wild under cracked glasses until they fixed on Veshak.

"Is he hurt? Dead?" Cayde's voice was laced with panic.

Felix sat back on his heels and tore the captain's shirt away, revealing a wrap of cloth around his chest and ribs. It looked similar to the one that he had bound around my foot, and Felix shook his head. "No, he's breathing. We got to get this shit off 'im."

Cayde swept forward and pushed past me, producing a dagger from his boot. He slid it beneath the wrap and sliced clean through the first band, and I held my breath in anticipation.

The two worked together quickly to release his chest, and Veshak breathed deeply as soon as he was free.

"When did he last sleep unbound?" Felix asked.

Cayde shook his head. "I'm unsure of the last time he slept at all."

They both looked to me, and I chewed on my lower lip. "He gave me his cabin, but would not tell me where he moved to."

Felix swore and touched the black and purple bruises on Veshak's ribs. His chest was compressed and indented with wrinkles, and his nipples had turned white. Felix stood and pulled a blanket from the chair, throwing it over him, and Cayde moved to pull the captain's boots off.

"He will be okay?" I asked, forcing my voice to steady.

"He must rest," Felix commanded, then turned to me with a glint in his eye. "So, you're the troublemaker from the sea?"

I startled at the accusation and scrambled for what to say.

He waved a hand and looked me up and down. "Don't worry 'bout it. Stay and I'll get you fixed up."

I obeyed, unsure of what to make of his clipped speech. He sounded unlike the other crew members.

"Are you from the same place as Veshak?"

"No, I was born on an island. Tamarai, named for the flowers bloomin' there."

He lifted a case from the ground and set it on the desk. The brass buckles creaked when he opened the lid, and he produced a dried padma from its belly, displaying its pale petals in his palm. "These grow wild at home, and 'ave great medicinal practice."

I barely stifled the gasp that caught in my throat, and he raised a brow. "You know the flower?"

I shook my head and changed the subject. "Do you take care of all of the ship's ailments?" I asked.

"No," he said, returning the flower and shuffling bottles around. "That's the carpenter's job. I doctor the people." He winked, and I smiled.

The tinkling sound of glass clinking together and books thudding onto the desk filled the silence between us, punctuated by soft sighs from Veshak, until Felix rounded the desk and knelt down.

"What happened?" he asked, lifting my foot. The wrap fell away easily, and the skin around my wound throbbed.

I winced against the pain as he examined it. "I was shot with an arrow. It didn't start hurting until the kraken attack, I think I walked too much on it. Or the slide down the deck caused more damage. Now it's nearly excruciating."

He nodded and pulled a satchel from his belt. "When was it? You get treatment?"

I hesitated, biting my lip. The sea slapped the side of the ship, as if in answer, and I shook my head. "No." I could not reveal my hand here, if Veshak was also unable to tell the crew of his truth.

The doctor nodded, glancing up. His cool golden eyes fixed on mine, and wrinkles formed around them as he spoke. "I can help with this."

I pulled my leg back and winced. The memory of the pain from losing my tail surfaced in my mind, and my stomach churned. "Can I not let it heal on its own?"

Felix shrugged. "You might, but you risk infectin' it. Rather you want, I can douse it in alcohol. With a hole like that, I reckon you'll limp for weeks yet." He leaned back on his heels and pressed a knuckle to his lip. "You afraid of me?"

I shook my head quickly, and he jerked his chin to my leg. "I'll relieve the pain. Anything I need to know?"

"Of course not," I answered hastily.

His touch was gentle as he guided my leg and set it on a crate. His thick brow arched and lips pursed, but he continued to his case, where he pulled out a few bottles of red and brown liquids. They sloshed in their vials, and I wrinkled my nose at the smell as he popped their corks.

"Magic works as directed by mantrik. If I tell your skin to stitch, but that skin is hiding somethin' else by anoth'r, it could cause further damage."

Felix lifted a glass with a pointed top, which he flicked. The top cracked and flew across the room, shattering onto the floor, and I winced at the sound. “An ampule, keeps metal from gettin’ mixed,” he explained as he caught sight of the look on my face. He poured a few drops from the red liquid into the brown vial, then handed it to me. “Drink, to help infection.”

I obeyed, then nearly vomited. The taste was rank, like the smell of fish laid out on the beach for two days, only slightly covered by the essence of honey. “What is that?” I choked out, snatching the canteen of water from his hand.

“Bit o’ garlic, honey, turmeric... dash of arsenic,” he said with a shrug. “It’s experimental.”

I drank deeply and let out a heavy breath when the vile taste had left my tongue. “That’s awful.” I wiped my mouth with the back of my hand and handed the canteen back.

He waved his hand. “Keep it, you’ll be needin’ one onboard.” Lifting my foot and taking the chair, he settled my heel against his knee. “Last chance to tell me somethin’.”

A twinge of phantom pain shot through my calf where my fin used to be, and I grimaced. “No.”

He shrugged. “Alright.” His hands were warm on my foot, and fingers gentle as he held the spot just below the hole. “You’re goin’ to feel tinglin’, then it’ll knit itself back together.”

Warmth seeped from his skin into mine, followed by a hum of energy. It felt similar to the first touch of Navya’s power, but lighter. He pressed his fingertips in a circle around the arch of my foot, and I winced when he grazed the raw flesh. The tingling became more pronounced after a few moments, then uncomfortable. My skin grew hot, and I was tempted to pull my leg away. He continued to work his hand around, applying more pressure and heat, and the hum of his magic grew louder. His eyes closed, and my skin burned.

"Ow!" I tried to pull away, but he gripped me tighter, and my skin screamed under his touch, pulsing with the power he pushed into it.

"Shh." He squeezed me tight for a last moment before releasing his grip, and I pulled my legs up into my chair.

I cried out in shock at the burn that faded as quickly as it had come on.

"That shouldn't 'ave hurt." His eyes flashed with a knowing look. "You feel more than a pinch?"

I hesitated but shook my head no, and he clapped his hands to his knees. "Let me know if you need anythin', and rest. You'll walk easy on the morrow."

He left as quickly as he did everything else, and I sat in stunned silence, absorbing the weight of what had just occurred.

Magic, true magic, healed my foot. I lifted my toes to the air and wriggled them. The foot that shouldn't even be attached to my body. Would omitting that piece cause an issue with my flipper later?

I curled into the chair and looked at Veshak. His face was calm in the setting sun, the blanket tucked under his chin and the bags under his eyes fading.

My eyelids drooped, and the ship rocked. The linens over the chair were warm, but dreams evaded me. I tossed and turned with the tide, clenching my body against the pain in my foot.

I would do anything to return home, to have my tail back. For a brief moment in my sleepless rest, I forgot why I left.

And then I remembered the arrow in my foot, the reason for my pain, Juhi's bloodless lips and her burial. Navya's fading voice as she granted me this new body.

I could not lose sight of my mission. I had to stop the rot.

20

VESHAK

PAIN SHOT FROM MY side, and I threw my arm up to grasp at the wound. My eyes rolled heavily behind my closed eyelids, and a groan slipped through my lips.

"Shh, it's okay." Zara's voice murmured nearby, and a cool rag pressed down onto my forehead.

I grimaced at the touch, at the pain that radiated through my skin, and pried my eyes open.

I blinked slowly, clearing the salt caked over my eyes, and peered through the dim light.

A dull thud pounded through my head, my neck felt weak and kinked, while pain stabbed at different parts of my torso and thighs.

Another groan escaped me as I tried to roll, to stand, and gentle fingers pushed me back.

"I think the kraken did more damage than you know. You need to rest," she said. "We're heading to dock."

My slow gaze wandered up, and, finally, I met her large dark eyes. Her hair was loose, the curls a frame around her round face, and her mouth was set in a frown.

I opened my mouth to speak, but my throat strained, and her brows furrowed.

"Drink some water." She produced a canteen, tipped it to my mouth, and let a trickle drip between my lips. "How are you feeling?" she asked, sucking her bottom lip between her teeth. Her brows knit together in concern, and her face was flushed.

I tried to speak again, but only a groan came out, so I nodded once.

"Felix is tending to men on deck, with only minor injuries." Zara's hand landed on my calf, and she fixed her gaze on mine. "Are you in pain?"

"No," I lied. I lifted my hands to rest on my chest and lean back, and panic gripped me.

My binding had been removed.

I tried to move, but attempting to sit set a fire roaring through my bones. Pain ripped through my ribs. I reached out, looking for a blanket to cover my bare chest with, and found nothing. My mind raced. I was obviously hurt, I needed Felix, he could help, but he and Cayde were the only two on the ship that knew the truth about me. Zara seemed to have good intentions, but I didn't know that I could trust her.

I tried again to lift my head, to see what was happening with my body, and an unintentional hiss escaped my lips.

Her hands found my shoulders, and she gripped them, helping me to lie down properly.

"It's okay, relax. Tell me what's happening."

I desperately gulped down air and strained to speak. "Felix. I need Felix." The words came out like shattered glass and splintering between letters, but she nodded.

"He was just here a moment ago, he checked on your bruising. I'll fetch him again."

When she returned from the door, her face fell. "There are many injured. He can't be here." She braced her arm next to my leg and met my eyes. "Do you want to wait, or would you like me to help?"

The repercussions raced through my mind again, but as the pain pulsed in my torso and I tried to catch my breath, I nodded, letting my arm fall away from my body.

Tears stung the corners of my eyes. "My wrap," I murmured. I felt weak, admitting I needed it. I covered my chest further with my hands, as if I could will my breasts out of existence, or have her not notice that my chest was not flat like the rest of the men on the ship. That I was not like other men.

"Oh!" Her exclamation sounded less surprised than I expected. "Yes, he had to remove that, you have bruised bones. You're healing now, but it will take the night, after those mixes he gave you."

I studied her closely, the way her mouth was relaxed and her eyes sincere.

"Are you uncomfortable?" she asked.

I hesitated. "No one knows," I said, then stopped. How could I explain myself?

She nodded and rose from her chair, shuffling around the small room. She produced a blanket and held it up. "My sister is like you," she said, quietly, as she let the blanket unfurl.

I startled at her words, turning on my pillow. "What?"

"Mhmm." She tucked the linen around my legs and around my shoulders. "Our elder, Navya, has magic and helped her to look as she saw herself. Her name is Sai."

My brows furrowed. "Navya is a mantrik?"

"No," she paused, as if rolling the words around on her tongue. "Yes. I suppose I never considered it. She lives with my people and helps with some magic as needed." She sat back on her heels, her brow furrowed.

"Did she change you, too?" I asked.

Zara's fingers trembled as she jerked her head to the side. An uncomfortable silence fell between us, and the distance between where I lay and where she sat felt like a chasm. I wanted to reach out and touch her, to place my hand on her knee and tell her that she could trust me. Something clearly haunted her.

She cleared her throat and crossed her ankles. "She did. Change me, I mean. Navya is the reason that you pulled me from the sea."

I leaned forward, and a gasp of pain slipped through my lips.

"I hope that I can trust you, as you can trust me," Zara whispered, nodding to my chest, and heat rose to my cheeks. I released my grip on the blanket and reached out. She let her fingers fall into my hand and said, "I am not human, I did not come from a shipwreck."

I searched her face, roaming over her wide-set eyes, her curved nose, the dark brown of her lips as they parted around pearl teeth and formed the words "I am katalval."

My chest warmed, and I stroked the back of her hand.

"You are still Zara, and I'm still Veshak," I said. "I look different under my clothing, but I haven't told the crew the truth of who I am aside from Cayde and Felix."

Zara chewed her lip and nodded, fidgeting with her sleeve. My heart thumped hard before I nodded once.

"Why can't your crew know of this?" Zara motioned over my body. "Do you fear your men?"

The restrictive skirt I was raised in, the heavy gold anklets and strict laws I was bound by crossed my mind. Followed by the image of my father and his stern voice. I jerked my head to the side. "This is who I am, and I fear they would not follow my word. I come from a place—a family—where privateering is the last expected career..."

Zara nodded. "My family also does not agree with me. The surface has been explicitly forbidden, I should not be here."

"Where are you from?" I asked in a hushed voice.

"Mautakheli Isle." She pulled her hand away and brushed hair from her face, and I tried to lift myself up, but fire burned down my spine, and she placed a gentle hand on my stomach. "I was under the impression you hunted my kind, but clearly it seems that I may need your trust as you need mine."

I swallowed thickly.

"I left my people to stop the rot that has been killing them. There is a sickness spreading through the sea, and my sister died a few days before you found me. I fled after we laid Juhi to rest. I cannot just wait to lose more family."

"Oh, Zara. I am so sorry," I murmured.

She waved her hand. "Rest, we can speak later," she insisted.

"I have a ship to run."

She let out a *tsk* and moved to fix the blanket. "Cayde said that he can handle everything. We will reach Raktam tomorrow evening."

I lowered my head and bit the inside of my cheek, unsure of how to manage the strange mix of feelings swirling inside of me. Before I could muster any more words for her, she vanished, leaving me to my thoughts.

A katalval was aboard my ship. This beautiful woman who was so intriguing was the very bargaining chip I sought. She swam willingly to us, and now gave me her trust. I released a heavy breath and closed my eyes.

Did I deserve it? Could I execute this plan in Raktam while keeping her safe?

I could not hide it from her; I had to tell her the truth as she had trusted me with hers. I would take her to Raktam and help with whatever she needed. But I needed her to stand by my side as I took Dorian's place.

I struggled to rise but forced myself to roll out of bed, gasping for air as I did so. The temptation to use my own magic to help me was too much, but Cayde's many warnings over the years echoed through my mind, and I gripped my knees and breathed hard, willing my back to straighten and ribs to stay where they should.

I stumbled to the door, and each step I took was easier than the last. The ship was quiet under the waxing moon. I took a deep breath of the salty air and looked around. A handful of crew scrubbed the deck, and I became suddenly aware that my chest was unbound. I grabbed my shirt and wrapped it tight around myself, crossing my arms, and turned to the stairs. The glow of the moon was broken by Zara's profile above me, where she leaned out over the ocean.

"I must tell you something," I said as I approached her.

She spun on her heel, stumbling back, and threw a hand to her chest, but released a breath. "Of course," she said.

"I will do anything I can to help you save your people." The words left my mouth before I knew what I was saying.

Zara leaned in, her eyes wide. I fought against the pain in my ribs and the pain in my chest as I tried to think of how to tell her the full truth of my plan.

"The man you saw in the brig is my brother."

Zara let out a gasp, and I snapped my mouth shut.

Her fingers trembled as she touched her lips, and emotion swirled in the depths of her eyes. "You would torture your own brother so?"

My mouth suddenly went dry, and I tried to find some words to offer her, some reassurance.

She shook her head. "I could never do such a thing to my sisters." Her voice wavered. "To my sister." She backed up abruptly and turned to the steps.

"Zara! Wait!" I called after her. "There is more!"

She froze on the step below me, waiting. "What else could you possibly need to tell me?"

I swallowed, hard. "He is my brother, but he did not know that before we invaded his ship. I had him taken so that I might take his place in Raktam. His father ordered the death of katalval, with a reward, and I planned to leverage that against the kingdom."

I did not get to finish explaining—she was already running away. My body sagged, and I leaned against the railing and swore.

The sun began to peek over the horizon, and warmth seeped into my limbs, but the pain moved from my ribs to my heart.

21

Dorian

CLANKING SOUNDS YANKED ME violently from a sleep drenched in stars, sending me tumbling from the hard bench and onto the harder floor.

I had spent my countless hours alone trying to traverse the void that my mind fell into, with no luck, and only now did I see the pile of trays in the corner, full of cold food. My stomach growled, and I sat up as something shuffled in the dark.

"Who's there?" I demanded.

The woman emerged from the shadows, a brass cup clutched in her hands.

I slumped back and rolled my eyes. "I am not Veshak," I groaned.

"You are his brother." There was a question in her voice, and I looked her up and down.

I sighed heavily and nodded. "I suppose so."

"I am Zara," she said. She knelt and set the cup between the bars. "I fear that we are both prisoners."

"How can you be a prisoner when you walk free?" I asked, but I fixed my attention on her.

Zara.

She stepped back and wrapped her arms around her body. "He told me that he captured you and intends to take your place in your home. But he intends to use me as well, to aid in his quest."

A chuckle slipped through my lips and died on my tongue a moment later.

Hari... I thought. I hadn't seen him since the first time he came to see me. I could only imagine what he had been subjected to above decks.

"Are you well?" Zara asked. "You look pale."

She stepped close to the door, and pain exploded through my head. The echo of the woman from the sea grinding my bones under her tail filled my mind. I gasped, blinking through the haze, and the creak of the door punctuated the waves of pain.

Keys dangled from her hand, and I searched the room. The door was open, and she was so close.

I reached out and wrapped my fingers around her arm as the mantrik had done to me. "I don't want to kill you," I said through gritted teeth.

As I stared at the woman through tear-filled eyes, the pain from the sea-mantrik flooded my senses, and I grappled with Zara, dragging her to the ground.

"What are you doing?" she cried out.

My fingers wrapped around her throat. I did not know if I moved them or if they choked her of their own accord. Her face contorted in my vision, and I was staring at my father again, at the spot in his neck that had dissolved under a pool of star-specked darkness. I couldn't fight back the pain as I thought of this woman beneath my fists and suffocating my father in my vision.

"Help!" Zara screamed and I screamed with her. I did not want to kill her. I wanted to be free of the hold the mantrik had with her vicelike tail on my mind.

I wrenched myself away from the woman, panting and blinking the stars clear. The pain in my head faded to a dull thud, and Zara scrambled back.

"I am not a murderer," I whispered. "I am not a murderer!" I screamed.

My chest heaved with the effort of forcing the visions of the woman in my mind down and fighting off the pain that she had planted in my mind. Zara's steps faded into the creak of the ship and the splash of sea against the wall of the brig, and I finally pushed myself up from the floor.

I scrubbed the fatigue from my eyes and froze where I stood.

She had left the door open.

I took a step toward it, and the floor creaked. I froze.

It could be a trap.

But what if it wasn't.

I moved quickly and as quietly as possible. The door creaked on its hinges, but I did not have time to fear the sound, turning down the hall and walking on my toes to the steps.

I glanced up the stairway, and a throb of pain flared through my skull. I did not want to follow her.

I turned toward the men's voices down the hallway. I needed to find Hari.

A small kitchen sat on my right. No one was inside, but my stomach ached at the smell of meals past, and I ducked into the room.

A pot of something red and thick sat on the stove, with a pile of flatbread wrapped in cloth beside it. I picked up a loaf and tore into it greedily, my mouth watering at the powdery texture on my tongue. I swallowed rough chunks of the bread whole, too hungry to chew.

I ate three loaves before looking in the pot. The smell of vegetables filled my nose, and I dipped a piece of the bread in it, scooping up a bit of potato. It tasted of tomato and some herbs, and I relished the flavor. It didn't burn my tongue as the soup had, and my stomach ached for more food.

I dipped a whole piece of flatbread in, soaking up the sauce. After my fifth piece, I picked up the pot instead and tipped it to my lips. The stew gathered at the corners of my mouth, but I gulped it anyway, desperate to fill my belly as much as I could. I should have eaten when they fed me. I should have woken from the dreams, but it was too late for regret, and I swallowed every piece of potato and every bean pod from the pot, then used a last flatbread to wipe the sauce from the sides of the pan.

"Rudra's balls, aren't they feeding you?"

The pan clattered to the floor, sauce splashed like blood over my feet, and I swung around to see Hari in the doorway.

I swiped my arm over my mouth, smearing red onto the sleeve of my tunic, and fell against him, wrapping my arms around my best friend.

"Hari!" I cried out in a broken sob, forgetting for a moment that I was not supposed to be out. My fingers found his jaw, kneading into the soft flesh of his cheeks, while tears stained my own. Emotion flooded my body, and I reached up, pressing my lips against his. He froze for a moment before pressing into my kiss, his mouth soft and warm against mine, hands fisted into my shirt.

"Who let you out?" he asked, pulling away.

"C'mon, let's go," I said, grabbing his hand. It felt so good to touch him again. "We'll take a longboat—"

"Wait, we're still a day from Raktam."

I straightened and looked at him, fully looking him over. He had discarded the gray jacket of Raktam and wore a different black vest. A thick stubble grew over his jaw, and I lifted a hand, scraping over the beard growing on my own face.

He didn't appear to be starving or abused at all. In fact, he seemed to be in peak health. The rush of need faded as quickly as it had come on.

"Why haven't you come to see me?" I asked.

He hesitated before pulling away. "I've been put to work. And you shouldn't be out here, you have to go back. If the captain sees you—"

"The captain?" I scoffed.

Before I could say anything else, a man bounded around the corner and asked over Hari's shoulder, "Are you coming back to the mess?"

His wide grin died on his lips when he saw me.

"Ay! What are you doing out!" he yelled.

I backed away from Hari, eyes flicking between them. The hand on Hari's arm, the closeness of their bodies. I turned to run down the hall, but a blow to the back of my head sent me flying into the hard ground.

22

ZARA

I CREPT THROUGH THE ship, careful to avoid the helm and the places I knew men would be working. The early morning mist that Veshak had warned of before shielded me from view, but also hid everything else from my sight. A scraping sound filled the air that must have been one of the cabin boys scrubbing the floorboards with a soapstone, and I walked slowly around the outer edge of the deck. Groping sightlessly, I worked from memory, searching for the ropes that would lead me to the longboat.

I didn't know exactly how far Raktam was from here, but according to Cayde's direction, it was due east. I'd just have to row. I couldn't be their captive, only to be turned over to the crown. I had to save my people.

When I finally found the ropes—only two, barely visible in the thick fog—I wished for my tail back. It was a two meter drop to the boat, which was covered in canvas and seemingly filled with crates of supplies.

I sighed and tried to twist the ropes, pulling and moving to lift the boat, but to no avail.

"Only traitors flee," a voice said behind me.

My pulse quickened, and I turned slowly. Veshak stood five paces away, hand on the pommel of his sword.

"What are you running from?" he asked.

My eyes grew wide, and I glanced around, looking for some escape. He stood between me and the rest of the ship, with barrels to my left and the helm to my right. I lowered my hands and swallowed, gripping the railing. "Nothing," I said. My fingers wrapped tightly around the wood, and I turned slightly. Something sharp wedged into my palm, and I worked my fingers under curved metal.

"Crew only leave like this if they've stolen or killed. Which is it?" he pressed.

I jerked my chin to the side, and in the same moment yanked the sharp stick free from the rail. When I swung it around and pointed it at him, I saw it was a harpoon, rusted from disuse, and he frowned.

"What is so important to hide that you turn a weapon on me?" he asked.

I scoffed and motioned to his sword. "I could ask the same of you. You corner me on deck and accuse me of stealing from you, yet you planned to turn me over to the crown of Raktam."

His jaw dropped, and he released his sheath, and I took the opportunity to rush him.

I swung the harpoon at him, both hands braced on the thick handle, and he recovered quickly, yanking his blade free and sending it glancing off the flat side of my weapon like a wooden stick. I jabbed at him, and he bent away, defending himself, turning to allow me the space to continue attacking.

"I don't want to hurt you, Zara," he said.

"But you'll sell me?" I spat, aiming for his side. He blocked my jab easily, and I huffed at the effort of swinging such a heavy piece of metal around.

"You're mistaken," he said, raising his sword to block another swing and turning so his back was to the rail. I glanced at the open deck, which was a wall of white. I could run, but he would hear my footsteps, and there was nowhere to go. "Just let me explain."

"You said they offer a reward for me," I spat, throwing the harpoon at him and darting away.

I dashed toward the main mast and leaped onto the net. I could not see him from my perch so I could only assume he couldn't see me, and I began to climb, looking up to the mast. The only sound I made was an extra rustle underneath, quieter than the flag.

"Zara, I would never deal in the trade of another being. It's immoral, and unjust." His voice rang clear, though quiet, as if the mist knew he only wished to speak to me and not wake the whole ship. I said nothing and continued to climb, clambering into the fighting top.

"The sun is going to rise soon, please come down," he called up from just below me.

My heart began to race, and I ducked down into the nest. How did he find me so quickly? Surely the mist would have hidden me better and he would've searched at least around the deck more.

"I'm not going to hurt you, but you will get killed if you stay up there."

"That sounds like a threat if I have ever heard one," I scoffed.

"The navarin hunt at dawn, and they will eat you. Please, come down," he pressed.

"The navarin are safer than you. What of the reward?" I threw back.

I heard his footsteps stop, and I held my breath.

"I need your help," he said. "Do you think I would let you stay on board if I intended to harm you?"

Perhaps he had a point. "And what of your sword pointed at me?"

"You drew on me! I need you to hear me out, please. I tried to explain it all."

"I'm listening now," I said, raising my head. The moon had begun to set, and the first rays of light streaked across the sky, tinting it with shades of purple and red.

"Come down. It's not safe up there."

"It's not safe down there so long as you hold a sword," I retorted.

I looked down, but still could not see Veshak, but I heard the clatter of metal and then light footsteps. "There, I've dropped it."

"Okay, now speak your piece. I'm listening," I said, rising fully to stand.

He let out a groan of frustration, and I squinted, trying to see him through the fog. The sky had cleared considerably, and I had a view of the sun rising, and birds in the distance, but the entirety of the ship below me was still blocked out by a shroud of white clouds.

"You have mere minutes, get out of there!" His voice was frantic. "They're going to attack!"

My brows knit together, and I opened my mouth to question him again, but as I did, a flash of red in the distance caught my eye. I squinted against the glare of the rising sun, lifting my hand to shield my eyes, and watched as the red mark grew in size and broke apart into three.

"Get down!" he yelled. "The navarin are coming!"

The red shapes grew quickly, and their wings became clear. My eyes widened as I recognized their large forms.

"They're just birds!" I scoffed at him and straightened. "Calm down."

"Zara, this isn't a game!" As he yelled, the first bird hit the mizzenmast with a thud, and the other two circled, releasing bone-chilling calls. I crouched and watched them, my stomach dropping.

The navarin were nearly as large as the blue dragon that had brought me to Veshak, and their wings threw great gusts of wind around that should have cleared the fog, but it stayed in place. The bird on the mast dug its claws in, splintering the wood between razor-sharp talons.

A scream erupted from my throat, and I ducked down into the nest as cracking sounds filled the air. One of the birds echoed my cry with an earsplitting caw, and the mast next to me shuddered. A shadow fell over me, red wings blotted out the early morning sun, and sweat beaded on my neck and back.

I crouched down further, paralyzed with fear as the birds shuffled and croaked to each other. I'd only ever seen them from afar, safe in the water as they flew from coast to coast. I never knew they were so large.

The sounds of the men shuffling around beneath me steadied my heart rate, and I shifted my arms from over my head, rising a few inches. "What do I do?" My voice barely carried over the now incessant cries of the birds.

"Stand back," Veshak said.

I opened my mouth to ask why, but a moment later, a shrill whistle filled the air, and a blade sunk into the thin wood in front of me, the tip buried deep enough that it poked in toward me. I moved to stand, but immediately three more projectiles followed. I waited a beat before moving.

"Are you done?" I asked.

Before Veshak could answer, one of the navarin swooped down. I scrambled up and watched the bird dive toward the fog, its wings spread from mast to rail. Thuds rang through the air—the sound of bodies dropping—but it pulled back up before it touched the fog. I released a heavy breath and snatched one of the daggers, pulling it back into my nest, and tucked it into the waist of my pants.

The bird across the ship shrieked, and a shudder racked my frame.

"You have to get down on your own. We can't shoot while you're up there or we might hit you," a man called up.

I nodded before I remembered that they couldn't see me, then took a steadying breath. Dagger gripped in my palm, I stood. The leather handle was warm against my skin, and the blade came to a short, sharp taper—it was meant to be thrown. I cocked my arm back as the bird took off to plunge again.

I threw the knife, aiming for the navarin's neck, and the dagger flew handle over head. It missed completely as it arced high over where the bird was when I aimed and sunk between waves.

The bird cawed and rose again, and I dashed for the wall to gather the last three knives.

"Aim for where it will be, not where it is!" Veshak yelled. The fog was still so dense around the ship that I could see nothing below, but it had cleared from the rest of the sea.

I pressed my back to the mast and circled, looking for the navarin again. The other two still perched on opposite ends of the ship, and as I faced the helm, my pulse quickened. The sea bird was massive, at least four times my height. Its red wings hung loose at either side of its body, and a great black beak opened and shut, dripping saliva from its maw.

It turned beady red eyes on me and spread its wings, sending a shiver through them and a cascade of tiny color shifts through its feathers. I cocked my arm back, lifting the second blade, and aimed for its neck.

The blade sunk deep into the wood of the mast, above the navarin. It lowered its head and released a cry, and the crew below me shuffled and yelled and orders were thrown about.

"Jump down! We have you!" was yelled up in the same moment the bird launched itself from the mast, beating its great wings and snapping at me. The knives fell to the ground with a clatter, and I threw a leg over the edge of the nest, heart pounding and blood rushing in my ears.

The fog was still thick beneath me; I couldn't see the deck or the crew. I could fall right through the wood if I jumped, but Veshak's voice came straight up. "Trust that we will catch you."

I froze. I had so many reasons not to trust him, let alone the other men in the crew.

The bird's talons dug into the wood next to me a moment later, and I released my grip. The wind tore through my hair and pulled a scream from my mouth as I fell.

My heart thudded in my chest. And I bounced against a net, into the air, and fell back into the tight hold of it again. My hands found the hard knots of rope, and I took great gulping breaths, tears stinging my skin, and my body shaking.

Hands and arms grabbed me, pulling me from the net, and I allowed the crew to gather me up, pushing me into someone's arms as a shuddering cry racked me.

"It's okay, we have you," Veshak said in my ear.

"They won't reach you down here, Willy-Will is keeping the fog," Cayde assured.

"What?" I asked, blinking up.

"He's our weather mantrik," he explained. "His family brings storms, changes the tides, so on."

I nodded, vaguely aware of what that meant. He was likely the reason that the rain hadn't affected our travels or the storms had never destroyed their ships.

Veshak looked over me as I leaned against the mast. "You are unharmed?"

I nodded, but eyed him, and glanced around the still-misted ship. "How could you see me up there? I can't see anyone else."

He shrugged. "I have good vision."

It all came flooding back then. The betrayal, his brother, the deal he had made with my life before we even met. He had saved my life three times over, but still wanted me to join him in Raktam.

I looked up into his eyes, and my heart thudded hard. "I don't want your help," I murmured.

A bird screeched above us, and he pulled a dagger from his boot, glancing up before launching the blade into the sky. It disappeared into the thick mist, and the navarin let out a croak and fell, shrouded in shadow, into the sea behind him.

Veshak leaned in close, causing my pulse to quicken as he breathed, "Maybe you don't have a choice." Then he straightened and held out a hand. "I make a better ally than enemy."

A shiver raced down my spine, and I swallowed when he finally stepped away from me. He barked orders at the crew to raise the sails, and Willy-Will emerged from the mist, arms held high above his head to keep us hidden as we sailed away from the hunting ground.

23

VESHAK

WE STOOD ON THE sloop under the shroud of mist, preparing to leave my galleon in the North Kotik. She was solemn against the unbroken sea, sails raised and decks quiet. The crew would hold steady and wait for my return.

Cayde slapped my back, drawing my attention away.

"Pining does not fit a pirate captain!" he teased, pulling a flask from the inside of his vest and offering it. I shot him a withering look before snatching the drink and taking a swig.

"I do not *pine*, quartermaster. I plan, and I watch." I handed the flask back with a grimace. The wine inside was as stale as week-old bread. "And, anyway, I do not trust that Ward will turn over the ship on my return."

"You stare at that boat as if it holds your very heart, or you left your fire inside its hull."

I startled, turning my gaze on him, and raising a hand to the spot between my ribs and stomach. The fire that normally burned inside me dwindled, and I sighed. "Do not speak of my fire," I said. "You may curse me from ever seeing my flames again."

He chuckled. "You will see the sun soon, I am sure. There are more ships, should anything go awry. We will finish the job and return to the desert, and you can roll in the hot sands of Paalaivanam."

I looked back at the galleon before turning toward the captain's quarters without answering. Cayde didn't understand. Cayde did not fear the days that the sun did not peek out from behind the clouds.

He did not have to doubt his own capabilities, or have parents that did for him. He had the privilege of appearing as he was born, without fear of persecution, or execution. He did not have people behind him that asked for his brother first, when faced with battle or strife.

He did not lock a drawer of secrets on a ship that he left behind.

I heaved a sigh as I faced the door, where I could hear Zara shuffling about on the other side.

Cayde did not have secrets to hold for a katalval, either.

She looked up when we entered and glanced past me before I snapped the door shut.

"Is the mist gone?" she asked.

"No, Willy-Will brings it in every day to block the navarin from spying us. It will disperse by midmorning once they fly back inland."

Zara nodded and studied a map on the desk, and I stepped up beside her. I resisted the urge to reach out and stroke her back.

What was wrong with me?

"Where are we?" she asked. "I know the layout of the ocean, but here... I feel adrift."

A smile curled my lips, and I lifted a paperweight from the edge of the table, setting it two hundred clicks from the coast of Raktam to indicate our ship.

"Eight hours travel from the coast. We will release the crew from here."

"Why?" Her large eyes seemed wider than normal, and her voice laced with fear.

I shook my head in response but lifted a logbook from under the desk, turning the cover open to show her a chartered course from Dorian's previous captain. "We have their course. They planned to travel south, then around Mautakheli, cutting past Cankili and grazing the Navarin Strait. Either they're stupid or have a death wish, as that strait spells disaster. We'll take this route instead," I said, drawing my finger east from our position. "If we are questioned, we will explain that we were attacked and lost the big ship."

The door opened, and Orion and Hari walked in. Orion set a bundle of cloth on the table before standing behind Hari.

I grinned and pulled a leather patch from the pile. It was triangular and rounded on the corners, and I pressed it around the socket of my eye that was scarred and different from Dorian's.

"I have to blend into Dorian's image as much as possible. It is easy to explain that Dorian was tanned at sea, or that he lost some weight. But I'll have to say that my eye was injured when we were attacked by the very pirates we stole a ship from."

"Where do I stand?" Zara asked. "What is the assurance that you are not going to sell me?"

"Dorian must marry in order to take the throne and become king. That is where you come in, my dear," I held out a hand, and she hesitated before placing her fingers in my palm. The touch was like the first time I breathed fire, swirling heat and smoke inside my gut, and burning the inside of my chest. I swallowed hard and continued, "I need you to masquerade as my fiancée. Then you will have the freedom to go where you need and do what you will to help your people. I can execute orders on your behalf. I will kill Eudo, and once we have accomplished your goals, we will return to the sea."

A slow smile spread over her face, and her grip on my hand tightened. "Okay," she said.

"Okay," I agreed.

I looked at Hari. "You are a part of this crew now, and your duty is to come with us. As Dorian's gentleman-in-waiting, it would not be right if I returned without you."

He frowned but inclined his head. "You want me to pretend that you're Dorian?"

"In name alone." I nodded at Orion. "He will be your escort, to ensure that you behave."

Orion clapped a hand on Hari's shoulder and saluted. "I still need to prepare the ship for dock. Anything else?"

"Yes," I said, straightening. "If Hari steps out of line, I have promised Dorian a long and painful death." I did not say which one of them were to die, I wanted that threat to land however Hari needed it to.

He swallowed hard and said nothing as they left the cabin.

Cayde finally spoke, and my heart sank as he voiced the truth I had been avoiding. "You mean for me to stay behind?"

I turned to face him. The hurt on his face sent a pang of guilt through me. "Yes. You are the only one I trust with the galleon. Dorian must be kept alive and safe, and the galleon can't turn over to Ward."

He took a heavy breath before lifting a finger to his brow. "Aye, Captain."

The hours passed by slowly while we sailed toward Raktam. The sun rose, peaked in the sky, doing nothing to warm us, and began to set again before we saw the coast on the horizon.

Zara stood at the helm of the ship, fingers clamped tightly on the rail at her hip. I studied her. The way her dark curls cascaded down her back, her curved nose and apple-like cheeks facing toward the sun.

As if sensing my gaze, she turned from the water, and I glanced away before my eyes fell back to her face.

"Worried I'll jump?" she asked.

Heat crept up my neck, and I swallowed hard. "Wondering if we both should," I corrected, the corner of my mouth ticking up.

I closed the gap between us and held out a hand to help her descend the step.

Men ran around the deck, and their gray coats lifted the hair on my arms. They belonged to my crew, but the ruse still made me uncomfortable.

The ripple of the flag raising was loud above us, and the purple blotted out the little bit of light that still shone.

"I assume this will be your first city visit?" I asked, my voice low. The ship rocked hard as it was turned into port, and shouts became loud and clear from the deck. Cries of "It's the prince!" and "Fetch a carriage" carried to us on a breeze.

Zara gripped my arm while the ropes were thrown out. "Your crew was my first interaction at all. I know I won't fit in."

A vast boardwalk stretched out in front of us, and the smell of the town hit me before the view did. Litter lined the road, and the distinct rot of garbage hung around the water, further tainted by the smell of death. A few people milled about, paying our ship no mind, and I wondered at the fact they would ignore the return of their prince—that only a few royal carriages trundled toward us, and no common ones.

"I wish I could say those feelings go away." I smiled back at her and placed her hand on my shoulder to keep our descent on the gangway steady. "But I reckon no matter what type of people one is adjusting to, there will always be space for feelings of unease." I glanced at the dirty road again, the shacks of homes, and frowned.

No color splashed their walls, no vegetable patches sprouted outside. People wore rags, not clean clothes.

"Something is very wrong here," I murmured.

She fell silent behind me, but her hand stayed put, finger barely grazing the skin of my neck with her palm rested against the collar of my coat.

"This is not how I imagined the land," Zara agreed.

A guard of five surrounded us, iron armor clanking loudly, and they ushered us toward the first carriage. A severe middle-aged woman with hair in a tight bun waited by the door.

"Dorian," she said, reaching out as if she might hug me. She turned the collar of my coat down instead.

"Imogene," I tried.

"You must get to the castle quickly, the board will be concerned with the loss of a ship."

"Of course—"

A gut-wrenching scream sliced through the air, cutting me off, and I slapped my hands to my ears, spinning to find Zara.

Her mouth hung open and tears flooded her eyes as she fell to her knees beside me.

"Zara!" I called, trying to break her trance, but her cry did not stop.

I fell down beside her while Imogene threw open the carriage door. I wrapped my arms around Zara, pulled her to the side, but she did not budge.

Her eyes were fixed on the dock in the distance.

I squinted, and my stomach dropped.

A multitude of ropes hung between timber pilings, coated in algae and barnacles. Hung from the middle was the decaying body of a katalval. His long hair covered his face while birds pecked at his bloated belly and tail.

Bile rose in my throat, and I scooped Zara into my arms. "Shh, it's okay," I whispered. I knew damn well it never would be.

I sat her on the seat and said to Imogene, "She comes from a nonviolent people" before clambering in and slamming the door.

"Take a breath, Zara. You'll let them know," I said, brushing her hair back.

She hiccuped over her cries, and I wrapped my arms around her, the knife twisting deeper into my gut.

The cart finally began rolling as her sobs quieted to whimpers, and she slumped fully into my embrace.

"Who was that?" I asked.

Her voice came out as no more than a rasp, and she swallowed hard, knitting her fingers together in her lap.

I squeezed her knee, letting warmth seep into my limbs in an attempt to ease the tremor in her body. Her shiver did slow, but she still sniffled.

"Zara, who is he?" I asked again.

"My father," she whispered.

My jaw tightened, and I pulled my arm back. I glanced out of the window, where guards marched so close that I could not see the city around us. "We will make sure his body is retrieved. You should not see your own family treated so disrespectfully."

She began to relax the further we rode, drying her tears on her sleeve.

The wheels below us screeched to a halt behind angry sounds from the horses outside. I lifted my head from where I leaned back and straightened the embroidered vest that was the slightest bit too large. "Those horses sound as if they've been worked too hard. They don't like their handler."

She lifted a brow. "Is that what those animals are?"

I nodded grimly. "I suppose you will have some adjusting to do."

Two raps sounded on the door, and I turned and offered an arm. Zara placed a hand on my elbow, gingerly stepping onto the box that had been placed in front of the carriage.

"I am here for you," I offered in a low voice.

She shot a startled glance up at me before nodding once.

I swallowed thickly and lifted my gaze to the sprawling estate. A fountain large enough to swim in broke my view of the grounds, with spouts spraying into the sky and a seat worn rust-red on the edge facing the gardens. I was struck by how similar it was to the fountain at my own home, where my mother enjoyed sitting every morning for tea.

Gardens and woodland stretched out to either side, and a wide staircase climbed to a grand iron door in front of us.

"Welcome home, Your Highness," Imogene said.

I nodded to her as I continued to take in the castle. My mouth parted at the walls that reached for the clouds. Ivy climbed the stone, and blackened iron statues holding swords to the sky stood guard beneath the steps. A heavily sweet scent filled the air from pointed purple flowers dotting the grasses.

I set my hand over Zara's before we ascended the steps.

When the doors swung open, I felt as if I had stepped inside of a tree.

Walls of glossy wood surrounded us, broken only by panels of hand-carved flowers and animals. The floorboards pointed toward the hallway ahead, and iron flowers hung from the edges of the ceiling.

A stout man emerged from the doorway in front of us and clicked his tongue, drawing my attention. "Come, Your Highness. The board has already assembled."

I looked between him and Imogene, immediately stepping into the role of concerned prince. "What's happened? Is everything okay?" I asked.

Imogene shook her head, turning to the man, and he pinched the bridge of his nose before ushering us down the hallway. Zara clung to my arm, stumbling to keep up, and I laced my fingers between hers. Her hand still trembled, but she stood tall, unwavering beside me.

"It's your father."

"Where is he?" I asked, heat rising in my throat and voice straining.

"He wanted to speak to you before your ascension, but as his advisor, and now yours, it is my duty to pass on his last wishes," he said. "King Eudo grew gravely ill soon after you set off on your journey, and suffered a broken windpipe. He has found you a suitable bride and we'll have your ceremony in a fortnight."

I stumbled back in shock. "So, he's passed?"

"No, Highness," the advisor said, confusion tainting his tone. "He is simply unable to move, or speak. He is incapacitated beyond help."

I placed a hand over my chest and inhaled sharply. "Sky's above, you scared me."

Imogene gripped the advisor's arm. "Perhaps this is too much, Lewis. We should let him rest." Her gaze suddenly fell to Zara, as if seeing her for the first time. "And we have a guest, we must call the maids." Her voice clipped.

I would like to see my father before he falls any further into his sickness."

Lewis hesitated. "There are other matters to attend to, Dorian. The board waits for you."

I hesitated but fell silent as we were ushered through the castle. A group of guards stayed close behind us and marched in unison, their armor clattering with each step.

Iron sconces guarded each archway we passed, and every window to my left offered a grand view of the city and sea.

The meeting room he led us to was much plainer than the rest of the castle, with only a long wooden table, which was set with high-backed chairs in the middle of the room. The walls lacked art, and the only warmth of the room came from a band of instruments in the corner—though they were unmanned.

"Let's get started." A heavyset gentleman clapped his hands together and stood in front of the first seat. His wool coat was fastened with metal buttons, and his boots covered his knees. His face was clean-shaven, though ruddy, as if he'd been drinking. He caught me looking at him and nodded a hello. I returned the gesture and looked around the table.

"The crown prince returns to face his wedding day after all."

My head snapped toward the snide voice, and my gaze landed on that of an old man. His back was hunched but his blue eyes sharp. He towered over the table, and I swallowed as I saw that he stood in front of the king's chair.

"Take your seat, Hastings," Lewis snapped.

The duke, I realized. Dorian had warned me that they had a rivalry.

Hastings grumbled under his breath and moved to the side, sitting hard onto his own chair.

"There are a few matters to attend to. The first of utmost importance is the hunt for the katalval," the heavy man said.

"How did your travels fare, Highness?" Hastings asked.

"Just fine," I replied, slowly.

"Did you have any success in catching or tracking any of the creatures?" he pressed.

"Duke Hastings only wonders, as His Majesty the King brought the initial approval for your trip to us." A woman to my right motioned to the first chair, flapping the feathers that adorned her plum dress.

I nodded slowly, breathing in hard as my hand twitched toward Zara's. "I had no such luck," I said. I hesitated, then cleared my throat. "Should we not take a roll call before we start any discussions? I'd like an agenda to hold all names in this room."

The duke chortled and slammed his hand down on the table. "Look at that! Time at sea brought sense to the prince's head!"

The man to his right shot him a dirty look and shook his head. "I don't think that's necessary, we all know one another, aside from her." His face contorted into a sneer as he nodded at Zara.

"Who is she?"

"Why is she here?"

"And where did she come from?" a thin woman with a beak-like nose down the table asked.

I jerked my head to the side, but a guard approached Zara from behind. I felt her fingers tighten around my wrist, and the fire in my stomach roiled, my shoulders tightening in response.

"Prince Dorian, is your guest affecting your ability to answer our questions?" the first woman asked.

"She could be escorted to her quarters," Duke Hastings suggested.

"She's fine," I choked out.

The beaked woman interrupted, "She's a distraction!"

An ironclad hand grabbed Zara and wrenched her away from me, and she cried out as the guard squeezed her.

"She is my fiancée," I snapped. "And she will not be taken anywhere she does not choose."

The duke flicked his hand, and the guards behind us stepped back. I stepped in front of Zara, shielding her from the view of the table.

The woman with the feathered dress motioned between herself and Hastings. "Eudo has offered your hand to our daughter, Lady Bernadette. You can't bring back a woman unknown to the kingdom."

"I do not wish to marry anyone but Zara," I said slowly, addressing the duchess, then turning to the rest of the room. "We were attacked at sea—my ship, I mean, by pirates. The ship went down, and we narrowly escaped with one stolen from the pirates' fleet. Zara was on board as their captive, and I fell in love with her. I'm lucky to have my life."

"That is unfortunate," the man to my left said.

"The kingdom might not take to her. They know Lady Bernadette," Duke Hastings pressed. "But this... stranger..." He trailed off and motioned to Zara.

My mind raced as I looked around the table. The aging faces pressed in around me, clearly urging one of us to offer them a solution that they would enjoy. I gripped the edge of the table and looked at the wall behind the group.

"What if we see the kingdom? The people can decide for themselves if they like her, and if we make a match."

"That is absurd," Hastings protested, but Lewis raised a hand, silencing him.

"The king would want Dorian to have some choice. It is a valid option. And the people should know that the crown prince has returned."

"And they will love her," I added. "She saved my life."

A few raised eyebrows were directed my way.

"So it's settled, you will be taken through Raktam this week. If the people respond well, you will marry her within the fortnight," the Duchess Hastings said, her face pinched.

My chest tightened, but I nodded my agreement. I was in too deep now.

24

Dorian

MY BENCH HAD BEGUN to cause sores on my back, and there was a fierce ache in my shoulders. I tried to concentrate on one thing at a time. The swaying of the ship; this brought sickness to my stomach. The yells of the men above me; this angered me, as I remembered why I was in the brig to begin with. The feel of the falling through starlight; the mantrik's grip on my mind flooded me, and pain lit every nerve.

The sun set and rose twice over before I could finally focus on the fact that Hari had been allowed to walk freely yet had not released me from my prison.

We had the chance to leave together, and he did not run with me. The pain of those thoughts was far worse than anything else.

Eventually, I began counting.

"One hundred, ninety-nine, ninety-eight..." down to one, and then I started again. I mumbled the numbers under my breath, I said them in my head, I repeated them until they no longer sounded real and the feelings in my body faded.

I fell into an uneasy sleep, where I crawled through the tear in the Tala Mountains and tumbled into a dark void that wrapped me in the soft branches of ancient trees.

The woods around me were dark, crowded with gnarled trunks that made it nearly impossible to see the ground at my feet. I stuck my arms in front of my body in hopes that I could feel the way, but they were as blind as my eyes. When I found my face with them, horror struck me as I realized that I had lost both of my hands.

"Hello?" I called. "Can someone help?"

Where did my hands go? I wanted to ask.

"Prajapati guide me," I prayed under my breath. I shuffled on what I assumed must be a path through the forest.

"What am I doing here?" I called to the empty woods again.

"Praying to the wrong god, me thinks," a voice whispered on the wind.

I turned and stumbled, but caught myself against the trunk of a tree. "Who said that?"

"I have a riddle for you. If you answer correctly, I'll tell you. If you answer incorrectly, I shall not. But you must carry me on your back, for I have no legs, and do not look back," the voice said.

"I have no hands to carry you," I replied.

"I have hands to hold on to your neck. Together we make a whole person." They sounded like the rocks under my feet, like the bark of the tree I clung to, and I swallowed hard.

Something about the voice's logic made sense, but they unsettled me as well. "What if I do not answer at all?"

"Then I will kill you," they replied, bluntly.

I looked down at my wrists. This had to be the answer to get my hands back.

"Okay."

A loud rustle sounded, and a weight landed upon my back—not heavy, just enough to notice.

"Continue walking, and I shall tell a story."

"I thought it was a riddle." I tried to turn my head, but the grip around my neck tightened.

"The riddle is in the story, listen closely. And do not look back!"

"Okay," I agreed, beginning to walk.

"A poor man in Aatma had a son named Talleen who stole often from his parents. He was unfulfilled in life and only found joy in gambling. At night, he would go under his father's pillow and take what coins he had earned for the day, then sneak to the smokehouse and trade it away on whores and bets. This continued on for many years, until finally the man could handle no more.

"He called the bailiff and asked for his son to be taken away.

"The poor man thought that his son might only be arrested and punished with a few days in jail, as they were family. He wanted Talleen to learn a lesson. But when the boy was taken in, he was charged with theft a hundred times over, and as a result, his hands were cut off in front of the town so that he may never steal again. Then, still wounded, he was sent into the woods to survive alone for one hundred days."

I grimaced at the thought. The sentence sounded like something my father would do to a child in Raktam as a display of power. Inspired by folktales but not far-fetched enough to raise a riot.

The demon on my back continued their story.

Talleen stumbled into the woods, bleeding and tired, and slept under a banyan tree for seven days and seven nights. He wept, he prayed, he starved. He did not know it, but he acted as a brahmin performing for the gods.

On the eighth day, he woke to see a man standing before him. Harsh sunlight shone against his bald head, and he clasped wrinkled brown hands against a small chin.

"Who are you?" Talleen asked.

"I am the sage of these woods. What are you doing here?" the old man replied.

"I have been banished from my home and had my hands cut off for trying to make money for my family."

"I see," said the sage. "Well, you are causing quite a raucous under my tree, and I cannot have it anymore. Come inside. You may stay for one day and night, and then you must leave."

Talleen followed the sage around the trunk to find a door, which swung open wide. Though he had seen no walls outside, a grand entrance was revealed, fit for a Maharajah, with plush carpets, colorful walls, and tables lined with oil-filled lamps. Talleen removed his shoes and was immediately greeted by the most beautiful woman he had ever seen, dressed in a saree the color of the sea. Her thick dark hair was plaited down her back, nearly brushing the floor, and a gem adorned her brow. She took his shoes and placed them on a table by the door before offering him a bowl of rose water to clean his hands.

The man led him deeper into the house, made of twisting halls and grand rooms, and he met more people like the first. One in a green saree offered him a bowl of fruit, which he accepted gratefully. A man in a shade of sunset pink held a tall glass of mango juice, and he drank as though he'd die of thirst. All the while they did not stop walking.

Finally, they arrived at a room hung with thick curtains. A man with a sapphire-studded lungi wrapped around his waist stepped aside to reveal a plush bed made with silk sheets and more brightly colored carpets.

"You may sleep here. One of my spouses will bring you dinner, then please join me for breakfast in the morning."

"Your spouses? You are married to these people?" Talleen asked, incredulous.

The sage looked at him in bewilderment but did not answer, leaving him to his bed.

In the morning, Talleen found that the table was as grand as the rest of the house. Long enough to fit the sage and all twelve of his spouses, plus four guests. The platters were piled high with foods of all sorts: dosas and oil, idli, tandoori. There were platters of the freshest fruit, already cut up into pieces. Yogurt and mango drink sat at intervals along with rice, okra, and stewed lentils.

Talleen sat down next to the old man at his beckon, and two of the husbands served him a helping of fruit, rice, and yogurt.

"Thank you for your hospitality, Uncle. Might I ask a question?"

"Of course, my boy."

"How do you provide all of this wonderful food in the middle of the woods?"

The husband in a white lungi with crystal stones on his shoulders reached over and scooped rice with a piece of dosa, offering it to Talleen. He inclined his head in thanks and accepted the food.

"Have you not put two and two together yet?" the sage asked, raising a brow.

Talleen looked startled and shook his head, peering around the table.

The sage waved his hands over the table, and all of the food disappeared. He repeated the motion, and the food reappeared just as quickly.

"You're a true sage!" Talleen said.

"Yes, now eat, please. You're to leave shortly."

Talleen dropped to his knees beside the old man. “Please, you must teach me your ways. If I knew what you do, it would solve all my problems. I could provide for my parents and return home.”

“No, no, it cannot be taught.” The man waved him off.

Talleen continued to beg, asking what could be done all through the day until finally the sage gave way.

“Fine, but you must practice strictly. There are no breaks, and you will begin the first task immediately.”

Talleen agreed. “What must I do?”

“Go sit under that banyan tree and meditate for one year. Three hundred and sixty-five days. On the last night, I will fetch you.”

Talleen’s heart sank, but he bolstered himself and fled through the house, forgetting even his shoes.

He sat under the banyan tree. His hair grew, his nails curled, his stomach caved in. The summer sun blistered his skin and the winter moon bit his toes. Still, he kept his eyes closed, and legs crossed, and did not move.

Finally, the sage placed a hand on his shoulder and roused him. “You have done well.”

He invited him inside, and they shared a meal together.

“Am I ready?” Talleen asked, his back still bowed in the form it had taken for a year.

“You have one more test to complete first.”

“I miss my family terribly. I was supposed to return after one hundred days. Would it be possible to visit them before we continue?”

The sage observed him and nodded. “If you are sure that you wish to put off the task.”

Talleen leapt in excitement. “I wish to go, and then I will return to you.”

The old man stroked his chin. "I will send you with gifts to take to them, if you must leave. But if you stay, then we can finish now."

Talleen considered the offer, but could not risk another year of not seeing his family.

The sage had gifts brought for Talleen to take home. Jewels, fruits, sweetmeats, and cloth secured atop a parade of a hundred cows that would bring the boy's family riches. Talleen set off with a full heart, excited to pay back the debts that he'd accrued.

His family welcomed him with open arms, thrilled to have their son back and also relieved to no longer be poor. His mother arranged to have the cloth made into new clothing for him, and his father had the jewels set into bangles and necklaces. The fruits and sweetmeats were put on the altar to thank Prajapati for their sudden wealth, and half the cows were sold or traded for land, while the other half were put to pasture.

Talleen enjoyed a short stay with his family, and on the seventh day, he told his parents that he had to leave once more. They urged him to stay, but he promised that he would return someday.

When he set out into the woods once more, he was surprised to see the sage sitting by the river's edge. The old man held a basket in his lap, and a jar of rice was at his feet.

"I have returned as promised, Uncle," Talleen called.

The sage did not acknowledge his greeting, but set the basket down. "Your last task is to clean and cook this rice in the river's water. When you have done so, return to me."

The handless boy protested and sputtered, raising his arms. "Uncle, I cannot possibly! I have no hands to hold the basket, nor to scoop the rice. The basket has holes and will let the rice leak out. The water is cold and unable to boil the rice properly! Surely your spouses have told you such."

"It is possible," the old man said. He left the boy alone with the jar, the basket, and the rushing river.

When the old man left, Talleen wailed to the skies. "Surely this is punishment for leaving!"

But he had already sacrificed one year. He thought of the riches that the sage hid in his tree, and his mother's joy, and he set to work.

Talleen used the stumps of his wrists to push the jar open, and he carefully gripped the tin cup inside, dumping the rice into the basket. A few grains of rice leaked from its holes, but he paid them no mind, continuing to scoop until the basket was a quarter of the way full. Sweat broke over his brow as he looped his wrists through the handles and swung it toward the freezing water with much effort. The rice was heavy, and it hurt his arms to work with no hands. The coursing river shoved him this way and that, and when he lifted the basket from the water once more, the rice had all drained from the bottom, and it was empty.

Frustrated, he tried again. And again. And again, until the sun set. He continued this for three days, expecting the jar to run out of rice, but each time he scooped rice from the jar, it was replaced just as quickly.

"Have you cooked the rice yet?" the sage asked from behind the boy.

Talleen pulled himself from the river and showed him the empty basket. "I do not understand. This is the last thing standing between me and the lavish life that you possess. It is impossible. There must be another way to gain the magic."

The old man said nothing as he scooped rice into the basket until it was half full. He hefted the basket up into his arms and carried it, with himself, into the middle of the river. He stood there for no more than five minutes before reemerging, soaking wet from the chest down with the basket still clutched to his body. When the sage tipped it toward Talleen for a look, the boy was bewildered to see that every grain of rice inside was cooked through.

"You must have used your magic in there!" he cried. "You have undoubted advantages over me. You have hands to perform the magic with, I have none. That's where we have gone wrong."

The old man shook his head sadly and began to transform before his eyes. His hands disappeared, and he was left with frail stumps at his wrists. His body bowed around the basket of rice to hold on to it harder, and his face shifted.

Standing in front of Talleen was an aged version of himself.

I reached a break in the woods as the demon on my back finished their story. I felt them flop a bit with a strong sigh, and then they asked, "So, what was the moral?"

I thought for a moment. The main character had clearly been reflective of myself, with a similar loss, and trying to conquer a power. The sage did not make much sense, though. Who would stumble upon an old man like that in the woods and walk through a door with no wall? Why would Talleen only care for the riches?

"Don't get hung up on the details," the demon demanded.

Heat flushed my face, and I nodded, wondering how they knew.

If the sage had no hands as well, perhaps he had also been exiled. But the last line of the story was that he was an aged version of the boy. Which should be impossible, but so should the door with no walls and a house so large in the woods—and also making yourself new hands from nothing.

Then the man did the same task that he was instructing the boy to. Perhaps the boy did not earn the magic because he lost focus from his mission. But that seemed too easy.

"Tick tick, Prince," the demon taunted in my ear. "You must answer if you've a chance of learning who I am."

And why would the old man find such comfort in the woods but still conjure himself such obedient spouses, while the young version of himself craved the attention of his family.

Perhaps it was much simpler than that.

I cleared my throat. "You must believe the impossible if you are ever to achieve it," I said.

The demon on my back laughed. They suddenly grew heavier, and I heard a thud on the ground behind me before the unmistakable *sling* of a sword being drawn. A shiver ran down my spine, and I stopped walking. The footsteps rounded me, and I blinked hard, not ready to face my death.

"Please, make it swift," I whispered.

I opened my eyes and looked into the deep-red eyes of the god that had been haunting my visions. The familiar knot of silver on top of his head and the scythe he had forged from his own hands.

"You are the god that tore our rift," I said.

"And you are the prince that wields it," Rudra replied.

My hands burned as he said it, and I looked down to see the same darkness I fell through filling my palms.

His hand reached out and settled on my chest. "Do come visit me again," he said with a smirk, before shoving me backward.

Stars flashed around me, pouring from my fingertips, and I fell with a thud, into my body, my mouth tasting of burning flesh.

25

Zara

SMALL DROPLETS OF WATER gathered in the hairs on my arms and legs, and a shiver graced my spine. The stone balcony I sat on collected water in pools, which reflected the vision of the moon, so there were many tiny universes captured beneath my feet, until the dew began to overflow and drain between the railing. Crickets chirped to announce the end of night, and the sun peeked over the horizon, casting warm amber into the sky. Juhi would love this sunrise.

A quiet tap came from the inner door of the bedroom, and I peeked back through the balcony curtain. Veshak poked his head through the cracked door, glancing around my untouched room until his eyes landed on me. His face brightened, and he strode through, a servant following on his heels.

"I brought breakfast, I thought we could dine together?" He paused in the arch, and I nodded, shifting from where I lounged on the bench and unwrapping the heavy wool shawl from my shoulders.

"Thank you," I said to the man, who set a tray beside me. I recognized fruits and yogurt, but a large white shell with something yellow inside caught my eye.

"I'm sorry, what is this?" I asked.

"Soft-boiled navarin egg," he said.

A sour taste filled my mouth, but I murmured my thanks again, and he inclined his head and hurried from the room. Veshak sat opposite me, blocking my view of the ocean.

He picked at the egg yolk with his spoon. "I wonder how these are sourced. I only knew them to be laid in the straight." He shuddered. "I cannot eat it after nearly watching you be eaten by them."

"It feels like a message from the birds," I whispered, staring at the broken egg.

He nodded and set his own back on the tray, then turned his gaze on me, and it was hard to look into his single uncovered eye. "Do you worry that you have made a mistake? By coming here, I mean."

I swallowed and stared at my plate. A deep part of me did not want to offend him. "I dreamed of my sisters. Sai is strong, but if the rot can kill Juhi, a warrior, what might happen to my baby sister?"

"I think I understand," he said. "I worry that you'll be hurt here."

"I fear for my people now that I have left," I said, looking up into his eyes.

The corner of his lips twitched down.

We sat in silence for a long while, spoons clinking against porcelain.

"Your bed is undisturbed, did you wake early?" he finally asked.

I shook my head. "I slept out here, it was cool and wet, and made me think of home."

Veshak's face fell, and he looked back over his shoulder before moving out of the way to join me on the bench. He adjusted his robe, and a long beat passed before he cleared his throat. "It's not too late to go back. We can call the whole thing off."

I lifted a piece of fruit—a sliver of red-skinned berry—and shook my head as I bit into it. The white flesh was soft, but the skin crunched under my teeth. The fruit itself was mild, and tangy, like biting into a flower. I set it down and lifted a spoon of the porridge, dotted with yellow pulp and black seeds. "I have to see this through—we have to. There is a king to slay and a metallurgy system to overturn."

He quirked a brow at me but did not argue. I nodded firmly, more to reassure myself than him, and reached for the gilded teapot. His fingers grazed the top of my hand as I grasped the handle, and I jerked back, feeling as if I'd been burned.

"You're boiling!" I threw him a startled look and touched the side of the pot again. The tea inside had long since cooled, and I was certain that I'd felt the heat on the back of my hand.

Veshak folded his hands in his lap and shrugged. "I run warm."

I reached out to touch him once more, and he shifted away. "Don't worry about it," he said.

"Are you sick?" I asked, my eyes wide. I was overtaken with the sudden need to touch him. I wanted to feel his skin and make sure he was okay.

He shook his head. "It's probably from sleeping in front of the fireplace."

I nodded slowly, still unsure, but didn't press for more information as a knock sounded on the door.

"How many people come barging through these rooms a day?" I muttered under my breath.

He laughed and rose to escort Imogene to my hiding place.

"I'm not sure what's gotten into you, Dorian. It is improper to be alone with the lady in her chambers," she chastised as she pushed the curtain of my window back.

"We're only having breakfast. Nothing sinister is happening."

"I would like him to be here," I offered.

Imogene's voice fell into a stern warning. "I don't care if you were playing Pachisi or skipping ropes, no visiting without a chaperone."

Irritation worked through Veshak's jaw, and he shot me a glance before ducking inside. His footsteps quickly receded, followed by a slam of the door.

I chewed on a piece of tart fruit, and Imogene appeared by my side a moment later.

"I've come to offer you a tour, my lady." Her voice was strained, and I nodded, rising as swiftly as possible and forgetting breakfast.

"Will it only be us?"

I shed my dressing gown, taking in the pile of clothes on the bed, and Imogene turned away as Veshak had. I spoke to her back while I pulled the bundle of clothing apart. A thick white cloth with curved cutouts and a puzzle of laces sat atop the bundle. I raised a brow at it, holding it to my waist, then torso, before discarding it to the floor.

The pants were straightforward, similar to what Veshak had given me on the ship—a layer of cloth with an opening between my thighs, followed by a set that had only holes for my legs. When the gown rustled loudly, its many gems clinking against each other, Imogene turned to help tie it.

"I do not wish to be a bother, but I do wonder if there are lighter clothes that I might find somewhere?"

Her face pinched but she nodded. "There is a seamstress in town. Though, your gowns there were hand-selected from the old collections."

"I do not mean any disrespect." The words rushed from my mouth. "I am not accustomed to wearing such extravagant garments." I pressed my palms against the tightened bodice, and her eyes softened.

The older woman motioned for me to turn around. Her wrinkled fingers worked through the laces at my back, adjusting the cords that held my breasts in place, and then moved the heavy chains at my hips.

"My late queen had a hard adjustment when she arrived in our humble kingdom, gods rest her soul. His Majesty was adamant about marrying into Aatma, and joining the lands, much like Dorian's insistence that he take your hand."

She pulled tightly at my waist, and I felt as if I might lose my breath.

"She tried to see the people, but became a recluse in this castle, only spending time with the king and aching for home."

My heart dropped as Imogene circled to face me. "I do not want to see that happen to another queen. I will arrange an escort to the seamstress."

I offered her a small smile through short breaths. "Thank you."

Two guards waited outside the door for us, and Imogene breezed past them, clearly expecting me to keep pace as she strode through the castle.

It had been so late the night before when we were allowed to retire that I didn't get to see any of the halls we ventured down, or even note what the path to my rooms was. In broad daylight, the castle was beautiful. Imogene led me down the stone hallway and pulled back the curtain on a library. Great shelves lined the walls from floor to ceiling, carved with small scalloped patterns between rows and rows of books. Couches and chairs scattered the floor, accented by handwoven rugs in rich shades of red and purple.

"This is where the king worked most often—the central library," Imogene said, motioning to a desk near the window alcove. The sea waved jauntily in the distance, beyond the city walls, and the ghost of a smile traced my lips before she turned abruptly from the room.

Her heels clicked furiously as she led the way through the maze of the castle, pointing down hallways and gesturing here and there. "That way is the kitchens and servants' quarters, you'll never need to worry about that." She referred to a dingy hall lacking rugs on the floor. "Passageways linking the halls and various rooms are behind teal curtains, lavatories behind cream, and meeting rooms shielded by purple." Imogene stopped and pulled an exceptionally heavy plum curtain back to reveal a small room lit by lanterns from above. Two chairs faced each other with a three-legged table in between them, and she explained that the double layer curtain muffled sound to allow private chats between diplomats.

We toured through a vast ballroom, the floors shining marble and walls painted with murals of the kingdom's heroes slaying great beasts. Imogene showed me through a maze of hallways that all looked the exact same.

"This is the oldest part of the house," she explained. "It's quite easy to lose your way. When Dorian's eight-times grandfather built his home up here, it started as a vast mansion. After his son donned a crown and erected the first wall around Raktam, a carriage house was added, then roads and gardens built." She pointed to paintings of men wearing crowns and holding scepters as she spoke. Most had large bushy beards and great capes of animal fur. "It wasn't until Eudo's reign, when he joined our land with Aatma, that the newer wings were built."

As we reached the end of a hallway, I noticed a tall man leaning on one of the frames to a meeting room. I recognized him from the board meeting, but couldn't remember his name.

I raised a hand in greeting, but he narrowed his eyes at me and closed the curtain.

"Who is that?" I asked.

"Duke Hastings," Imogene murmured. "You'd do best to avoid him, ma'am. He'll only bring you trouble."

I hesitated while Imogene turned down the opposite hall. A woman emerged from the shadows and ducked into the room, her face shielded by the curtain.

"Come quickly," Imogene called, and I obeyed.

We passed a multitude of stone staircases, all overlapping one another with curved iron handles.

"These are the main steps. If you are ever lost, find them at the west of the castle, and they will take you to the same place on every floor."

I nodded, but my head was spinning as we entered the wood-paneled foyer that Veshak and I had stood in the evening before.

"I don't understand how we ended up back here," I murmured.

Imogene chuckled and pulled a piece of waxed canvas from her pocket. "Worry not. Most guests get lost. There are seventy bedrooms in this castle, most of which are not in use at any given time." She set the cloth in my hand and pointed between the careful drawings on it. "This is a diagram of the main three floors. You won't ever need the attic or the dungeons. Just remember what I said about the stairs. If you're lost..."

"Find them in the west," I confirmed.

She smiled, seeming much warmer than when she had greeted me in the morning. She patted the back of my hand. "Good girl. Now, let me see that chain around your waist."

I held my breath as she lifted the egg-shaped ball from my belt and cupped it in her palm. Tiny flowers began to grow from inside it, and I gasped as they sprouted between the intricate metal lace. White jasmine and a large pink rose. She pulled a peony from her apron and tucked it beside the others.

"Wow," I whispered, and she smiled.

"I prepared our previous queen in this same way when she faced her future husband. Each flower's scent does something for you both and will promote romance between you."

I felt a blush rise in my cheeks, and I dipped my head to thank her.

"Let us go and view the gardens over tea while we wait for the prince."

I was quiet as I followed her, caressing the small iron ball filled with flowers.

How could something so deadly be so beautiful?

"This is one of Dorian's favorite places," Imogene said, leading me to a trimmed hedge. "The arch opens to a maze, and when you reach the center, there is a garden table. We can have tea there this morning."

She smiled, and I nodded, moving to follow her, but stopped suddenly when she disappeared around a corner. I heard her footsteps rustling over the grass, but they sounded like they could be coming from any direction.

Dorian loved the maze. Not Veshak. He would get lost inside, or not know where to find us.

"Imogene?" I called.

"Yes?" Her voice echoed through the air.

"Could we take tea elsewhere? I don't think Dorian would enjoy being here today."

Her head popped out around the bush before she asked, "Why is that?"

I scrambled for some excuse, trying to think of what would be feasible. "He did not sleep well. His head aches," I lied.

Her face fell into a solemn expression, and she nodded. "Perhaps by the fountain, then. The water is quite calming."

I forced a smile and thanked her, and she led me back out around the castle, down a long and narrow path. I recognized the stone road that the carriage had driven on when we first arrived, the iron doors, and the water spraying from the dolphins' mouths.

A quiet hum sang through the air, and I looked around to see a group sitting in front of the steps to the castle.

The instruments from the meeting room sat between their legs and on their shoulders, and they slid their fingers up and down the strings, coaxing soft music from the wood.

"Here you go, dear," she said, patting beside the rippling pool. "You relax here and I'll fetch the tea from the maze, and Dorian."

I obeyed, turning to look at the fountain.

I had never seen anything like it before. The structure was the same color as the iron at my waist, and a group of three dolphins leaped from the water in the middle. Spouts sprayed a rainbow into the air, while water trickled from the dolphins' snouts. Their bodies curved around each other in an unnatural dance. I leaned and pressed my palm to the one closest and sucked in sharply at the texture of its body. It wasn't silky like it should be, but cold and dense.

"There is one of these in the courtyard of the Mahal, too," Veshak said, and I yanked my hand away, turning to face him.

"It is strange, but beautiful," I said. "The music, too. When I heard instruments from the water, it hurt. But here..." My heart swelled, and tears pricked the back of my eyes. The colors around me seemed brighter as the notes floated through the air. "I don't know how to explain it."

He smiled and sat, holding out a cup. I savored the warmth on my fingertips and the smell from inside.

"I decided to make it myself. It is chai, like my mother drinks while sitting by the fountain at home," he explained as I lifted the drink to my nose.

I inhaled deeply and sighed before taking a sip. It was creamy and spicy and savory on my tongue all at once.

"This may be the only thing I enjoy about being human," I whispered into my cup.

Veshak laughed and sipped his own chai. "It is pretty incredible," he agreed.

26

Veshak

STEAM FROM MY BATH fogged the mirror, obscuring my reflection. Closing my eyes, I rolled my neck down to look at where I gripped the basin of the sink. The last water from washing my hair drained, full of bubbles, and left a slick of oil on the rim. I moved to turn the tap on and rinse the sink again, but the granite sliced into my hand, and I swore.

Blood pooled in my palm. I scrambled for a towel, shoving my hand into it and to mop up the drops of scarlet. My breath came out in long ragged gasps, and I glanced at the door before raising my hand to my mouth.

My tongue raked along my skin, flicking between the layers of my flesh that had split open. My blood tasted bitter, salty, but I swallowed it down and left a trail of saliva over the puckered edge of my wound. I curled my fingers in and raised my clenched fist above my head, until gooseflesh pricked my skin and the steam cleared from the air. My hand still ached, but when I looked at it again, only a bloodstain was left.

I dressed quickly without looking in the mirror, donning my wrap first. It proved difficult to bind my chest with an aching hand, but I was practiced in fastening the strip of cloth in worse scenarios. I held the end secure between my rib and elbow, pulling it taut around my back and around my front. Using one hand, I made a quick switch to overlap the strip on its end, pressed my fingers to the now covered end again, and began to wrap upward, switching between squeezing my arms down to secure the cloth and pulling my chest outward as I worked.

After only a few minutes, I was left with a flat enough chest, aside from a few wrinkled spots, and an end of a strip which I tucked into the last row, along with a wooden pin.

The clothing I'd pulled from the prince's closet was awful and nearly as complicated as the wrap to work myself into. There was a pair of stockings, first, followed by a restrictive undergarment and puffed pants. The shirt was similar enough to the linen I wore at sea, but also layered with a vest, cravat, belt, and jacket. His socks were silken—I immediately understood the need for the stockings, as they kept the frilled bits of fabric from falling—and his pointed shoes had a heel that clicked when I walked.

I nearly forgot the patch for my eye, and I swore when I saw it still on the counter. The small piece of leather was hard and smooth, and I pressed it against my eye socket, pulling the straps on either side around to secure it behind my head.

The sun flooded Dorian's—my—room by the time I emerged from the bathing chamber. The early morning fire had long since died out, and the large bed had been made.

I let heat rise into my throat, turning to spit embers into the fireplace, and froze in place as someone coughed.

My gaze fell to the window, where a man stood, a blade in his hand and towel over his arm.

The seat of the vanity was pulled out, and a set of tools laid out next to him.

I choked down the flames. "Hello?" I said, trying to shield my surprise.

"Highness," he replied curtly, motioning to the seat. "I assumed you would need a shave after such a long trek."

"Thank you..." I said. He flicked his blade open, and I strode to the chair. "Simon," I said.

He gave me a look as baffled as many of those I had received throughout the castle.

"I must apologize, I have suffered some sea sickness, and many old names and faces have eluded me," I explained as I met his gaze in the mirror.

He dripped some water into a wooden bowl and began to swirl a brush vigorously. "I've never heard of such sickness, only that which causes vomiting. Did you receive a blow to the head, Dorian? Or perhaps fall violently?"

I startled at the name.

"Yes, a few times over, in fact; we were attacked by pirates."

"Pirates! By the seas. That must have been an awful first excursion. How did Hari fare?"

"Well enough," I replied, pulling at the hem of my jacket.

The man's eyes widened, then narrowed at my jaw as he strode around my left side. He stroked a finger from his ear down to his chin. "And did you take a groomer on board? You should have grown a neck-length beard by now."

I watched my throat bob in the mirror. "The navy had blades of their own," I lied.

The man dragged a rough finger from my lower lip, over my chin, and down to my neck, tipping my head back. "You show no signs of a shave. In fact, no sign of a beard ever. Your face is like it was fifteen years ago." His eyes flashed between mine, and he scratched his nose. I waited, unsure of what to say.

He changed the subject. "We kept the barber on."

"Oh?" I asked. Dorian had not mentioned a barber.

"He can help with your hair, it seems to be in a different state as well."

"Thank you," I said. The tone of Simon's voice was strange, the way he moved. This felt like a test, and I was sure I was failing.

He did not reply as he packed his tools, and I waited impatiently for him to leave.

When the door finally snapped shut, I released a heavy breath and ran to the vanity mirror to examine my face.

"Fuck," I whispered. I stroked my bare chin, gliding a finger down my jaw and brushing the smooth skin above my lip. Another curse of my birth.

A teal-clad guard was waiting by my door when I emerged from the room, and he guided me to the front doors of the castle, where Zara waited with Imogene.

"Wow," I breathed, taking Zara by the hand and looking her up and down.

She had dressed in a lavender silk gown, with gem-studded sleeves that fell off her shoulders but covered her arms and wrists. The bodice was fitted and the hips flared to allow her any movement she might need, and she held a wool coat, royal purple and fixed with the same silver buttons as my vest. Together we looked the proper head of Raktam, and I smirked as I realized the irony of that.

"You certainly look more alive in this than in the blanket."

She hid a laugh behind her hand, and Imogene shot me an alarmed look. I stifled my own laugh with a cough.

“I understand that we are to tour the kingdom today, Imogene, but has anyone considered a tour of the grounds instead?” I asked.

“Why ever would you need a tour, Dorian?” she asked, her severe frown pulling her brows into a furrow.

I shook my head quickly, recovering. “Not me, for Zara. I thought it would be a better welcome.”

“Where do you think we’ve just come from?” Imogene retorted.

“I would also like to see my father.”

“He is too ill for visitors,” she said, her tone harsh. “Now, if you wish the lady to win over your people, you have limited time before the markets close.”

I snapped my mouth shut and allowed the old woman to usher us out the door.

An ornate carriage waited for us at the bottom of the steps. The iron cage around it glimmered in the sunlight and curled into floral motifs. The curtains inside were pulled back to reveal seats studded with the royal crest. Zara hesitated beside me, her fingers trailing off my elbow. I caught her eye and squeezed her fingers before addressing Imogene.

“I think we’ll walk, Zara does not enjoy closed spaces.”

The older woman’s face flushed, and her expression turned sour. “That’s not traditional, we use the carriages—”

“I understand,” I said, “but I’d like our guest to be comfortable, and unless we have a topless carriage available...” I trailed off, leaving space for Imogene to offer another solution.

“We do not.”

“We’ll walk, then.” I offered my arm back to Zara, which she took, relief evident on her face.

The road leading downhill was made of uneven stone. Though we’d asked not to ride in the carriage, it still followed behind us, and the horses snorted and stomped while they were pulled to match our slow pace.

"Thank you," she whispered at my side.

I glanced back at the guards behind us and leaned in. "I would not want to sit on a seat of iron either," I murmured.

Her smile was wry, and we slowed as the hill sloped into a deep descent. As the trees thinned around us, the guards formed a tight circle, blocking us in on all sides.

"I understand safety, but it is hard to take in the sights like this," Zara said.

I nodded my agreement, but said nothing as we entered the main city.

The buildings were tall, nearly stacked on top of each other, and sandwiched between narrow alleyways. Intricately woven iron beams supported the outer corners of each home and shop, meeting in metal pergolas that shielded entire portions of the road. The farther we drew into the city center, the more things hung from the beams above us: flowers and lights at the first café, then a street market where vendors hung their wares on ropes and hooks from above.

The guards pressed in closer around us while we broke into the crowd of people milling about, and we began to draw looks.

I tried to point out a fresh fish stand, but my arm was shoved away by one of the men in armor. Zara moved toward a stand with fragrant soap and nearly ran into the back of another guard who stepped right in front of her.

"Let's find somewhere to sit," I offered.

"What?" she asked over the hum of the crowd.

I motioned and pointed farther down the road to a café with seats pouring out into the street.

She nodded, and we shuffled our group toward the buzzing restaurant. The smells of freshly baked bread and warm tea wafted through the air, and my mouth watered.

The guards tried to stay with us when we stepped through the door, but I turned and raised a hand. "That is quite enough! We mean to eat in peace. You can wait with the carriage."

They hesitated before obeying, and only Imogene stood nearby after we were seated.

Zara snatched her hands away when she touched the tabletop, and I set my hands where she had, feeling the cool metal of it bite my skin.

"What the fuck?" she hissed, leaning down and squinting at the vicious edges.

"It seems that iron invades this land as well," I observed, before pulling out her seat. "The castle was drenched in it, from the ceilings and sconces to the bed frames and door handles. Then there was the carriage..."

"It's vile," she said, sitting.

I leaned back in my chair, and the arch of the seat's back dug into my coat, and I swallowed.

A server approached our table, wiping her hands on her apron before asking, "What can I get ya?" Her voice turned up when she spoke, like a bell tinkling, and I turned to smile at her.

Her face drained of color, and she dropped into a curtsy, pulling out the heavy fabric of her woolen dress on one side. "Oh, Your Highness, I'm so sorry! I didn't know you were coming into town!"

"No matter," I said, waving my hand. "We've decided to take a stroll, see the people, and introduce my fiancée." I held a hand out to Zara, who inclined her head to the woman.

"Oh, pleased to meet you, ma'am," she said, and Zara stood, returning the bow.

"The pleasure is all mine. I am honored to be in Raktam."

The corner of my mouth twitched up as I watched Zara play the role of perfect future queen, speaking to this stranger as if they were old friends. She introduced herself as the owner of the café and explained that she had been open since the trade routes between Jihva were established.

"Before that, there was no tea here!"

"Wow, and how were the routes established?" Zara asked.

The owner looked puzzled, glancing to me and then back to her. "The war, of course. When King Durling joined the states."

"Ah, of course," she said. "Dorian has said something similar."

They finally separated, Zara giving the other woman a warm pat on the arm and requesting lunch and a pot of tea that the woman insisted would be the best she'd ever had, and I grinned at her as she sat.

"What?" she asked.

"Nothing," I said, raising my hands. "You'll gain approval in no time."

She leaned in after we had been served lunch and gripped my wrist. The fire in my stomach roared in response.

"Was she serious? About Eudo, I mean."

I nodded as I chewed on a sausage. The meat was bland, barely spiced, and I swallowed it with a shudder. "Yes. This is why we are here. Forty-nine years ago, he married my mother. Two years later, he waged war on her homeland and forced every other state to bend to his will. I'm not sure what happened after, she wasn't here to witness it, but considering how Dorian turned out... I wouldn't be surprised if everyone here reveres the king."

"I wonder if the people near the docks feel the same. Their homes did not seem as decorated as these ones, and the people did not crowd around you, like they do here."

"Perhaps we need to go out there," I said.

She looked thoughtful as she chewed on a bread roll. The crowd still bustled around the market behind us, and more couples began to sit at the tables around the outdoor café. Cautious glances were thrown our way, and I ignored them, sipping the tea. The owner was right that it was good, but certainly not the best.

I let my eyes drift to the sky, reaching my arms back and stretching out my shoulders, and listened.

"—before he's to marry."

"—is the wife?"

"I applied to take his hand and was denied for lack of title."

I had to stifle a chuckle at the conversations around us, but Zara sat up a little straighter and tapped my arm. "Listen," she whispered.

"—three suits of armor due to the military in two days, and a full suite of weapons," someone said.

"You'll be at work through the night," a woman complained.

I snapped my head around to see a woman in a pale-blue dress. Iron buttons decorated the front, and chains bound the corset, wound between an external stay instead of laces and soft cloth.

The person who sat with her wore a thick leather vest over a black blouse, and their sleeves were rolled up to reveal blackened fingertips. I glanced at Zara, then back at the blacksmith. They would hold the answers to her questions about iron.

"A blacksmith." I rose to approach their table, but Imogene stepped forward as the blacksmith spoke, and I missed their next words.

"It is time to return. There is much to prepare and not much time."

"I must speak with them," I said.

"You must be fitted for your wedding suit," Imogene corrected, grabbing my arm and coaxing me away.

I pulled away from the older woman and stepped back. "Imogene, I am your prince, and therefore your superior. I will go when I am ready."

A storm raged behind her golden eyes, but I did not back down, and Zara stepped between us. "Please, Imogene. It is important to me to meet them."

She finally sighed and grumbled. "Fine, I will wait in the carriage."

We approached the table where the blacksmith sat, and I held out my hand. "Hello, I am Dorian," I said cheerily.

They stumbled over a greeting, shoving their chair back to stand, bowing slightly, before enveloping my hand in their large fingers.

"Your Highness!" they exclaimed. "To what do we owe the pleasure?"

I wrapped my arm around Zara, beaming as wide as I could. "I would like to introduce my fiancée. She is fascinated by ironwork, and I know you to be a smith?"

They inclined their head, a pile of braids teetering precariously, and greeted her. "Yes, of course. My name is Smith. Byron Smith." They turned to the woman, who curtsied. "This is my partner, Tavi."

"It is grand to meet you both," Zara said, reaching out to shake both of their hands.

Their eyes widened at the gesture, but they obliged, and a silence fell over us.

"Can you tell me how the rings are disposed of?" Zara finally asked.

"Rings?" Byron asked, his brow furrowing.

"The iron that rusts in the sea," she clarified. "It breaks apart, and the rings open with two sharp ends... from armor, mostly." Zara hooked her thumb over her shoulder at the guards behind us, and I sucked in a breath. She had not pointed that out before, had not mentioned exactly what was causing the deaths of her family.

"We have a place to dump refuse, of course. And I try to recycle what doesn't get used into new pieces."

Zara nodded, but frowned.

"She wishes to get involved in the city, to understand how it all works here before we marry and take the throne," I said, hoping it would ease any discomfort they had at being questioned.

Tavi narrowed her eyes. "I thought you were betrothed already." Turning to Zara, she asked, "Why do you wish to take the crown?"

Byron smacked Tavi on the arm, but I cocked my head at the direct question. She did not back down from the confrontation.

"I strive for peace between lands, but especially care for the sea and seek to clean our ocean and stop our dumping into the Kotik," Zara replied. "Which is why I wanted to speak to you."

Byron sniffed, drawing my attention. "That is an interesting policy to stand for." I caught his eye, and he hesitated before continuing. "I only mean that we did not see the queen before, Your Highness. To hear directly from our next that she cares for the sea and not the people, after our previous queen did nothing for us..."

Heat crept up my neck, and I snapped at him. "She gave everything to Raktam."

They dipped their head, and Tavi lifted a hand to their arm. "They only meant that we never saw her in city appearances. The years she sat on the throne, the doors were only opened publicly once, and she only promenaded with the king twice."

I loosened the hand I had clenched at my side, searching Tavi's blue eyes, then Byron's solemn face.

I stepped back beside Zara and nodded. "I must apologize for any ill feelings. I still mourn for my mother, though it has been many years. And I have only just learned of the state of my father."

Tavi gave me a simpering look. "Of course." She offered another bow. "Excuse me, Highness, we must get back to work. I'm truly sorry for your trials."

"As am I." Byron followed, bowing again and clapping their hands together. "The flames will not bellows themselves. Please, excuse us."

"Wait," Zara called as the couple turned away.

"Might we come with? I have ideas about bettering our metal disposal here," she offered, uncertainty wavering her voice.

Byron's cheeks strained, but they smiled. "Of course."

Three guards followed close behind us as we strode down another unfamiliar street.

The neatly lined bricks turned to mud-slicked rubble under my boots, and the houses lining the road grew closer together until they were nearly stacked on top of one another. The protective cages around the buildings were sparse in this part of town and had rusted in many places, while corrosion overtook them to the point of futility.

Zara walked closer to me as we descended a narrow path, weaving toward the wall that guarded the inner city. Her cheeks turned a pink hue the closer we drew toward the ocean, and when we rounded the corner to a dark alley lit by rusty lantern light, she pulled the collar of her coat around her face.

"Are you okay?" I leaned in to ask.

She nodded vigorously. "Of course." Her voice was muffled.

Byron glanced back at us before pointing ahead, and I raised a brow as they ducked through a passageway in the wall.

We emerged in the northernmost section of the city, where rubbish littered the street and the road was cracked and overtaken by vines. The outer wall of the city looked far larger up close, stretching high into the sky, and I frowned at its proximity to the homes here.

Lanterns sputtered out around us, choking out their last drops of oil. The rocky path under our feet gave way to dirt, and the buildings around us began to look much smaller than those in the Mid. There were no stairs leading up to high apartments with a view of the ocean; instead, rickety fences blocked in overgrown yards.

"We're just through here," Tavi said, stepping past Byron to unlatch a rusted gate.

Zara gripped my arm tightly, and we ascended the thin steep steps into the back of the blacksmith's shop.

A wave of delicious heat was the first thing I noticed, as it washed through me and warmed my bones. The room we stepped into was lit by a roaring fire on the back wall, and a scattering of workbenches filled the room along with barrel seats, with tools and chains hanging from every possible space on the wall and ceiling. The air was still thick with the same moisture as the rest of the city, and my limbs felt heavy as we entered.

"What is this?" Zara asked. She held her hair back as she peered into a metal vat of something emitting an acrid smell.

Byron peered around a chain hanging in their line of sight and gasped loudly before dashing toward her. "Please, ma'am, don't touch anything!"

I followed as quickly as I could, dodging barrels and nearly tripping over a pile of deformed copper.

"Why is it so lumpy?"

Byron stuck an arm out in front of her. "I must insist that you step back, my lady." They cleared their throat as I snagged her arm.

"What nonsense do you have going on here?" I demanded, looking at the faintly glowing mixture.

"Oh, Your Highness, it is incredible technology I have been developing. This is a new alloy which contains an unnamed metal—only a small portion of it can generate a great explosion. It's quite dangerous, but I feel the large amount of force behind it has great potential!" Byron's eyes were wide with excitement as they motioned around the floor to pieces of burnt and blackened wood.

The fire in my stomach rose into my chest as my body warmed, and I swallowed, uneasy. "Wonderful," I said, stepping away.

They cleared their throat and clapped their hands. "Allow me to show you around the shop." We left Tavi in the great cavern we'd entered into and passed into a room full of fireplaces and molten metal.

"This is where all of our iron lives before it is shaped. It is most important that one does not step too close to the flames or touch the raw material." Byron tossed a sliver of metal into the glowing pool in the middle of the room, and it dissolved immediately. "Lest an injury occur."

Byron led Zara and the guard to the next room, and I knelt when they turned their backs. The surface of the pool was as bright as the sun over desert sands, and I breathed a sigh of contentment as I dipped my hand into the molten metal. The heat felt incredible seeping into my skin, and the fire inside me coiled like a gleeful child, leaping to escape from my mouth. I hadn't felt such warmth since I had been home. But I bit back the urge to stretch my ability and pulled my fingers from the metal quickly, careful not to drip any onto the floor, before following the group.

"Where does iron come from?" Zara asked.

"Right here in Raktam," Byron answered, beaming. "My father, Baldric, was the smith who discovered the correct compound that allowed the kingdom to be built as it is now."

"The king rewarded him handsomely?" I asked.

Byron dipped their head. "He was blessed with a barony."

The title of baron was not a light gift to pass on. To give only a blacksmith a name was unheard of, in any kingdom.

"Why is your home here if you have a title?"

Byron nodded and smiled. "The titles in Sariram are more of a formality, since the king united the states. But this shop is part of the land granted to my father. As well as a section of the wall"—they hooked a thumb over their shoulder—"and some to the north."

"Don't you have the wealth to live in the inner city?" I asked.

They shrugged and turned to lift their hand to a piece of scaled armor behind them. "You'll like this. This is one of the first prototypes of armor. My father worked for a year to get the design just right for the king. He is the reason that Raktam has the protection it does, the reason our city is so great." Byron beamed, and my stomach dropped.

This was the shop where it all began. I stepped forward and reached out, and an aching sadness filled me as I brushed my fingers over the smooth texture of the links all chained together. Pieces of my mother, hung on a wall. To think that these people held so much pride in what they had taken from her.

"I'm most interested in the weapons and armor that are disposed of in the ocean," Zara said. I dropped my hand from the armor, fighting the urge to snatch it from the wall.

"I'm afraid that I'm unsure what you speak of, my lady," Byron said. "We have a dumping ground, yes, but when it gets too full, we remove some from the bottom and bring it back here to filter and recycle."

I swallowed at the sharp expression on their face and at Zara's easy command for information. If the gods were on our side, he wouldn't suspect that anything was amiss.

"Across the oceans, masses of the iron from this city have sunk deep undersea and released rot that is killing—"

"Rot? What do you mean?" Byron asked, their face pulling into a puzzled expression.

"Rust. It flakes and gets breathed in by fish, or the rings, the links get swallowed. It kills life out there."

Byron shook their head quickly. "That can't be right. I'm sorry, my lady, for disagreeing." They strode to a large stack of barrels turned sideways and mounted together on wheels. "At least half of all iron here is refined, and these are full of metal scrap just waiting to be smelted."

They turned to a slab of metal on the wall, reaching from floor to ceiling, and gripped a handle, which I hadn't noticed before. The muscles in their arms bulged as they pulled, and the door cracked open.

A waft of rancid burning smell flooded the room.

"This is the hub of our recycling. It comes in and goes out through here, all directly to the king's carts."

"How do you manage that on your own?" I asked.

They slammed the door shut again, and a hiss of pressure released from behind it.

"I do have some help, just a little, from the outer kingdom. It was all arranged by the king."

"And what of the waste in the ocean, then?" Zara pressed.

"I wish I could offer you an answer."

Fury twisted the features of her face. I gripped her arm, pulling her away as the stories of the war surfaced in my mind.

"Come, let them work," I murmured before addressing the smith. "Thank you, Byron."

The road was slick with a drizzle of rain when we emerged from the shop, and Zara's voice was furious. "Their father made the iron," she ground out.

Irritation needled the back of my skull, and I shook my head. "The iron came from my mother, remember? The blacksmith only used it. And if they have a way to dispose of it, that is all there is to it."

"That can't be it," Zara said, her voice breaking. "I couldn't have come all this way for nothing."

"No, I know." I sighed and turned back toward the café. "We will find the answer. For now, we must focus on winning the people over."

"You promised to help," she said. The drizzle thickened to a sprinkle of rain, dappling my skin, and I glanced back at her, at the pain on her face.

"And I will. We will find the answers and save your people from their suffering."

27

Zara

Hundreds of flower bouquets stretched out in front of me. A pile of colorful linens sat in the corner of the room, and stacks of dishes with varying patterns on them decorated every surface in the dining room.

I studied the two flowers that Imogene held in her hand and sniffed. They looked the same to me, and smelled the same. I said as much.

“One is a daisy, and one is a sunflower,” she said, exasperated.

I pointed at the sunflower. “I like the way this one points up in the center?”

She clicked her tongue and set it down on the table. “That one says ‘encouragement,’ which is *fine* for your wedding day, but the daisies are a symbol of new beginnings. They would really be better.”

Frustration leaked acid on my tongue, and I bit back a snide remark, taking a deep breath. I was painfully aware of too many sets of eyes on me. There were servants in every corner and guards at all windows and entries.

“Of course, then the daisies.” I reached out and touched her hand. “Imogene, you are an expert with flowers. Why do you not choose all of the arrangements?”

She hesitated before setting the daisy down and taking my hand. "I would love to be in charge, Zara. But this is the role of the future queen. You must plan the wedding, and you will be tasked with choosing the decor for the castle, setting the menus, and making any changes to the grounds or even to the architecture of the city. The king has only done this for so long since there was no queen."

"What would the king normally do, then?"

"Before King Durling ascended his father, I am told that the king was only a figurehead. Sariram was a matriarchal society."

I pressed my lips together as the weight of her words sunk in. The king has only made the choices since the queen was gone.

"Let's do the daisies. And bring in white and gold linens. I do not want to see teal or purple at the wedding."

Imogene smiled and inclined her head. "Wonderful. Now, for the guest list—do you have family nearby?"

My heart felt as if it had dropped into my stomach.

Yes.

"No."

I could not tell her that my father hung outside of the city.

"They wouldn't be able to be brought in," I murmured, tears pricking the backs of my eyes. Anger bubbled in my stomach, and Imogene reached out and cupped my cheek.

"I'm sorry, dear. I've lost family as well."

I swallowed back a choked breath and looked up at her. I nearly broke, nearly asked to have my father taken down. But I remembered what Veshak had said about giving us away. I remembered how Barun's tail looked, caved in from where the birds had begun to eat away at him.

"Who will come?" I asked.

"We invite all titled citizens," Imogene said, and began to list names. Most I did not recognize. "Durling, of course. And Girish Aatma and his new wife, he is Dorian's uncle."

"I would like to extend an invitation to the blacksmith," I said.

Imogene startled at that. "Which one?"

"Byron. We ate next to them the other day."

"We will send a messenger," she assured.

I looked around and realized that we had been working for hours. "Where is V—Dorian?" I asked.

"He and Hari have training weekly. I am sure that they are keeping their regular appointment since they have returned."

"Thank you," I said, "I should like to find them."

"Would you like an escort?" she asked.

I shook my head and left her with the arrangements. "I'll return soon."

The castle was still confusing—a maze of stone hallways and teal cloth that one could drown in, but I had begun to spot the differences in each wing. The west side had more wood, the south held more art. The north was where Veshak and I stayed, and there were more windows and light stone walls there, and the east was dark and new, all iron inlay and cold air.

I walked the halls toward the north, aware of how my footsteps echoed through the silence, and the hair on my neck raised. I passed the hallway with my bedroom and turned down another. The windows lining the wall displayed the city being drenched by a downpour from the gray sky. I frowned. Surely Veshak would not be training outside in the bad weather.

I turned down a hall with no windows, and the sound of metal on metal cracked like lightning. I jogged down over the plush rugs and past a handful of closed doors until I reached one covered with iron bars. Rain pounded against the glass, and rust sprouted around its hinges.

The metal clanged again, followed by grunting and a cry of pain.

"Dorian?" I called out, shoving my shoulder into the door. It creaked open, and the jeers of men fighting filtered through the sheet of rain. I squinted, shoving wet hair from my face, and wove between overgrown bushes.

A field opened up behind the castle, a barren circle in the center with ropes wrapped around stakes. And in the middle, Hari lifted a sword in the air, high above Veshak.

Dread filled me as the weapon began its descent, and I screamed, "No!"

Hari slipped as Veshak slashed upward, and he let out a cry of pain. I ran toward them, and Orion leaped into the circle from the sideline.

I reached for Veshak, sure he was dead, or dying, and rage and fear and sadness all filled me at once.

"Why would you do that?" Orion snarled at me, lifting Hari from the ground. Blood blossomed from his side, and Veshak dug his blade into the ground, standing easily.

I stuttered over the tidal wave of emotion, my voice trembling. "He was going to kill Dorian!"

Orion hoisted Hari over his shoulder and moved toward the castle. "Medic!" he called out, and guards rushed around him.

Veshak scrubbed the back of his neck. "We were sparring, Zara."

I looked between his eye and eyepatch, and shame bubbled in my stomach, followed by anger. "How was I supposed to know? I thought training meant, I don't know, something with books!" I yelled. "Why would you slash swords at each other for fun!"

"Just as a blade must be sharpened, so must the skills of a swordsman." He looked tired as he spoke, and I stepped closer.

"Have you slept?" I asked. I thought back to what Felix had said about him unbinding. "We have been here for three nights, if you have not unwr—"

"I'm fine," he snapped, then breathed. "It is too cold and damp here to sleep."

"As opposed to a ship?"

"If you must know, yes," he said, closing the gap between us. "My home is very dry. A desert, in fact." His voice was barely above a whisper. "So this heavy, mist-laden air is filling my lungs to the point that I can't *breathe*, and I can't even go anywhere to fix it because I have you to worry about and a guard on my ass at all times."

He had moved so close that his breath mixed with mine. My lips barely parted, and I could taste his black-tea breakfast on my tongue as I scrambled for something to say. "I'm sorry," I finally said.

"For what?"

"For making you stab Hari."

He chuckled, and his laugh caressed my mouth so softly. "He'll be fine. But Dorian may not be when he finds out what I did."

I searched Veshak's face, looking over the bow in his lips and curls falling over his forehead, and reached a hand up to run a thumb over the dark skin under his eyes.

"I'm fine, I'm safe," he murmured, stroking a pattern over my bare shoulder.

"Felix was worried about your sleep." I forced myself to take a step back. "What can we do?"

He pointed his sword toward the wood in the west. "While we were prone to weather change on the ship, we mostly sailed in the south and east. But here, the city is landlocked in a cold place. The woods are protected from the weather of the coast. They'll be cold, but not as damp."

"You want to sleep in there?" I asked.

He nodded. "If I did not have you, I would spend every night there, sleeping on the ground by a fire."

I swallowed hard and picked up Hari's discarded sword. "Okay, let's go."

Veshak laughed, a deep and hearty belly laugh, before sheathing his own sword. "You can't be serious?"

Heat flushed my cheeks, but I nodded. "I have been working on wedding preparations with Imogene all day. But I can't very well plan a wedding for one. We must make sure that you can make it to the altar."

"And what of the trip into town this evening?"

"We'll postpone it," I insisted.

He shrugged and held out his hand. "Alright, then."

I looked at his palm, the deep bronze of his skin and the calluses on his joints, and my stomach fluttered as I slid my fingers between his. "Alright, then," I echoed.

Veshak ordered a servant to fetch an overnight satchel while we changed into travel clothes. I stripped from the heavy gown I had been dressed in and pulled the linen tunic from the ship on. It felt so light on my skin, almost like I was wearing nothing, and I breathed a sigh of freedom now that I was out of the Raktam-style dress.

I promised myself that I would make it to the seamstress Imogene spoke of once we returned.

The trousers still smelled like seawater, but I ignored the pang for home and pulled a pair of boots on, tucking the cuffs in tightly.

Veshak was waiting outside my door when I emerged, a bag slung over his shoulder and a lopsided grin on his face.

"Are you ready?" he asked.

I smiled and nodded and swung my borrowed coat around my shoulders. "Did you tell Imogene where we are going?" I asked.

He scoffed. "No, but I told Orion, and he will pass it on. He and Hari are still bunked together."

"Perfect."

We crept through the north wing, careful to duck behind purple curtains when we heard the clink of armor.

Once we were free of the castle walls, the trek to the edge of the woods was easy, and we laughed at the fact no one had stopped us.

"It's incredible how diligent they are in the city, but to think that we could die in the castle and no one would be the wiser," Veshak mused.

My chuckle died down as we stepped onto the path.

"Something about that is terrifying," I said. "I thought the castle would be the safest place here."

"We are in the heart of enemy territory," he mused.

"Do you think they know? Could that be why they leave us unprotected within the walls?"

"No, there's no way. I'm sure this is how Dorian lived. He must be very lonely."

Pine needles cracked under our feet as we hiked, and the air grew colder. As the sky darkened, the tree trunks around us became thicker, more gnarled with age. I couldn't help but flinch at every unfamiliar sound: the chirps of insects, the slithering beneath brush, the flutter of wings in the canopy above.

As Veshak promised, the deeper we ventured, the lighter the air became.

Soon, it was even easier for me to breathe, and I noticed his shoulders straighten and his chin lift.

"How will you decide where to camp?" I asked, after the moon had risen complete and whole in the sky.

"My mother told me stories of these woods when I was young. She would hike through them and hide in the base of the larger trees. We should be nearing them soon."

"The island, Mautakheli, only has palm trees that we can reach," I said. "They grow easily in the grass nearest the water and drop coconuts into the sand, which are brought to us on receding tides."

"That sounds lovely."

"Yes, it is," I said. "But our access to other fruit of the Isle is also limited to the will of the tide, so it is not as lovely. We have sakka trees that grow in the sand but mango and banana trees grow inland. We are only lucky enough to get food from those if the perfect storm hits and knocks their fruit into our tide pools."

Veshak slowed and pointed to a tree wide enough to wrap ten men around. It had a cavernous entrance and was dark inside, with moss-coated walls. We ducked into it, and he began to empty the satchel.

"Can Navya not give others legs as well? Or change herself to bring you food from inland?" he asked.

He spread out a blanket roll that had been strapped to his back and set a bundle of food on top of it.

I chewed on my lip and considered what he said. I had known Navya my entire life, but had never considered her magic before she changed me.

The sound of cracking broke through my thoughts, and I turned to see Veshak yanking roots out of the wall, his bare hands coated in wet mud and splintered sticks tucked under his arm. He stepped back into the center of the cavern and set the pile into a pyramid.

"I wonder about the outer kingdom, in the same way," I said. "Do you think that Eudo holds food over their head or keeps those walls up like some warning for the people to stay in place?"

Veshak looked at me, startled, and my eyes widened as I watched an ember flick off the end of his tongue. "Of course. That is why so many guards accompany us outside of the castle. They must look the part of the king's muscle."

"Are you okay?" I asked.

"Yes, I'm building us a fire." He turned back to the pile of wood, and a small stream of flame poured from his mouth.

I stifled a gasp as heat washed over me suddenly, along with the memory of heat radiating from his body.

"That's why you run hot?" I asked. It wasn't truly a question, but he nodded in confirmation anyway. He did not offer any further explanation, but sat back on his heels and scrubbed his chin.

"Eudo must have worked out this plan to conquer Sariram long before he married my mother. It likely took years of planning to break down the borders and build such an empire for himself that he could keep even the people within his walls so docile, that the poorest part of the city would not feel strong enough to riot."

"We must go and visit them. There has to be a link between the walls and the iron and the rot in the sea. If Eudo built his kingdom on destruction using the blood of his queen, surely he wouldn't have changed the system."

"Especially since he was never able to invade the other continent," Veshak said. "Or your waters."

"And that is why they must hang their enemies. As a threat," I whispered, fighting past the ache in my throat.

His face fell, and he was at my side in a moment, his arms warm around my shoulders. "Oh, Zara, I am so sorry."

I let myself collapse into his chest. I did not fight back the tears that fell, but no sobs accompanied them. The pain in my gut was more than just sadness. It was fueled by rage, as I thought of the way Eudo's men had hung my father so carelessly in front of the docks. I could only imagine the pain he experienced in his last hours, the betrayal he felt at being banished.

"He was only there because of me, and Navya." My voice cracked as I admitted the sin out loud.

"It's not your fault," he whispered, pressing his lips into my hair. He stroked his fingers down my spine, pressing between each ridge of bone. "You didn't know what would happen."

"You don't understand," I choked out. "My sister died, and he broke our sacred laws and risked her essence."

"I don't understand," he agreed, pushing my hair away and stroking my cheek. "But I still understand your nature. You're kind, and caring, and you set out on a quest to save your people because of what happened to Juhi. A person like that would not banish their father to certain death, I am sure of that."

He cupped my face in his warm hand and brushed a tear away with a calloused thumb. I curled harder into his embrace, and he pressed gentle kisses into my hair as tears fell from my eyes.

"I am so sorry that you were made to feel as if any of your trials have been your fault," he said.

I let myself soak in his warmth as we lay together and he continued to murmur assurances in my ear, until the fire began to sputter, and until my eyelids were too heavy to hold open anymore.

I only stirred when he moved away, and I watched through my lashes as he unwrapped his torso, holding my breath while he revealed black bruises on his back.

28

Veshak

Zara's body was entwined with mine when I woke. I kept my eyes closed and forced my breathing to stay even so as not to disturb her. Her breath was hot on my neck, and her hair had come undone, falling over my arm and tickling my nose. Her leg was twisted between my own, and her arm reached across my torso, her hand cupping my bare chest.

Heat flooded my stomach, spreading to my chest and between my legs as I felt everywhere that her body touched mine. I willed the thoughts to go away, tried to remind myself that we had just left the castle to sleep.

But I could finally breathe again, I felt like myself, and the way she curled into me felt so right. My heart rate picked up, and I breathed out, low, a tendril of smoke trailing through my lips.

She shifted beside me, and I turned to watch as her thick lashes fluttered against her full cheeks. Her eyes cracked open, and a small smile broke across her face, more dazzling than the sun after rain, and I couldn't help but smile too.

And then she looked down, and her smile fell, and she yanked her hand away. My heart plummeted.

"I'm sorry, I didn't mean to," she whispered.

Fear gripped me for a moment. Did she not want to touch me? I lifted my hand, and she touched her palm to mine, wrapping our fingers together. "I didn't mean to sleep like this," she said.

"I am happy that we did," I murmured, pulling her hand down to kiss her fingertips.

She touched the soft skin under my eyes and traced my cheekbones. "You look rested."

"I feel much better." My heart raced, and I glanced down at my bare chest, where bruises marred my skin and my nipples had puckered.

"I shouldn't have touched you," she said.

"I enjoyed it," I whispered. It felt like a dirty secret to share, and the embers in my stomach flickered in response.

"Me too."

I glanced at her, then pressed another kiss to her hand before setting it gently on my chest. "I'm happy to have your touch, if it does not bother you."

Zara hesitated for a moment, breathing slowly, before gliding her fingers over my collarbones. The contact felt like a thousand tiny pinpricks, and I craved more. But I held still.

She moved her hand down between my nipples, tracing a path of flame to my belly, where she let her palm rest.

"I would very much like to kiss you," I said. "Not just as your fake fiancé."

She nodded as she lifted herself up on an elbow. She hovered above me, and it felt like an eon that her breath mixed with mine.

I pushed myself up, closing the gap between us. Her mouth was so soft on mine, giving way and pressing back with as much need as I felt. She wrapped her hand in my hair, and her tongue split my lips, and I couldn't help the quiet moan that fell from my mouth to hers.

I shifted my weight to kiss her harder, and she pulled away, sucking in a sharp breath.

"Are you okay?" I asked.

She nodded, pressing her fingers to her lips, but she sat back and looked around. "Imogene will wonder where we are."

I couldn't help the disappointment that flooded me at her withdrawal, but I nodded and moved to stand. "Of course."

Our hike back to the castle was quiet. I wanted to ask her if I had done something wrong, if there was something wrong *with* me, but I kept my mouth shut tight. We snacked on apples and bread from the satchel and stopped to rest when the sun peaked in the sky.

We broke through the tree line near sunset to a wall of guards, with Imogene, Hastings, and Lewis at the front of the line. I swallowed hard and stepped forward.

"I—"

Imogene raised her hand to silence me. "You had us all worried sick! We thought you had been killed, or kidnapped. Get into the castle. There is a meeting waiting."

I glanced at Zara, and we trudged inside, a wall of men closing in around us.

The room was abuzz when we entered, the board around the table arguing loudly over one another. The duke slunk around behind me to take his seat, and Lewis cleared his throat. No one noticed, and he repeated the sound.

The third time, he picked up a heavy tome and dropped it on the table, and a hush finally fell over the room.

"We have recovered the prince and his fiancée, so the meeting may commence."

Hastings stood, raising a finger to speak, and Lewis rolled his eyes. "For the gods' sake, do you ever fucking shut up, Hastings?"

The duke looked as if he had been slapped, physically recoiling. "I was only going to say that I still think this Zara woman is a bad idea for the kingdom. One week home, and she's already absconded with our prince!" He sat with a huff, and Lewis rubbed his temple.

"For once, I actually agree with you."

Murmurs broke out around the table, and I looked around, shocked. I glanced behind me and realized that Zara was gone, and so was Imogene.

"Wait one moment," I commanded. "She did not *abscond* with me. I left of my own free will."

"You said you brought her off of a pirate ship, did you not?" the woman with a beaked-nose asked.

"Surely that is an indication of her intent," a man at the other end of the room agreed.

"And none of this addresses the concerns that have been raised about you," the duke said, looking directly at me.

I sat back, folding my hands into my lap. "What concerns?" I asked as calmly as I could.

"Some say that you are not fit to take the throne," he said. His nasally voice made a nerve in my neck twitch, and I wanted nothing more than to jump across the table and tear out his heart.

"It is not too late to step aside," he continued. "I am the king's second, of course, so I can always fill the vacant position."

"Absolutely not," I said, slamming my fist on the table. "I will marry Zara. I will ascend. And you all will stop questioning me."

"Actually, Dorian," Lewis said. "It is our job to fill in and ask these questions while the king is unwell."

"Perhaps we would feel better about Zara if we knew where she came from," the bird-beak woman chirped.

"Perhaps someone should fetch the king to remind you all of who I am," I said.

Lewis shook his head sadly. "He cannot speak. But you can, and you can tell us why we should allow you to make this woman queen."

"She is part of the diaspora," I said. "Just like my mother was forced to be." It was a lie, I knew it was, but it wasn't like anyone within these walls knew any better, and the quip forced an uncomfortable air between us all.

"And she saved you from pirates?"

"A kraken, after the pirates." My voice was clipped. They were digging for things to find wrong with Zara, and I would give them nothing.

But pirates...

"Would you all feel safer if the pirates were captured?" I asked.

Murmurs of agreement circulated, and Lewis cleared his throat. "Perhaps, if we knew the location of the ship that attacked you, we could ease the guard while you visit the city," he said, motioning to the teal-clad soldiers stationed every few feet around the room.

"Get me a map."

There was a mad shuffle around the room while someone searched, and finally a piece of papyrus and an inkpot were placed in front of me. I dipped the nib of the pen into the pot and searched the map. My gaze passed over the north section of the Kotik where I knew my ship to be and moved further south and east. I let my hand hover, and I finally dropped a dot of ink and circled an empty spot of ocean.

"There," I said. It was where we had encountered the ship from Kallu.

Lewis peered over my shoulder. "I'll mobilize the navy. We must appoint the new commander."

"And I would like to go to the city without being jostled about by guards," I said, inclining my head to Lewis. My heart thumped nervously.

The board began to protest, but Lewis held up a hand. "We agree."

I nodded my thanks and left before anyone could change their mind.

Hari and Orion sat in the hall when I emerged, with a pile of fern leaves between them.

"—land is better. There's no debate," Hari said, and I stopped, leaning on the doorframe to listen.

He clutched two pieces of the leaves between his fingers and pointed at the strips that Orion held between tattooed hands. Hari lifted his own strands and demonstrated crossing the first over the second, and back again, weaving a hexagon pattern. Orion furrowed his brows and shook his head.

"I think the sea makes more sense. You need cover, you go below deck. There is no need to craft a hat from straw," Orion said.

Hari threw his head back, sounding exasperated. "Weaving has been around far longer than that. This was passed down by the people of Sariram before cities were even built. It was vital to Aatma before ships were ever thought of."

"Who will you pass it to now?" Orion's voice was serious as he attempted to fold the strips again.

I smiled as Hari nudged him. "You. Clearly."

I cleared my throat and stepped toward them, and Hari leaped from his seat.

"What happened?" he asked. Orion set his weave down carefully, grimacing when it unfurled itself.

"They've called the guard off in exchange for information on the ship's location."

Orion rubbed his temple and looked around before asking, "You told them?"

I inclined my head. "I showed them," I said, dropping my voice. "Where we met Kallu."

Relief eased the tension in his face, and he straightened.

"And how is this arrangement?" I asked, motioning between them.

A blush tinged Hari's cheeks, and Orion nodded. "All is well. No trouble."

I opened my mouth to ask for him to elaborate. Was Hari staying away from castle staff? Were there friends he had met with?

But guards began to march around us, and I snapped my mouth shut. Lewis and the other advisors swept by and began to direct people around. Hastings dashed past, his cane tucked under his arm as he ran down a hallway.

I nodded to them and wandered down the hall instead.

When I passed by one of the purple curtains, I thought I heard the duke speaking behind it, a hushed whisper caught under the heavy fabric. A woman responded, but then they fell silent. I moved on, wondering if I had been hearing things.

The castle was abuzz with ship preparations for the rest of the evening, as Lewis directed guards to change uniform from teal to iron armor and gray naval jackets. Weapons were brought in from some level of the castle below us, and carriages were loaded to equip a ship with enough food for a month, in case they encountered trouble.

I hid in my room when I began to hear Dorian's name circulate. I did not want to be asked any more questions about pirates or locations. I gave them what they asked for and would do no more.

A few knocks came throughout the evening, furthering the anxiety I felt. I sat on the floor in front of my door, spinning a knife in my palm. Waiting.

I had asked to see Eudo twice and been declined both times. As Dorian, I was not a threat to him. There was no reason I shouldn't be allowed to visit. Now, with the guard called to sea and the board distracted, I had my opportunity.

As Veshak, this would be the night I killed Eudo.

I waited until the half-moon rose into the sky, and listened for the silence outside.

The door to my bedroom swung open easily, revealing a dark hallway. The oil lamps had been snuffed for the night, so I lifted my own from my bedside table and tucked a dagger in the waistband of my pajama pants before stepping onto the scalloped rug that pointed east.

It was funny, I thought, that the rugs would point toward where the king slept. As if whoever chose it knew that someone would need the direction to find him. That someone might get lost on their way to kill him.

My steps quickened as I wove through the maze of hallways. I snuck past paintings without seeing the faces in them, wondering briefly what they witnessed through their days.

I felt as if I walked for half the night, navigating the new wing of the castle and its intricate maze of doors. Every wall looked the same, every turn took me to a new fork in the halls, and when I finally rounded the seventh corner with the same stretch of iron-handled closed doors on either side, I breathed a sigh of relief at the door waiting at the end.

The rug ended a step before Eudo's bedroom, and there were no guards. They were all occupied on the other side of the castle.

I studied the shaded panels in the wood, the heavy hinges, and the ornate crest in the middle of the door before I raised my fingers to the handle.

The room was quiet aside from the low crackle of a fire. The curtains were drawn, and the lamps blown out. I could make out the outline of a grand bed and chairs nearby, but nothing else.

A large form lay under piles of blankets, unmoving, with bandages around his neck and head. His eyes were covered by a cloth, and his feet stuck out atop a small pillow, toes gnarled and blackened.

I closed the door behind me as quietly as possible and crept up to the foot of the bed, where I had a clear view of the crown on the empty pillow beside Eudo's sleeping form. The iron handle of my lamp was hot in my hand, and I set it silently on the wood floor.

The blade tucked against my stomach was heavy, the handle curved to fit my palm. I crept to the side of the bed that Eudo lay on.

I would bury it in his chest, swiftly. And then Zara and I would leave. My mother would be free. Raktam would gain a new king.

The king's body looked slight under his sheet. His cheeks were flushed and skin slick with sweat. I couldn't see his eyes beneath his nightcap, and I paused, considering pulling it away. I thought of waking him, of telling him who I was, so that he knew who delivered his death and why.

Or telling him that I was Dorian, so that he felt a sliver of the betrayal that my mother had.

He took in a rattling breath before a cough shook him. His arm moved, and he tried to lift it into the air, to cover his face, but his fingers only rose an inch before falling down again. The bed quaked with the force of his movement, and I froze, letting my knife fall to my side.

I couldn't kill him like this.

Where was the great king that slayed an enemy with one swipe of his sword? Where was the bastard king that stole my mother's blood? Where was the Iron King that ordered armies to swarm Aatma and stole people for his gain?

I bolstered my courage and spoke. "I've come to tell you that I'm getting married. I thought you should know. I've chosen my wife from away."

A beat passed. I thought—I hoped that he would rise from the bed. No response came from the broken king.

"I'll take the throne next week."

I sighed and turned to leave the room, but the rasp of his voice followed me out.

"Dorian," he croaked.

My heart raced as I snapped the door shut behind me. I slid to the floor against the wall and held my head in my hands.

29

Dorian

A GRIMACE PASSED MY lips as I tried to force the starlight to coat my hands as it had in my vision. Nothing happened. I tried again, and again, to no avail.

I could wield the void. I traveled through it; I had seen it leach itself from my skin.

Unless Rudra lied.

Perhaps I was thinking too big. When my mother felt iron coursing through her veins, did she immediately form a sword?

Pain tingled against my skin, and tears pricked the corner of my eyes. A spark of dark energy released from the fingers on my right hand, and I sucked in a sharp breath. It was only a few stars that sparked radiant heat and then sputtered out just as quickly, but it was something.

I thought of Hari, of the fact that he had not been to visit me, and of Dorian's promise to keep him safe. Had Dorian hurt him to keep him away from me?

My skin split across my palm, and a small stream of the star-speckled ink swirled in my hand, dripping onto the bench before it was sucked back in. I gasped at the pain, and at the way my skin stitched itself back together so quickly. Sweat broke out on my brow as

I touched the spot where the tear had appeared. The skin was smooth, like it had never happened.

The woman in the sea had said that magic had a price. Did I have to pay mine in pain?

I gritted my teeth, pressing my palm to the edge of the bench, and slid it hard and fast along the rough wood. A cry slipped through my lips as my skin tore open on its sharp surface, and I lifted my shaking hand.

Drops of starlight fell to the seat, mixed with my tears, and disintegrated spots of wood beneath me.

I leaped up from my seat and ran to the door, wrapping my hands around the beams. I gritted my teeth and stifled the cry that choked up in my throat. My chest constricted and muscles screamed with the effort of pushing this strange magic through my body, and the tiny cords I urged to writhe around my fingers were weak, sputtering in and out of view as the stars winked with the darkness they were wrapped in.

I felt a piece of wood crack open under my hand, and I pushed myself harder, gasping against the effort, the burn on my skin, the pain in my chest and head. Bright, silvery light poured from my fingers, and inky tendrils wrapped around the wooden bars, melting the fibers away in a whisper of dust. The only sounds were the crackle of embers popping and my dry sobs.

I released my grip on the dark coils of stars in my palm. The rest of the door splintered, and a crack filled the air as shards of wood fell to the floor in front of me.

I pressed my aching palms to my mouth, my tear-soaked cheeks, and let my whimpers fade before I stepped out into the dark hallway.

No one had refilled the single lantern in the brig for days, so I turned to where I thought the stairs were and winced as my bruised fingertips brushed the other cell doors while I walked.

I couldn't remember the last time I had felt the sky or tasted the sea. The moon was beginning to wane, and I looked up at it when I emerged onto the main deck, letting it lull me for a moment.

This is what Mother felt, when she finally left, I thought. Painful darkness dripped from my fingers as the image of iron and blood dripping from her arms filled my mind.

And Eudo, gripping her so cruelly, hurting her so easily.

I had been so stupid. I could not let the throne go to anyone else. It had to be me; I was the only one who could change the city, break down the iron gates that her blood had built, and ensure my father never hurt another soul.

There were so few people on deck, most bent over their work, and I pressed my palms to my sides and walked toward a longboat. I peered over the edge of the ship, and sick roiled in my stomach. I swallowed hard before jumping, throwing a leg over the rail. My body teetered on the edge, and I was suddenly aware of the gap between the longboat and galleon. Waves licked the curved belly of the ship beneath me, and I looked to the sky.

"Rudra save me," I begged, hoping that the god that had granted me magic would help me now.

I threw myself back, and salty air caught in my lungs for too long.

And then I hit the canvas.

The longboat rocked under my weight, but I shuffled around to climb underneath it, wriggling through bags, lifting them and trying to tuck myself away. I needed the oars and a knife to free the ropes.

But before I could dig for any tools among the storage, voices echoed over me.

"We need that ammo thrown below deck."

"Not another ship on the sea, like it's cursed."

"There's ammo in here."

I held my breath as footsteps drew close. The boat started jostling and rising, and bright light flooded my vision as the canvas covering me was yanked away.

"How'd you get in there?" a burly man exclaimed, shoving a lantern in my face.

The acrid smell of burning whale fat filled my nostrils, and I shoved it away. "Please, I don't know who you a—"

"It's Cayde!" he growled.

He reached out and grabbed my arm, his thick fingers wrapping around my bicep as I tried to back farther into the boat. "Where do you think you're going?"

I hesitated, and more of the crew appeared behind him. A laugh rippled through the crowd, and they pressed in around us.

"Throw him over!" someone behind Cayde yelled.

"We need him," Cayde threw back.

"Kill 'im," another voice insisted.

His brow twitched, and he turned to see who had yelled. "Veshak gave explicit instruction."

Someone else shuffled in the crowd, sandy hair falling into his eyes before he shoved it away. "I agree, Cap isn't here, and he's not capable anyway. Kill the prince."

Cayde spun on the man. "We will lock him up again."

The man that stepped forward frowned. "He's already escaped before. What of the third time, and the fourth?"

"I just want to go home," I said. "A katalval is heading for my throne."

"What was that?" the man snapped, turning and drawing his sword.

Cayde glanced at me before looking back at the smaller man. "We have orders, Ward. He is a prisoner."

"He said there was a hybrid!"

I cleared my throat. "Veshak took her to Raktam. I need to kill her, or just get her out of the way. I need to get back for my coronation."

Another chorus of "Kill him" rang through the crowd, and Cayde raised a fist to silence them. "Our captain has a plan!"

"Veshak has been galivanting with the prize this whole time. He captured her and is turning her in for himself! He is no captain, he is a traitor," Ward said, his voice low. "And, as I see it, you might be the only one that stands by him."

"You better remember who saved your life," Cayde said coldly, releasing me and turning on Ward.

"Disagreement will lead to mutiny," I mumbled.

Ward chuckled. "I like you." Then he stepped onto a crate and looked around the deck. "Who is tired of Veshak tossing you all around like sacks of meat to be sacrificed?"

A round of cheers went up.

"You chose to fight!" Cayde yelled.

"Who wants better wages?" Ward called out, ignoring him.

Louder cries rang through the air. I inched back toward the longboat, my palms itching, but Cayde caught me by the arm.

"Who's your captain?" Ward screamed loudly, and the crew screamed back, "YOU!"

Cheers went up around the deck, and Cayde scrubbed his face. The crew shuffled below Ward, and soon a jacket and sword were carried on hands raised high and handed to him. A slow grin spread across his face.

"My first order as captain is to hang the prince!"

"Wait!" I cried out as Cayde tried to step between me and the men that grabbed at me. Fingers twisted in my clothing and knotted in my hair.

"I told you about the hybrid!" I cried out, but the crew did not release me, hoisting me high into the air and carrying me toward the mast.

"A wager!" I screamed. "Let's wager!"

"Stop," Ward called, and the crew slowed.

I fell with a hard thud to the cold deck and scrambled up as their new captain dropped from his perch and strode toward me. "What's your wager, then?"

"I'll bet my life, for your captaincy," I gasped.

"On what terms?" Ward asked.

I swallowed hard, but forced my shoulders back. "Your choice."

I expected him to say a sword fight or draw of arrows. But he grinned and slapped my back. "I'll take that wager over Pachisi. If I win, you die. If you win, you take my place."

My stomach sunk. I was no good at the game; Hari had beaten me every time we played as children. So badly that I had not played since we took separate rooms.

The crew shuffled around us and laid the cloth cross out on the ground, and I sat, crossing my legs in front of one side, while Ward took the opposite side.

"Partners?" he asked.

I shook my head. "That would mean equal shares of the bounty, wouldn't it?"

He grinned with malice and picked up the six cowrie shells, while I placed our wooden pieces down into the middle square.

He threw his hand; the shells tumbled and clinked together and fell onto the cross. Three faced up, three faced down.

"Balls," he said before motioning to me.

I gathered the shells, shaking them loosely in my palm, and blew out a low breath. Taking the first turn would not decide my fate. But it could give me a great advantage.

The silky white pieces fell from my fingertips like stars, and for a moment, I feared I had melted them away. But then they rolled and revealed five faces.

"I suppose my near death has given me an advantage," I said.

The men around us were eerily quiet again as I shook the shells and threw them, and Ward's jaw clenched in anger when no faces showed.

"I prayed to Rudra just before you caught me. He may have already granted me his favor," I said, moving my first piece out of the home square.

My second turn earned me a ten, with only one shell facing up, and I moved my second peg from home.

Ward said nothing as he threw his first turn, revealing no faces. He released one of his pieces from home.

My next turn only advanced my first piece by one spot, and we continued on. As the game progressed, the sun peeked over the horizon, and sweat broke out on my brow. Ward also began to look tired, but did not say as much as he taunted and insulted through his turns.

By the time dawn broke, we had each returned three pieces home. My last piece had ten spots to move, and his had four.

I took the shells into my hand, and rolling them between my palms, I threw them at the board.

They seemed to fall in slow motion, clicking against each other as they floated in the air, turning over and over while they decided which way they would land.

I held my breath.

The men didn't move.

The shells fell.

And only one faced up.

"Yes!" I cried, moving my final piece into home.

I leaped up from the deck, turning to celebrate, but my smile fell quickly. I had no one to celebrate with. The crew around me looked dumbstruck, and Ward stalked toward me, glowering.

"I'm not turning the captaincy over," he growled.

"We wagered," I said, backing up.

"You're a cheating jackal," he spat.

I looked around for some sort of weapon as he advanced, but he pressed me into the rail of the ship.

"I don't want to captain the ship," I said, trying to steady my voice. "I just wish to return to Raktam. Take me back, and I'll consider the wager done."

"Or I kill you now and call it done."

"And how will the crew react if you go back on a deal?"

Ward paused. He lowered his fist from where it hovered in front of my face, and he ground his teeth, backing away.

"Fine," he muttered, then to the rest of the ship, "We sail for Raktam!"

30

VESHAK

"YOU CANNOT LEAVE WITHOUT a guard! It is unheard of!" Imogene snapped as I pulled my coat on.

The foyer was finally empty. The newly appointed naval recruits were gone, the weapons loaded on the ship, the food packed.

I frowned. "I understand your concern, but I can assure you that we will be okay. We are just going into the city."

Zara reached out and patted her arm, then sat on one of the small leather stools to pull her boots on under her fluffed gown.

Imogene scoffed and lifted her own skirt, spinning to search for shoes. "I will accompany you."

"We do not need a chaperone, Imogene. We are to be married in just a few days," I said.

She stuttered, looking back and forth between us, before pursing her lips.

"Also, Hari will be coming," Zara said.

Imogene's cheeks turned red, and a nerve in her forehead pulsed. "This is abhorrent. Your mother would be ashamed, your father irate. The board has lost their minds!" She turned to march down the hallway, then stopped, turning back and glowering. "I am going to cancel this wedding and you will have to elope somewhere that allows unchaperoned couples if you are so desperate to rebel!"

I looked at Zara, who watched the older woman stomp down the hallway. I wanted so desperately to reach out and touch her, to take her hand. But I balled mine into a fist and slid it into my pocket instead.

Orion and Hari passed Imogene, leaping out of her way, as they strode toward us. "What's got her pants in a twist?" Orion asked.

"We slept in the woods," I said.

A blush rose to Zara's cheeks, and I continued hastily. "I was claustrophobic. And then Lewis traded freedom from the guard for information."

Orion raised a brow, but Hari offered me an understanding look. I had asked them both to accompany us to town. We didn't need the muscle, but it would seem wrong if I didn't take Hari with me, and Orion needed to be close by.

The pair called the carriage around, and I offered Zara my arm to descend the steps. She hesitated before taking my elbow.

"I am sorry to confine you in the carriage, but Hari says that it is a rather long walk."

"That's alright. We spent so much of yesterday walking, I don't think I'll mind," she said.

The trip down the steps was over too soon, and she released my arm, taking the warmth of her hand with her as she settled into the seat next to Hari. I released a sigh and climbed in, making space for Orion, and the door shut with a loud snap behind us.

The horses on this carriage sounded milder than the ones that had brought us in from port, and the ride was not nearly as bumpy as our first.

After a few minutes, Hari glanced out the window and said, "This is about the spot where Dorian always asks to get out and walk."

I looked at him, blinking.

"Should I do the same, then?"

His amber eyes betrayed some unsteadiness before he shook his head. "I'm sure you can justify staying inside. You have Zara now. Besides, I always had to walk with him. Most of the time I just started out walking, since I knew we would end up that way at some point."

I wasn't sure what to make of his confession. The words seemed so simple, yet it also seemed like a betrayal to Dorian to divulge the secret.

So I thanked him and turned to the window.

I recognized the café as we trundled past, then the alley with Byron's shop. Before long, we were rolling down another hill.

"I didn't pay attention when we first came through," I said, noticing the obvious difference between the middle town and upper.

There were no rich houses around us, there were no iron supports or wide side roads lined with greenery. Everything was just a little duller, and a lot smaller.

"All of Raktam has a purpose," Hari said, with a sniff of indignation. "If you get to talking to people here, you'll find that most of the Mid is made up of Aatmans. They're all working class, people who have jobs—specialties, even. But they're not important enough to hold titles. The only reason they were brought here is because Eudo deemed them worthy of joining his new civilization."

"And you were one of them," I said. It was too clear. The shade of his eyes, the curve of his nose, the way he spoke of Eudo.

"Yes," he said, but he did not elaborate.

"And lower Raktam?"

"Hard laborers. The less desirable jobs are out there. The smiths and masons and leathercrafters that take up space and create refuse. There are a lot of houses, too."

We passed through the lower city, and I could see what he meant. We had only seen Byron's street before, after traipsing through the shortcut, but now we passed many large workshops that looked similar before reaching the outer wall.

There was some arguing outside over if we were allowed to pass through, but the gates rose for us, and we exited the city.

The carriage rolled to a stop moments before the stink of the dock reached us. I took a deep breath and tucked away the disgust that surfaced. A footman rapped on the outside of the carriage door, and it was flung wide open to reveal a muddy stretch of road. The man held out a pristine glove to help Zara down from the carriage, and the edge of her new dress soaked up water from the dirt under her boots.

I clambered out after Orion and threw my arm around Hari. A pang of guilt struck me as I wondered if he had been used by Dorian his entire life, but I shook the thought away. “Have we been here before?” I asked.

He nodded and leaned in, and I froze as his breath tickled my ear. “Years ago. Dorian tried to speak to the people here. He offered them money and wanted to change the town.” His lips lingered on my ear, and he curled his fingers into my arm. I hesitated. The show of intimacy didn’t feel forced, but it did not feel as nice as Zara’s touch.

I pulled away and looked at him with wide eyes, but he ignored my hesitation and continued walking.

“I believe I made a mistake last time I was here,” I murmured.

Zara glanced at me and reached up to her braid to unfasten the end. Tugging the cloth from her curls, she wrapped it around her neck and pulled it up to cover her nose and mouth.

“Well, let’s go rectify that and win some hearts.”

I watched her curls swing around her freely, catching the light in their oily darkness, and I couldn’t help the smile tugging my lips up as I reached out and brushed the back of my hand against hers.

The corners of her eyes crinkled with a smile, too, and she entwined her hand in mine. I breathed a sigh of relief at the touch.

The great wall that separated us from the rest of Raktam towered behind us, casting a horrible shadow over the land. We passed a few small farms, their soil wet and bare. The houses that lined the road were in various states of disarray, from ivy poking out between stone bricks and window panes to roof tiles sliding down and doors overgrown with moss.

The few people that passed carried satchels of their belongings or pulled hand carts and cast wary glances in our direction, as if we were here to steal from them.

A woman walked by with a bag clutched in her fingers, her knuckles white around its handle. The child on her hip fussed and threw his tiny body back. She tried to move off of the path, but she tripped, and the bag in her hand fell into the mud. Wrapped packages rolled out as the infant screamed with indignation.

The child beat his small fists against her back while she reached for the lost groceries.

When we had docked and been ushered into our carriage, we had missed seeing all of this, too wrapped up in our own worries.

"Ma'am!" I called out.

She looked up, startled, and scrambled to finish collecting her belongings as I took a step in her direction.

"Ma'am," I called again, running toward her.

"Please, I don't want trouble," she begged, grappling to hold her baby and pick up the bag.

I knelt to scoop up the largest paper pack and the satchel and clutched them to my stomach.

"I just want to talk," I promised.

Zara approached her slowly and reached a hand out to the child. "Hello," she cooed. "What is your name?"

The woman hesitated. "This is Deven, and I am Lue." She reached out, and I released the bag. I couldn't help but look at her hands, at the veins popping out from her thin skin.

"We are visiting the city, working to find improvements to make," I said, and she paled.

"To help Raktam," Zara corrected. "We want to learn what the city needs and where the sources of pain stem from."

Lue glanced behind her. "We are barely part of Raktam. No one would come here if it weren't for the docks."

"Doesn't every part of Raktam have its purpose?" Zara asked.

Lue turned back to the road, still not meeting my gaze. "You will do best to leave, you will not be welcomed."

I opened my mouth to protest, to say something else, but Hari's hand fell heavily on my shoulder. "Come, let's keep going."

I let him steer me in the opposite direction, and the guard fell into step behind us.

"I don't understand," Orion said from my side. "Why would people live out here if they are opposed to the crown?"

I shook my head in disbelief as the road narrowed around us and houses began to grow closer together. "I have no idea, but I intend to find out."

It was far more damp in the shadow of the wall, and I glanced up, expecting to see sunshine through the clouds. Instead, a dull gray coated the sky as far as I could see out into the harbor.

I raised my hands to my mouth and blew into them, calling the fire up from my belly, but it barely sputtered, and I coughed embers onto my fingertips. Why was it so cold up here?

People seemed to spot us from far away and ducked into their homes to avoid us.

Hari pointed at some buildings we walked past, explaining that they had been here long before the walls went up, even before the kingdom was only a town, starting at the edge of the woods.

The structures he pointed out were no more than ruins, left alone while homes had been erected around and on top of them, and I looked on, confused.

"It makes sense, with the castle being so far west of the city, but why shut out such a large part of history?" I asked. I didn't really expect an answer, and no one offered one.

When we passed the docks, the carriage behind us hit a bump, and the horse let out a snort while the metal on the carriage rattled furiously. A man sitting on the edge of the dock glanced back and dropped his rod, shooting to his feet and running away.

I turned back and hailed the footman, who looked bemused when I asked him to leave us alone and take the carriage back to the castle.

"I can't do that, Your Highness. I could be jailed for returning without you," he said.

I rolled my eyes and scratched my chin, looking at where Orion and Hari huddled together, and where Zara stood with her hands behind her back.

"Take the boys to a tavern, then," I said, waving them over.

"Which one?" he asked.

I looked at Hari and raised a brow. "Remind me, where did we go to drink last?"

"Cloak and Dagger," he said.

Orion held the door open for him, then stopped to look me up and down before turning to Zara. He unfastened the sword holster from his waist and held the leather sash out to her, blade and all. "Here, you should take this. Just in case."

She took the sword in both hands with a small smile. "Thank you."

"We'll meet you later," I assured him, and clapped him on the shoulder before turning back to the main road. Zara slung the holster over her head and settled the sword at her hip.

"Do you know how to use that?" I asked, remembering her less than efficient rapier use with the kraken.

"No," she said, giving me a lopsided smile. "But I won't need to."

I wanted to laugh, to feel as confident as she sounded, but as we turned into what could be called a town square, I heard voices chattering low and the sound of a fire crackling in the distance.

The road curved, turning us north. The edge of the docks fell away to sharp cliffs feeding hungry waves. The buildings around us crumbled to ruin, and we were cast deeper into shadow.

The longer we walked, the more our path seemed to give way, forcing us to hug the kingdom wall on our left or brave the sharp rocks on our right.

Zara sniffed, and wrinkles furrowed her brow. "What is that smell?" she asked. "It's familiar, but... not?"

The air was still thick with sea, but an added heat drew sticky drops of sweat over my skin, and the rotting smell that had filled my nose since we left the carriage was denser. The cracking and burning sounds grew more intense, and I glanced at the sky. The sun had been blotted out completely by clouds of smoke.

I inhaled deeply, and the acrid smell choked the fire inside my own belly.

"It's metal," I realized out loud. "The same smell from the blacksmith."

The hair on the back of my neck rose as we crested the hill, and I gasped at the scene in front of me.

A valley stretched as far as I could see, buried deep in scrap. Houses lined the edge of the heap, coated in a layer of ash. Hundreds of people worked to scoop chunks of the metal into carts, wheeling them along narrow paths, clambering through the piles to throw buckets of it into steaming geysers. Others wore helmets and gloves and dragged satchels of the scrap away, toward a waiting carriage.

And the outer wall of Raktam stretched all the way around the valley to the edge of the cliffs, blocking the people in, only broken by vents high in the air. The only way out was the road we had walked on.

I jumped as a rumble like thunder filled the air and one of the vents slid open. My eyes widened as a flood of iron pieces spewed out, sliding down between two homes and sinking into the scrap heap.

The people working below did not react, only continuing to mill about.

"What in the skies is happening here?" I whispered, horror twisting my gut.

Zara turned tearful eyes on me, and she pulled the cloth down from her nose. "This is what the gulf looks like. Where fish go to die, where the rot floats from and kills my people."

"We have to do something."

She nodded and yanked the cloth from her neck, securing it to her waist. I turned my sword so that it was behind my back. Whatever the outer city had been subjected to, they did not need to feel as if I was approaching them with a weapon.

Heads snapped up to face us as we ran toward the center of the valley, and the fire heated my chest as I looked at the people working.

Scars marred ashen skin and bones jutted out from ill-fitting clothes. Wary gazes tracked us—eyes in shades of amber, blue, and black, fixed on our faces—and hands were raised. I thought first that they clasped their fingers together to ask favor, and then we slowed, and I watched pale lips whisper the gods' names, and rage lit in me over again.

They feared me, and they prayed when we passed.

Iron poured from the wall again, tumbling into the mass around us. I felt as if I were swimming through a dream from how thick and deep the metal refuse was.

I tried to speak to a woman with hair cut to her shoulders and skin worn like leather, and she shook her head, backing away and dropping to her knees. Her gnarled fingers knit together and captured Prajapati's name as she chanted it over and over into her palms.

Zara touched the shoulder of a child, and he screamed and ran.

I turned away from her and found myself facing a man hunched with age, his narrow nose nearly pressed to mine and sallow cheeks trembling in anger.

"You will not take any of us! It is not time!" he declared, raising an iron pole in his thin arms.

"We are not here to take anything," I said, slowly. "We are here to help." But as the words slipped from my mouth, I realized how foolish they sounded. I didn't know what that meant, for myself or him.

"What do you mean by 'it is not time'?" Zara asked.

He opened his mouth to answer, but a feathery sound filled the air, followed by a shriek that sent a tremor down my spine.

My eyes shot to the sky in the same moment that Zara unsheathed her sword.

"No!" the old man cried out.

The crowd of people around us began to dive into the iron heap, burying themselves and each other, pulling masses of metal over their heads. Anyone that was still high on the ridge, near the homes, ran into cover, yanking doors shut or piling into the carts full of waste.

He moved to hide as well, and I grabbed his arm, pulling him close. "What is that?"

"It is not my time to feed them!" he insisted. "Release me!" His voice was so shrill, so scared, and I loosened my grasp enough to let him fall beneath the surface of iron.

The valley was eerily quiet without the shuffle of metal being moved, filled only by the piercing cry coming closer and the shooting of the geysers. I turned and looked at the wall around us, at the cliffs on the other side of the hill, listened to the scream in the distance and peered through the smoke-filled sky.

Feed them...

"It's a navarin," I murmured.

Zara squeezed the pommel of her sword harder and stepped in close.

The heavy sound of wings grew louder, and I spun around in a circle.

"Come on, get up! You have to run!" I screamed.

Zara left my side and jumped into the iron, echoing my cries.

We waded through together, and I sifted my fingers through the shards, trying to grasp hands and arms, feet and legs. Every time I thought I grazed someone, they disappeared, sinking deeper into the metal.

Sweat soaked the collar of my shirt. My hands stung. Blood blinded me. But something shifted nearby, and I flailed toward it and finally wrapped my fingertips around a soft leather boot.

"We have to run!" I screamed, yanking the old man out of the heap with me.

He and I stared at each other for a moment before he wound up his fists and beat them against my chest, trying to wrench himself free. I held fast this time. I wouldn't let him escape again—I needed him to help warn the others.

"You fool! There is nowhere to run to!"

"We can escape to the city, the inner kingdom!" I yelled back. "That will kill us!" I pointed to the sky above the strait, where three navarin circled closer by the moment.

"The gates will not open for us, the only choice is to hide or die," he snarled.

I looked around frantically, searching for Zara, but she was still beneath the metal's surface.

"We will take you to the castle, but we must hurry," I said, yanking his arm.

He dug his heels into the shifting scrap and howled a protest.

"Leave us be! You have done enough by summoning those beasts!"

He pried at my hands with his curled fingers, tearing at my already raw skin, and I released him.

"Please, let me help you," I begged. "You can't die out here. None of you should be here." I motioned around the valley of metal, blood dripping from my fingertips.

"You put us here." He pressed a wrinkled finger into the crest on my vest. "With your walls and your farming."

I opened my mouth to try and explain, to tell him we would fix it, but it was too late.

The shadows of great wings flew overhead, and I was deafened by the screech of the hunting bird directly above.

I shoved the man away and whipped my sword from its sheath, turning to meet the beast.

Eight shining daggers speared toward my face, and I dropped to my knees, swinging my blade in a high arc.

The navarin screamed in pain as I severed one of its feet, and a spray of blood coated my already damp face. The talons fell with a sickening thud behind me while the bird tumbled down into the valley, tucking a wing and twisting around.

It opened its maw, revealing rows of needlelike teeth, and staggered up onto its single foot.

Its red-feathered wings spread wide, black eyes piercing through me, and I ran toward it with my sword raised.

I slashed toward its neck, but it snapped at me, nearly biting my arm. I rolled over a discarded iron wheel and jumped up by its side, stabbing my blade into its shoulder. It shrieked and tried to fold its wing in, and I twisted, shoving my foot against its muscled body and yanking my sword back.

The navarin's wing fell to the side, half torn and useless, and it flapped the other one, trying to remain balanced. It took a step toward me and fell forward, croaking miserably as it moved.

The smoke stirred around me, and I stumbled back, looking at the sky.

A second bird circled around, but it looked unlike any navarin I had seen before.

Its wings were not the shade of crimson of the others, but black as night and stretched twice as wide.

"Rudra's balls," I whispered.

The navarin dove, and I stumbled back, breaking into a run, but it did not swoop at me.

I watched in horror as it landed atop the bird I had incapacitated and tore into its neck. The pained cries from the smaller navarin ceased, and moments later, the behemoth turned its beady eyes on me.

Blood dripped from its beak, staining the iron under its feet. True fear settled into every bone of my body, and I looked around. The surface of the metal sea was still. Every door was shut tightly. Even the geysers were calm.

I swallowed hard and willed my fire to life, stoking the embers in my belly.

Heat simmered in my chest, surfacing to my throat, but it wasn't enough to use as a weapon—although I escaped the dampness of Raktam for a night, I still had not gotten enough sunlight or pure heat to feed my flames.

I turned to run, and it launched from the ground behind me.

The beat of its wings was deafening. I raised my sword above my head, turning to face it as it dove toward me, but it pulled up. It flew in a tight circle, swooping and chomping with its bloody teeth.

I was too exposed out in the open, and I needed help.

"Zara!" I screamed in the same moment that I was knocked forward. I rolled to my back, and the beast atop me knocked the air from my lungs. A talon dug into my side, sending pain shooting through my stomach and back. It lowered its jaw, and a guttural clicking sound choked out from its throat.

The soft pink part of its neck was so close. A vein pulsed above me, and I stretched my fingers, wriggling underneath its grasp. If I could just stab upward, it would all be over.

I moved to lift my sword, but found my arm trapped on the other side of the talon that was shredding through my skin and clothes. The embers in my chest flickered, but the heat was fading, and I coughed out a wisp of smoke.

"Please," I begged no one in particular.

A thick drip of bitter saliva poured over my face, and I choked at the iron tang in my mouth, suffocating on the smell and taste. The image of the bird tearing out the throat of another filled my mind.

My eyes fell shut, and I turned my head, willing the navarin to grant me a quick death.

Its throaty groan pitched into a shriek, and it fell back with a grunt, releasing me. I gasped and scrambled up the hill, wiping goop from my eyes and dragging my sword with raw fingers.

"Run!" Zara screamed.

She sat atop the navarin, Orion's sword clutched between her white knuckles as she dug it into the bird's back. She speared the blade down between its shoulder blades over and over, tears streaming down her face as she screamed in fury.

I hesitated for only a moment before sprinting up the hill. She couldn't keep the beast at bay forever, and we needed some defense.

Its scream pierced my ears, and its wings began to beat the air. It had too much space to fly and attack us from out in the open.

I dashed toward the closest part of the wall and pulled my throwing blades from where I hid them in my boots.

The navarin began to rise into the air, and a cry of surprise escaped my lips—Zara clung to its back by the handle of her sword. Panic enveloped me as they soared together, and I watched her twist the blade deeper into its back, climbing higher onto it and wedging her heels between its body and wings.

The bird screamed but continued to fly, jerking to the side every time she moved.

"Zara!" I yelled, and they both swung their heads in my direction.

The bird dove, she turned her blade, and its wing tucked.

I threw a dagger, aiming for the soft spot under its beak, but it rolled in the air and narrowly missed. I cursed as I raised my hand to my eye, feeling the patch and flipping it up.

Time slowed while they spun. Zara released the sword and threw her arms between the thick feathers on its back and clung on. Her legs slipped, and she was suspended upside down for a moment, until the navarin straightened.

It beat its wings, sending a gust of wind over me, and Zara disappeared from view.

I released the breath I held and called out for her to force the bird lower. I didn't know exactly how much control she had, but it couldn't reach her while she was up there, and we had an advantage as long as she didn't fall.

The dagger was slick from my sweat and the blood between my fingertips, but I lifted it in front of my face, pressing my back to the stone wall and aiming for where I thought it would be.

I threw the blade. Zara screamed. The bird screamed.

Its talons stretched toward me, and I fell to the side. Its wing caught my face, slicing into my cheek with the ease of a butcher's blade. I let out a cry of surprise but flattened myself into the dirt. A crack like lightning echoed around us, and a quake rumbled under my body.

And the world went silent.

31

Zara

My body felt so heavy.

Stone rubble fell from my back as I shifted. I slowly unwrapped my fingers from the pommel of the sword, my knuckles aching from the effort. Dust filled my eyes, and I blinked over and over to clear my vision.

We had crashed through a section of the wall, and I could see over the roofs of the lower kingdom, moss coated in grime and soot, tiles cracked from the impact.

Smoke pouring from the blacksmith's shop beneath us.

The bird under me was unmoving, and blood trickled from the wound I had torn in its back, mixing with the particles that were beginning to settle from the sky.

I coughed and sat up fully, pulling myself up from where I had straddled the beast.

"Zara? Zara!" Veshak called from nearby. I stood on shaking legs. My gown was shredded from the navarin's razor-edged feathers. My palms coated in blood. My throat raw.

I stumbled over the bird's body, through the gaping hole in the wall.

Voices were beginning to fill the air from both sides of the city. Veshak was by my side in an instant. He wrapped an arm around my waist gingerly, supporting my weight.

"Are you okay? Where does it hurt?" he asked.

I shook my head. Pain burned all over my body, but I hadn't sustained any true injuries that I could feel.

He helped me climb over the broken stones anyway, an arm wrapped around his own torso. We leaned on each other, careful to avoid the navarin's wing that was still stretched up to the sky.

A piercing cry pulled my eyes up, and I flinched, but watched as the third navarin flew away.

"It's over," Veshak whispered.

"Thank the gods," I replied.

People began to surface from the metal sea as we reached the path, and their murmurings grew louder.

"The wall has fallen."

"The beast has been slayed."

"Is that the king?"

Veshak scanned the hundreds of faces, then pointed to an old man wading through the scrap.

"You!" he called out, and the man staggered forward, lifting his legs high to run toward us.

More people began to swarm from over the hill, from behind the houses atop it.

"You broke down the wall!" the man called back.

"You've been trapped out here?" Veshak asked, breathless, as we met the man at the base of the hill. "That's what you meant."

He nodded, reaching out to grasp Veshak's hand. "You mean to let us free? To join the kingdom after all this time?"

Thousands of bodies marched through the metal valley, moving toward the wall, reaching over each other to touch it. Scrap was thrown into the hole. Stones were thrown out.

"Whose orders kept you here? Why are you outside the walls?"

"The Baron Smith. We were trapped here after the war, and we had no means to travel to a different state or hire a ship."

"Who?" I asked.

He turned his red eyes on me, and the wrinkles around them caught a loose tear.

"We have no title as the humans in Raktam. We are not mantrik, or jagarving, or katalval. We fought against Eudo, to preserve the lands as the gods intended, and were cast out when the walls were erected. I came from Aatma, as did many others. Some from Jihva, or Kallu, or Ceyi."

The crowd surged forward around us, swarming faster up the hill and growing denser as we spoke.

Veshak shuddered. "You are responsible for refining the iron?"

The old man nodded. The people around us yelled and threw the rocks that had kept them out of the city, and others passed buckets of iron to the front, dumping it back to where it came from.

"Your people feed the navarin, which feed the kingdom?"

The old man nodded again and motioned around. "We feed the kingdom, we clean the ships, we trim the iron, and we have nowhere else to go."

I reached out a hand and placed it on the old man's shoulder, and Veshak dropped to a knee in front of him. "You will go into the kingdom, you will tear down the walls, and I will issue orders from the castle to get you whatever you need, after my ascension."

"Thank you, Your Highness."

"Dorian," Veshak lied.

The cries from the crowd were so loud we couldn't hear anything else the man said. He was swept away as people pressed in around us, and the crowd became suffocating. My skin felt as if it may peel away from my bones as they worked their way past. We were pulled along, and I watched as fingers tore at the stones; skin flayed against the grout and blood stained the dirt where it fell from cracked palms, desperate to reach the path beyond.

There was such a cacophony of sound from the carts of metal scrap being thrown back into the city, from the rumble of the wall crumbling away. Tools began to get passed forward. And dust and rock flew into the air, mixing with the smoke that still filled it.

Veshak and I watched in silence before he finally offered me his arm, and we turned away from the scene, trudging back toward the narrow road through the crumbling ruins.

"You told them you were Dorian, and that you would issue orders," I murmured.

"I had to," he said. "I'm their prince now. Who else will help?"

I thought about that as we walked, and of the valley full of metal pieces. Not rings, like in the gulf, but sharp shards of iron. Far more deadly to flesh. Could he really make a difference? And what if Dorian didn't care, when we released him?

My muscles screamed in protest as we walked, and I finally collapsed on the sand before the docks. Veshak fell down next to me, and air hissed through his teeth as the sand was stained pink beneath his fingers.

We could still hear the cries of people swarming the wall, and pride bubbled up in my chest.

"I can't believe that after everything it was the very residents in his own city that Eudo has been using to maintain power. To think that he chased his wife away and trapped others instead."

Veshak sat and pulled his knees to his chest, brushing clumps of sand from his fingers. "I hope they find a home."

A beat of silence passed between us.

"When was the last time you were home?" I asked. "Have you been since you set sail?"

He sighed. "No, and I miss my mother terribly, but since I took the ship, I also took the vow that if given the opportunity, I would kill her captor. We've docked in Paalaivanam, but I have not stepped foot in the Mahal."

I dug my hands into the sand and looked out over the sea.

I let the silence settle between us. A wave rolled over my toes, and he reached forward, rinsing his hands.

He licked the salty water from his fingertips, his narrow shoulders slumping forward.

"Are you okay?" he asked.

"I can't stop thinking about my father," I said, lifting my hands from the sand and picking grains from the wrinkles in my palms. "My sister had a proper burial. But my poor father was never granted the mercy of return to the sea."

Veshak stood suddenly and held a hand out. "The sun is about to set. It's the perfect time for us to visit the docks."

My heart twinged as I saw Barun's hands rise in the distance, still suspended in the air.

"Why?" I asked.

"No one deserves death like this, let alone a lost afterlife. Imagine if that navarin killed either of us."

My stomach dropped. "You mean to take him down?"

He swept his arms out on either side of himself and bowed low. "I am at your service, just as I am the rest of the kingdom."

I opened my mouth to protest, but he turned and continued walking to the dock.

"Barun must be released to the sea so that Rudra might escort his essence to a reincarnation," I rushed out, jogging to catch up.

"What law did he break?" he asked over his shoulder.

I lowered my voice as our boots clacked onto the salt-worn wood.

"He stole from Juhi after her death. You are not meant to touch the dead while rites are performed."

"That must have been very hard for you," Veshak said, turning and looking down into my eyes.

I said nothing, unsure how to respond. I remembered watching him do it, how the shame had curled like a finger in my belly, how I should have been banished too. The way Navya yelled out his crime.

My father was in the same position as when we landed. Bile rose in my throat, and tears pricked my eyes, but I forced myself to continue to look at him.

"What are you going to do?" I asked.

Veshak lifted his vest, revealing two long daggers. "I have to cut him down."

My jaw dropped as he slammed them into the wide pole, one on top of the other. His hands wrapped firmly around the handle of each curved blade, then he dislodged the right. He swung his body and reached his arm high to dig the blade into the pole, and repeated the motion with the left, using his feet to climb as well. I watched in awe as he wrapped his legs around the pillar, leveraging his weight and throwing himself to the top. He pulled another knife from behind his back to saw at the rope that bound Barun's wrist.

My father's left side was free in a moment, and I gasped in horror as he began to swing down.

My mouth gaped as the ropes fell and the dock dropped out underneath me. Barun hung half a meter away from the walk's edge, and Veshak would have to swing my father as he cut. Sweat gleamed on his brow in the moonlight as he worked. There was a loud snap, and I cried out. In fear? In anguish? I didn't know.

My father's body fell with a wet *thud* in front of me.

I tried to breathe in but the stench of death filled my lungs, and I fell to my knees. The cavern of his belly was blackened with mold; barnacles clung to the matted fur of his tail. I could taste his decayed flesh on my tongue, the sulfur of his half-consumed liver.

"Zara!" Veshak called, and a moment later, he was beside me.

I rolled toward the water and vomited.

It took a few long minutes to recover myself, but once I did, he was there with a canteen of water, which I sipped carefully.

"I didn't think he would be so..." I trailed off as I looked at Father from afar.

"Dead?" he asked.

"Consumed."

I couldn't even recognize my father's face. I knew it was him, with every fiber of my being. But he was not wholly Barun.

"What do we do?" Veshak asked, his voice gentle.

I sniffed and turned. "We must get him into the sea and face Paalaivanam. Give thanks to the gods and ask for them to guide him through the veil." I adjusted the cloth at my waist. "Normally flowers are affixed to the hair, but I have seen no padma maut here, so I must have faith that the gods will accept our intentions."

There was no hesitation as he stooped to pick Barun up from the ground. I opened my mouth, about to protest, or offer my help, but he jerked his chin toward the water. He looked small under my father's great form, and I rushed to the sand where we could step into the tide.

The sea was cold on my feet, far colder than it had ever felt before, and I was shivering before the water reached my knees. By my waist, I struggled to stand, but I watched Veshak march through the waves as if he could part them by force.

The salt stung the scrapes in my skin, but I ignored the pain, pushing forward.

We waded out until the waves were at our necks, and we had to spit foam out to speak. Barun floated in front of us, his face and belly barely above the water.

"Om namo Matsya," I said, teeth chattering together. Veshak looked at me before repeating the prayer.

"Om namo Rudra," I continued.

Veshak caught a passing piece of seaweed and offered it to me. I smiled half-heartedly and placed it in my father's hair. "Om shanti om."

"May Rudra guide you through the veil," I said. As he began to float away, my breath caught in my throat.

He should have never been out here. I should have fought for him. The way he floated, half decayed in the sea… It could have—should have—been me.

I worked my fingers through the knotted fabric at my waist, desperately trying to free myself from the anchor to my mother. It was wet and stuck together in the dusky light, and I began to panic as I couldn't work the knot loose.

I couldn't hold onto this stolen thing anymore.

Foam splashed my face, and I took a breath, plunging beneath the surface. Salt stung my eyes, and I blinked hard, trying to see my fingers. The water was filmy in front of me, and my lungs burned after only a few moments. My heel caught on a rock, and I lowered myself deeper into the wake, squinting through the bubbles that formed from my thrashing.

Finally, I could see the knot at my hip, and I slid a finger into the largest loop, yanking it free.

I kicked up, turning my face to the light above me, and gulped the air, coughing before swimming toward my father.

I dragged the black strip through the waves behind me and collapsed onto his hollow chest. "Take this to Mother," I begged, draping the cloth over his body.

Veshak dragged me back to shore and half carried me up the road toward the gates.

"Thank you," Veshak said, breaking the silence.

I turned to him, startled. "For what?"

"For allowing me to help with such an intimate task. For allowing me to experience your culture. For saving my life."

I twisted my fingers together, looking down at my shredded gown. Tiny scraps of iron had embedded themselves in the netting; the silk hem was coated in blood and nearly disintegrated. My skin was still raw and painful from where I had held on to the navarin.

I couldn't do this anymore.

I swallowed thickly. "I want to leave," I said.

"But the wedding?"

I shook my head. "I can't. You offered to leave before, and I am taking that offer now. Seeing those people, how deeply the corruption runs. I can't risk losing my life here and not seeing my sister again."

He nodded. The sky was beginning to lighten with moonlight, and my bones ached nearly as much as my soul.

"Okay. I will see what we can do. Imogene will know how to get us out of here."

I glanced over my shoulder long enough to see a flash of green pass over the horizon.

32

Dorian

WIND WHIPPED THE SAILS and saltwater stung my eyes. I swallowed down the sickness in my stomach and focused on the stars above, blurred by the pouring rain. Shouts from the crew were barely audible over the wood splintering around us.

I was huddled in the doorframe of the captain's cabin, unsure of where I belonged. I couldn't hide in the safety of Veshak's space, and I felt useless slinking below decks. I could not help the crew that desperately threw rigging about the rocking boat.

So I curled in on myself and watched the storm while Ward fought with the wheel.

"You'll drive us into the heart of the storm!" Cayde screamed, stomping toward him.

"Mind your place!" Ward called back, bracing an arm on the wheel spokes while Cayde tried to shove him away. He yelled commands to the crew that I didn't understand, and I swallowed, lowering myself further to the floor. The deck shifted hard underneath me, and I grimaced at the thought of dying on the sea.

"Drop the sails, batten the hatches!" Cayde yelled over the boom of thunder.

Ward shoved him back. "I'll lock you in the brig if you don't shut up." His voice was laced with such venom, even I shuddered.

"You would have us killed," Cayde yelled, pushing him away.

They collided in a flurry of fists. A spyglass fell from Cayde's belt, and Ward knocked the wheel into a wild spin, sending the brass piece rolling toward me.

I watched them grapple and lifted the glass to my eye, ignoring the roiling in my stomach and their screams at each other.

The horizon was stained with ink, and the sea drank hungrily from the sky, spitting foam back into the clouds.

I turned to the west, searching for Raktam, for some sign of home, and sucked in a breath.

"I believe there's a ship approaching," I said.

The men continued to fight, ignoring me, and I squinted at the ocean's surface. It was dark, but there was certainly a shining break in the sea.

"A ship approaches!" I called out, louder.

Ward stabbed a trident-shaped lever between the spokes and wrenched the glass from my hand.

"Shit," he mumbled, and thrust the glass at Cayde. "Prepare the men, the navy approaches."

I leaped to my feet and followed Ward. "The navy? How do you know?"

"Their belly is marked in iron, and the ship is too large to be anything else coming from the west." He turned on me with appraising eyes and hooked a thumb over his shoulder. "You might be going home sooner than you thought, Prince."

Something about his tone was unsettling, and I swallowed hard. Hands caught my wrists from behind, and a cloth was shoved in my mouth before I could protest.

"Throw him in the longboat," Ward ordered.

I looked around frantically for some escape, but large fingers pressed down on my hand, yanking my curls to guide me toward the same boat I had tried to escape on.

I was shoved into its now empty bottom, and my face smacked my knees before I fell backward.

A couple of oars were thrown over, and then Cayde came tumbling down beside me.

"Safe return," Ward said with a laugh as he began to lower the pulley.

I tried to protest, I tore the fabric from around my face, but the storm beat the belly of the ship at my side and muffled my cries anyway. Cayde hung his head on the seat opposite me, refusing to look up at Ward, who watched with wicked eyes as we floated away from him.

The wake of the galleon shoved us further into the storm, and my body was racked with shivers and my boots flooded with water as our dinghy spun through rivulets of foam.

"We're going to die out here," I muttered.

"No, we're not," Cayde said, picking up an oar and spearing it between the waves. "We're going to get picked up by that royal ship and rot in their prison. We'll die in Raktam."

I fixed the harsh linen shirt that scratched my collar and lifted the second oar, mimicking his movements.

"If they gather us, why would we be arrested? I am their prince."

The man-o'-war was gaining on us, growing closer by the minute, and I swallowed down the fear that we might be split in half by its bow.

"Because they already have their prince," Cayde said.

The broadside of the ship pulled alongside our tiny rowboat, and I grimaced as we sloshed to the side. We stood together, waving our arms and yelling.

"Help!"

A man dressed in a silver brocade coat, who proudly displayed the crest of Raktam upon his breast, waved.

A rope was thrown over the side of the ship, and I wrapped my arm in it. I began to climb, and my muscles burned from the effort. When I reached the rail, a multitude of hands grabbed me and hoisted me onto the deck, straightening me and brushing me off.

"Thank you. We thought we would die," I said as Cayde was pulled up beside me.

A sharp sting of pain erupted in my jaw. It took a moment to register that the captain had struck me, and my tongue darted between my teeth, seeking out the tang of blood as it pooled in the crevices of my mouth.

"Stop! What do you think you're doing?" I demanded as the naval recruits shoved me roughly to my knees and locked iron bars around my arms.

"Shut up, pirate," he spat at me, meanwhile gesturing at the rest of his crew. "Throw them in the brig."

"Stop this at once!" My command erupted from my belly like the roar of a volcano. "This is no way to treat your prince!" I tried to summon the void to my palms, to slam it into the captain, but the pain that accompanied the stars last time didn't come, and my eyes fell to my empty hands.

The captain's eyes widened a fraction of a centimeter as he studied me before sneering. "You're no prince."

"Who the fuck else would I be?" I mumbled before I was grabbed by the collar and dragged across the deck. The stormy sea slapped the ship, punctuating my words. "He is an impostor!" But no one listened.

I was shoved into a cell and did not bother trying to rise. The wood was cool against my skin, my clothes damp on my back, and a shiver racked my body. I studied the black knot in the plank beneath my face, the way it curled in and diverted like a scar. I wanted to press my nail between its grooves and further dig away and splinter the floor. To press the darkness that leaked from my skin into it and tear a hole into the ship and sink us all.

But what would that accomplish?

I would not make it home. My brother would still take my throne.

I closed my eyes and tasted hot starlight on my tongue, swallowing the sweet call of the void. I began to count backward and thought of Veshak. I wondered how he decided to take my place. What led him to steal my face?

Where did he come from?

The smell of acrid burning filled my nostrils, and I opened my eyes to see the knot in the wood filled with darkness. Finally, it poured out of me. I leaned over and pressed my face to the pool, breathing it in, blinking through the stars.

When I opened my eyes, I was falling through the sky. I reached out to grab onto something, anything, but only blue spanned on either side of me. I blinked, and everything looked different, grainy. The air was so hot, and the stars that had filled my vision were replaced by the pulsing beat of my heart.

I opened my mouth to scream, and a growl erupted from my chest, followed by a burst of flame. I moved my arms again and looked over to find large, bony wings stretched with tight flesh flapping, then holding steady to glide through the air.

My stomach dropped as I tumbled down, and I frantically tried to flap my arms, but to no avail; I—or we—were gliding downward. Mountains of sand stretched as far as I could see, and a great wave of it plumed around my clawed feet as I landed hard. A shiver ran down my spine as I stretched up and fell back into the warm sand. Nothing had ever felt quite as good as landing in this desert. But I quickly rose again—I came with a purpose.

A quick beat of my wings lifted me just over the sand, to glide along its surface and head east.

More winged beings gathered. Their great bodies stretched out in the sand, or buried in various positions, soaking up the warmth. Their translucent skin was stretched tightly over their bones, and their inner flame burned brightly through their chest. Sharp teeth poked out from their maws, and their eyes burned like suns in bulbous sockets.

I walked over a hill, swinging my tail to stay balanced, until a glint of gold caught my eye at the bottom of a valley. I craned my neck to the sky and shivered, pulling my wings into my back and arms and swallowing my flame until it fell to rest in my stomach.

I brushed the sand from my loose pants and turned to face the head of Prajapati, admiring him with awe. He had not changed in the centuries that he sat in the desert. His golden crown sat untarnished atop his head of curls. His dark skin was unblemished, and golden eyes were warm and welcoming. The only thing that would change about him was the patch of grass under his neck. It sprouted fresh daily, then died through the night, and would be replenished again.

I removed my shoes before falling to my knees and bowing my head. "Great Prajapati," I said in a voice deeper than my own. "I've come to seek your wisdom."

"Yes, young jagarving. You have an offering?"

I raised the coin he asked for toward him before stumbling forward. He opened his mouth, and I placed it on his tongue.

He chewed it thoughtfully for a moment, then his eyes went dark. I felt as if he looked directly through me. "He can only grow to take your throne."

I gasped as I opened my eyes to see the familiar walls of Castle Durling rising up in front of me. A guard banged on the cage I was cramped into, and he shouted, "Wake up, jackal. Time to march to the dungeon."

Hot starlight pooled in my palms. I would not stay in another jail, certainly not one in my own home.

33

ZARA

MY PALMS SMOOTHED OVER the engraved arms of my chair, and I curled my fingertips around them, sliding my nails into the ridges of its carved sides. I pulled at the seam of the cushion where it met the wood, then smoothed the silk edge over, marveling at the different textures.

A heavy purple curtain hung in front of me, but I still held my breath, careful not to make a sound as I leaned back and closed my eyes and relished the feel of this seat, the warmth of the small room, the smell of the long-dried flowers hanging from my belt.

I shifted in the seat and picked up the pastry I had brought with me. It had a golden flaky crust, and a servant had dolloped a heavy hand of jam atop a spread of cream. I had to fight the urge to bury my nose in the dough with how sweet it smelled, and I picked just a crumb from the side instead, marveling at how gently it gave way.

I would miss the food when we returned home. But nothing else.

My chest warmed, and I swallowed.

I would miss Veshak, too.

I took a bite, and muffled voices froze me in place.

"There are things I wish to do. I need change in this city," Veshak said.

"It is always some change with you. First you want to leave, then you come back, now you rush to take your crown. Tomorrow you won't want it again," Imogene replied.

I lowered the pastry from my mouth and leaned forward, careful not to let the chair creak.

"There are people dying out there!" he growled, then heaved a sigh. "I ordered Hastings to fund a new division of homes, and he laughed at me."

I recognized the pity in her voice. "No one will take your orders until you take the crown or your father passes."

The hair on the back of my neck rose as the weight of her words sunk in.

"We must hurry the wedding preparations along," Veshak urged.

A cold finger of dread curled in my chest.

"I told you that I would cancel the wedding." Her tone was cold. "You cannot even abide by the rules already in place."

"I am sorry for acting an ass, but I need the wedding moved up."

He wasn't going to take me home. He meant to betray me and force me into this marriage.

A beat of silence passed between them.

"Alright, then. I will send out the announcements."

I heard footsteps recede, and my cheeks burned. After helping all of those people break down their walls and flood the streets with iron. After laying my father to rest.

After agreeing to leave.

I threw my plate on the table and shoved the curtain aside, and a gasp slipped through my lips.

"Sky's above, dear!" Imogene threw her hands to her own mouth, stumbling back. "I didn't know that you were in there."

"I was having breakfast, alone," I said, anger simmering low in my stomach. My fingers trembled, and I gripped my skirts to hide my whitening knuckles.

The older woman looked over me and reached out a hand, but I stepped away before she could touch me.

"You are not my friend, so long as you serve *him*," I spat.

"I served the queen and only accepted Dorian's request to stay in order to watch over him."

I scoffed but said nothing.

"Shall we go to the seamstress?" she asked.

My chest burned with the laugh I choked over. "To confine me in a wedding gown?"

She frowned and closed the gap between us, reaching up and tucking a strand of my hair back. "To gather the clothing that I promised you, to make you more comfortable."

I swallowed hard but resisted the urge to smack her hand away.

"Because sometimes the best weapon a woman can have is the shield she places around her own body," she whispered. "And it does no one any good to hide in confined spaces feeling alone."

I finally nodded and took the arm that she offered.

A hand of guards waited outside as they always did, and when I tried to walk past them, they moved into a line in front of me.

"The city is no longer safe," one said, and I startled. I had never heard them speak before.

"We must insist that you ride in the carriage from now on."

"There are riots in the lower kingdom," Imogene explained as we climbed into the cart. "The outer wall was torn down, and they are moving inward."

I froze, unsure of how I should react, unsure of how much she knew.

"The seamstress is nearby, so there should be no concern of crossing into the invasion."

"That's good," I breathed.

She cocked her head. "Is it?"

I pursed my lips and turned to look out the window. For the first time since we had docked, the sun was shining, and the bright golden light revealed the vast iron skeleton of the city. I picked at the tiny scabs on the inside of my hands while our carriage rolled through the belly of the city, and rust flakes drifted through the air like molting navarin feathers.

The stones of the road were so dry when I stepped out of the carriage, I was shocked to see people sweeping the dirt from them. I looked down to study their shape and grimaced as I recognized the same shades of gray and blue I swam past every day in the sea. Tiny tulip and cockle shells were embedded in the dirt between the rocks.

Imogene tugged on my sleeve, and I looked back up to see her watching me. I pulled myself away from the patch of road I had been studying and followed her beneath a sign engraved with a spool of thread and needle.

A bell on the door clanged as we entered, and I was struck by the colors—every shade I could imagine lined the walls. Someone had captured the night and stitched it into a gown that hung from a woman's form in the window, with stars embedded in the midnight train. The sun rose through a skirt at the end of a rack, bleeding red and pink through its waistband.

I reached out and touched a black scarf, swirled with ivy. Its ends were dotted with gold, fusing into a mix of red floral patterns.

I lifted the silk to my nose and breathed deeply. The smell was intoxicating. This impossibly thin cloth was woven with layers of soft incense and oils from the fingers that had stitched it together, the mild scent of soap, and a hint of salt from the air outside.

"Do you want that?" Imogene asked.

I opened my eyes from where I had fallen into a trance with the colored cloth and nodded vigorously. "Very much, yes. It is divine."

She chuckled and held out a hand to take it.

"Hello!" a voice called out, and we turned together to face a woman, not much older than me, with hair plaited to the floor. She held out a short arm, reaching to wrap both of her warm hands around mine.

"Welcome, I am Subba," she said, smiling wide.

"Hello," I said. I could not help but return her smile.

"I understand that you don't like the dresses?" she asked, motioning to the one I wore.

It was another one pulled from the armoire, pale yellow and heavy. The top was laced too tight and dug into my ribs, and my muscles pulled when I walked. I thought of the purple one I had stashed in the back of the closet, with the shredded skirt and bloodstains.

"They look beautiful..." I said, lifting the skirt. "But are impractical for moving around. What if I must fight? Or defend myself? And the cloth is so hot!"

Subba raised a brow and glanced at Imogene, and I held my breath.

She laughed suddenly. "I like you. A queen should be ready to battle, you are right. Come," she said, turning to the back of the shop. "I have some clothing that I think you might prefer."

The cloth in the shop hung from ceiling to floor, on various metal poles suspended between thin ropes.

"Here we go," Subba said. "Can I help you undress?"

We turned into an alcove with a mirror. Imogene took one of the two seats, and I faced the mirror so that the seamstress could unlace the back of my dress. It fell to the floor with a thud, and I threw Imogene a pained look, noting her wide eyes, before beginning to untie the stays under my breasts as well.

"Oh, no, you can keep those on," Subba said.

I met her gaze in the mirror and pulled the tie free. "I am tired of being restricted. Please find me something that will allow me movement."

Imogene stood and patted her shoulder. "Something like Maryana's gown should do."

Subba nodded and pulled a curtain around us, and I let the undergarments fall atop the pile of fabric at my feet.

The woman pulled a long stretch from a shelf, holding it out in front of my waist. The color shifted from pale pink at one end to gold at the other. She wrapped it once, then again. Pinning the pink side with her finger to my hip, she folded it on itself over and over until she held a fistful of pleats, which she tucked in at my navel before pulling the gold end over my shoulder.

The hand-fastened skirt flared out at my ankles like fins, and for a moment, my reflection showed me as I should be.

"This is perfect," I said.

She nodded with a smile and produced a matching blouse. It slid through my fingers like silk and fell against my skin as gently as sunlight. There was no added weight, no sharp bones or metal, and no confinement.

"This is a type of saree that the queen wore in Aatma. I have many here, though most people find it too cold to wear them."

"It is exactly what I wanted."

"I will gather more, and some salwar trousers for you," she said, beaming.

Subba disappeared behind the curtain.

I smoothed my hands over the pleats of the skirt, touching the soft billows at my hips, and Imogene caught my fingers.

"What happened here?" she asked, turning my palm toward her face. She trailed her finger over the tiny cuts from the metal, and the larger ones from the navarin that had been covered by my sleeve.

My heart rate picked up, and my skin flushed, and I suddenly felt more naked than when I had dropped my dress.

"Where did you get these injuries, Zara?" she asked. I flinched at her use of my name. "They are fresh."

I wet my lips and whispered, "The outer kingdom."

Her eyes narrowed a fraction, and she released my arm.

"The navy captured the pirates that held you captive," Imogene said, her voice low.

I sucked in a sharp breath and dipped my head. "That's good," I said, trying to level the pitch in my voice.

"They were brought in early this morning, along with two that had been set adrift in a rowboat. The guards said that one looked like Dorian. So much so that they nearly believed his claims that he was the prince."

My mouth felt so dry as she spoke.

"You wouldn't know anything about that, would you, Zara?"

I fumbled for something to say, tried to cough a lie up from my throat. Nothing came out of my mouth except an unintelligible hum.

"Here we go," Subba said, pulling the curtain back. Her arms were laden with boxes and satchels stuffed full of clothes. "You can wear that one out, and I will have your footman load these into your carriage.

"Th-thank you," I stuttered, glancing between her and Imogene.

The stewardess stood and placed a hand on my back, so gentle, and said her thanks to the seamstress as she led me from the shop.

"What are you going to do?" I asked once we were locked into the carriage together.

She leaned her head back against the seat, the iron crests on either side of her ears looking like adornments for her hair. "Who said that I needed to do anything?"

34

Veshak

The sounds of ceramic scraping mingled with the smell of roast chickpea and cod, fried egg, and spiced tomato sauce. I glanced up at Zara, who sat at the opposite end of a long table, and she glared into her lap. I stabbed at the fish on my plate, and I scooped the bite up, looking at it, then her.

"I like your dress," I said.

The only response was the clink of her knife against porcelain.

I had tried to speak to her when she returned to the castle, but she'd ignored me then. She had ignored me at lunch. She'd kept her mouth closed when Imogene brought our wedding banquet menu to us. She had not spared me a look when we crossed each other in the gardens.

A line of servants, maids, and guards stood on each wall of the dining room, unmoving and more silent than the night outside. Great dishes piled high with cakes and fruit separated us, and I cleared my throat.

"How is your meal?" I called across the room.

She did not answer, and I waited a long moment before scraping my chair back and standing.

One of the servants in a pale-gray tunic stepped forward, but I waved my hand and looked over the pile of nonsense to Zara. She dropped her fork and startled at my gaze.

"How is your dinner?" I asked again.

She stood as well, slamming down her silverware. "It tastes of sand."

My mouth went dry, and I pushed my chair back, moving toward her. "Zara..."

"Don't," she snapped. "Don't try to pretend like you care."

"What are you talking about?" I asked. "I have tried all day to speak to you!"

Her mouth twisted down, and she bared her teeth. "You said we would leave!" Her voice wavered, her face reddened, and my heart thumped in my chest. "I heard you with Imogene. I told you that I can't do this anymore."

My jaw dropped, and I let my fork fall to the plate. "Zara, I—"

"You what?" The venom in her voice stung, and the air thickened with tension. My mind raced.

I looked around the room at the servants and raised a hand. "Leave us be," I commanded, and she scoffed.

"Don't bother. *I* will leave."

She turned from the room, and I chased after her, letting the dining room door fall shut with a bang behind us.

"Wait, please just listen!" I begged.

She spun on me in the narrow hallway, fury in her eyes, and jabbed a finger at my chest.

"I have listened to you! I have listened since you pulled me from the sea. I listened when you told me your plan to benefit us both, when you offered me a way out, and then when you betrayed my trust. I am done listening."

I looked around frantically, hoping that no one could hear her. That she would not say the wrong thing. I stepped close to her and spoke low. "I never meant to hurt you. I will keep my promises, but I need the crown to do so."

A mirthless laugh erupted from her, and she threw her head back. "You do not need the crown to kill Eudo."

The tap of metal on stone clicked through the air, and I looked past her to see Hastings strolling toward us. His cane clicked too loudly on the sliver of floor that was uncarpeted, and a woman that I didn't recognize walked with him.

"Zara!" I hissed, and grabbed her arm. I yanked her into the nearest room. The lock clicked softly, and the sound of the duke's cane faded.

Great windows covered the walls and ceilings, letting the warm evening sun in, and I briefly wondered how we had missed this room before. Plants lined the floor and shelves around us, but couches dotted the space.

I turned and pinned her to the door, my arms locked on either side of her head. Her chest heaved from her anger, and I looked over her face. The wrinkle notched between her brows. The flare of her nostrils. Her lip tugged back over her bared teeth.

"I cannot do it," I whispered, turning away and releasing her.

"What do you mean?" Her voice had softened.

"I saw Eudo. I already tried to kill him, but I am too weak."

I felt her fingers wrap around my wrist, and I turned to find her dark eyes searching for some answer in mine.

"I don't understand. Help me to understand."

I sighed and fell heavily into one of the plush chairs, gazing up through the glass. "Eudo can't move. His body is so frail. I raised my dagger, and when I had the opportunity... I froze."

"That is all you came here for," she murmured.

"I know. All I want is to make a great enough impact. I tried at home, and I was told that it was not my role. I tried here, but this is not my place to change. I tried for my mother, but I am too weak to kill the man that hurt her." My head fell into my hands.

Zara's fingers touched my cheek, and she leaned down, pressing her mouth on the top of my hair. "You are not weak. You are strong. It takes strength not to kill a broken man."

I looked up. Her face had softened, her eyes warmed.

"Promise me that we will leave," she said. "Promise that it will be as soon as possible, and you will tell me what hinders our plans."

I touched the back of her hand and said, "I promise."

Zara leaned down, her hand still cupping my face, and pressed her soft mouth to mine. My fingers found her waist, thumb grazing her bare skin. She kissed me hard, her lips parted, and I caught her moan with my tongue, sliding it against hers. Her bottom lip gave way to my teeth. The longing I had felt for her since we met crashed down around me, and I was suddenly drowning in the feel of her.

She lifted her skirt and swung a leg over my lap, deepening our kiss as her knees pressed into my hips. I stroked my fingers down the river of her spine, and she shivered under my touch. I pressed my body into hers, drinking in the taste of her tongue on mine. Reached for her chin, licking over her bottom lip, up her cheek, to her ear.

"I want to taste every part of you," I moaned. "I crave you."

I pulled her chin back down, and her teeth enveloped my bottom lip, sucking, before she rose up and let a drip of her saliva fall to my tongue.

She pressed down harder onto me and slid the cloth from over her shoulder. "Untie me," she gasped.

I obliged, reaching up behind her neck and feeling for the strings of her blouse.

She pressed her face into my chest, inhaling deeply before kissing my collarbone, my neck, my shoulder.

The pink silk fell away to reveal her naked breasts, cast in golden light from the setting sun, and the flames inside of me roiled at the sight of her above me.

"Zara..." I said, leaning in and kissing the space between her ribs. Her skin was soft and smelled of sand. "I believe you are a goddess," I breathed. I wrapped my hands around her, pulling one nipple into my mouth.

Her head fell back and I felt her moan through my throat, and I let out a hum of appreciation in response. I flicked my tongue over the soft bud, sucking as the heat traveled from my chest down between my legs.

I cupped her other breast, turning to drag my flattened tongue over it. "Your skin is like sugar," I whispered, biting her gently before kissing a trail over her chest, around her breasts, down her ribs.

Her fingers worked through the ties of my shirt, and she shoved it back off of my chest. Her hands lowered over the wrap, but she did not try to remove it. She caressed the cloth as if it were a part of me, gliding her fingertips up and over, touching the bare part of my skin.

I lifted her gently off of my lap to stand, then knelt to the ground before her. She was radiant against the waning light, her hair cascading around her shoulders, her brown eyes alight like I had never seen them before.

I kissed through the fine hairs on her stomach and stroked the line where her belly met her hips. She shivered when my fingers found the edge of her skirt, right at the top of her pubic bone.

It came away with a gentle tug.

"Sky's above," I said, touching her hips, dragging my fingers down her legs. I kissed everywhere I touched, gliding my tongue over the soft spots of her skin, down to her ankles. I gripped her calves and pressed my nose into the patch of hair between her thighs and inhaled deeply, savoring her scent.

"Let this be my last meal," I begged.

She moaned in response and lifted a leg, wrapping it around my shoulder, and I leaned deeper into her, flicking my tongue to the wetness that waited for me.

"Please, Veshak."

A quiet gasp slipped through her lips, and I fell back to the ground, pulling her over me me. My tongue slipped into her, and she squeezed her thighs around my head. She writhed atop me, moving in rhythm to the stroke of my tongue, her moans filling the air.

I felt her turn, and her hand reached back and pressed into my stomach, the flames that waited inside me heating under her touch.

My muscles tensed as her fingers slid under the waist of my pants, but she wrapped the fingers of her other hand into my curls. A soft touch, a reminder of our morning in the woods.

I licked over her clit and groaned my approval before sliding my tongue inside her. Her gasp made my cock throb between my legs, and her gentle touch grazed over it, sending a thrill through me. She pinched my head between her fingers, stroking me up and down before dipping down into the pool that had leaked from me.

I flattened my tongue over her clitoris, pressing my face farther into her, moaning as she swiped that heady need back over me and used it to massage in a circle.

She cupped her fingers around me and pressed in, and I groaned at how good it felt to be touched. To feel wanted like this.

"Please," I begged against her flesh.

Her moans filled my ears, and her wet need slicked my face and chest. Her fingers worked faster and faster around my cock, slipping inside me when I licked her. We mimicked each other's patterns and echoed each other's cries.

As I tried to pull away, to warn her that if she continued I would come, she pulled my head harder into her and called out my name.

I came undone underneath her, shaking violently and pulsing under her palm. She fell forward and rolled, and we lay like that for a long moment, with my cheek pressed to her warm, sticky belly and her hand tangled in my hair.

The moon rose over us in the glass room. Crickets sang loudly somewhere nearby. It was the first time I had heard them in Raktam, and I hadn't known they lived so close to the beach. The windows fogged with dew, the day-blooming flowers turned in on themselves, and I began to doze off.

"Veshak," Zara said, scooting her body down to lay next to me.

"Zara," I replied, eyes closed with bliss.

"How will we leave?" she asked.

I opened my eyes and looked up at her. She still lay next to me, her naked body bathed in moonlight. Her stomach pressed against my chest, and her breasts fell to one side. She laid a leg over mine, and I smiled, pressing a kiss to her shoulder.

"After weddings, there are honeymoons. If you can wait until then, there will be a ship to take us on a trip. I can try and arrange one before, but with the wedding and ascension so close, I'm not sure how feasible it is."

She chewed on her lip and nodded slowly. "What does this wedding mean for us? For the future?"

I leaned up on my side, propping an arm under my head, and placed a hand on her hip.

"It can mean anything you want. I will also swear any vows to you that you would like. I will be your partner in all things—treason, quests, and schemes included—until the end of time. Or if you would rather think of it as a task we must do to escape, that is fine too."

I raised her hand to my lips and pressed a kiss to her fingertips. They tasted like both of us, and I smiled. "I hope the whole court saw us through those windows, to witness my devotion to you. I was yours the moment I laid eyes on you."

35

Zara

Dawn broke and poured sunlight over the kingdom. I lay back on the plush bed, staring at the embroidered tapestry hanging above it.

It depicted a woman and a man, standing together over a crowd of people. The people held aloft fruits and baskets of bread and animals that curled up to fit into their fists.

I pulled the soft quilt to my chin, curling into the feather pillow, and savored the feel of the bed. It was the first time since we had arrived that I truly let myself enjoy this comfort. And now we would be leaving it. I would be going home.

A pang twisted in my gut. Something between longing and regret, confusion and also pain.

I had seen things I never would have had I stayed in the sea. I had learned so much and experienced so many wonders. I would miss the flowers that bloomed from Imogene's fingertips. The rainbow in the water fountain. The food. I would miss the food so much.

I would miss the feel of Veshak wrapped around my body. His hands, his lips, the scent of him. I lowered my hand, brushing it over where he had rested on my stomach.

I wondered if Navya could give him a tail so that he could stay with me, but I shook the thought away. He had to return to his own family.

A sharp rap of knuckles sounded on the door, and I sat up as Imogene let herself in, followed by a few servants.

I met her gaze, and my pulse quickened as I remembered that she knew what I had done to the walls.

"It is time to prepare for your wedding breakfast," she said, her voice cheery.

I threw back the blanket and rose, smoothing my nightgown against my hips.

A saree was laid out on the bed, red with gold edges, and a tray of tea and fruit set on the table.

Imogene waited while I tried to wrap my own skirt, but the pleats fell all wrong, so she stepped in to help.

I sat in front of the vanity while she combed my hair, then plaited it.

"I brought in flowers from the garden," she said, pulling a bundle from her apron.

"Thank you."

I watched her as she tucked the blooms into the crevices of my braid. My hair became thick and heavy, the white and yellow petals building a ladder to the crown of my head.

She left me watching myself in the vanity mirror until I felt hands touching my shoulders. I jumped from my chair, spinning to see Veshak smiling at me.

"I knocked," he said.

I touched my palm to my chest and swallowed. "I didn't hear you."

"That is okay. I only wanted to bring you a gift."

Veshak knelt down. He took one of my bare feet in his hands, smoothing his thumb over the arch and squeezing my toes. "I wanted to give you something for this important day. It may not be a true wedding, but I want you to know how much I care for you."

He pulled a pouch from his belt and emptied it into his palm, revealing two polished, gold anklets. They were set with emeralds and rubies, and I gasped at the way the light sparkled against their surface.

He placed my heel on his knee and unclasped one chain. "I belong," he murmured, clicking the jewelry into place around my ankle.

He lifted my other foot and stroked the top of it before securing the chain around it. "To you," he said, rising up onto his knees in front of me.

I gathered his face in my hands and kissed him, closing my eyes and enjoying the gentle touch of his lips.

"And I to you," I said. "They are beautiful."

He didn't move from the floor, and I stood, looking down at him.

"Did you kneel before Imogene like this? To beg for the wedding?" I asked, joking.

He wrapped his hands around my ankles, his warm fingers sliding beneath cool gold, and a moan slipped through my lips. He leaned down, pressing his mouth to the inside of each leg before sitting up. "I will only kneel before you, goddess," he said with a smile.

Bells began to chime in the distance, and he rose from the floor. "I guess that is our cue. It's time to get married."

The garden had been set with rows of tables with golden linens. Chairs were wrapped in yellow and white bows, and vases of daisies sat by every place setting.

Raktam residents were filtering in, greeting each other, greeting the advisors. I watched as women touched each other's arms in gentle displays of affection. Men clinked glasses and nudged elbows. People picked seats next to each other, quick to switch the placards that had their names on them in favor of a friend.

More bells tolled, and a line of servants emerged from the castle, large silver platters clutched in their hands.

I turned and glanced at Hari as he stepped up beside me. "Weddings are a big deal here. Especially royal ones. You should both go take your seat."

Veshak clapped his shoulder and thanked him, and I followed him to a smaller table at the end of the garden.

Music hummed through the air from the stringed instruments, and a smile tugged at my lips. People bowed and curtsied as we passed. Even Hastings looked less miserable than normal, with Imogene hanging on his arm. The breakfast guests were dressed in an array of colors, and when I spun around to sit, they reminded me of the coral reef.

Veshak lifted a glass of wine toward me, and I raised my own. "To our successful, though temporary, occupation of Raktam," he said, voice covered by the chatter from the growing crowd.

I smiled and watched a tiny spotted bug fly in close, landing in his mess of curls. He reached out a hand and stroked the end of my braid, and smiled, pinching a flower between his fingertips.

"Stop!" someone yelled.

Time froze as I looked at the soft yellow petals of the flower clasped in Veshak's hand. The music grated to a halt, and voices fell away. I turned to find the source of the yelling.

Dorian stood atop the garden steps, fury etched into his face. Iron stained his clothes, and a half-melted cuff clung to one of his wrists.

He pointed a trembling hand at Veshak, tripping down the stairs toward us. "Somebody arrest that impostor!"

Nobody moved, but a flurry of questions broke out through the crowd.

"Who is that?"

"What happened?"

"Where did he come from?"

Dorian shoved his way through the crowd, snapping at a man who refused to step aside, and approached our breakfast table. He studied me, disgust twisting his features. Veshak raised his arm between us, as if he could shield me from the spite in this man's glare.

"I do not care to kill you," Dorian said, stepping close to me. I lifted a hand to my throat, and the memory of his fingers around my neck washed over me. Who could enlist royalty to perform such an errand? I was no one to these people. I had come to accomplish my own task.

"But your friends have threatened my throne twice over now, and I want what is mine."

"Leave her be," Veshak warned, stepping around the table to stand in front of me.

Dorian glanced at him, eyes widening a fraction, before looking back to me.

"You have no say in this, Veshak."

Hari moved toward us then, standing at my side.

"She will do you no harm. The pirates saved her life, it is cruel to threaten it now."

"We can find a solution," Orion agreed, stepping up to my other side.

"I was going to release you," Veshak murmured. "After this wedding, we were leaving."

Dorian took a step back, looking over all of us, eyes searching Veshak's, then Hari's face.

"You two don't know how to treat your family."

He shoved Veshak back and yanked his sword free, swinging it around toward Orion, who took a step back.

Pressure dug under my chin, and he lifted my face with the tip of his blade to look him in the eye. "I am sorry for this, but if I don't kill you, she will take my throne."

My mind raced. "I don't know who 'she' is," I said.

The duke caught my attention from the corner of my eye, stepping sideways toward Dorian, while Imogene narrowed her eyes, looking over the scene and fixing her glare on me. Dread pooled in my gut. Something had gone very wrong.

Veshak leaped forward then, shoving back at Dorian and wrestling him to the ground. They grappled and rolled, each trying to gain a hold of the sword. Bile rose in my throat as they struggled. Finally, Veshak stood, the sword clutched in his fists and pointed at Dorian.

"I do not want to kill you, brother. Please, concede."

Hastings ran forward, Imogene at his heels. "Leave the prince!"

The woman shoved past him and screamed, "Get up, Dorian! Kill her!"

I looked at her, startled. She was the one who wanted me dead?

Veshak did not move his blade from Dorian's neck. "Release him," Hastings commanded. "You're an impostor and have been caught!"

The brothers stared at each other, and Veshak commanded to the air, "Go and get Eudo. He will recognize me."

"Enough of this!" Imogene screamed.

I leaped back as her sleek bun fell away, lengthening and turning black; her eyes darkened, her skin sunk in and paled, and her nails sharpened. She grew in size as she stomped toward us, towering over me, as if she had tied two chairs to her feet.

She slammed a hand against Veshak's chest, throwing him back through the air. I gasped as he fell onto our breakfast table and did not get up. Screams cracked through the air from some guests, and retreating heels clicked along the stone, toward the castle.

I looked back as Navya's grin spread across the woman's face, and my stomach dropped. Imogene wasn't Imogene. She was the mantrik that had taken my tail.

"Navya?" I asked. "Why would you do this?"

"To take the throne, of course!" she cried out. "The king dies, I marry the duke, I become queen, happily ever after, the end," she gushed.

I looked around at the fleeing wedding guests, their pastel skirts clutched in their hands and hats pressed firmly to their heads.

"And what about the duke's wife?" I asked, looking at the duchess across the yard.

"Easy," Navya said. She made eye contact with the woman and waved her hand through the air, fingers wriggling. I watched the duchess stand from her seat across the lawn. Her pale-green dress crumpled as if someone had wrapped their fingers around it, and her head snapped to the right before her body fell with a *thud* to the ground.

I stifled a gasp. I shouldn't have been surprised, but something about seeing her snuff out a life like the flame of a lantern sent shivers down my spine.

I took a step back, and another, and turned and ran through the garden, weaving between bushes.

Navya's disconcerting laugh filled the air, and I shuddered. The bush I crouched behind wasn't very dense. I could make out her figure through its twig branches. The way her body continued to grow in size and tentacles slithered out from underneath her skirt, stretching out through the manicured grass and snaking around bodies as if she could smell what she was looking for. The way she picked up Veshak's discarded sword and flung it around as if people would just run into it.

"Come out, come out, Zara!" Navya cooed. "I need you to play nice so I can have your throne too."

Hari and Orion were still so close to her, my heart thudded in my throat when she slashed her blade down and Orion narrowly avoided the blow.

"Get up, Veshak," I whispered through the leaves. I cursed myself for not thinking to don some type of weapon in the morning, for not looking to the future when we had faced so many dangers already.

Navya lifted a tentacle, and it thumped down over the gazebo where the band had played. The splinter of the wood and shattering of stone tiles raised the hair on my arms, and I crouched further into the grass.

She turned away, facing the castle, and began to move toward it. "Dorian," she called, "you better bring her body forward or I will start crushing everyone you love."

I watched her slither away, her tentacles slapping wetly over the grass, twisting around bodies as she swung her head this way and that.

No one was dropping dead, like the duchess had. Some people got knocked down, but they scrambled up again quickly and ran for the castle.

And then I remembered the day she took my tail.

Look into my eyes.

She needed the eye contact to manipulate our bones.

I ran out from behind the bush and lifted a broken branch from the ground, hefting it over my shoulder like a spear. I rushed toward her, grunting from the weight of the wooden shaft in my arms.

Pointing the splintered end to her kraken-like bottom, I stabbed it as hard as I could into her slimy, writhing flesh.

She screamed, spinning to face me, and one of the thick tentacles knocked me back. The air left my lungs and darkness encroached on my vision when I hit the ground.

"Zara!" Hari yelled.

I saw him above me, two of his faces floating.

"Are you okay?" Orion asked nearby.

"She has to look in our eyes to change us," I gasped, moving to sit up. Hari ran away, lifting his sword and turning his head down. The wedding guests that remained had taken cover under their chairs or behind bushes. Orion left my side, swearing.

A flood of guards poured into the garden from the castle gates, joining the fight against the monster that Navya had become.

Spiked bones unsheathed themselves from her skin, and she leaped toward Dorian with daggers for nails. She slung barbs from her arms into the confused men around her and knocked them down as easily as pachisi pieces.

I ran across the garden while she was distracted, blinking in surprise as I passed Cayde, who was locked in combat with Hastings.

Veshak was staggering to his feet when I fell down beside him.

"Who's battling whom?"

"I'm not sure anymore, but we need to get out of here," I said, wrapping my arm around his shoulders.

Before we could escape the shadow of the broken table, Navya let out a screech from across the garden.

"You!" she screamed, pointing a twisted finger at me. New pricks erupted from her forearms and crown. "I'll have your heart with or without the throne!"

I stood from my hiding spot, pulse thundering in my ears, and yanked a sword from Veshak's back. The sound it made upon being drawn was reminiscent of the sea bird's caw, and I took a deep breath as I stepped forward.

"Come kill me, then," I bellowed, with more courage than I truly felt.

Veshak ran up as Navya flung her fist toward me. "No!" he yelled, and flames sputtered all around.

I lifted my weapon, expecting to swing at Navya's spikes, but instead found myself trapped in a ring of flame. The projectiles sizzled as they met the wall, and I found Veshak's eyes on the other side of wavering heat.

Navya let out a scream of frustration, turning back on the guards that swarmed her.

"What did you do?" I asked, looking at the circle around me. The fire reached my shoulders, and there was no way I could escape it.

His eyes were pleading before he turned to face Navya.

Rage redefined her features, and she lifted her arms above her head. Her fingers knit together, and she pointed them to the sky. As she swung her arms down, her hands transformed into the head of a scythe. The gut-wrenching scream she released melded with the whoosh of the blade as it swiped through the air.

Dorian raised his blade toward Navya. Veshak stepped up beside him, and I knelt behind the flames, assessing how to escape, with my own sword ready.

36

Dorian

Veshak stood at my side, and I lifted my sword, letting the pain of burning stars flood my skin and envelop my blade. A wall of ink formed between me and the monster that was Imogene, and a guttural roar broke the air around us, followed by the sound of tearing.

My heart stuttered in my chest, as I thought the sound came from me, but I looked around as screams of fear and surprise tumbled over each other.

Long leathery wings tore themselves from Veshak's back. He rose up on clawed feet, and talons unsheathed from his hands. His face stretched and jaw unhinged into a razor-lined maw, spitting fire into the sky. He swung his now massive head around and fixed his beady golden eye on me before flapping his wings. The sound was like a sail tearing through the sea air, and fire poured from his mouth as he shot upward into the sky.

One of Imogene's tentacles wrapped around my blade, and I squeezed my hand around its hilt. The blood in my veins heated and the muscles in my arms screamed with effort as we battled over my sword. She pulled hard, and my thumb popped.

A string of curses flew from my mouth as I was thrown back, crashing into a set of chairs. Splintered wood and dust filled the air around me, and I coughed, forcing myself to blink the debris from my vision and stand.

"She will suffer," the Imogene-monster hissed, slithering toward Zara.

I sprung forward, gathering a broken piece of wood in my arms, but a scream from the left caused me to falter.

Hari was caught in the rubble of the gazebo by her tentacles.

"NO!" I screamed, turning to run toward him.

His shrill scream beat my eardrums as her spears twisted through his stomach, and my heart shattered.

I stabbed my blade into the limb that held him. She yanked me back, away from Hari, and flicked me away like a fly.

The ground spun and air taunted me, kissing my lips, but I could not inhale. Stars speckled my vision as darkness tinged the sky. It was Hari's next scream that allowed me to fill my lungs, and I bounded upward from the ground, staggering toward him.

He was still pinned against the wall, and both of his legs were twisted upward at an odd angle. He cried in earnest. I stumbled toward him, an arm outstretched. As I felt along the ground for anything to use against Imogene, my vision cleared, and I heard a battle cry.

Orion bolted between me and Hari, slicing through the tentacle and lopping it clean off. The monster screamed and fell back, letting Hari slide down the wall as Orion ran to his side and held him, yelling for Felix.

I fell to my knees and surveyed the garden. Dozens of guards lay in the grass, blood pooled around them. Cayde leaned against a far sculpture, a wound in his side. Hari cried with a red face, his stomach torn open, and Veshak flew overhead, snapping at the monster's face.

My fingers curled around a dagger in the grass, and I launched myself toward her.

The Imogene-monster arched her back, the tentacles around her quivered, and her bones began to ripple along her spine.

"Die!" Zara screamed. She threw herself forward, through the sputtering wall of flame, and heaved her blade into the soft part between the beast's tentacles.

Veshak dove down, spewing fire into her face and sinking his talons into her stomach.

With a clear shot of her back, I sprinted toward her. But as I reached up, ready to sink the short blade into her skin, I realized that stabbing her would do nothing. We had been throwing everything at her, but she was still able to transform unscathed.

I lunged forward, diving to the side at the last second for a writhing tail of scales that still had not finished moving, and stuck my knife deep into her muscle. She let out a surprised cry, and I called forth a surge of stars onto my skin. Darkness filled my vision as I let the void fill every crevice of my body and urged it to overtake her.

I screamed from the pain of summoning the void. She screamed as inky tendrils wrapped around our bodies. The earth quaked, and the ground opened up beneath us. My skin burned with the effort of clinging to her, of feeling every tear between our world and the darkness I shoved her into.

"Rudra!" I begged through the tear, and the pitch black reached up and sucked us both in.

We landed hard, and I yanked my dagger free of her skin and looked around. The last star floated from my finger to a crevice in the air behind us.

Black clouds roiled overhead, thick and threatening, and thunder boomed in the distance. The field at my feet was barren, the dirt dry and spotted with tufts of dead grass and a path that led to a crumbling stone wall.

The monster that was not Imogene stumbled back, her newly split snake tail writhing under her. Fury twisted her features, but when she tried to move toward me, her body twitched.

As quickly as she'd healed earlier, her previous wounds opened up. Gashes tore themselves along her arms, her scales receded and left her standing on two legs, and her calf was left hanging free from her leg. Her cry filled the air as blood poured from her stomach.

"What have you done?" she cried out.

Before I could answer, a booming voice from above echoed around us. "Your soul will be sorted once your body has found its death. Welcome to Underworld."

My stomach turned, and I stepped away from her decaying body. Her cries of pain and anger cracked through the air, and I ran toward the small rift of stars we had entered through.

Something stung my back as I touched the edge of the rift, and I spun to see her swinging spiked arms toward me. Thorns the length and thickness of my fingers flew through the air, and I ducked as one whizzed past my ear.

"I told you I would kill you!" she cried out, her voice stunted as her throat began to disintegrate under burned flesh. She crawled along the ground anyway, pulling herself forward with withering hands.

My shoulder protested as I raised my arm, and I stumbled backward, feeling along the ground. My fingers wrapped around the sharp edge of a rock, and I flung it as hard as I could toward her. Pain shot through my arm as the rock tumbled through the air and hit her square in the head with a *thwack*.

She fell to the side, finally unable to chase me, and I reached for the stars once more before the guilt of killing my stewardess could wrench my stomach.

Pure darkness spotted by billions of stars surrounded me. The space was devoid of sound and scent. The air felt cold as it filled my lungs, but familiar against my fingertips. I closed my eyes, finding no difference in what lay behind my lids, and let the knots in my body ease. I might have floated there for a thousand years, or only a second, before I wondered about the state of the castle gardens.

I reached out, feeling for the seam between this realm and mine, and slipped into the salty air.

The screams from the courtiers had died down to whimpers, but the cries and quiet reassurances were not much better. My body sagged in on itself, and it took more energy than I could muster to stay upright. I staggered into the grass and fell against a pillar of the fallen gazebo, gripping the rail to keep myself upright.

The duke's grating voice called out from across the courtyard.

"You don't belong here!" he spat, descending on me. He scurried across the gardens, yanking a sword that had been embedded in the ground.

"I thought you died, old bastard," I mumbled, swaying on my feet.

The blood-smeared blade glinted in the afternoon light as he pointed the tip at me.

"Seize him!" the duke screamed, barely moving on bleeding legs. He motioned between me and Veshak, who knelt behind me. "Both of them."

Thirty men circled behind the duke, and the smug look on his face was sickening. His nose wrinkled and the corner of his mouth lifted as he motioned at me once more.

The guard behind him did not move, and he spun on them. "Come on, then, get going!" he yelled.

Eudo's creaky voice filled the air, breathless but commanding. "Leave that boy alone." He stood at the top of the gardens, body swaying.

The duke let out a cry of anger and lifted his sword, swinging it high. Veshak leaped forward, shoving me back, and I cried out as the blade fell.

It did not strike.

Four teal-clad men grappled with the duke, arms wrapped around his, hands covering his mouth and working to yank him back.

"Take him to a cell," Eudo commanded. His shoulders were hunched, his neck covered in blackened bruises, and he descended the steps slowly.

"Where is your wife, my boy?" he asked, voice barely audible. "I was told that the wedding was today."

I looked over the garden, at the destruction that had taken over. Tables lay in broken pieces, bushes were smashed, and flowers shredded. The gazebo had collapsed, and a ring of ash surrounded what would have been an altar.

"I have no wife," I said.

"Then, who is that being held by another man?" He pointed to Zara and took a step toward her.

Veshak's arms tightened around the woman, and I pressed a hand to my father's shoulder.

"No one. I won't be taking a wife. Just the crown."

Eudo barked a laugh, falling into a fit of coughs, and he tumbled forward into my arms. I dropped to my knees and lowered him to the ground.

"I have not fought to stay alive so long, only for you to dishonor me so," he moaned.

"Why is it so important that I marry?"

Eudo's chest rose and fell heavily in my arms, and I studied him as his skin paled. The wrinkles in his face cut deep rivers for sweat to drip away, and thick stubble patched his jaw. His eyes fogged as he blinked slowly at me.

His fingers trembled as he lifted his hand, and I gritted my teeth against his brazen touch on my stubbled cheek.

"Why, Eudo?"

He sucked in deeply, and the rattling breath forced a cough to rumble through his body before he could answer.

He choked against the effort of speaking. "It was the only request your mother made before we wed. Magic follows the matriarchy."

My stomach dropped, and he coughed out another breath and gripped the collar of my jacket. "You must swear, Dorian, that you'll remember her." His voice was pleading and his eyes wide.

He had to know how wrong he was, but he pulled me down harder with strength only Rudra could have lent him. "You must carve your own path now, as ruler."

I froze, fingers trembling where they held him, and leaned back farther.

A coughing fit overtook Eudo, and his body shook violently. I dug my fingers into his back, holding him as upright as I could as the fit wrenched blood from his throat.

There was a sick irony in his pleas for me to remember my mother as I had begged of him when I was young. I wondered, as he died in my arms, if this was a last trick, if there was some secret law that I was not privy to. If I would sit on the throne.

As he trembled in my arms, I was struck with the urge to find some words of comfort, some reassurance that he would find peace beyond the veil.

The memory of Imogene's rapidly decaying body in the middle of the dark field surfaced in my mind, and my stomach turned.

If Rudra willed his death, then so be it. I would not interfere.

I swallowed hard and studied the deep wrinkles around his eyes.

"Mother is alive, and I will see her again," I finally said. "Free of you."

His cough subsided, his eyes widened, and before I could force any words of warmth from my mouth, his chest fell and did not rise again.

His sweat-soaked head lay heavy on my lap until the sounds of the crowd around me broke the spell of his death. Hari's voice was an anchor through the din, and I laid my father on the ground as gently as I could, releasing him to the dirt where I was sure some courtiers would care for his body. I followed my best friend's voice blindly through the crowd, which pressed together hungrily to get a good look at their fallen king.

His calloused fingers found mine before his golden eyes.

"Are you well?" he asked, breathless and hunched to one side.

I nodded, unable to form a sentence, or even a word, as I grappled mentally before throwing my arms around him. I could not hold myself away from his touch another moment, from the familiar embrace of my closest friend. No matter what rift might grow between us, I needed him like the sea needed the sky.

Tears stung the backs of my eyes and grief burned my nostrils, but he gripped my back tight, and we slumped over one another. The branches of a guava bush cushioned us and tall grasses wrapped around our legs, and I let my tears fall freely as I laid the burden of the day onto the blood-soaked grounds at our feet.

Eventually, the chatter stopped, the footsteps ceased, and a gentle hand pressed into my collarbone.

"Your Majesty?" a fair voice spoke, and I looked up from Hari's still embrace to see a young boy's face, flush under white hair.

"Might we relocate you? The lord may be more comfortable, if not in the infirmary, than in a bed," he said, nodding to Hari.

I glanced down, my vision clear for the first time since the sun rose, and took in the state of him. His face was pale, drained of the color in his cheeks and the sparkle in his eye. The bone in his thigh was exposed to the air. His arms still held tight around me, but his breaths came in ragged bursts.

I leaped up and shouted, "Ri! How could you!"

A weak smile turned the corner of his mouth up, and he lifted a hand for help. "I am here to serve, Your Majesty."

I let the joke fall to the ground beneath us as servants rushed to lift him. There was no humor in my new title or his continued service as advisor.

My mind screamed at him, screamed for me to follow wherever he went, but my feet were planted firmly in the weeds as his limp body was carried into the castle. Hari would be best cared for by the staff. Clearly, I would only drain him further. He would not seek his own help while I was in need.

The garden was empty when they left. My only injury was internal, and no servant or maid asked if I needed assistance.

Surely a king couldn't die without more fanfare. My father couldn't pass away in my arms without someone interfering. Why had no god stepped down from the sky or up from the sea?

Was that all that death was—a quiet whisper between bodies, an exhale from essence, before being swept away by staff and having your title thrown to the next of kin?

My shoulders sagged as I walked around the perimeter of the yard, searching for more proof of what had occurred, and I found my feet carrying me through the maze where I had enjoyed tea every morning before I left for sea.

Would anyone remember the Iron King tomorrow? I wondered.

Tears pricked my eyes, and I blinked them back.

It was too easy to find the middle, and the hedges were undamaged by battle. My fingers caught on the tiny leaves of the bushes, twisting around my knuckles as I turned corners. Left, then right, left twice again.

The middle of the maze was just one large circle, broken by cardinal paths, and a table sat in the middle underneath a tree.

My tea tray should have been waiting for me, cups clean and turned upside down, chairs tucked under the woven iron table.

But a long shadow was cast over the west path, and tears filled my eyes as I looked up at the hanging form of Imogene. A hemp rope wrapped twice around her neck, and her feet dangled above the kettle. Crisp, dry flowers poked out from her apron. A similar bouquet to what she held that day I was ushered to the docks.

I collapsed under the tree and cried. For her. For myself. For my family. For our future.

EPILOGUE

DORIAN

IT HAD BEEN TWO weeks since the battle over my crown, and a strange sense of normalcy settled over me. Living among Veshak's crew, sailing on my own ship, fighting for my life. It made everything else easier. Closing the east wing was my first decision. Appointing a new board of advisors made of residents from all over Raktam had been my second. There was a lot to clean up. Too much to announce and explain.

The days passed in a blur, and I was grateful, because at the back of my mind, always, was Hari.

I had not been allowed to see him for the first week of his healing. The mantrik doctor said visitors could cause stress. Then, as the second week passed, my anxiety grew. I had an awful, gnawing feeling that something was horribly wrong. That I would open the infirmary door and Hari wouldn't be there.

I paced outside the infirmary door, nerves stuttering my steps with every groan of the floorboards beyond.

The door creaked open. My heart leaped as I turned, expecting to see a maid exit.

But my gaze did not fall on a white cap and frock. Instead, a thick crop of curls darted out of the room.

"Orion?" I asked, confused, as he stumbled to a stop.

The privateer squeezed the satchel in his arms so tight that the fresh scars on his hands thinned, and he dipped his head.

"Your Majesty," he said, not quite completing his bow, but not rising from it either.

"Is the formality necessary? I was your prisoner," I said, shocked by my own words.

He rose but did not meet my gaze, and I looked from him to the infirmary door, which closed with a snap.

"Are you visiting someone?" I asked. As the question flicked from the tip of my tongue, I saw the answer in the depths of his eyes and remembered the way that he looked at Hari during the battle.

"Yes," he said shortly, tucking the bundle of cloth under his arm.

I offered him a small smile and pressed my palm to the door. "Happy sailing, Orion."

I held my breath as the hinges squeaked, and I swung the door open. The sound took me back aboard the galleon for a brief moment, and I shook my head. I did not have time for visions.

Hari sat in a sloping wooden chair affixed to four great wheels, a long bar arcing above his head so that one might push him around. His legs were secured in front of him in an iron cage, and he gripped the arms of his chair as the nurse jostled him about.

He looked like a stranger.

I paused in the doorframe, taking in the scene, before stumbling forward and dropping to my knees beside him.

I reached out to touch the back of his hand, but he pulled away.

"I am so sorry, Ri," I started, my voice hoarse as the pain of seeing him so close to death filled me again. "I should not have let you get hurt. I should have noticed that you were bleeding and broken and—"

"Yes, you should have noticed," Hari said, and his tone felt like a slap across the face. His voice softened, "But I am healed."

I breathed out heavily, my hand frozen in the air between us. There was so much to say, but where could I start?

He broke the silence and asked, "Will you roll me out of here, Dori?"

"Of course," I said. I looked over him as I stood and walked to the back of his wheelchair. His cheeks were rosy again, his muscles plumped over, and his hair brushed back from his face. My stomach clenched when he did not meet my gaze, but I swallowed back my unease and pulled him into the corridor.

I could handle anything as long as he was okay. I never wanted to see him like that again.

The wheels on his chair squeaked as we rolled through the castle, punctuating our silence. The bubbling of the fountain expanded the calm quiet, muffling the sound of the brake as I pulled him to a halt in front of the worn metal seat.

I wanted to say something, to offer a better apology, to assure him that I would never let it happen again.

"I'm glad that you are better," I said, unsure where else to start.

Hari inclined his head, his eyes softening as he turned his face to the sky. "I am as well. I was afraid for a moment that the vision of you on my chest was a picture from beyond the veil."

He fixed his light gaze on mine, and suddenly I felt small. "But that is not what my afterlife will look like. I had enough nights while healing to think, to imagine what I might want. I had time alone in the castle, too.

"I love you dearly, Dorian. But I cannot continue to spend my life serving you. I was chosen from a handful of children to be your companion. I have lived a good life with you, I would not argue otherwise, but it is time for me to pave my own path. I will set sail today and will not return."

I sat back, stunned.

"You mean to leave?" I finally asked after a long beat of silence.

He nodded, reaching out to grasp my hand. The contact burned, a flood of emotion released from my chest, filling every crevice of my mind and body, and I choked back a sob as I studied him. His pale, freckled skin. His fine hair. The amber eyes that bore deep into my soul. And as soon as the floodgates opened, they closed, and he pulled his fingers back.

"Why must you go? Am I not enough?"

"I want to sail, Dorian. I want to get back out on the ship and leave. Things are better away from the city—we could go together. You could leave this behind," Hari offered.

My heart raced. "Together, as we always have been?"

Red tinged his face.

He motioned back to the bar of his chair and looked to the sea. "Push me to the docks?"

I looked at his chair, for some sign of a trunk or satchel with his belongings, but I obeyed anyway.

"You have insisted that you will not bed anyone..." he said.

"I will not," I confirmed. "But I will love you in other ways. I will write prose that lures the sun from the horizon to warm your cheeks. I will paint the night sky in the sand for your observance. I will slay the armies that march into the land with my hands alone but offer the same touch that has only ever been yours. I would offer you my sword and lay at the foot of your throne, should you ask to free my head from my body."

Hari reached back and held my fingers in his for a moment, then released me. The surge of warmth I felt when he held me faded, and I was left empty, cold.

His hands fell to his sides, and his tone was sharp. "I have stood by you since I was in leading strings, thus sacrificing another man's touch since I knew to crave it. It is time to choose myself."

Pain stabbed through my gut, twisting my heart around.

The trek through town was slow, tedious under the weight of his confession.

Every shop was closed, some had signs up, most did not. The hill was tricky to navigate with wheels to steer and the remnants of rubble in the road, but I gripped the cart as firmly as I could and used every muscle I had to hold him steady as we navigated the winding path.

Soon enough, the docks came into view, much closer than they used to be.

Orion stood atop a gangway, the flags of a man-o'-war billowing above him.

"You are enough, and will be for someone else. But I need more for myself."

His words fell heavy on my heart, and I finally understood. He wanted a lover, a partner, not just adoration. In the same way that I would love anyone, but touch no one, he could touch anyone but could not live without it.

"I love you, Hari," I said, my declaration more a plea than a statement.

"I love you too, Dorian." He turned and held my gaze for a long moment before nodding to Orion, who marched down the plank and began to push my best friend, my greatest love, onto the ship.

Veshak approached from beside the ship and pressed his palm against my shoulder blade. "Cayde will take care of him. He is a more than capable captain."

"And you'll let me know if anything happens?" I asked.

"Of course. I am sure that our paths will cross. Zara and I are taking the fleet to Mautakheli first. But I have a feeling we will meet them back in Thandu."

I turned to study him, the scar over his one golden eye, his smooth, high cheeks. Then I noticed how his hair split unevenly down the middle. That wrinkle that was beginning to divot his forehead. His smaller than normal ears. And I smiled.

"I see Mother in you," I said.

He squeezed my arm and motioned up the road. "Would you like to join Zara and me for a drink before you rush home?"

I followed him, scrubbing my palms together. "I wanted to see you anyway. I've been working with our Uncle Girish on the plan that you gave to Hastings, and I have his proposal with me."

The bell on the door clanged, and Bromios lifted a hand in greeting from behind the bar.

I searched through the dimly lit tavern for some familiarity, but tables had been shoved aside and chairs removed; the patrons had changed, too. Short people with red eyes mixed in among lanky builds with amber. Stout blue and deep brown danced together, and the corner of my mouth lifted.

Veshak slid onto a bench beside Zara and pressed a long kiss to the top of her head while I sat across from them. I couldn't help but notice how they always touched when they were together. Fingers intertwined, a hand on his arm or a kiss on her head.

They had done something amazing, while I was on the ship, by showing Raktam their care.

The papyrus in my pocket was soft, and I unfurled it across the table between us. A map of the city was drawn out in charcoal, the boundary of the old outer wall marked out in gray lines, and new roads pressed into the fibers with harsher drawings.

"There were over two thousand people living out beyond the wall," I said, and they both inhaled sharply. I nodded, knowing. I pressed my finger to the faded lines of the three kingdom walls. The inner one still stood, but not for long.

"We will divert the military to cleaning efforts. The army has already been called in from patrolling trade routes, the guard is working now, and the navy will be redirected once they dock. The inner wall will be torn down once the first two are cleaned up."

"Where will the waste go?" Zara asked warily.

"There are some large, empty valleys to the south. They are uninhabited by people or wildlife, and we will build a rock quarry there to recycle the stone."

She nodded, and I pointed to the maze of roads that was previously the lower kingdom. "Girish has agreed to oversee the funding of homes that you suggested," I said, looking at Veshak. "He and his new wife are looking forward to expanding their responsibilities. They also have a letter for you to take to Mother."

He beamed and gave Zara a squeeze around her shoulders.

"And the katalval?" Zara prodded.

"Already declared safe. Whenever you make contact with your sister, we will be waiting for word of what needs done here to open Taimur to them."

Zara reached across the table and grasped my fingers. "Thank you, truly. I know it will take my family time to come around, but I am glad for the chance."

I smiled and nodded. "And I will do away with the land division of the barony, the duchy, and so on. All of the land will be farmed and titles rescinded."

Veshak breathed deeply, his shoulders straightening, and I smiled, pride swelling in my chest. "Your fleet of ships will be ready and waiting at the docks at dawn."

"Do you think it is too much at once?" Veshak asked.

I scratched at the beard on my jaw, pulling a hair and twisting as I looked around the tavern. I recognized titled residents dancing with those from the outer city, and Bromios pocketing coin from each patron without issue.

I shook my head. "Change can be good."

"I hope that your changes bring peace to your people," my brother said.

"They were your changes," I corrected. "And we need them. I needed this, needed you. I think that we will heal from Eudo and move into a new age."

"Oh?" Veshak asked.

I stood as the bells to mark my ascension began to chime. The door to the tavern swung open wide, revealing residents marching toward the castle.

"I think it will be an age of revival," I said.

"What a notion." My brother grinned, and I threw an arm around him, and Zara, and we turned with the crowd.

"Ascension time?" Zara asked.

"One last ceremony before you two sail off to your own future."

The End

Acknowledgements

Sam, I don't know what I'd do without you. I'm so grateful to have you as my best friend and most sane accomplice in all things writing. Cheers to two years working on this with you, and all our changes through that!

A massive thanks to Lauren for dealing with me through deadlines and continuing your incredible work on my books.

To my beta and ARC readers with special thanks to Christoph for reading this three (or more?) times over. Your feedback is invaluable, you're a literary genius, and my book would never have made it off my desktop without you!

To Aamna, Sarah, Lia, Jade, Daniel, and the countless others who helped with this book from conception to print. You all did amazing work with the covers, edits, art, and all the things in between.

Last, but certainly not least, thank you, Reader, for joining me in this corner of my world. I hope you enjoyed the story.

Ari is a trans author and editor from Oregon. Writer of mythology and fantasy novels, he spends his free time reading, listening to nerdy podcasts, and playing board games. Follow him on Instagram, Facebook, or TikTok @darkmythauthor to stay up to date. To learn more about him and his books, visit:

www.abdanielsannachi.com

www.ingramcontent.com/pod-product-compliance
Lightning Source LLC
Chambersburg PA
CBHW020244030826
48979CB00030B/2612/J

* 9 7 8 1 9 2 2 9 3 6 8 4 4 *